MARMALADE

BY ROLAND BLACKBURN

READ UNTIL YOU BLEED!

For Cecily,
who never stopped
believing

CHAPTER ONE
A WARNING

If you say his name, he'll come.

He left my life in ashes. He cost me everything. But he taught me that.

Miles. Years. Neither made any difference.

My oldest friend.

Names have power, and his—

But I won't say it. No matter how hard they press here, how much they cajole or threaten or promise here, I will not say his name. Every time I have, someone dies.

And it has to end.

Once, I used to think I was the only one that could see them. It made me feel special.

Later, I thought I was the only one who chose to see them. It made me feel strong.

Now, I think I'm the only one who *doesn't have a choice*. And it terrifies me.

His memory feels like a curse. His dark figure, the wide-brimmed hat slung low, the course of stubble along his jaw. A handsome devil in every sense of the word.

My oldest friend.

I hope he never finds me.

I know he's looking.

To tell you about him would set him back on my path, and I won't wade through the blood again.

My oldest friend.

How I miss him.

I know what you're thinking.

I'm not crazy, though I know only the insane feel obligated to weigh in on their general sanity.

2   MARMALADE

I'm not crazy, but I'd be lying if I said that makes me sane, either. The problem with perception is subjectivity, right?

If there's no common ground to start with, nothing one party says is ever going to make sense to the other.

Maybe it's crazy, then, to even try.

You really want to know? Where I think it all started? That's easy.

Don't say I didn't warn you.

In my backyard, looking down the hill from the pink plastic table, I could just make out the sunny afternoon giving way to dusk. Little streamers of cloud had settled in just the right spots for a spectacular sunset, and I had my tea set out.

I was holding court with Sarah.

The cups were pink. The saucers were pink. Even the little romper I had on was pink with pink hearts. My father draped everything I owned in it, like he wanted to make sure the world recognized that he had a little girl. There was probably a deep-seated neurosis there, as the clicks would say, but at least my mother could tone it down when it came to accessories.

She loved me fiercely. It hurts a little just thinking about it.

Our little fingers were extended to the point of dislocation. The two of us laughed and giggled as we toasted Dr. Bear and Alfred the Giraffe, our gentleman callers for the day.

Sarah herself had no time for pink, always dressed in what I now would recognize as vintage handmade clothes.

Maybe I'm just getting my memories crossed. Even cheeking your pills for a while, you start getting some pretty bizarre notions. After the first couple of weeks, I started thinking I was Daphne du Maurier every six hours.

But I asked Sarah if she wanted more tea. Tupenny jam? Marma— no. Wait. That was close.

She shook her head and pursed her lips, her sandy ponytail bouncing as she glanced back at the stand of woods at the foot of the hill, nose wrinkling as if she'd sniffed something rotten on the breeze. You know, her sense of humor was wicked, and I'd never met anyone else who knew so many old games, but sometimes she could be a hell of a downer. At times she'd stare off into space as if she were looking for something or listening.

Some nights she'd sit at the foot of my bed and weep.

Sarah came back from wherever she'd gone and grinned. Two of her front teeth were missing. "Thertainly, milady."

I lifted the teapot and poured her an imaginary draught. She raised the tiny cup to her lips, and we giggled again. Even as little as we were, it felt ridiculous.

I noticed one of the dolls was on the lawn before the trees, a plastic effigy in the dimming light. Maybe Sarah had dropped it playing hide-and-seek or come-into-my-castle, but Dad would have burst a vessel if he saw my toys strewn about the yard. "Be a dear and fetch Aunt Edna, would you?"

"Of course." Sarah set the teacup down with a little curtsy, skipping to the edge of the woods. Dr. Bear and Alfred sagged, their tea having gotten the best of them, and I helped prop them up in the meantime. The shadows were starting to stretch across the yard as I rearranged the cups and saucers to their proper spots.

The last I saw of her, she'd bent over to pick up the doll.

I imagine Sarah saw a pair of black scuffed boots.

Having finally resumed our high tea to its stately position, I heard a wet green crack, as if one of the branches had split off in the forest. The muffled thud came after, and I looked. If the woods were going to start coming apart around us, high tea could be moved to the palatial gardens of the living room.

Before the scrappy stand of trees stood a scruffy long-haired man, tall against the stretching shadows. A wide-brimmed hat hid most of his face, and old work clothes hung off of him like loose skin. Glancing up, he caught me staring and waved broadly with one large hand. Not sideshow, mind you. Just big.

Lying behind him in the tall grass, a second effigy was barely visible, motionless and pale. The man waved again and took a step forward, obscuring the image.

I never saw her again.

I gave him a tentative wave. "Hi."

"Hello yourself, little raven." His mouth parted in a sideways grin, the timelessness of middle age draped about him like a cloak.

"I'm not supposed to talk to strangers."

Does it sound a little penny dreadful? It's hard to explain how natural everything felt, like something had finally fallen into place. There was nothing threatening about him, just a heat that felt as if it filled the yard.

I wonder if that's what love at first sight is supposed to feel like, but I doubt it. Poets usually have more class.

"Wisdom beyond your years." He nodded, as if weighing my words. "Well... they've called me lots of things in my day, but you. You may call me—."

Well, you know. It's in the file, after all.

I won't say it. Not even here.

Then I nodded too, as if a deep and thoughtful secret had passed between us. "I'm Prose."

"What a beautiful name." There was something sad about him, a forlorn haunting in his eyes. In the moment I wondered where he had come from.

Even now, that's a question that's never really gone away.

"So we're not strangers?"

"Assuredly."

"What's up with Sarah?" I asked. She still hadn't moved.

"Sarah's playing possum," he said. "Don't you fret."

I shook my head, relieved. "Do you know how to play tea party?"

He glanced up at the house. "What else you got?"

And after that, we were inseparable.

Sarah never came back, but I didn't miss her. No one ever came around asking for her. I suppose I should have thought that a little weird, but then again I had another friend now.

Despite everything that's happened, all the lies, all the blood between us, I think I still do.

Poe forgive me.

If only Mom had left a note.

CHAPTER TWO

WHERE THE DEAD FERN GROWS

The room is a mess of beige and brown. Institutional colors, I think, only because the paint is cheap. Our ceiling's the shade of rotting eggshells, and I let my eyes wander across the holes and crevasses like my own galaxy of constellations for almost twenty minutes. It's not hard to kill time when they make you take meds before shift change.

Over by the sprinkler head, my archer finds his pegasus, and they entwine into something greater, hungrier. Before it fully takes shape, there's a knock at the door.

Phoebe glances over. We rochambeau. Scissors beats paper, again.

A glance through the glass panel unveils Monique, who hollers through the door that Osgood needs me. I refuse to consider the panel a window. A window shows you things; all this panel reveals is a three foot by five section of cinderblock wall.

Dutifully, I put on a clean T-shirt as soon as Monique ducks out of sight, black with a green DHD and a skull motif, and slip out into the hallway. My tour of the Eggshell Galaxy can be put on hold, and an excuse to skip shift change isn't something to be taken likely.

Monique rolls her eyes at the metal shirt but steers me out into the dayroom. It's a wide and clear space with contractor-made furniture and high ceilings that reflect whispers. A wide flatscreen TV is mounted on the near wall and tucked towards the back is a dining area adjoined by an efficient little kitchen. Since Everbrook has a full cafeteria and kitchen staff that handles most of the meals, right down to county-approved snacks, the dining area's only for burnouts and ITLs. If you're Everbrook Strong, you'll never have to sit there, and the kitchen's only there for the sporadic occasions when the staff want to fire up the grill, fry quesadillas, or both.

As institutions go, it's just askance of prison.

Osgood's sitting in a plastic chair at the dining area, his briefcase tucked beneath him. A legal pad and a gleaming chrome pen rest on the table before him that he's promised to bequeath to me when we're finally through. He stands up when I enter and doesn't flinch, a tight little man in his late thirties, hair kept short like he's ex-armed-forces. My guess, that he has never confirmed or denied.

Not a bad egg for a click. This is visit sixteen.

"Hi, Prose." He breaks into a catalogue grin, and I have to remind myself that he's being paid to be here, "Are we good to talk here?"

He knows better. "Outside?"

Osgood makes a show of checking the weather, which is gorgeous, a clear Oregon autumn with the green slowly bleeding out of the world. Truth be told, it doesn't matter. He'd allow us outside in a blizzard if that was the only way I would talk. "I guess we can."

I barrel through the slider before he has a chance to finish. The breeze on my face feels good, tulips and pine, and he follows along behind me as I cross the little walkway to the 'Sip, a two-ambulance-wide sidewalk that stretches to the Admin building on one end and the gymnasium on the other. Tributaries spring off to the other lodges, each separated by genders and ages. Ours is the big house, Girls Intensive. Girls Adolescent & Junior Girls spring off behind me, and the corresponding boys' lodges are on the other side of the 'Sip.

No, I don't know why they call it that. I haven't found anyone that remembers.

The seventh building is the alleged victim of budget cuts. With no name, it now sits dark and vacant. The old-timer staff and repeat customers back up the financial woes angle, though Melyssa says that when she was little something really bad happened and they had to close it down. Melyssa makes dolls of her own hair, though, so let's not lose perspective.

We walk towards the field, a wide expanse of grass framed by tall stands of pine and Douglas fir who do their best to hide the dirty grey wall surrounding the complex. A looming skeletal man in a brown suit passes by, and Osgood gives him a professional nod before turning to me. "Do you want to sit down?"

"I think better when I'm walking."

"You mean casing the joint, right?" It's old banter, but there's a weariness to his voice I don't like.

"Any word on what's going to happen?" I change the subject. The clicks work for the county, and thusly with the court. What exactly their level of input is has been kept shrouded and Byzantine, but one would think it's more than lip service.

"You've got another hearing in two weeks." He shrugs. "They're still in the preliminary stages of your case. Any decision's a long way off."

I nod like I've been working in juvenile court all my life. "Right."

"If you've got any specific questions about it, you should speak to your lawyer. Right now, I'm here to talk to about you."

My lawyer's a frazzled public defender whose caseload is slowly crushing them to death. We've met once for five minutes. He doesn't return my calls. "Okay."

His legal pad steps in front of him like an aegis. "How are you doing?"

It's such a banal question that it's hard to hide my disdain. "I'm being given meds I don't want three times a day and forced to stay in my room for long stretches at a time. When I'm not, the food's terrible and it's a heavily monitored mixture of board games and movie nights as we wait for our futures to be decided by strangers. Shit's grand."

"How are you getting along with everyone?" Another question he knows the answer to. He's talked to the staff and teachers. Right now he's just establishing a baseline for how this conversation's going to go.

"Not." Which is true. Except for Phoebe, I don't try to connect with an ever-changing sea of faces, even if they weren't already freaked out by the Red Orphan.

I know their nickname for me, hear it shouted by morons at the cafeteria. Every now and again someone like Nelly gets in my face, tries to front like a well-timed boo wouldn't send them wetting themselves.

It helps to adopt a Gandhi-like stance. Non-violence, not the starving thing.

"Do you want to?"

"I just want to leave."

He nods and jots something down. My father could have watched his hand move and tell me what he'd written, but I'd never learned the trick. "How are you sleeping?"

"Like I've drunk deep of sweet nepenthe." The Poe went over his head, and I was a little disappointed. We'd been learning to joust with minor literary lances, but this time he hadn't even bothered to horse.

"Are you dreaming at all?"

"No." Lying this time. Of all the things I didn't want to talk about, the ever-changing kaleidoscope of nightmares was third on the list. I couldn't even blame the meds.

He raised an eyebrow. "No live organism can continue for long to exist under conditions of absolute reality."

Just when I thought he was out. "I love Shirley Jackson, Osgood, but that's not the problem here."

"Are you still seeing things?"

Left out of the sentence was *that aren't there*. "A little."

The pen flashes again. "Do you want to tell me about them?"

I start walking in a different direction instead. My steps take me towards the gym, and Osgood hurries to keep up. The battered doors are heavy but unlocked, and I step briskly through the foyer, past the meeting room, and towards the basketball court, no doubt funded in the heyday of America's economic boom. I can't imagine anyone signing off on building a full indoor basketball court for crazy kids in the austerity era.

The lights are out, giving the doorway the appearance of a gaping maw. Interstellar steps echo off the scarred hardwood beyond as I find the switch. The hanging overhead lights click on like luminescent stalactites, and in my head I hear the bats fluttering away.

Osgood looks a little flustered as I sit down on the row of bleachers, most likely uncomfortable at finding himself behind closed doors with a seventeen-year-old girl. There are rules for the staff about ever being alone with the clientele, and while he technically doesn't work for Everbrook, the fact that I've pulled him out of his glib comfort zone brings me the smallest amount of pleasure.

I scan the gym for signs of life, but we're on our own. Worn hoops hang from either side, college regulation, and the walls and floors are scarred from sixty years of adolescents. For no known reason, a small stage has been cut out of the north corner of the wall, its curtains currently drawn. What production you'd ever hope to put on here is beyond me, and now the space is just used for storage and surplus.

A small wooden door marked EMERGENCY EXIT blurs into the scenery in the northwest corner of the room. There are a number of doors out of the gym, and all but the ones out front lead directly to the legends and apocrypha of Everbrook: phantom showers, an old daycare, an old barracks-style bunkhouse before licensing stepped in. There's even supposed to be an attic, and one girl swore up and down the staff had taken her down to a bomb shelter. I've never snuck off to explore, much less verify. There's enough trouble here without going looking for it.

Osgood says something, and I snap back to attention. For a moment I thought I saw a head poke out from behind the black curtains of the stage, but this time I'm sure it's my imagination. I try to focus and hear him a second time.

"Can you tell me when they started scaring you?"

I was seven. He'd been around already for years.

No, I'm not going to tell you about him. Right now? Try never. We talked about this.

We were in the brown house on the little hill. The woods in back had grown thicker, crept closer since he came.

There was still a lot of yarn left on the sweater at this point. Mom remained great, and her smiles lit up my heart like it was full of helium and birthday cake. After school we'd play games and watch reruns of old shows on Nickelodeon once I'd scribbled down my homework, and every week we'd take a trip to the library. It was like a spending spree, and we'd get Slurpees at the corner market and read new books sprawled out in the living room until Dad came home. My grades were rock solid, and there were already hushed whispers of college and careers. My dad was teaching English at Chapelwaite, wrote novels in his spare time, and was just coming off of his best-selling work to date, a book about a Washington lobbyist uncovering a government conspiracy called *Shadow Players*.

Mind you, *best-selling to date* was not the same thing as best-selling, but he was content to plug away as his readership grew, albeit glacially. He wasn't *that* Thomas Harden yet. I remember asking him what conspiracy meant, and he told me it meant that if book sales kept up, Bigfoot was going to be signing our checks.

Maybe I'm remembering it wrong.

The night it showed itself was just like any other.

It was raining outside. Life in the PNW, right? The thick, dark clouds had shut out the moon and removed the stars. He'd been gone for four days then, which was rare but not unheard of. He never explained why or where he'd go, just "Matters need tending, little raven. See you soon." Most of the time it was a day, maybe two. Rarely longer.

Shit. I said I didn't want to talk about that.

Did he bring it? I don't know.

It would have explained so much.

It would have made hating him so much easier.

Anyway, I was in those wee thin minutes between going to bed and getting to bed. My room was a standard kid's sanctuary, with my little purple bed and posters thumbtacked to the wall. A bookcase that was already starting to swell sat next to the little desk my mother had bought at the Grange garage sale, but the real prize was hidden in the closet. Behind two folding slatted doors was a massive orange toy box, overflowing with blocks and action figures and dolls and stuffies and old crayons and drawings— you get it. In retrospect, it was almost certainly something my father had banged together with a couple beers and five minutes in the garage, but still. I loved it.

Yeah, I loved my toy box.

This still isn't about that.

After brushing my teeth, I padded down the hallway to my room, pulling the door shut behind me and crawling into bed through the dark by pure memory. Dad had encouraged that from early on, something about confronting my childhood fears.

Of being alone? Being in the dark? I don't know. I never asked him what he was afraid of.

Mostly, I think it was because he liked to watch old movies with the sound up after I'd gone to bed. His sole capitulation had been a night-light, a crystalline pixie in a glistening gown, purple wand casting a faint blue radiance across the room.

Under the covers for maybe a minute then, counting sheep and failing, I decided I wanted Harrison, my stuffed rabbit. I picked out a book from the shelf, *The Witches of Worm*, maybe, and snuck out of bed to pry open the closet doors. Something smelled different in there that night, earthy, but I connected it to the rain outside. By the dim glow of the nightlight, I started to rifle through my toy box, pushing aside old models and teacups. Then I saw it blink.

It was gone just as quickly, lost in the slurry of plastic and children's dreams. My hands jerked back of their own volition, and I took a deep breath to get a hold of myself. Maybe watching *Creature of the Black Lagoon* last week hadn't been such a great idea.

Trying again for Harrison, I was brushing aside a scribbled crayon drawing when I revealed it. A face, shriveled and concave like a dried apple.

Its palsied eyes opened and fastened on me. My blood flowed to ice, and a hand slid from beneath a pile of old blocks, long nails clacking as it parted the detritus sea. It was cold as it seized my wrist, its palm like sandpaper.

Throwing myself backwards, I fell out of the closet. My head bounced off the leg of the desk. I could still feel the insect scratch of its flesh against my skin, and white lights dancing I rolled to my feet, shoving the closet doors shut as it began to emerge, toys dripping from its skin like water. Breath trapped in my throat, I shoved the little desk in front of those doors. I remember thinking as the stench grew worse that this couldn't be real, that I needed to wake up, just wake up.

When it pounded against the closet doors, I wanted him there so bad I said his name.

But he didn't come.

The thing slammed against the doors again, and they parted, just a crack, but then nothing. The room was icy still, but the reek of it had intensified, and I stumbled backwards to my bed. The silence in the closet grew almost painful. With my little flashlight I checked the corners, the crack between the bookcase and the wall, behind the dresser. Finally I got down on my little hands and knees and shone the light under the bed, waiting for that dried hand to clamp onto me and crush my wrist like paper.

Beneath the bed the shadows parted, and besides a second-grade science project, nothing was there but dust bunnies and the far wall. Warily, I got to my feet.

It snatched a claw down from the ceiling then, impossibly long, and yanked me up by my hair. I screamed, the stopper finally out of the bottle, and screamed and screamed and screamed as it lowered its wrinkled face to mine, breath like old tombs. Its eyes were black stones in cold fires.

Everything fell apart. The door burst open, my father yelling incoherently, and the thing hissed. Something snapped like bad elastic. A whisper, and then it was gone.

My father's hands were on my shoulders, alternately hugging and shaking me. A barrage of questions poured out of him that I couldn't answer, and I just sobbed until he held me close, his scent of sweat, cologne, and the hint of lager driving everything away. Mom stood silhouetted in the doorway, tears welling up in her eyes, and we went downstairs for cocoa and marshmallows, a rare and luxurious treat. Dad read me a story, then another, until I was asleep in the sanctuary of his arms.

In the morning we decided I'd been dreaming.

That didn't explain why Mom's eyes had flickered to the ceiling.

Osgood chews on the base of his pen for a moment. I'm afraid to meet his eyes.

When he speaks, it is with the calm, measured tones of someone who doesn't want to get stabbed with his writing implement.

"Not a current episode, then. That's something. What do you think it was?"

"I don't know." The memory alone had kept me up at bedtime for a year, a sore tooth that needed just the slightest pressure to howl. "I don't know what they are."

"Do you think you see ghosts?"

"The ghost of a shriveled worm monster? Yeah, I'll check the historical record."

He pauses. I'm getting the feeling it's just for effect.

"Be honest, now. You did say that you'd gone to bed."

"Not a dream."

He sighs. "Of course, and no judgements. But no one else saw anything."

"That they told a seven-year-old about." I'd turned the night over and over in my head for the last decade. He wasn't going to point out any weak spots. "The furniture had been moved. The closet door was open."

"People can do fantastic things in their sleep." His pen twitches across the paper. "Cook meals, drive cars, crack safes."

"So you think I dreamt it." It's not a question, even though a fragile kernel of my heart hopes he's right.

It doesn't matter. At this point truth is as relative as nightmares.

"I didn't say that." He runs a hand through the thinning front of his hair. "We're just looking at possibilities."

"Right." I rise from the bleachers in a lithe burst. Osgood starts.

Does he think I'm going to run?

I grab a basketball off the rack, bouncing it to check its weak inflation. In a group home with a hundred kids, they have the shelf life of Easter eggs.

Osgood looks down at his notepad for a moment. "Have you seen anything else? Recently?"

My eyes involuntarily twitch towards the stage. *There's someone behind the curtain*, I almost say.

That's not going to speed up my chances of release, though, so I shake my head and try for a layup. The ball falls in with a reassuring swoosh.

"No more appearances by the Man?"

I stop in mid-layup. "What?"

"Do you want to tell me about him?"

I shake my head. "If you've read my file, you already know the answer."

"It's going to be necessary for your treatment, Prose. You've invested so much in this character, this Marmalade Man, but you've walled him off us completely."

"Free advice? Don't say that name."

He shrugs. "I don't agree. You're not going to get better until you're willing to face what he represents. Until you're willing to talk about him."

"If I talk about him, he'll hear me." I bounce the ball over to Osgood. "If he hears me, he'll come. If he comes, someone dies."

"He came up twice today, even if you walk around the name. That brings us to---" he checks his notes. "-forty-three times, in total."

I shoot the ball again. It clanks off the rim.

Osgood sighs. "So what, then? Is he coming for me?"

"Maybe. I hope not. For your sake."

"You're talking about him." He tries a jump shot that fails spectacularly. "Trust me. You just need to get deeper."

"Stop telling me to trust you. The implication is that you're lying. And I don't want him anymore. Sometimes lost things need to stay lost." I fetch his miss and lay it back in. ""I want to go back now."

We walk back down the 'Sip as a group of boys are coming in to appropriate the gym. One of them checks me out, then whispers to his friend. *Spooky.*

Word gets around.

Osgood drops me off in the Girls Intensive dayroom. It's full of teenagers talking, playing games, Lo and the staff just within eavesdropping distance. Chapman rises from his chair by the back desk like a toad emerging from his pad, a pale man going to fat with the demeanor of a fading jock. His beady eyes graze over me and I groan. If Chapman's here, he's running the shift.

My click sets his briefcase on the table and shakes my hand, mumbling platitudes about my behavior to Chapman, who nods, not really listening. The click is an interloper in his pond, and Chapman can't wait to see the end of him.

Osgood presses the catch on his briefcase to slide his notepad back in, and I see it. A hardcover, jet black, red letters. *Thomas Harden.* I read. *House of Razors.*

With both arms, I've snatched up the briefcase, swinging it at Osgood even before I'm aware of acting.

"You fuck! You want Red Orphan? I'll fucking give you Red Orphan!"

It smashes his nose with a wet crunch and sends his glasses scything across the room as I howl.

Bringing it back around, I catch him with a shot to the temple before he can raise his arms. I'm arcing it back for a third when the hands clamp down on my arms and I'm hoisted up and away. Furious tears burn my cheeks as I scream something else I can never take back.

Osgood's clutching his bleeding nose on the tile, his eyes the white of a deer in the middle of the road. The rest of the room falls burial silent as I'm wrenched away towards the blue seclusion room in the back.

All except for the big blonde, Nellie, who then spits on the carpet. "Crybaby."

"Settle down." Chapman growls it as I'm hauled through the big double doors and into the hall beyond. I can't even see who's touching me, and with a shove I'm stumbling into the padded space. The heavy door slams shut with a magnetic click, and I'm trapped with nothing but blue padding and my thoughts.

"Make good choices, Prose," someone drones from beyond the door.

If only I had some.

CHAPTER THREE

TOUCHING BASE

It's hours later when I wake up in my assigned bedroom. Old sunlight filters through the plastic curtains in a dull patina that creates shadow plays across the floor. From the angle of the light, it's late afternoon.

Still groggy, I try to sit up, wincing at the soreness in my back, my shoulders. Events replay themselves across a bone-white screen, and a dull fire kindles in my belly that I don't bother to quench.

House of Razors. House of fucking Razors.

I pull the thin sheet back over myself and try to go back to sleep. In the distance I can hear the voices of the other girls, watching movies or talking with conspiratorial tones from the dayroom, and I groan.

Crybaby. Cry, baby, cry.

When knuckles rap against the door again, I realize what woke me in the first place. A muffled voice mumbles that I have a visit, and embarrassment turns to panic. "It's not the cop, right?"

I've only succeeded in confusing them. "Cop?"

"Detective Holcomb."

"Not unless your uncle's a cop, kid. Come on."

I wait for them to step away from the panel, then throw on the first outfit I can put together and step onto the hallway. A man's sitting on a plastic chair just across from my room, and I realize that I must be on some kind of punishment status, but that's at the back of my mind as I scamper into the public restroom and check myself out in the mirror. My dark hair's locked into insufferable tufts and wild animals, and the brush I grab from my hygiene box doesn't do much to tame it.

I try to pass for normal. Under the halogen lights, my eyes look tired and haunted, but there's nothing I can do about that now. Gloomily, I tell the stranger I'm ready. He gives me a tired smile.

I've seen him around maybe half a dozen times, but never caught his name. Neither does he offer it, which usually sets off alarm bells but today is the least of my problems. He probably works with the older boys but got stuck pulling a double shift. There's a lot of turnover here, only never for the minors.

My name is smeared in red on the dry-erase board, scrawled under the Teaching Level column.

Poe wept.

Escaping the dayroom with nothing more than bemused glances, I follow him down the 'Sip to the big building known as Control. Part administrative office, part nurses' station, part visitor center, the three-story building is more medieval keep than personnel center.

Cheryl's behind the desk, and she offers me the reticent grin of someone who doesn't want any trouble as she asks me how I'm doing. I shrug and roll up my sleeve. They try really hard not to leave bruises, but a knot of yellow and green is already forming on the inside of my arm.

It's all she needs to know. Her disappointed eyes scan a logbook below my range of vision. I notice a couple of scattered clusters, single parents and children playing, chatting or outright flirting. *What a place to pick up chicks.*

A small girl sits alone in the corner beneath a plastic plant, a book open before her handmade sweater. There's a glint of silver iris as she looks away.

Cheryl clears her throat and buzzes my visitor in. Like an old gameshow, my excitable bachelor's about to come strolling down the aisle, but instead of lithe and devastatingly handsome I get mousy and exasperated. His hair's lighter than mine, a series of waves that end just below the frames of his glasses, and I give my uncle Mark a hug. He returns it, now thinner than I remember, and Cheryl directs us to a private room with a plexiglass wall. The stranger following me pulls up a chair and sits just outside the door, a low-grade haunting. I've had worse.

After a couple of false starts, Mark asks me how I've been.

"Wow, Mark. Week seven in residential care, but you want to know how's tricks?"

He turns a little red and pushes his glasses up on the bridge of his nose. "Easy, now. I'm on your side, remember?"

He's not who you're pissed at, I remind myself. *It's not his fault.*

Taking a deep breath, I catch the faintest hint of vanilla, and gooseflesh pricks my arms. "I just don't want to be here anymore. You know?"

"I get it. Rowan used flip out on me during my little trip inside."

I had almost forgotten. Whispered family lore had my smiling, carefree uncle being institutionalized when he was sixteen, the reasons for which had never been explained. That my parents would both bring it up when the bickering turned especially sour was reason enough to keep quiet.

"I was so—angry. But after the first week, I put the pieces together. You've got to play their game, Prose. Answer questions. Solve riddles. The progress is so slow it feels like nothing's happening, but then suddenly you'll wake up breathing free air again. The staff are only trying to help."

"No one grows tired of reminding me." I glance back at the door. The stranger is leafing through a magazine on his clipboard, pretending not to eavesdrop. It's an awkward look. "Help doesn't usually leave bruises."

"Sometimes it leaves scars." Mark leans in a little closer. "I'm jumping through the county's hoops on my end. Jump through yours, and we'll meet in the middle. Get you out of here."

"How does it look?" My court-appointed defender couldn't pick me out of a lineup.

"Preliminary." Mark pushes his bony hand back through his hair, and I realize how much he's aged. At some point his gawky post-adolescent self wandered out into traffic and died. "They're running background checks on me. Analyzing the apartment. Turning over rocks and pointing. The county's angling towards my lack of parenting experience and arguing that I can't support you, much less be responsible for someone with your, and I'm sorry, *special emotional needs*."

"Poe wept."

"On the plus side, it doesn't look like they're ready to charge you with anything. Yet. Some people don't seem very happy about it, either. If Holcomb or the other detective come back in, don't say a word to them."

"Mark, they're cops."

"To whom you've already given a statement. Their only job right now is to poke holes in it." He sighs, and how much he resembles a tired scarecrow chills me. "They're looking to put you away, Prose. For a long time. They're not your friends."

"Really?"

My sarcasm's lost on him. "Don't say anything without Baxter here. Promise."

"Fuck Baxter. But I promise."

Mark nods and reaches into his battered coat pocket. The man by the door leans forward, interested for the first time. Mark pulls out three paperback books. "To pass the time. We're going to get you out of here, Prose, but you have to do your part. Remember that."

The books go directly to the stranger outside the door, who riffles their pages and hands them back to me. No tabs of acid fall out, no hundred-dollar bills. I'm sure he's at least a little disappointed. I glance at their covers.

"I heard about today. That shit's going to keep you locked up in here."

"Language," the stranger says. He doesn't look up.

"It wasn't my fault, Mark." Something clenches inside me. "The click went behind my back. He read the book."

Mark shakes his head. "Everything you do in here goes to a judge out there. Mistakes will cost you months, Prose."

He's right, and it stings a little. Hot blood rushes to my cheeks, and I fight it back. I'm not going to cry in reception. "I just want to go home."

"And you will," he smiles, and rises to leave. It's a lie, but a sweet one.

After we say our goodbyes, the stranger and I walk back to the Lodge. The silver-eyed girl watches us from behind the thick glass door, one palm pressed against it like a pale starfish abandoned in high tide. Something about her is troubling, and I walk a little faster.

The stranger might not know my backstory, and so I take a chance. "Do you see her?" I ask, looking back to Control.

He turns. "See who?"

"Nothing." *It's irrational*, I think, but my feet blur faster down the 'Sip. *Magical thinking.*

Osgood likes to hold court on that particular topic, more than a little smug as he retreats behind his degree. Challenge your thoughts, your paranoia, your fear. But there she is, the starfish still breathing softly against the glass.

A guilty worm starts to wriggle inside my head.

I don't take my meds. Dad always said there's nothing wrong with someone that can be fixed with chemicals, which is kind of funny considering how things worked out, but feeling sleepy or bloated or constantly confused is just as appealing as it sounds. One of my bed's steel legs has a broken cap, and my pharmacopeia of wonder finds a home there more often than not. I'm up to a hundred little capsules, white and orange and somnolent blue piled against each other like exotic spices. Storing them serves no purpose, but it feels right just having them there.

In case of insanity, break glass.

The dayroom of Intensive Girls is thick with bodies as if they're staging an intervention. Nellie shoots me daggers, but everyone else only looks bored as I cross to the back hall and main desk. Chapman sits next to it like a toad on his pad, pleased with himself. His eyes fix upon the three books I'm carrying, and he pushes a folder with my name on it over to me. "Sign them in," he says, like this is Ellis Island, and I flip to my property log sheet and dutifully write their titles. Already done with me, he asks my haunting if he checked them for contraband.

"Do I have a one-on-one?" I ask.

"After what you pulled? What do you think?" he growls. "You're considered a danger to yourself and others until a clinician says different, kid."

I catch his eye, already turning back to the dayroom, and ask if I can put my books away. At Everbrook, it's always better to ask permission than beg forgiveness.

He nods, dismissing me, and I slip down to my room and stash them away in my closet. Phoebe's nowhere to be found. My haunting floats outside my door, careful not to enter. When I come back out, Chapman's in the dayroom, and he signals me to have a seat with one thick hand. I shake my head and point to my status on the board, for once a little thankful. A little crimson, he waves me off, either annoyed or embarrassed that he forgot. Chapman's not big on forgetting.

I walk back down to my room and seal the chamber as Chapman begins his group session, explaining the shift and what everyone would be doing, scores from the previous morning, behaviors and little rules that need polishing.

Everbrook is a bureaucrat's dream, with behavioral management down to the smallest decimal. Everyone's name goes on the board next to their honor level, either One, Two, or Three. Different levels have different privileges, and to lose them is to enter the dim world of Teaching Level. No groups, games, or television. Thirty minutes of recreation and a bedtime that a toddler would complain about. The Puritans had a wilder social life.

Spreading the paperbacks out on my off-white comforter, I try to decide between them when there's another knock on the door.

I appreciate the formality. Not everyone here knocks.

When it opens, I see my haunting's been transformed into Graham. The staffing switches happen a lot. When you get the red 1:1 next to your name, it means that they're waiting to see if your violence was just an episode or angling towards a whole series. Someone gets specifically assigned to watch you and make sure you don't eat your mattress. Staff stay within fifteen feet of you all day, a little spook on your shoulder, and they rotate without warning or feedback. It's disconcerting to have different people following you at all times. If you weren't paranoid before, welcome to your new complex.

Graham is holding a stack of paper and a little crayon, which actually makes me laugh out loud. "Really?"

Embarrassed, he shrugs. "Doctor's orders. Finish the packet and you move off of Teaching tomorrow."

I take the stack of paper and flip through it. It's a series of assignments, essay questions, and required reading. A small child might have written these.

Someone else I might have given a hard time to, but Graham has the apologetic eyes of a substitute teacher. He's younger than most, light brown hair in tightly glued spikes, and he gives me a little grin. "Take your time. And whatever you do, don't turn it in to Chap."

I nod and he shuts the door between us. *Play the game,* I think, but the stack of paper still goes on the floor.

I come to slumped against the window, my neck and shoulder at a crooked angle against the brittle stucco. My legs are twisted beneath me against the wholesale mattress, one of them now completely asleep. One of the problems with cheeking your meds is that, even when successful, they still begin to dissolve. You end up taking low quality doses of whatever cocktail they have you on. Mine has Atavan, Zoloft, Halidol, and some other heavy hitters I'm still too foggy to name. Even in small quantities they strike like a velvet hammer if it takes you too long to spit them out.

A rustle of sheets next to me, and I look over at the opposite bed. Phoebe's laying on her stomach, feet crossed and kicking at the air. She's commandeered one of my paperbacks, and she pushes her bangs out of her face with a manicured finger. Her hair's night incarnate, one of those bob cuts from the twenties, when everyone said *doll* and *clyde* and acted like they were trapped in a Chandler novel. She catches me looking and twiddles her fingers. "Morning, Zelda."

"Don't call me that." I yawn, my back arcing. "What time is it?"

"Little after seven." She sits up and nudges the papers with a foot. "Taking a break, huh?"

"Something like that." I get up to look through the door. Monique's sitting in the plastic chair this time, chatting with someone down the hall. *Night falls, and now my watch begins.*

Sitting up, I glance at the packet. The pages are still blank and willing them to be otherwise has been remarkably ineffective. "This sucks. It's like being trapped in the same day over and over. Like I've been here forever. *Will* be here forever."

"Nothing is forever." She smiles as she says it. Her left hand stays close to her hip, as if she were cradling a baby bird. "'Sides, you could do worse. Three hots. One cot. All the board games a girl could ask for. Plenty of *male supervision.*"

Her eyebrows waggle at the last. I groan. "Ew. I'm fine."

"Are you?" Phoebe slides across the space between our beds and sits down next to me, pushing the hair out of my eyes. "Think about your answer, for real, and think about it hard. Yours is the only mind you're ever going to see the world from, kid. If you're okay, you'll know. If you think you're not, though—"

There's a knock before Steve enters. There's a greasiness to him that defies explanation, and I lean back instinctively. In a chino shirt and jeans, you can see the softening muscle of a faded athlete, blonde hair cut short to set off a narrow brow. His hands are huge, disproportionate, pink spiders that are constantly roaming and exploring. In one of them is a plate, the other a carton of milk. He sets them on the foot of the bed and takes half a step towards me. I will myself not to flinch.

"Dinner's up." His eyes are dirty ice by the side of the road. "Did you finish your packet yet?"

"This guy." Phoebe says to the room. He pays her no mind.

"No. I fell asleep." He makes a clucking sound, and I look past him, uncomfortable. Monique is still across the way, manning her post. "No rush. It'll be done by tomorrow."

"Good." He leans in closer. "You can't go around hitting people, kid, especially the staff. You want to get out of here, right?"

Out of this room, out of this building, out of your presence.
"Yes."

He spreads his hands like he's just uncovered a great secret. His fingers cast long shadows against the wall like warped puppets. "There you go. Just play along, and everything will be all right. Don't make waves."

Does he know why I'm here? If he does, I wonder if he'd rethink that statement. There's a file somewhere with a case summary that would stand your hair on end. "Good talk."

"Yeah, now skidoo." Phoebe makes a flitting *shoo* gesture with one hand.

"I worry about you girls, that's all." He smiles like it hurts him and backs out of the room. Monique watches him go, eyes shrouded. I can't read her face.

Dinner is fish sticks and steamed vegetables, bread and butter on the side. The fish is salty and the vegetables bland. They still haven't figured out a way to screw up bread and butter, though, and I eat a few bites before my stomach begins to ache. Something with the meds, maybe. Phoebe watches mealtime behind the cover of a paperback.

I push the plate down to the foot of the bed and pick up the packet again. Phoebe grins. "You're really going to finish that?"

"Looks like."

"Please, dollface. You don't have to jump through that hoop," she says. "Your Man would say the same thing."

It's the wrong thing to say, and my face must show it. She tries to finish. "All I'm trying to say is that playing their games might not be as important as you think. There's more than one way to skin a cat."

"Meow," I say, and get started.

My eyes snap awake. I'm a light sleeper, always have been, exiting the land of Nod at the slightest provocation. It made it a real bitch for my father to play Tooth Fairy. After the first few times I'd caught him heavy-footed, he'd given up on the tiptoeing around and began wearing a green tutu for the occasion. He'd even purchased a tiara.

The memory, pure and clear as spun sugar glass, throbs painfully in my chest, but then there's the noise again. Muffled voices, the brief flicker of a flashlight, and I sit upright, A glance outside the window shows only the dark, deserted hall, so I tiptoe over to the door. There's something odd about other people sneaking around that makes one try to outmatch them,

I raise an eye to the panel, standing a few feet back to keep my face in the dark. The only light is from the desk in the hallway, and the black sockets of the other doors stare out into the void. Right now, the whole Lodge could be up with me, peering out. Watching.

Chapman walks by, a kraken breaching the surface, and I take another step back. He's got a battered logbook in one hand, trailing down lines with one pudgy finger. Angel is behind him with a flashlight, a weathered old member of the night staff that could pass for Danny Trejo after a wildfire. He slinks by without a glance in my direction.

Over his shoulder in the far corner of the hall, a dark smudge by the fire door, is Marmalade, his pale jaw a sickle of bone beneath the black wide-brim hat, his faded work clothes blending him into the lightless stone. Without a word he rushes them. I have time to think *Osgood, what have you done?* before his long fingers curl around Angel's chin and pull, hearing the snap of dry cartilage, the old man hitting the floor, the door slamming open as he comes for me.

Little raven, he says, the scent of vanilla filling up the room as his arms coil around me. *We're all down here in the dark together.*

I shake my head. My heart is thudding wildly in my chest, and the far end of the hall is empty, no man in black buried in the dark. *Did I just drift off?*

Somehow I'm still on my feet.

Leaning closer to the window, I can make out a huge man sitting at the desk, three hundred pounds or more compressed into a hoodie sweatshirt and baggy jeans. I haven't seen him before, and he whispers something to Chapman upon his return that the latter doesn't like. Chapman barks a stage whisper at him, and the big man starts walking in my direction. Dimly the teaching level comes back to me, the 1:1, and I slide from the window to beneath my sheets with liquid grace. There's just time to close my eyes before the room light flickers on and off, a random starburst. I had forgotten the bed-checks.

A count to ten, and I wander back to the window, every nerve singing. They're going through the contact sheets now, everyone's court-approved family and friends, and Angel mumbles something to Chapman. It dawns on me that this is strange, Chapman here so late, but then he looks up from his papers. His eyes pierce the darkness. Somehow he finds me.

Angel mouths two words to him, and the spell is broken. Darting back beneath my sheets, I pull the comforter over my head. Dawn seems a long way away, and I gaze up at the Eggshell Universe, willing myself to be back amongst the stars.

Two words. *She's gone.*

Graham's behind the big desk, a styrofoam cup of coffee cooling by his elbow. The sheaf of papers comes apart before him in the bustle of the hallway, half a dozen girls going about their morning rituals, but somehow his focus doesn't waver.

"You put a lot of time into this."

It's not a question, but I nod anyway. Most of it was multiple choice with some light reading comprehension thrown in for balance. A lot of the pages had been filled with cartoons.

My pride isn't exactly fluttering.

"I've never had anyone quote Orwell in their teaching packet," he says, and staples the mess back together. It gets dropped into a plastic file folder in the big pull-out drawer, and just like that it's locked away forever. "You know how this works?"

I shrug, trying to remember what someone might have once told me. I haven't seen Phoebe all morning, and her absence makes everything a little grayer. "I move up?"

"You move up, but you stay back here for breakfast. Your one-on-one stays until the county clinician sees you and takes it off, but you'll get to go to Academy."

In other words, someone would be following me around until Osgood told them to stop. The Academy is what passes for school here, a gray stucco building where not stabbing your neighbor with a pair of play scissors is worthy of an A. Supposedly the tiny classes of remedial work count as high school credits, but I think Miskatonic is the only college they'd get you into. "My heart soars."

He ignores the sarcasm and takes a question from a delicate girl a little younger than I am. Taking the cue, I grab my hygiene bag and run through the essentials. Sandy follows along behind me, a tiny, sincere woman with green eyes too large in her elfin face. "Good job finishing your packet so fast," she says. It sounds genuine as I step into the communal bathroom. Everyone gives me a wide berth at the sink.

"It's not a big deal," I say. Praise of any kind makes me uncomfortable, and I start brushing my teeth.

"To you, maybe," Sandy continues from the doorway. "Not everyone accepts their consequences."

Was she here yesterday? I glance down at her little hands, wondering if they had been part of the set that had hustled me off to the blue room, if her little fingers had left the bruises on my arms.

Not that it would have taken much. Hell, I've always bruised easily.

A half-dozen girls have already cleared out, lining up to go downstream to the cafeteria. It sounds lame, but like everything else here it's an experience you have to earn. If Everbrook has taught me one thing, it's that anything can be transformed into a privilege.

I spit into the sink. "I shouldn't have hit him."

Sandy nods, and I set about trying to tame my hair. Today it's a battle, and I finally settle for just tying it back before putting my things away and walking out into the Lodge. The dayroom has the vodka smell of industrial sanitizer, empty except for the delicate girl and a raven-haired toughie who came in yesterday, Harkness or Darkness or something. Both are sitting at the table, separated by a plastic chair. Lo's unassuming at his perch in the hallway, his back to the desk as I sit.

We don't say anything as we wait for breakfast to arrive. Harkness keeps glancing over my shoulder at Sandy, who's probably haunting me from a couple of yards back. Up close her bottle-black hair frames a face that's all angles with a jaw that looks like it could take a punch. There's a fresh bruise under her right eye and she's cut the sleeves off her t-shirt. I'm guessing it's not her first tour here.

It's been six weeks, though, and I realize I really don't know any of girls.

Harkness gives up the ghost first. "Is it true?" she asks in a stage whisper. "Not judging."

"Is what true?" By the way everyone inches forward, it's the elephant in the room.

"You know."

"Yeah, I hit Osgood a couple of times. Not my proudest moment."

"Not that. The real question." She waggles her thin eyebrows conspiratorially. They look like shadows against the pale milk of her skin. Her black hair's cut short, pretty in a goth-Peter-Pan kind of way. "Red Orphan."

"It's okay." The delicate girl leans forward as well, her green eyes striking against the warm sienna of her skin. Her thin bones could be made of porcelain. "We all have our secrets."

"I'm not supposed to talk about the case." I'd seen an episode of *Bones* where the defendant's cellmate had been an informant, another of *Law and Order* where the cellmate had been an undercover cop. Neither had ended well for the blabbermouth.

"But of course." The delicate girl put her hand on mine, and I jerked it away. There was something unwholesome about the heat of her touch, the feathery lightness of her hand. "What other secrets do you have?"

Harkness looked at her funny, which was a relief. For a moment, I wasn't sure that anyone else could see her. "She doesn't want to talk about it. That's fine. Plenty of other chatter on the wire."

The delicate girl smiles, thin-lipped. Her teeth are very long. "Common knowledge is so— common."

Uncertain, I nod. The smell of Sandy's coffee is driving me crazy, and I'd wrestle Hemingway for a cup right now. "Did either of you wake up last night? Hear a noise?"

"Sinatra?" The delicate girl laughs, a tinkling of damaged bells. Harkness glances over my shoulder at Sandy, who I can only imagine looks none too pleased with this turn in the conversation. The delicate girl's voice drops to a whisper. "Did you see his eyes?"

"What?"

"It's our resident ghost story," Harkness explains, but the other girl shushes her with a wave of her finger.

"*Made of dark, and tone so true. You'll know if he's been watching you,*" the delicate girl intones, dropping her voice. She lets her eyes roll back in her head for emphasis. "*Claws of ice, and eyes of gold. Where he takes you's never told.*"

A chill ran up the nape of my neck. I wasn't sure if it was how weird the delicate girl was being or that someone had bothered to construct a folk poem. "Give me a break. It has a nursery rhyme?"

Vanessa nods. "He's been here forever. I heard it from an older girl when I was in juniors, who heard it when she was little from someone in Intensive Girls, who heard it— well, you get the idea. He's this flowing black mass, like an ink stain on the world, only with these piercing yellow eyes. He'll serenade you before he comes and takes you away. I've heard that when staff find what's left of them, they just clean it up and say that the kids ran away. The price of doing business. Too bad, so sad."

"She's being dramatic." Harkness shoots her a look that says *tone it down*. "Every institution has its spooks."

"And every ghost story its tragedy." She folds her hands, birdlike on the table in front of her.

"It wasn't— whatever the hell you're talking about," I say. "The night staff were running around with flashlights. The taxpayers would go nuts if they were playing ghost hunters."

"Maybe Chapman was looking for the stick up his ass," Harkness grins, and shrugs at whatever glare Sandy's giving her. "What? Guy's kind of a jerk. No, Yesenia ran last night."

"Or was taken," Vanessa says sweetly.

"Girls, change the topic." There's a thread of irritation in Sandy's voice that threatens to become a tapestry.

"We're not being disruptive, are we?" The delicate girl smiles again, sharp enough to shave with. "Just three sisters, having a conversation. Civil as can be."

I think of the walls, grey and stretching tall. How could you just go over?

"Doesn't matter, Sandman. She's not the first, won't be the last." Harkness puts her elbows on the table and stretches. "Reed blew out two months ago, Maddy the month before that. Us teens get itchy feet."

Sandy doesn't say anything, but the tension's welling behind me. I blurt it out before my rationale smothers it. "How do you get out?"

"Old state secret," Harkness pushes back from the table. "Fire tunnels below the gym. Put there so that there'd be a way past the walls if the place burnt down. Get the keys, make the right turns, and there's a hatch that drops you off on the other side."

"That's enough," Sandy says. "Let's go, Prose."

"How do you know?"

"Been here long enough," Harkness says. "Off and on the last two years. Vanessa here's been around longer than that. You pick up a thing or two."

"*Now.*" Sandy's will is a physical force that's pushing me towards the hallway. Her glower power is awesome to behold.

"You need anything else, hit me up. It's not like it's an achievement, cycling back and forth between foster homes and bad ideas. When I turn eighteen they'll wash their hands of me." Harkness shrugs. Her eyes don't match her words.

Sandy's directing me back to my room, even though I'm not the one speaking. The food comes in behind her, smelling of pancakes, syrup, and institutionally scrambled eggs. I follow directions, not needing the friction, and Vanessa brightens right before the door shuts. "You would have liked Reed, Spooky. You're even in the same room."

CHAPTER FOUR
THE NEW CLICK

The Academy was everything you'd think it would be, and I was back in my room reading Agatha Christie by three. Off of 'teaching level', there's yet another day before privileges are restored, meaning I don't have to work but also have zero to do. Minus the paperbacks, I'd be yellowing the wallpaper.

For a place designed to help you, so much of it only made me feel sick.

The group of strangers had just landed on the island when I hear a knock. I look over for Phoebe but she's wandered off. The timing is weird, and I smell something like burnt copper as I put the book down and answer it.

Lo's waiting outside. Though there's a snowdrift of white piling up at his temples, his face is unlined, almost like a child's. I chalk it up to a lack of stress. "You're still on your one-on-one, right?"

Not sure if he's actually asking, I nod. In the six weeks I've been here, I've gotten the measure of most of the regular staff, and Lo is by far the most laid-back if not completely detached. For him, if it's above the bare minimum necessary to stay employed, it's not happening.

In a way, it's endearing. No pressure to fix things, no inkling to save the world. If you're copacetic, he's more than happy to let things keep going how they're going.

"Cool, cool." He looks back at the desk. Chapman sits in front of it, thick arms folded. "Your clinician's here."

"Shit." He's unperturbed. "Sorry. I'll be out in a minute."

My socks stay practically glued on at all times, a testament to my mistrust of industrial carpet, but I slip my shoes on at the slowest rate possible. An apology would be in order, at the least, if not full prostration.

Poe wept.

Yesenia's room is being cleared out on the way, her belongings stuffed into green nylon laundry bags, sealed shut with masking tape, and tossed into a wide white laundry cart. Harkness gives me a grin from the couch, a controller in her hands. Bright lasers and alien carnage flash by on the screen in front of her. Some of the other girls give me scowls.

I turn back to Lo. "Where is he?"

Lo shrugs and turns back to Chapman. Chapman sighs and points to the door. "Right there."

The light is behind the standing man, shining through the paneled window by the front door. He is immensely tall, six-six or better, but what stands out about him is his unhealthy leanness. If he turns sideways, he might disappear.

"Osgood's my click. That's not Osgood."

"No more." There's an accent in there, Eastern European, maybe, but exactly what it is had always been my mother's trick. To me, everyone sounded like they were from one of four places.

He takes a step closer, and I'm stricken by the gauntness of his features, his sunken cheeks leaving eye sockets deep and retreating. A black fedora sits atop his closely-cropped hair, and a graying handlebar mustache serves as an odd accoutrement to his conservative features. Where Lo's features are almost childlike, his are those of an ancient, the face of a brooder prone to plotting.

His eyes are chips of flint that survey me dispassionately, "I am Dr. Svara. I will be taking over for Osgood." The clinician says the last with a touch of distaste that borders on the bizarre.

"No," I hear myself saying. "I see Osgood."

"Alas, your case has been transferred to me." Svara murmurs. He pivots to the door. "Please, let us talk outside."

I look around the room for help. The scowling girls are watching me expectantly, and Nellie mouths to another *drama queen*. Harkness rolls her eyes and waves her controller at me to just get on with it. By the desk, Chapman is showing enough emotion to qualify him as asleep. "Fine," I grumble, and follow him out.

Outside, the air has already started to cool, and dry leaves blow down the 'Sip. The wind smells of smoke and Douglas firs refusing to die. A weird impulse compels me to just take off running.

Maybe the gym story's true. Once outside I could call Mark from a store, get him to pick me up.

We could just disappear.

But the thought's ridiculous. I don't know where the tunnel is even if it were real, and besides being the first place they'd check, Mark has less of a chance disappearing than the Statue of Liberty. The way Dad always talked about him, he was only marginally an adult, bouncing around from one dead-end gig to another, staying afloat through goodwill and a network of friends that wouldn't let him drown. How the court was going to appoint him a caregiver was a question I hadn't liked to ask myself, because he was all that was left.

Svara clears his throat behind me, snapping me back to the moment. He gestures to a small wooden structure next to the Lodge that could arguably be a gazebo. "We can speak here."

"I really prefer to walk and talk." I struggle to find a reason. "It's relaxing."

"Osgood must have thought you, mmm— very relaxed."

This isn't going well. "Somewhere else, then. It's too close—" *to home*, I almost say, and catch myself. The thought is so alarming that my eyes begin to water, a knot in my stomach tightening and intense. In that moment I miss my parents fiercely. "—To everyone else. I don't want them to know my business."

"Very well. The field, then. There are many places there." The doctor nods sagely. He would have to put on twenty pounds to look vampiric.

"Thank you." I force it out and start walking, each stride a tug on the knot in my stomach.

Watch your words. This one's different.

Osgood had been easygoing, playacting with the idea of us becoming pals. Svara does not seem to care for the illusion.

I hear Lo breathing behind us as we pass the other Lodges. Boys are outside playing basketball on a plastic hoop, younger girls on another patio coloring figures in with chalk. The world seems so normal, so reasonable that I feel another pang of homesickness.

All that's gone, my dear. All gone.

We're all down here in the dark together.

We make our way onto the field, and I hear the local owl offer its eternal question. The earth is damp and squishy beneath my shoes, and Svara gestures to an identical gazebo-like creation.

Sitting across from me, he frowns. I must look like I'm about to bolt, because he relaxes the moment I draw my feet up. "I have been going over your records for several days now. Would it surprise you to find that I have some concerns?"

"No." I watch Lo behind him, ostensibly watching me but more interesting in bouncing a soccer ball to himself. Landon Donovan doesn't need to feel threatened.

"I am going to ask you to talk about several things that may make you feel uncomfortable." He draws a digital recorder and lays it down on the bench next to us. "Rest assured, I am not a policeman. Our conversation is protected against any criminal proceedings. Our only purpose here is to establish a picture of your overall mental health."

I sigh. "Okay."

He raises an eyebrow. "In your sessions with Osgood, you mentioned figures. Autonomous figures, that no one else can see. Do you recall this?"

"Yes."

"How long have you been hallucinating?"

"I'm not. Have they found her yet?"

"Hm?"

"Yesenia. Has anyone found her?"

He shakes his head. "I am not here to talk about other girls. Truth be told, I have no interest but in you."

A small notepad rests in his palm. I didn't see him take it out. "Nice to feel special."

"You claim to not see figures?"

"No." I sigh. "I don't hallucinate."

Svara smiles, his mustache rising in a friendly wave. It doesn't meet his eyes. "As you say, then. These figures that no one else agrees to see. When did you first notice them?"

I shake my head. "Everything started when they noticed me."

It wasn't always this obvious.

Even now I still get fooled on occasion. It took me reaching an age where I realized that not everyone dresses like they're going to a costume party before I put it together, but to be fair, not all of the irregulars do. I don't know if they have any control over their outfits, but unless it's Halloween, I can spot them about nine times out of ten. Sometimes higher.

Right, right. When.

The day was dark, grey skies drizzling so lightly that it was like walking through a haze to the bus. Mom had my hand, and you should have seen her in those days, young and bright-eyed. Her smile ignited the furnaces of my little heart, and I was overflowing with love, the way I think you only can be when you're really little, that lizard-brain response so deep inside that it's actually instinctive. The very meaning of unconditional.

The sidewalk was wet and some of those little red worms were fighting their way to higher ground, and my shoes splish-splashed through shallow puddles as we went down the hill. We'd made the left turn on Barrister and everything smelled of moist earth, wet leaves. Clean, you know?

He had stepped out of the trees halfway down the hill before I first noticed him. The man was young, younger than the kid who drove our bus, and he had this dark blue coat on over pants the color of the sky. The traces of a mustache were struggling for life above his lip, and he had this weird black hat, like a cap, but taller. As I got closer, I could see gold buttons, little straps on his shoulders. I didn't recognize the outfit, not then.

Little girl, remember?

Anyhow, he was approaching from the other side of the street. Above all other things, he was a stranger, but I figured we had a pretty good chance of getting right by him. He was scanning the clearing before the next patch of woods, as if he were looking for something he'd lost, and we'd almost passed by when he chanced to glance behind him and caught me looking.

There was something in my gaze he didn't like.

He took a step towards us. I remember squeezing my mother's hand so hard it hurt, and I tried to drag us along a little quicker, because something was about to happen. "We're going to be late," fell out of my mouth. Below, the yellow behemoth charged towards our corner, hooking a right off of the state route and bulling its way into our neighborhood.

"We'll be fine," my mother said. She smiled down at me, then something broke. She almost stopped walking, and I tugged her onwards. "Prose? What's the matter?"

"Please!" the man in the blue coat gargled out behind us. He was waving one arm in a desperate bid for attention. "Please!"

My heart was thrumming a bassline in my chest. I squeaked it out. "We're going to miss the bus."

"Don't be silly," my mother said, but the color had slipped from her cheeks. Her eyes were wide and white as she put the back of her hand against my forehead. "What's gotten into you?"

"Miss!" the man screamed. "Miss, please!" He was twenty yards away and closing. The closer he got, the more I could see what was wrong with his face.

He rattled his arm in our direction as he hobbled towards us.

At the corner, I could see the other children clambering up the black rubber steps, a line of innocents fed into the belly of the beast. Shelley McCaffrey and Bobby Something were the last to climb up, and then it was just me. My mom knelt down and gave me a kiss on the cheek as the figure advanced behind her.

She asked me if something was wrong again, but I was already racing up the steps. With a *whoosh* like releasing a breath the door shut. Relief poured out of me. I found my way back amongst staring eyes to the naugahyde bench in the back, struggling to catch my wind.

A fist hammered against the windowpane, inches from my face. "Please!"

He shouldn't be alive, I thought. *How can he be alive?*

Again, then a third time as the engine lurched us forward. In my mind the glass had already shattered.

"We need you!"

The bus yanked me away, and the stranger let out a raw howl of frustration. His pinwheeling hand brushed against my mother's arm as he screamed, and through the grimy plastic window, I saw her turn around.

She stood there for a moment, questioning the very air around her, before turning and trudging back up the hill.

I can guess what the police record says. No, I am answering your question.

No. He is and he isn't. He's something—I don't know. If you read Osgood's notes, you know I don't want to talk about him.

Really.

You don't want to hear about the native in Stryker's Field? The hanged man at Shelley's eighth birthday party? The black mass that grew inside Mrs. Gutierrez's second-grade classroom at Harrison Elementary?

I said no. I don't want to talk about him.

It was a cloud, you know. Full of eyes, and fingers, and hungry little mouths. It begged to be noticed, it pleaded, it cajoled.

It made promises when her back was turned.

Not the kind you wanted kept.

If you don't want me to tell you about it, that's fine. Don't do your job.

Because you're not the first click to come in here and take a shot at fixing me, okay? I have a pretty good guess as to what's in my file, what the police wrote down, what Holcomb opted to omit. I know what I saw.

I know what I see.

Fine, write that down.

For the last time, I am not going to talk about him. Even if it's the root of the problem, the seed everything springs from, it's not going to happen. He...

That's not it.

No.

That's not it.
You don't understand.
He'll hear me. And he'll come.

"We're done," I say, and stand up. My legs are sore from the rough wood of the gazebo bench, the blocky angle cutting into my circulation, and I walk over to Lo. He sees me coming and misses the rebound, the soccer ball falling back to earth in a moist splat.

Svara stands up behind me. I can see Lo's eyes. "It is over when we are finished."

"I'm not talking to you. Bring back Osgood."

Lo looks back and forth between us, uncomfortable. I take his hand, large and baby-smooth against my palm. "We're going."

He glances to Svara again. I wonder what the power balance is between the county clinicians and the staff, who overrules who. I give Lo's hand a tug. "I'll make it easy. Either you take me back or I run."

Lo shakes his head and the spell is broken, and I let go of him and start walking down the 'Sip. He follows me like the newly damned.

A rush of cloth and Svara is there beside me. The faint aroma of cloves and dust exudes from his coat. "We are not done here, young lady."

"If you won't respect my boundaries, I'm done talking." I don't bother to turn around. Lo waves a hand as we pass the younger Lodges, girls with chalky fingers lining up with curiosity, the basketball players being hurried inside. Am I making a scene?

This is how they see me. Everyone's been warned.
The Red Orphan's here.
Lock up the barn and pass the ammunition.

Monique raises an eyebrow, her fingers smeared with greens and blues as the younger girls scurry inside to clean up.

I didn't know she was here today and I say hi. She nods. "Make good choices, Prose."

When I reach Intensive Girls, I walk through the dayroom and go straight to the back, past the staring teens and looming Chapman, heading right into my bedroom. Chapman mutters "That was fast," before the door shuts behind me.

I pull the covers over my head as I hear the door yanked open. Svara is saying something, but I'm repeating in my head

— And travelers, now, within that valley—

—Through the red-litten windows see—

—Vast forms, that move fantastically—

—To a discordant melody—

until his voice fades and is replaced with vacuum, the sound between the stars. Eventually the room goes silent, and tears well up.

These aren't the choices I'm supposed to be making. This isn't going to get me out of here any faster.

But the alternative is so much worse.

"You okay, kiddo?"

I peer out from beneath the thin blanket, one eye open in trepidation. Phoebe's on the other bed, a little smile curling her lip. "Don't mind me. I just work here."

"I'm good," I say, and wipe at my eyes. She's got of one of my paperbacks folded open in front of her, Shirley Jackson's *We Have Always Lived in the Castle*. I force a smile.

"Don't be like that. What's all the hubbub, bub?"

"Osgood's gone, I think. For good."

"Well, you did beat him around the head and neck, so— yeah."

I shake my head. "There's a new guy, older. Pushy. He won't listen."

She flips her bangs out of her face. "Sounds like most of the guys in my life. So tell him to go jump in a lake."

"It's not that simple. If I don't cooperate, I don't leave."

The book sinks to one side. "Uh huh."

"If I cooperate, if I talk about what they want me to talk about, I'm worried something will come. Bad things are going to happen."

"Is this about the Man?"

"What?" My features become blank, an ornate mask. "What did you say?"

"The Man. Marmut? Marmaduke?" Phoebe gives me an appraising look. "You say it in your sleep sometimes. Those dreams don't exactly look all rainbows and unicorns."

Even without knowing that Phoebe occasionally watched me sleep, this was an unsettling revelation. How often had I twisted in the middle of the night, calling his name? Worse yet—

I cage my bets. "Yeah. Nothing good can come from it."

"Don't be a pushover, then."

"What?"

"You'll be eighteen in under a year, right? They can't hold you here forever."

The thought of spending the next ten months in the company of Chapman and friends gives me a fresh chill. "I don't know if I can last that long."

"Don't be a maroon. You've got your old pal Pheebs, a charming paperback collection, more Jell-O than you can shake a stick at. If it's as bad as you say, up their nose and settle in for a while. These bars can't hold us."

I smile in spite of myself. "Don't be silly."

"Please." Phoebe rests her palms on either side of my face. "You know you're all right. I know you're all right. The rest of the world? Fuck 'em. They give you worksheets, you miss some TV, and a year from now we walk out of here with a fresh start and a middle finger raised. They won't know what hit 'em."

"My uncle Mark—"

"Will understand." Her eyes are a deep brown, threatening to black. "Just think about it. Even if you decide to start talking, spilling your guts to this guy, the doors aren't going to be thrown open tomorrow. Once you start giving people what they want, they only end up wanting more. You'll cut your heart up and serve it to them, a little at a time, until one morning there's nothing left. Let them keep their levels and their stickers and their gold stars. The only person you need to make happy here is you."

She stands up and gives me a kiss on the forehead, smoothing out her corduroys with one hand. "Sorry to go all revival preacher on you, dollface. If you don't mind, I'm going to catch some air. There's an old palooka a couple of buildings over I'm dying to acquaintance."

"No one's going to mind?" I smile as she crosses to the door.

"Not for little old me. The password is *shh*." Phoebe gives me a devil-may-care grin and slips out into the hallway. Lo's staring at his phone and doesn't so much as raise his head.

I lean back against the pillow and explore the Eggshell Universe, letting my thoughts whirl about me like so much interstellar debris. Could I just plant myself, unwilling and mute, for the next year in this room? A lost probe drifting amongst the stars? More likely I would just completely lose it, eating Jell-O from plastic cups with my fingers and painting triptychs in strawberry and lime. Would Mark understand why?

Worse, would he be relieved?

Deciphering the whorls of old paint and streaks of plaster, I get so lost that I almost miss the knock on the door. "Meals are back," calls Lo, who already sounds like he's on the move.

I step out onto the dark hallway. No one's in view, not even at the desk, and for a moment I wonder if it's a dream—if I should bolt. In the next the shadows seem to lengthen, and I realize that Chapman should be squatting behind the desk, catching bureaucratic flies from his pad with Lo flitting about like an absentminded skeeter.

It's a trap, I think irrationally, and have a foot back inside my room before I realize that it's ludicrous. I can hear people in the kitchen, the sound of trays being unpacked, and I force myself down the corridor.

The kitchen and dayroom are fluorescent cells amidst dark matter. Vanessa looks tiny on a plastic chair, a crisp round pizza that looks hatched from a microwave on the grey tray in front of her with a side of potato salad. The aroma of baked cheese and pepperoni hits me, and my mouth waters out of proportion to reason as Chapman sets out cartons of milk. I cross the dayroom expanse before my absence can be noticed and slide in next to the delicate girl. Lo sets a tray down in front of me, its contents identical to the others. He's already got a quarter of a pizza jammed in his cheek like a ravenous squirrel.

There are three chairs set at the table, I realize. I've taken a bite out of the pizza and crane my head around, hoping for Harkness. Instead I'm greeted by a wall of blue.

"You're in my seat," she says, and I look up. Nellie is far larger than I imagined standing up. Her blonde hair is tied back in some complicated braid, her eyes blue chunks of ice. With her broad, thick shoulders I imagine her astride a polar bear, ambushing centurions in the blackness of the Teutoborg, a broadsword flashing above her head.

I don't get a chance to respond. "Now. Move your ass, Spooky."

"Nellie," Vanessa chastises, but only until a glare from the scowling girl drops her eyes to the tray.

"No one was sitting here." Reality seems like a safe bet. It's a fallacy more common than you'd think. "I didn't—"

"Some of us were helping out around here, Spooky. Some of us have better things to do than make trouble." She kicks the legs of my chair, and it scoots six inches across the tile.

Bewildered, I look over to Chapman. He's behind the kitchen counter, gaze fixed out the window in pretend obliviousness. A stunned realization is dawning.

"Hey," I begin, and Nellie picks up my carton of milk. With a squeeze, it ruptures like a wet balloon, drowning my tray, drenching the pizza, the potato salad, even the fruit cup. Everything is a sopping white mess as I look back at her in horror.

"Eat up, drama queen." The words burn in a way I hadn't imagined was possible, white-hot and stirring up embers.

Something inside me catches alight.

I'm on my feet before I realize what's happening. Lo says something, but my hands are already shoving at the big girl's shoulders. "What did you say?"

"Red Orphan," she snorts. "My ass. You're not scary, and you'd better get with the program." Her hands find my shoulders and push, and I'm stumbling backwards, my stockinged feet not finding purchase on the tile. I collide with the wooden table in mid fall, and its corner punches into my kidney in a bolt of pain. For a second, I can't breathe. "You're a spoiled brat, taking up everyone else's time, and I'm sick of you trying to get attention. Some of us have real problems."

"Girls, stop," Chapman says, and takes another bite of his pizza. For all he moves, his feet may have been mired in concrete.

She steps over to me in three long strides and wrenches me to my feet, bending my arm behind my back at an awful angle. Agony sings in my shoulder as she breathes in my face. "You might be sick, but you can listen. They'll cart you off to prison, they'll shove you out in the street, they'll find another relative for you to kill. I don't care. When you're behind these walls, you get with the program." She gives my arm another twist, and a wrenching pain radiates from the tips of my fingers to the balls of my feet. "Or I'll start finding bones to break."

She throws me into the table, and I hit it at my hips and fold. The wind rushes out of me in a long wheeze, and my fingers find an empty tray before I know what they're doing.

With a spin I bring the tray back around, a screaming parabola that Nellie registers with dull surprise. With screeching effort I bring the tray to a stop right before it crushes the bridge of her nose.

We look at each other. I let the tray drop.

And then Chapman is there, breaking us apart. I grab another tray off of the aluminum cart and walk back to my room, the silence following me like an audience. Lo only stuffs another wedge of pizza into his gob as I shut the door behind me.

CHAPTER FIVE
START SPREADING THE NEWS

The room is dark when my eyes snap open, the dregs of nightmare already filtering down the drain. The Man had been there sitting by the stove, one coarse thumbnail popping a match alight, and I begged him not to do it, but he just smiled that damning smile.

Little raven, we're all down here in the dark together.

Outside it's diving bell black. The hallway inside's not much better. I peer out the window, trying to make out the small path that winds across the back, but the orange sodium light must have burnt out. The night beyond the glass is endless, no moon, no stars. I wait patiently for some monstrous angler to drift by, too shaken to drift back to dreams.

With a puff, my breath is cold mist, and I wonder if the heater might be broken too. In the brilliance of government contracting, Everbrook's Lodges each run on a single central unit, controlled by a lone thermostat. Fifteen different bedrooms, a bathroom, two utility closets, the blue room, a sprawling dayroom and kitchen, all regulated by a tiny plastic knob buried somewhere in a locked closet. Some rooms boil and others ice over, regardless of the settings. My room's perpetually Tahiti.

There's the faintest of scrapes, a metallic *scritch* behind me, and I turn back to the hallway. The dim orange of overheard lighting bleeds sweetly through the frame, so faint it's almost imperceptible. In the dark, I trace the latticework of the reinforced pane, trying to convince myself that I don't hear something muffled moving at the far end of the hall, footsteps shuffling closer, so slow that their host must be either infirm or playacting.

Bed checks, I think. *Bed checks on the psych ward, nothing more natural than that,* as they begin to come nearer and nearer.

Any member of the night staff would be just going through the motions, eager to get back to their desk and coffee to finish playing Candy Crush. No one in their right mind would draw the process out.

Scritchh, the sound of a nail file drawn down metal lockers, and now a faint melody, some old warbler from old-timey radio. Gooseflesh breaks out on my arms as a vestigial instinct awakens. I realize that the window behind me is virtually unbreakable. There's only one way out of this room.

If I don't take it soon, I might not be able to take it at all.

The footsteps draw nearer, mere meters outside the door. Something smells of earth and old pennies, and I slip from my bed to the corner by the cabinet, not wanting to be seen.

—*start spreading the news*—

An eternity seems to rise and dwindle before me, and just when I think it's long gone, the thing steps past the reinforced pane, a black mass of nightmares and delusions. Something long and haggard like a terrible claw scrapes against the window in a low metallic *scritchh* as my scream catches in my throat, a small mercy, and its baleful yellow eye peers into the room.

—*i'm leaving today*—

My heart turns to ice. Something in my mind tries to wrench itself free of its moorings as the thing lingers. A lifetime passes before it continues its measured pace down the hallway. My fingernails have dug bloody crescents into my palms.

I let out a pained breath. Part of me wants to dive beneath the covers and wait out the long hours for the sun. The other Prose goes to the door and looks out the paneled window down the hall.

It's empty, devoid of monsters or people. A chair tilts drunkenly across the hall from my doorway, and I take a deep breath before opening the door and stepping out. The darkness is thick and clouded, and rows of lockers cast unfamiliar shadows. I take three paces before one of the night staff comes back, a turkey sandwich in his hand, hot coffee in the other.

"Hey. What are you doing up?" His eyes flicker back to the desk, the phone cradled atop it.

"Just thirsty," I manage as I approach. The water fountain's set into the wall a couple of yards from the desk, and he steps away from me. As I lean forward, my lips parted to receive, I study the dayroom and the kitchen beyond, dappled in the pale orange sodium leaked by outdoor lamps. I take a sip of cool water, reinforcing that I'm awake.

A thin woman steps out of the utility closet by the kitchen, a faint glow in her palm as she tucks her cell phone away. She looks at me, then at the man behind me. I don't know what else passes between them, but there's a hint of embarrassment, as if being caught away from your post. "Everything good?" she asks.

I start to answer, but the other man replies first. "Yeah. She just wants to water, then she's going back to bed."

"Great. Make good choices, Prose."

My eyebrow raised, I take another sip. Without a word the thin woman slips back into the hallway and leans against the wall. I look around a little more, trying to pierce the shadows, but there's no point. There's no one else in the Lodge.

"Good night," I mumble, and find the way back to my room. The thin woman follows, taking up the chair and a paperback across from my door. *There is a thing that nothing is,* I think to myself as I slide beneath my sheets. *And yet it has a name.*

The room is icy cold, hours left before the dawn.

I'm staring at the dayroom wall for almost five minutes when Harkness sits down next to me. There's something in its dappled paint and oblique deformities that drags my thoughts back to Rachel's old farmhouse. A whorl that calls to mind the drowning of galaxies. A blotch that reminds me of a man stepping off a scaffold. A rough patch in the corner, scuffed by a bad roller or the repeated tread of scrabbling feet.

She hadn't deserved what happened to her. None of them did, but they'd paid the price all the same.

A chill runs up my spine at the memory, and as I become aware of being watched I push it away, back to the black well where such thoughts linger in the dark.

I had gone to the Academy with Graham tailing me for most of the morning but still got called back for lunch with Sandy, the penalty for my altercation at the previous dinner. Apparently the wide social milieu of Everbrook was supposed to be a reward. I was glad to soak up the penalty.

Shields raise. The company is unexpected in the almost empty dayroom, the appraising eye more so. I raise an eyebrow and she gives me a sly smile. "What bench did you sleep under last night?"

"What?" The long hours after the thing outside the panel came were spent in spastic hyper-vigilance. Every time I started to drift off, that awful melody and leering eye would leap to mind, snapping me awake. Most of the morning has gone by in a series of Rorschach blurs.

"You look like shit, Spooky." She smiles as she says it, and it takes me a moment to process that she doesn't mean any harm by it. It's just an honest appraisal. "Wanna talk about it?"

"What's there to say?" I ask, studying her face. "Late night and a lot of reading. I don't sleep well."

"You and me both," she says. Lunch today's sweet and sour chicken over steamed vegetables and rice, a rare delicacy in the tasteless circuit of meals. She wrestles a hunk of meat to her lips. "It's not easy to crash with ten other psychos and pair of strangers standing guard. I'm amazed we sleep as well as we do."

"Right," I say, and take a bite of my chicken. It's already cooling.

"Seventy-seven steps to transcendence, right?" Harkness smiles again and pushes her shoe-polish black hair back. "You don't want to talk about it, that's fine, but the only people here to help you are sitting at this table. No offense, Graham."

"None taken," he calls. He had pulled over one of the office chairs and was leafing through last night's logbook with slender fingers. For a moment I wonder what he's reading up on, and then Harkness pulls me away.

"Look, I thought you might want a sympathetic ear, is all. We're all in this together."

There is a genuine concern in her eyes, a welling openness that I want to fall into. I chuck the thought into the well.

If it's an act, she's playing it perfect. We're all in this together? I've heard that one before.

Thoughts of Marmalade flicker to the surface, that sickle of a grin, the *who-me* look he'd try to play off.

"Don't take this the wrong way—" I start, but she laughs.

"Oh jeez. Look, I don't want to fish for clues, bait you into giving up your checkered past. I'm not going to show up on the stand next month with a horror story and a reduced sentence to boot. I just want to know if you're okay."

Am I that transparent? That she'd reached in and plucked it from me so deftly makes me pause. I fumble to regain control. "It's not that."

"Prose, I've been in and out of these places since I was six. Masks don't work on me." She smiles and puts her hand on mine. Her skin is icy pale, her touch warm. "I don't want to crack your head open and pore through the gooey innards. That's for the clicks. I just want to know if you're okay."

"Why?" It's out of my mouth before I can stop it.

"We're all we got." She pulls her hand back, and I can feel the ghost of warmth. "My halo's in the mail, if you were wondering."

I laugh, and something seems to have broken. I wonder where to start. "Have you ever—I don't know, ever seen something here? Something—not right?"

That my condition makes everything I witness highly suspect isn't something I volunteer.

"Scrumptious." Harkness takes another bite. "Prose, I've seen some truly laugh-or-go-crazy stuff over the years. This is Intensive Girls. Not right is the default setting."

I open my mouth, but Vanessa walks in with a tray, pulling up a chair to the table. The words catch in my throat, but it doesn't seem to matter. Her green eyes are alive and dancing. "I *thought* you might be talking ghouls and ghosts."

"You see anything weird lately, V?" Harkness looks neither thrilled nor upset with the interruption.

"A place like this is full of oddities." Her voice is one note shy of singsong. She takes a forkful of broccoli and twirls it. "Some things are odder than others."

I wonder if I can go back to my room, but I steel my resolve. "I saw something in the hallway last night."

Her eyes twinkle. "Ah. We *did* speak of the devil. Sinatra?"

What the hell. I've come this far. "Maybe. Black, and flowing, with this sick yellow eye? Hums a little? I tried to go down the hall after it, but it had vanished."

"You went after it?" Harkness freezes with her fork halfway to her mouth. "No wonder they call you Spooky."

Vanessa's eyes are white saucers. "I wouldn't advise it. The metaphorical stones on you, right?"

"You think it's a ghost."

"My roommate three runs ago said it's one of the night staff that haunts this place. One November, Everbrook had gotten six cases of sparkling cider in for Thanksgiving dinner but made the mistake of storing it in the Lodge utility room. Two brain surgeons thought it was champagne. At midnight, they snuck out behind one of the night staff and tried to choke him out for his keys but didn't know what they were doing. Crushed his windpipe, and—" Harkness drew her finger across her throat. "-*Start spreading the news*."

Trying not to shiver, I fail. Graham looks up from the log.

"That's not what I heard." Vanessa folds her hands primly in front of her. "I understand it was one of the maintenance men fifteen years ago. They have to take out the garbage on the overnight shift, so they have to get the keys for the side gate. One of the teens pretended to run that night but hid inside one of the big laundry carts instead. When they came by, the teen stabbed him with a pen, swiped his keys, and their whole Lodge took off."

"What?" Graham looks up from the logbook. "That's dumb. There are always two overnight staff."

"*Now there are*." Harkness grins. "There didn't used to be. I've been here longer than you, Graham-bo."

He acts like he didn't hear her. "And no Lodge has ever taken off in the middle of the night. We'd have called the cops, Vanessa."

She shrugs. "The dashing corsair protests too much. What's the story, then?"

"This place was built on the site of an old mining town," Graham starts, spreading his hands, and Harkness rolls her eyes. His eagerness to spin the yarn is endearing. "You know that little hill with the depression out on the field? Once there were two prospectors who didn't much like each other, on account of a silver claim they both thought they had the rights to. One day, the first prospector ate a big breakfast of eggs and potatoes and bacon and coffee and rashers..."

"Is a heart attack involved?" I ask.

"Hush. But the second prospector had poisoned his vittles, and the miner was sick all morning. When he went down into the mine that afternoon, he found out that the other prospector had been in there first. Half of the vein had been tapped."

"I don't think you've got a real solid grasp on mining." Harkness says, and he shushes her again.

"And so he waited for the second to come back. When he did, later that day, *and* thinking the first prospector was still sick, the first prospector rose up behind him and buried a pickaxe in his back."

"You work with children?" Sandy asks from the hallway.

Graham waves his hands theatrically. "And then he blew up the mine and buried the second prospector alive, so no one would ever know the tale."

"You're telling the tale." It seems a little obvious.

He frowns. "Well, of course he was caught. And, uh, hanged. Probably."

"Lame." Sandy says. "There's no ghost."

"You would say that," Vanessa offers, but Sandy dismisses her.

"Of course, if there was, it would be the construction worker who fell into the cement when they poured the foundation for the first Lodge back in the thirties. They didn't realize it until the end of the day when they were a man short. Legend is he's still down there, buried alive beneath the first Lodge."

I knew it was coming but waited it out.

"The very Lodge you're in—right now!," she finished, and let out a madwoman's cackle.

"No, seriously. Get back to school."

In a rough semicircle of plastic chairs and institutional couches, I'm sitting as far as I can from the front, trying not to close my eyes and sure I'm failing. The other girls are sprawled about the other seats, faking interest or even consciousness as Chapman stands in front of the TV and runs a group therapy session. His narrow eyes scan the room as he speaks, going through basics (what we're doing today, what we're eating for dinner, what's happening later) and some kind of variety show on pro-social behavior. He might as well be having an out-of-body experience, his face and words completely detached as he lectures briefly on what seems to be the importance of responsibility.

"Prose?"

"Because we all need to get better, and the staff here are just trying to help us. We can't blame others for not succeeding." Boom. After a few weeks, I learned a few lines that are both the answers to anything and nothing, and I relax.

Chapman continues questioning the room, looking for challenges and finding none. Harkness mumbles something about not trying to run away. Nellie pitches in we can't be selfish and that there's no I in team. Vanessa's a little more spaced out than usual and only manages that she should behave, which earns her a bit of a dark look but no comment.

The only one with anything interesting to throw in is Alisha, leaning all the way back in her chair. "We should keep our promises to our friends."

Chapman nods and looks to move on, but she's not done. "Yesenia was supposed to call me so we could hook up. Bitch broke my heart."

There's a ruffle of nervous laughter, and Alisha corrects her language before Chapman come down on her.

"That's okay, Al. Maddy ditched me too." Harkness pops in.

"Enough." Chapman spends another couple of minutes burrowing through the topic. Afterwards the group dissolves like sand in a river, and I slip back into my room before I can draw his wrath.

With Lo perched outside my door, I pore through a paperback and try to put some of the pieces together. My thoughts keep turning back to Sinatra, which is a bad sign.

Dwelling on things gives them power, the Man had said. Was it a ghost? A particularly vile irregular? A simple dream? I have no way of knowing, but then thoughts of the black city, the last supper beyond the door, the scuttling pallor try to fill me, and so I absently read Bradbury to distract myself. For all the horrors in my past, I don't know if I've ever seen a ghost.

The irregulars were terrifying enough.

There's a courtesy knock at the door again before it opens. Graham's got the cordless phone in one hand, offering it to me meekly. The way he doesn't meet my eyes says I probably don't want to take this.

"Hello?" I step out into the hallway and slide into his chair. Phones in the rooms are a big no-no.

"Prose?"

The gruff voice is instantly recognizable. I shrink a little lower in my seat. "Speaking," I offer, and hope he hangs up first.

"I was looking over your statements, and I couldn't help noting some inconsistencies." He didn't bother with introducing himself. Holcomb wasn't one for formalities. "I was hoping I could clarify a couple of things for me."

"Clarify them with my lawyer. You know you're not supposed to be calling here."

There was a sigh on the other end. "You know I'm just trying to help you, Prose."

"Help me?" *Help me for fifteen years to life, maybe.* My cheeks burn, and I turn my face away from the hall. "You've already called me a liar."

"Standard consequence for lying." There's a long pause on the other end, enough so that I wonder if he's hung up. "One body, well, accidents happen. Four, now... four's a pattern."

Four? A chill starts in my chest and bleeds outward in slow pulses. He doesn't seem to hear it. "I don't pretend to know all of what happened, but it's not that hard to piece together a narrative. A jury won't find it so hard either."

"You don't scare me," I say. It doesn't sound convincing.

"Then you're stupider than I thought. Your uncle and your lawyer—" he stifles a chuckle at the last. "The county will try you as an adult. A case as high profile as yours makes careers, Prose."

"You can't be good cop and bad cop at the same time, Holcomb."

I can't keep the venom from my voice, and he laughs again. "We're all good cops."

"Then charge me." *Really. Stop this charade and just do it already.* The waiting is a slow flood into my bell jar. Eventually I'm going to drown.

"This isn't some cop show, kid. We don't have to wrap your case up in under an hour so we can go back to selling frozen yogurt. Loose ends are being tied up, statements checked. It's just a matter of time."

"I didn't do anything." The words keep coming out, even though I want them to stop. "There's not even any evidence. My lawyer—"

"Your lawyer is a gibbon in a three-piece suit. He practices law like a five-year old practices piano." Holcomb growls down the wire. "Don't believe the hype. We're coming after you, unless you come clean first. You're running out of chances to not make it hard on yourself."

"I didn't do *anything*."

"Really? Dean Koontz would have thrown your story away as implausible, and the jury's going to do the same. Think about what I said, Prose. Think about whether or not you want to get out while you've still got a life left to live. Think about whether you want to see the ocean before your hair's gone white."

There's an audible click on the other end. It takes every ounce of self-control I have to not smash the portable against the cinderblock, and instead it falls softly to the carpet. My hands cover my face, catching fire. I will myself not to cry.

It takes a moment to realize someone's speaking to me. When I lower my hands, Chapman's glaring up from the desk, brow furrowed. "Pick it up."

"What?" The hitch in my voice is unmistakable, and I don't understand.

"The phone. This isn't some barn where you just drop our things wherever you feel like. Pick it up."

I shake my head, the tears coming for real now, unbidden and damned. The words have lodged as a hard point in my throat.

"You've got no respect," he says, standing up now. Like a beetle, he scuttles down the hallway. My eyes flinch to the side, looking for help, but there's no one there at all. "For the staff here. For the other girls. This isn't your palace, and we're not your servants. You're going to learn who makes the rules around here."

The wet saltiness runs across my lips, the taste of bad memories. "What's wrong with you?"

"You're going to need to get with the program if you ever want get outside. " His words are cudgels as he closes the gap, each sentence a swing at my knees. I breathe in his stench, a blend of old sweat and pungent cologne. "The first rule is that you do whatever I goddamn say, whenever I goddamn say. If you've got a problem with that, just imagine how well that orange jumpsuit's going to fit. Now Pick. Up. The. Phone."

I look at him advance, and a piece of ice lodges in my heart. With every beat it digs deeper.

A voice calls from behind him, and when he turns his head, I duck back into the Eggshell Galaxy, pulling the door shut with a slam that shakes the frame. Graham's in the middle distance, telling him that he's got a phone call, Admin on the line, and I hear a muffled bark, something about staying down here, but the pillow's already over my head at this point. The room spins around me as I stifle my own voice. There are more threats, more edicts, but I ignore them all. I'm not sure if I sleep or suffocate.

I pull back from sleep with the velocity of a falling astronaut. The nurse with her penlight had done a thorough mouth check for once, and my foggy rest is full of ghosts. As my body sits up with a jerk, my back already sore, I yearn to be free again amongst the stars before the smell of Lysol and carpet powder kills whatever dreams I have left.

For the past three days Svara's come to see me, a skeleton in a dark gray suit. To the gaunt man I sing the same refrain. *Osgood, Osgood, Osgood*, the song goes. *If you can get assigned to my case, someone else can just as quickly.*

Of course, the encore keeps ending with me in my room for the night. Say what you want about Everbrook, but it's predictable. Phoebe sticks around but eventually begs off and slips out. Apparently that ranch hand is just as handy as you'd think.

The Eggshell Universe and Agatha Christie are all I have to occupy my time, and it doesn't take long for my mind to turn inwards. I've seen enough cop shows to guess that Holcomb's just trying to scare me, but at the same time I've got to admit that it's working. There isn't a lot of evidence, but all of the circumstance paints a great red arrow squarely in my direction. Hell, roles reversed, I'd think was guilty too. The only hope I have is a jury that believes in monsters, magic, and multiple coincidence. That light is starting to fade, little by little, a slowly dying sun.

In the sodium lights of the walkway I can see little clouds of dead brown leaves scurry and whisper across the concrete. Summer dying fast, I think, and my thoughts travel back to the first house, my mother.

The Man.

It started escalating around the time I turned eight. I'm not sure when parents expect their children to start killing off their imaginary friends, but apparently that line had long since been crossed. While the other kids were building emotional rapports, I was still the sidekick of our dynamic duo. Marmalade and me. By the third grade, it was a little embarrassing.

To everyone else, it became something worse.

That day, my mother had called me in, giving me a shout out the window while I was playing in the yard. He and I were in the middle of a game, something simple like Raz-Ma-Tazz or Billy-Burn-Up. The Man rose from his hiding place and stared back at the house, swiping strands of long grass from the brim of his dark hat. "Looks like game day's going to have to take an interval, pumpkin."

"I'm not a gourd," I pouted, sticking out my tongue. "We'll just have to use our Big Timeout."

"We always forget where we were," he complained.

"I'm hungry, too. Maybe you can get a drink." I didn't know if he got hungry, or if he ever ate, but I sure knew he could get thirsty. We trudged up to the steps and went inside to the bathroom. A handful of Dial soap over my palms and we went to the kitchen, where Mom was stirring a pot on the stove with a shining stainless spoon. It was something simple with long noodles and veggies, sweet-and-sour-something, which was the usual fare when my dad was away. She told me to start washing up.

Marmalade coughed, and I stuck my hands out for inspection. "Yes'm. Already have."

"Don't say *yes'm*," she said, her back still to me. She raised the spoon as if trying to catch my reflection. "You've still got your boot-"

The spoon slipped from her hand, clanging against the tile with a jilting tone. My mother froze, statuesque for a moment, then whirled around. It looked like it cost her dearly.

Wide eyes fixed me, her healthy tan gone the color of old milk. I wondered if she was sick. "Mom? Mom, is something wrong?"

She stood that way for what seemed like forever, searching the kitchen for so long that tears filled my eyes. Panic welled up, and I wondered if I should try to call that nine-something number Mrs. Baltimore had told us about in class.

All at once she took in a hitching breath and released it, trying to smile. The result was ghastly. "Nothing's wrong. Mommy's just spacing out. Go wash up, honey."

"I already did."

That smile returned, ice chips floating in an empty sea, and I took a step backward.

"Scrub harder."

That was only the first. In the months to come, Mom would start *spacing out* more and more. Until it wasn't funny anymore, my father said she could have gotten a job at NASA.

When I came back to the kitchen, hands scrubbed clean *again*, both her and Marmalade were nowhere to be found. I grew roots and listened. Maybe a single croak came from the living room, where she kept her mellow juice.

It sounded like a sob.

The pot was bubbling in low chortles as the burner still blazed beneath, and I frowned and went to turn off the stove, Marmalade and Mommy forgotten. Even at eight I knew that an unattended stove was trouble.

On the counter were a couple of dry noodles. Little fragmented pastas, innocuous as breadcrumbs until you looked.

They'd been broken, shaped into three characters.

SHH.

CHAPTER SIX

THE DEVIL YOU GROW

A week has passed before they finally pull me out of the Academy. We're in the middle of a section on contemporary history, which I think is an excuse for the teacher to complain about the government and recite whatever diatribe he heard on Sirius XM during his ride in. My one-on-one status is ongoing, and Lo floats placidly behind me. I take it as a good sign. If they were really worried, Lo wouldn't be the one to watch me.

An apprehensive Graham knocks on the door and pulls Lo aside in the middle of a lecture about wearing guns in public. A couple of whispers, and they're both ushering me into the commons. Dark, heavy clouds squat overhead, and the autumn wind whips copper branches about without mercy. I ask them what's going on.

Neither answers at first, and alarm bells ring behind my eyes. A surprise ruling and early release sounds doubtful. Holcomb with a pair of handcuffs sounds a lot more likely.

My calves tense, my ankles loosen. I prepare to bolt. Maybe the tunnel's well-marked and unlocked.

Graham looks at me with a sad smile as he reads my mind. "It's nothing horrible, Prose."

His eyes are an overcast blue, and the line of his mouth gives nothing away. I sigh. "Nothing horrible means I'm probably not going to like it, either."

He shrugs. "Lo will get you through it, I'm sure."

I can almost hear his nodding and cast a glance back up to the admin building. The silver-eyed girl is playing before it, some kind of skipping game in front of the big double doors. Her skin is so pale it's iridescent beneath the overcast sky. She hops from one foot to two, two to one and one again, and Graham catches me looking and follows my eye. For a moment I almost ask him if he can see her, but I don't want to know.

The doors crack open like a vault, and I step inside the Lodge with sacrificial self-assurance. The dayroom smells of 409 and carpet powder, but beneath it is the stench of decay, an old building turning to dust. With no lights on, it takes a moment for my eyes to adjust to the gloom.

Jon is in front of the desk, a giant, square-jawed bear of a man who gives off an easy, paternal calmness. These aren't his usual digs, but his being here is a good sign. I wave a hand hello before the dark shape unfolds itself from the table and nods in greeting, a vampire rising from its coffin.

Lean as ever, Svara's dressed in a gray suit, a small black hat perched upon his cadaverous scalp. Before I begin to protest, he raises a hand. "Please, I think you'll want to hear what I have to say."

"Don't count on it." His fingers seem impossibly long. "You haven't wowed me lately."

"Is there somewhere you would like to go?" he asks. "We have some moments before the rain, I think. You say you like to walk and talk?"

I look at Graham, then I look at Jon. Jon sighs and stands up. "He just wants to talk to you. If you don't like what he has to say, tell him so and come back. No stress."

Svara gives him a look but nods. "No stress," he says, stressing the last -ess.

"Can Graham come with me instead?" I ask. If Svara burnt me at the stake, Lo would probably not rock the boat.

"Hey?" Lo murmurs, but the relief in his voice is obvious.

Graham smiles. "I'll take her. Sure."

"Cool beans," I say. "Let's go."

Our unlikely trio sets out down the 'Sip. I glance toward the Admin building to see if the silver-eyed girl is still hopscotching, but she's nowhere to be found. The sky has darkened, and dead leaves scratch and scurry across the sidewalk.

"Why are you here?" I ask Svara. One of his hands is clutching his hat to his scalp in the wind. It looks like an albino spider wrestling a fedora.

"In a moment," he smiles, and the first drops of rain begin to drizzle. "Perhaps the gym will suffice instead, yes?"

I sigh and veer right, one hand over my head to shield it. The gym is still, as if waiting in ambush, and only the rain and the wind can be heard.

The heavy double doors open with a grunt. The lights are off, and the cavernous mouth of the gym is a void. *Through the red-litten windows see,* I think, passing the meeting space, restrooms and into the mouth, flicking the switch as I go.

For a moment I get a weird afterimage as the overheads come to life, just a quick blur of figures on the stage that clearly aren't there when the light becomes final, and I shudder. The room is cold, and my Chucks squeak across the hardwood as I head to the bleachers.

Svara takes his hat off and shakes it before he enters, and Graham mull over the racked basketballs before going off to shoot baskets and kill time. He's at it awhile; half of the balls are deflated or leaking, the results of being drop-kicked to the ceiling in the hopes of pinging them off one of the overhead lights. Gym rules forbid it in white laminate all over the walls, but kids can't help but want the satisfying ring of high impact and the subsequent wobble as the light threatens to fall. I've never seen it happen, but they've got to be at least eighty pounds apiece and hang fifty feet off the ground. The impact would be damn near catastrophic.

Graham takes his first shot, never turning fully away from me. Svara looks me over with an appraising glance that makes my skin creep, like I'm a curious insect pinned to his collection board.

If you don't like it, tell him and come back. "What is it you wanted to say?"

He presses on his shirt pocket. *Digital audio recorder,* I think. "At your last *full* session, we were exploring the incidents leading up to your placement here. I have read the reports of your behavior in the subsequent week. If you overlook the entries from a—" He consults his notepad for a moment. "—Mr. Chapman, it appears to have been exemplary. Straight gold, top honors, and most important, a lack of oppositional-defiant episodes and outbursts."

I show him the inside of my arm. The bruises are faded to yellow across my bicep. "I'm a quick learner."

"Yet you maintain this belief in unseen forces. A cynical man might say you're doing your best to fake it and get out."

The words are ice water thrown into my face. "I just want to get better."

"And we all want to see that, believe me." He presses on his pocket again, and the recorder shuts off with an audible *click*. "Young lady, don't— how do they say it?— bullshit a bullshitter. I am a clinical psychiatrist with over forty years' experience working with disturbed juveniles. I can tell."

"Moreover, *I know*."

In the distance, Graham drains a three-pointer with a little *swish* of the net. He waves to me good-naturedly, and I give him one back. "What is it you think you know?"

He swats a hand at the question as if it were an errant fly. "I desire your total participation and confidence. The *real* answers, not just what you think will get you into my good graces or back with that uncle of yours."

"Like that's going to happen."

"It might interest you to know that the judge in your child services case is an old friend of mine from university. Chapelwaite. We meet for cognac every other Thursday and mull over the directions of our lives." He leans forward, and I catch the pungent scent of old tobacco. "He takes my opinion very seriously."

As I put the pieces together, my heart begins to sink. "Small world."

"Indeed. If you do, in fact, want to leave here, understand that I am the key to that lock. Not your uncle, not your public defender or that boor of a detective, Holcomb. For all intents and purposes, I am the difference between a pharmaceutical prison for the next ten years and your freedom."

I laugh. "How's that book deal coming along?" I ask, surprised to hear the words slip out of my mouth.

"A Red Orphan case study? It's tasty." He tries it along his teeth. "No doubt it hasn't escaped you that a client of your—how would you say?—notoriety commands a smidgen of public interest. As your practicing psychiatrist, I would also become—interesting."

"Aren't there rules? Client confidentiality?"

He flaps a hand dismissively. "Statements could come from anywhere. Undisclosed source on the staff. A roommate confidante, perhaps? It doesn't affect what we're doing in the slightest."

"My uncle's petitioning the court—"

"And won't succeed in without my approval. Your uncle is many things, but I can't imagine you hold a great depth of illusion for what he can achieve." He pauses, makes sure he had my full attention. "The terms are thus: complete and honest answers, paired with your good behavior. Combined, these will get you off the meds and back onto the street, at least until someone decides to file actual charges or you kill someone else. If I think you're lying, trying to game me, or fabricating any elements of your fairy tale to convince me of your sanity, the deal's off. You'll be behind padded walls long enough to collect Social Security. Are we clear on that?"

"A case study." Could I? Could I tell him everything before Marmalade came back?

"As you say. Are these terms not agreeable?"

I study his mirthless grey eyes in his sagging face, the flatness of them. Any hope of deception goes out the window.

Behind me, Graham puts in a lay-up with a grunt. All at once the wind seems to be gone from my chest, and all I have left are whispers. What choice do I have? "Yes."

He taps his chin with his pen. "This, of course, pertains to your special friend as well. There is to be no dodging, no evading. Do we still have a deal?"

"I won't say his name."

"Nor would I ask you to." There is the faintest hint of a smile. "Not yet."

The lump in my throat is turning to concrete. Hope springs infernal. "Then yes."

"Good." He presses his shirt pocket again and the device buzzes to life. "Today, I'd like to start with your first run-in with psychiatric care. Let's talk about the first incident at the farmhouse."

Okay, then.

The first thing to know is that didn't take long for me to always prepare for the worst. My father and I bounced around apartments for a while, but always staying in the same couple of counties. He was taking odd jobs that cut into his writing time as a way to piece together a living between royalty checks. His 'real time', as he'd call it. In retrospect, I think he had trouble finding work or just agreeing to do it. After the classes he subbed he'd come home, pat my head, knock out a couple of Widmers, and go straight to the old Apple my mother had bought him, typing away. Sometimes he'd throw something together for dinner, and sometimes he'd forget.

I got real good at making sandwiches.

Rachel he met at an art opening in Alberta, the result of some mutual friend of theirs in Portland whose name escapes me. I had been left home alone for the night to entertain myself, and I had just convinced myself that the wyrm had really and truly been left behind. When they came bursting into the living room, a little drunk and lots of fun, they scared the hell out of me.

But I wasn't resentful. Years had passed, you know?

No, really. She wasn't a bad person. Quite the opposite, in fact. Rachel was a free spirit, a fierce love, though maybe she sprinkled her trust around too liberally.

Would anyone have been perfect for my father? I don't know. That's not what I'm talking about.

Is that why—

I'm not going to dignify that with a response.

They hit it off really well. After the first few months and a gifted set of noise-cancelling headphones, we moved in with her. She had this old farmhouse a little off-town near Clackamas, a

Victorian monster in the center of a great field that had run in her family for a couple of generations. It had been kept in shape and was really well preserved, if you can discount the mice and the creaky steps.

And whatever lived in the corners.

I don't want to talk about that yet.

Because he wasn't there, okay?

I mean yet. He hadn't caught up.

I don't know how it works. He has trouble keeping up, especially when you're moving around all the time.

About half a dozen. It didn't matter. I never wanted to see him again, even when things weren't the happiest.

The pantry incident was the start. After that, the pallid things forsook subtlety.

I started to catch glimpses of them, hear them when I was in other parts of the house.

The inhabitants. From the city of dead light.

Who was there to tell? After Mom, my father made it pretty clear that he didn't want to hear about them anymore. About any of it.

Things were hard enough.

Summer was winding down when things picked up. I startled awake in the middle of the night, trying to punch holes in the heavy gloom, a black well drawing my attention beyond it.

Something was in there with me.

The old house had seemed much brighter, but now the light seemed to struggle. To choke. It was like being around a campfire and hearing something shift in the forest, just beyond the glow of safety.

I remembered going through some old boxes of toys we'd had in storage, sorting out what could still go in the massive chest in the closet and what we'd give away. I was old enough then to be giving away virtually everything, nostalgia a nickel a pound, and the toy box was a barren wasteland. But, in that moment, I heard something shuffle in the closet, just the slightest rasp of something rough slithering against wood, and I froze. Thoughts of the old house crept back.

Then I heard it again.

Are you kidding? No, I was out of there like a shot. My stuffed animal armada would have to fend for themselves. It wasn't until I pulled open their door that I realized my mistake.

My father gave me a look. The kind that said *you're not helping*.

I took to swiping a chair from the kitchen table and propping it up against the closet latch before bed. In the morning, my father would be properly vexed and drag it back downstairs. It became a little ritual for months: teeth brushed, hair combed, I'd sneak down the stairs and drag one of the heavy chairs back up. He'd haul it back down the next day, and we'd start the process all over the following night.

No, he was no help. Yeah, it still bothers me. I know he was hurting, but I was the one who was still alive, you know?

I remember sitting down to dinner one night, maybe three or four months after we'd moved into the farmhouse. Everyone had gotten a chance to get settled, but there were still plenty of sore sports, a glossary of rough edges.

My tween angst probably wasn't helping matters.

Rachel made the mistake of trying to spark up a little conversation, the first innocuous poke. "So, how do you like the new place?"

I shoveled another load of potatoes into my mouth. "'S okay. A little creepy sometimes."

There it was, the slide of grey, just above the mantel at the corner of the ceiling. Maybe it was just my eyes.

"It's an old house. I'm sure it'll get used to you."

Maybe she said it differently. Maybe it was *you'll get used to it*, which would have made way more sense. I've played it back in my mind so many times both are memories now, twins bound by barbed wire. "Not likely," I offered, and my father shot me a dark look past his fifth Widmer of the night.

Rachel considered, her lips almost touching the bowl of her wine glass. Whatever bouncers waited at the gate, she ducked the rope and pressed on. "So, is your little friend here yet?"

She'd never made mention of the Man before. I honestly didn't know that she knew about him.

It was her turn for Thomas Harden's glaring disapproval, but she seemed not to notice. He'd been calculating plots and character studies far more than he'd been my father lately. I flat out ignored it.

"We're not friends anymore, but no. He's probably on his way, though."

"Prose." My father rumbled it so low that I felt it rather than heard it.

"It takes him a while to find me again," I offered. "Last time we moved it took him a whole month to catch up with us. It was doubling back to Silverton that threw him off, he said."

She turned that over in her head. "Why didn't—"

I almost said it. Poe wept.

"—just hitch a ride with us, then?" she finished.

"Enough." My father's fist was clenched around the bottle, forearm rippling cords.

"You shouldn't say his name. It draws him. And he says it doesn't work that way. As long as he stays the hell away from me, though, I don't press."

The Widmer was airborne before the last word left my lips, shattering in a shower of suds and broken glass on the wall behind me, my father on his feet before the constellation of shards found the floor. His eyes were raw and wet. "That's. Enough."

Rachel's hand covered her mouth, like keeping silent would earn her some kind of door prize. I pushed back from the table calmly and felt a sliver of glass slide hotly into the ball of my foot. If I had tears in my eyes, that was the only reason why. "Can I go to my room?"

Rachel found me again. "Sure you can, honey. There's Neapolitan for dessert, with the strawberry excised—"

I was already moving, my injured foot leaving bright red splotches on the hardwood floor, up the stairs and through the last door on the left, door slammed and locked before she could finish telling me about the evils of ice cream. I put my cheap headphones on and was blaring the Misfits just as the yelling started downstairs. Plucking the sliver of glass from my foot, the thin crystal was about a knuckle long, red and gleaming in the desk light. I threw it in the wastebasket and was wrapping an old T-shirt around my foot and wincing when I saw it for the first time.

It had drawn too close to the closet door, pale skin wormy and cheap. Through the thin slat its queerly shaped eyes were visible, a sickly shade of yellow green that made me think of rotting vegetation. A grey tongue flickered between its lips, passing obscenely long through the gap in the door. It was looking at the wastebasket with something like longing.

Turning my back on it, I dove into my Jackson book, not sure I was following the plot, why Natalie kept visiting the professor, but I didn't think the thing in the closet could hurt me. As scary as some of them were, the irregulars never had.

I was naive. And, Poe help me, I was wrong.

He tapped his chin with his pen again. "Your father had an issue with your friends?"

"They weren't friends." I shake my head. "He had a really hard time of it when Mom died. I don't blame him for it."

"Again you say that." He pauses, checks his notepad. "Did you ever ask yourself why no one else ever— shared your experiences? Saw anything?"

"I don't know that. Most days Cthulhu could ride a unicorn through our living room and someone'd make a comment about the weather. People have a lot of trouble seeing what's in front of them."

Svara nods, the cap of his pen drumming against his lip for a moment. "Have you ever considered that the most obvious answer is almost certainly the correct one?"

I roll my eyes and stand up from the bleachers. "I could slit my wrists with Ockham's Razor. I'm not crazy."

"Of course. You have superpowers," he says.

Graham knocks down a jump shot and walks over, a sheepish grin on his face like he knows he's been goofing around for twenty minutes.

"I'm going to go back." My heart flutters. The cliff has been well and truly stepped off of, and I realize with something like awe that Svara doesn't believe me. Not a word of it. For some reason, this shakes me to the core. Skepticism, wonder, denial, those I understand, but this is different. Clinical disbelief. My lips form the words before I can stop them. "I'm not crazy."

"Of course not." He smiles, a crease of weathered lips. "They never are."

"Graham," I call out. "I'd like to go back."

"There's a first," he says, and tosses the basketball back towards the rack. It bounces off the metal with a hollow gong and goes careening towards the far wall.

"Wait." Svara has his pen and pad in hand, looking like a starved beat reporter hoping for the big scoop. "You still haven't mentioned the Man."

It's my turn to pause, to wonder how far I can push it before he reneges on our deal. What price freedom? "I'm not here to be made fun of."

"Mm. Tell me a story, Prose. A show of good faith."

Graham looks at me and shrugs. There are spots of sweat already soaking through on his T-shirt, and I give him a nod that's meant to be reassuring. *There once was a man no god had made. His name, he said, was Marmalade.*

Svara tuts. "Let's start making progress now."

"Get used to disappointment." I turn to go, then think better of it. "You know why I don't want to talk about him, right? The file mentions it?"

"It does." He looks amused, and my palm itches. I want to slap the grin off of his cadaverous face.

"It's not because I'm afraid to face my demons. It's not because I'm clinging to some childhood delusion. It's not even because people that I love have died." Standing on the bleachers, I look down. The smile has slipped. "I've stayed lost to him for so long. If I talk about him, he'll come."

"Prose..."

I hold up a hand. "Think about what you want before we really get started. Because if I start telling you about him, sooner or later you're going to meet him."

The dayroom is a confused mess when we return. Most of the Lodge is sitting in the dayroom under Sandra's watchful eye, playing games or talking quietly, moods subdued. There's a new intake getting processed in the back hallway, and from the sound of it she's none too enthused. The heavy double doors are shut but can't hold back the muffled shouts and shrieks. Something breaks, and from the padded grunts I guess she's being restrained. *Off to the blue room.* I look at Graham questioningly.

"She'll be fine," he smiles. His eyes aren't convinced, and I can't blame him.

Ladies and gentlemen, job security.

There's a nervous tremor in the air, a thin quavering hum as everyone tries to pretend nothing's happening. Another loud crash sets off a titter of nervous giggles.

"Bitch is taking away our free time," Nellie grumbles, her small eyes studying the room. Any merriment lies crushed beneath the thudding boot of her voice.

Sandra catches her eye. "Language. And we'll try to make it up later."

"I've heard that one before." Nellie's almost talking to herself. "I've heard that one *plenty*."

Sandra shrugs. "Remember how scary it was the first time you were here? You got used to it. You settled down. So will she. We all just need to be patient with each other."

Graham taps me on the shoulder. When I turn around, he's retrieved Scrabble from the game closet and gestures to the big table. I nod and pull up a chair as he starts shuffling the tiles into a bag.

He's not the greatest player, too obsessed with showing me the vocab words he can build to think about the ones that'll score him points. I chop him up with XIs and QIs, ZAs and JOs and HAJIs, and the first game ends with a difference of two hundred points.

Bloodied, he reshuffles the tiles and goes to grab a soda out of the fridge. Vanessa is over my shoulder like the apparition of conscience.

"We're going over the wall tonight," she whispers, fingering the dog tags wrapped around her throat. "It's all been arranged."

I fight to keep my face neutral. "Really."

"Tonight we'll depart this dread manor for the coast. No more levels and privileges and cardboard food, and there's going to be room for one more in the carriage." Her voice stays low, and I can feel the fire burning in her eyes. She straightens up as Graham returns to his seat. "Think of it."

Another piteous wail erupts, and an anxious ripple spreads, through the couches, the gossiping, the games. Something in it is primal, striking a raw chord that's pulling everyone askew. Pretending to ignore it, Graham pops the top on his can. *Years of practice.* "Think about what?"

"Whether or not to start playing you for sodas," I say. "Vanessa thinks I can get everyone here a drink in the next ninety minutes."

"Hey, that was just beginner's luck."

"Put your corn syrup where your mouth is."

In fifteen minutes I'm sipping a Sprite as the big doors open. The hall is a mess of thrown-about papers and overturned chairs that's even now being tidied by Lo and another man I don't recognize.

"Can I go to my room?" I ask Graham. "Figure I'll save you the trouble of buying me a case."

The margin of victory is a hundred and fifty, my last word using the triple word score on SQUAD. He throws his Ss away like they're nothing. "Go to it," he says, the grin on his face not entirely secure. "I need to wipe the blood off my face."

Chapman squats at the far corner of the hallway, sitting outside a door like a fleshy gargoyle. There's a clipboard in one hand and a series of fresh scratches glistening down the other arm. He's rubbing antiseptic on them with a paper towel but glances up as I cross the hallway to my room. "Who said you could be back here?"

"Graham." I try to keep it meek. "I just want to read in my room."

"Do you see anybody else back here?"

"Are you okay?" I ask, pointing to the raw gouges in his skin. "Do you need me to get you anything?"

"I asked you a question."

There's a glowering ember in his eyes, like he's hoping that I'll fan the flames. "No, I don't, but Graham said—"

"Graham's not running the shift, is he?"

"Well, you would know." There's a detached wonder that I can't quite disassociate. *Is he really trying to jump right into another crisis?* "May I be in my room and read? I promise I won't make any trouble."

He pauses, and I'm already turning back to the dayroom when he says "Fine. Reading *only.*"

"Will do," I say, and slip behind my door.

I eat dinner in my room, some casserole concoction I'm not familiar with. Graham's propped up outside my door, checking his phone and probably bored out of his mind. I've blown through *Hangsaman*, not sure if I got all of it, and have leapt into *Strange Wine* without a second thought. I'm thinking of scratching *Croatoan* across my door, but the implication would be lost on everyone.

What if Svara is just an accomplished bullshitter? The man shrinks heads for a living. If I pour my guts out in a sticky red pile at his feet, is he really going to help me, or just write his bestseller and walk away? (*Fatal Friend* was my favorite working title, shortly edging out *Murder and Marmalade).* Worse, if I give him what he wants, I need to make sure I can escape the blast radius before the Man comes and it's all over.

The string around my throat is growing tighter. I have to slip it before the trapdoor falls out beneath me.

Running away makes no sense. I don't want to tell Vanessa that, and selfishly hope she won't take Harkness with her. My face has been splashed under enough newspaper headlines to qualify me as a fourth-tier celebrity, probably just below the Sham-Wow guy. Red Orphan, remember? I'd be back here before sunset.

Unless there's somewhere to go, some safe house or secret track out of town and then out of state, but— please. Out of our band of cutters, rageaholics, and delusionnaires, I couldn't picture one who'd also head up a secret criminal empire with ties to some coyotes. More likely they just go to the mall and sleep in alleys, although no one who's run since I've been here has come back yet. Maddy, Yesenia, Reed.

Maybe there is a way to stay gone.

Of course, I have one hundred and twenty-two psychotropic pills in the leg of my bed that will take me pretty much anywhere I want to go, but then I see Mark, answering his phone in the middle of the night. Maybe it's raining.

I push the thought away, guilty and a little ashamed. Whatever else happens, I can't do that to him.

I know how it feels.

Deep pockets and hidden winds bleed across the back path of the Lodge. Beneath the orange sodium light, a figure passes by, the briefest image of a ten-gallon hat and chaps.

I start.

There's a knock on the door. A large man with skin like burnished copper stands in the threshold. His teeth are large and very white. I've never seen him before, and he takes my spoon and plate with accomplished grace. "It's time to take to your meds."

"Can I do it down here?" I don't want to run into Chapman again, but he shakes his head and sweeps a heavy arm into the hallway.

"Policy."

It's quieter than it should be, the lights already a sepia twilight. There's no clock in my room, so I guess that the med wagon is running a little late tonight. Only a couple of girls are still up and in the dayroom, the honors class who have perfected turning their damage inward. I spot Harkness playing Xbox with Graham, their eyes focused on the mounted flatscreen, hands and fingers beating a strange tarantella across their controllers.

Harkness whispers something to him as Graham hangs his head. *The malaise of the Master Chief.*

The nurse directly blocks the door. She never comes all the way into the building. Older than most of the staff, in her late fifties at least, a short, squat woman in scrubs and a zip-up sweater stands behind a wheeled metal cart that looks a little like a steampunk podium. Dixie cups of pills and water are in an outstretched panel before her, and my heart flutters, just a little. The younger nurses aren't as thorough, and this last one is all business. I might be taking one wild ride tonight.

I glance back down the hallway. Dr. Teeth is right behind me, and Chapman's sitting in an office chair, clipboard in hand, probably still writing up the incident report for the afternoon's festivities. Someone's bandaged his arm, and the thin reading light on the clipboard casts dark hollows across the fleshy pits of his face, turning him into a distorted jack-o-lantern. Before he can catch me looking, I fall into line.

Nellie's ahead of me, Alisha second. When a hand darts out to my shoulder, I choke down the scream at the back of my throat. "Shhh." Vanessa whispers, her bony hand giving me a pat. "My corsairs will meet us beyond the gate at midnight. The code word is *octopus owl*. We'll ride out and leave this dread manor behind us."

"I can't." My words come out strangled. Nellie passes by with a grimace.

"Of course you can. Much better than staying here, I'd imagine."

"I can get out now. Legitimately."

"You really think so?"

"That's what they told me." It's funny how any member of an institution receives the communal pronoun. Alisha walks past, and then I'm at the head of the line. "Fly right, eat my vegetables. They'll send me home."

"If you believe that, then you're a bigger fool than I thought you were." Her eyes are sad as she speaks, and she fingers the dog tags around her neck. It makes it hurt all the more. "You're in the system now, Prose Harden. Once you're in, it never lets you go."

"That's not true." How naive do I sound, I wonder?

She gives me a strange look, pity and contempt mixing across her brow, and then she's gone. A part of my heart chases after her, begging forgiveness, to tag along. I wonder what I've missed.

"Prose Harden?" The nurse looks at me with mistrust, like I'm a skinchanger lurking. I can feel Dr. Teeth nod from over by the bookcase.

"Present." With a fake smile, she hands me a Dixie cup. Little orange and white shapes dance at the bottom of it, the world's strangest breakfast cereal. Are there more now, I wonder?

I toss it back. With a swift flick of my tongue I press the pills between the outside of my teeth and my cheek. The nurse passes me another Dixie full of water, and I swallow it down.

"Mouth," she says, and I open up and say aah like a good girl. Her penlight probes my gums, and her eyes dance over to Chapman. "Swallow the pills, Prose."

Alarm and a grudging respect rise in equal measure. I have to take my bow. "Just checking." I say. "You're very good at your job."

She smiles humorlessly and hands me another cup. This time I wash them down in a burst of cold water. It's been a long time since I've had to take all of anything, and it occurs to me that this full dosage has been prescribed as if I'd been taking meds during my entire stay.

My tongue and cheeks go slightly numb. *Uh-oh.*

The back of my throat gets her light again, and she nods to the man in back. "Make sure she doesn't use the restroom for thirty minutes."

So she's doesn't yak them up goes unsaid. I move back to my room, my head already feeling loose, like a dirty balloon. "I'd like to go to bed now," I mumble to the tree trunk by the bookcase, and float down the hallway towards my door.

Chapman looks up from his paperwork at the far end. His small eyes and heavy cheeks lit from below give him the look of a homicidal jack-o-lantern. "Make good choices, Prose," he says. His mouth seems to grow wider and wider, and I shut the door behind me before anything else can take hold. Before I know it I'm on the bed, gearing up for a race around the Eggshell Galaxy.

Phoebe looks up from the next bed, one of my books outstretched before her. "Jeezy peezy, kid. You look like shit."

"Where have you been?" I ask. My voice seems distant. It echoes eerily, as if the room is much bigger than it should be.

"I met up with the cowboy again, out behind the empty Lodge. Joe or something. You sure you're okay?"

I cackle.

"No, really. He's a real sweet guy. Little too Texas sometimes, but you can hardly blame him for it. You've got to meet him."

"How did you?" The thought wanders off like a moth in a black room.

Phoebe shrugs and gives me a knowing wink. "The conventional way."

I have no idea what that's supposed to mean, but I play along. For a moment I can see myself, staring down from the ceiling with something like wonder. "Amazing."

"I'm going to match up with him after the place gets a little dark. Mum's the word, okay?"

My eyes are growing exponentially heavier. The strain of keeping them open or even thinking clearly is too much to bear. "We're all down here in the dark together."

"And these bars cannot contain our love. Get some sleep, sugar."

Giving up the ghost, I let my eyelids drop and am sucked away into the Stygian black. Strangely, there are no dreams.

The yellow eyes I see when I awake are real.

CHAPTER SEVEN
FALLEN LEAVES

She's shaking me, hard enough that my hair tosses into my eyes and one of my arms flops off the bed, colliding with the frame hard enough to bruise. My eyes crack open and daylight drives fresh nails into my brain, throbbing pulses of agony that curl me up into a kitten-sized ball. The hand on my arm doesn't stop.

"Rise and shine, kiddo. People are going think you jumped in a lake."

I grumble, waving an impotent hand. The pain subsides into dull waves, a tidal pulse I can at least live with.

Brightness seeps in through the window front, and for a moment I'm lost, lost as anyone has ever been. Then I remember Everbrook, the last six weeks of madness concentrated down into a fine cocktail of crazy and sit up. My room spins, the Eggshell Galaxy teetering on the brink, and then it all comes into focus with an audible click.

My other shoulder aches. Crusty brown dots stain the sheets. *Bloody blood blood*, and I trace with one finger the scratches on my upper back, a couple inches long and nowhere near as deep. My whole body's sore, but a brief check tells me I'm okay, that the worst has yet to be, and finally I look up into the patient eyes of my roommate and confidante.

"Jeez, did you get slipped the mickey." Phoebe gives me a half-smile that doesn't reach her eyes, and I realize with some horror that she's smoking, a half-finished cigarette pinched between her fingers like a strange specimen of beetle. My gaze flutters to the panel window, panicked that a face will be staring in, any face, and the shit will have well and truly hit the fan. *How in the hell is she getting away with this?* "What the hell happened to you?"

Yellow memories blur, the hint of a melody haunting, and I stare at the dried gore on the sheets, trace my wounds again. "That's a great question."

"Do you have any idea what time it is?"

My mind starts, skitters to a halt. "Nope."

"Almost noon. They think you've got some kinda bug." She gives me a hard, appraising look. "Maybe that's not so far from the truth."

Keeping my eyes on a fixed point, I wonder if I'm going to hurl. Nothing has ever felt this bad upon waking, not even when Brenda James snuck the two-liter of vodka out from the motel storeroom. To this day, I still can't drink cranberry juice. "It's my ass. I'll thank you to let me watch it."

"Toughie. You're doing a bang-up job so far."

I push the hair out of my face and almost succeed in gouging out my eyes. "How was your night?"

"It was lovely. Joe's a real gentleman. Don't change the subject." Her black hair wanders around her face like a nest of snakes as she paces the tiny room in a dark waltz, three steps to the left, three steps to the right. I giggle and feel a trickle of bile try to rise. "Seriously, what the hell happened?"

"They dosed me pretty hard last night. I don't remember." Which is mostly true. The kaleidoscope of images won't coalesce, remaining random fractals. Yellow eyes. Black mass. *Start spreadin' the news.*

Sinatra came back, I realize. And if it did this to me, who knows what's been done to the other girls?

With a lurch, a moment rushes back from our meeting. Alisha saying that runaways that never call back.

"Have you—I don't know—ever seen anything? Weird? Walking the corridors?"

"It's Intensive Girls, honey. Strange kind of goes with the program." She licks her finger and dabs my forehead. It comes away brown and bloody. "If you need to toss your cookies, just let me clear the space. You just dropped two shades of pale."

"I saw something the night before. Black. Like a humming cloud with yellow eyes." Trying to blot out memories of a deeper, darker melody isn't easy. The city of dead light rises before me, the piping tune calling me forward. I try to push it away.

Phoebe measures me up. "I don't believe in spooks, kiddo."

Nodding, I save it for another day. "Never mind. Probably psychosomatic. It was a rough afternoon with the doc."

She clicks her tongue and puts her hands on my shoulders. "They didn't believe you, did they?"

"Does it matter? *Whatever walked there, walked alone.*"

The look she gives me says it all. "Knock it off with the Shirley Jackson, will you? It's perturbing."

"Fine. They believed me, just fine."

Believe I'm crazy, writing on the walls with my victim's entrails. Screws loose and fancy-free.

"Uh-huh. Says your trip to Neverland last night." She sits down on the bed across from me and takes my wounded hand in both of hers. Her skin is soft and cold to the touch, and she smells of jasmine and musk. "Are you sure you want to go through with this?"

"It's not like I have much of a choice." Her worried eyes meet mine, and I reconsider. "Svara's my ticket out."

"You could always tell 'em nothing. Mum's the word. In fourteen months, you'll be on your own recognizance. Walk away clean."

"I might not have fourteen months. They're trying to put me away, Phoebe." The fact that I might deserve it was the farthest thing away from my tongue, but I was beginning to wonder.

Maybe they are starting to wear me down.

"You've already been put away. Give them a reason, and they'll make it permanent. Graduate you to the big state facility when you turn eighteen."

Or the local penitentiary. "I know what I'm doing."

She gives my hand a squeeze. "Kiddo, I don't think that's true."

Phoebe raises a thin hand to her lips and plucks the cigarette out from between them. Without a word she brings it down to her wrist, and the smell of burning flesh replaces the flowery perfume of her skin. I wonder if I'm dreaming. "You tell them about him yet?"

I don't have to ask. "No. I think I can hold off on that."

"You want to dance, they're going to want you to go all the way, kiddo. Don't think you'll get to stop with a long kiss goodnight." Phoebe lets my hand go with another squeeze and hugs me. It's so refreshingly sincere I begin to cry. "C'mon. Go clean yourself up. Get some grub in you."

When we leave the room, it doesn't take long for me to discover that Vanessa's gone. So's Alicia, for that matter. *The corsairs rode out, and our merry band dropped to six.* Lo gives me a nod from his perch in the hallway, and when I walk out toward the dayroom, he slips from his roost and follows me without a sound.

Chapman's on the phone, mid-argument with someone who doubtless is wondering why he can't keep the crazy where it belongs. He stops mid-rant when he sees me. "A client. Yes, Jeff, a client. I'll call you back."

Logbooks and permission sheets are scattered around him like a library riot. The look he gives me could pass for shrewd. "Good afternoon, Prose."

"Is it?"

He tries his best not to sigh and looks constipated. "What do you know?"

The question is so vague that I'm sure my pause looks suspicious. I glance over my shoulder, but Phoebe's already drifted back to our room. "All sorts of stuff, I guess. What are you talking about?"

"Your friend ran last night. So did Alicia. Any idea where'd they go? Who they'd reach out to? You guys were close."

"Not that close." The thought surprises me more than anything else. *Two or three chats and to the people who work here, you're their maid of honor.* "Have you found anything out yet?"

"Like what?" He points to the piles of paper stacked around him, for the first time out of his element, and I feel a twinge of pity for him. Not a whole lot, and easily forgotten, but there all the same. "They're gone. I need some Hardy Boys-level clues to figure out the where and why, but they don't exist. This doesn't stop the courts and social services from trying to violate me with a pointed stick, but I keep telling 'em it's the cops' job now. Maybe they'll listen."

"Maybe." My shields are up again, almost involuntary. He looks at me under lowered brows like a ferret.

"If anyone tries to get in touch with you, let me know. There could be some benefit."

"Sure." My foot takes a step back.

He considers this. "You've already missed school for most of the day. Grab a meal and hang out in your room until it's over and we'll do free time after that."

I nod, grab a plate from the cart, and tiptoe back. Somehow I've survived the passing, and it leaves me breathless and a little elated, like running out between wartime trenches to grab a soccer ball. Phoebe looks up when I close the door behind me. There's a knowing smile.

I shoulder the heavy double doors aside and head into the gym, grateful to be out of the perpetual drizzle and autumn wind. Svara follows, folding a small black umbrella into something resembling a police baton, and Lo still haunts me from a little farther back. For a moment, the three of us are cast in shadows like a coven, and I hear the Man over my shoulder.

We're all down here in the dark together.

My hand finds the switch. The will-o'-wisps struggle to life. Glancing over at the meeting room, curiosity stings me and I raise a hand against the glass, peering into the thick darkness. I can make out the shapes of desks and chairs, a dry-erase board, a podium. Somewhere in the back appears a threshold, another series of doors, and my fingers give the latch a tug before I can think better of it. Nothing moves.

"Come on, Harden," Lo calls, like I'm a dog on a tether.

My eyes are trying to adjust. They fix upon a long shape, dark and cylindrical. For an instant, I think it moves.

His hand is on my shoulder, warm and warning. I shrug it off, a little pissed at his touch, and push into the bright-lit cavern with the hardwood floor.

Svara's already perched on the bleachers. For the first time since we've met, there's a color to his cheeks. When Lo goes to find a basketball, I don't sit down but wander to the end of the wide chamber. There are two opposite sets of double doors, one windowless and scuffed, the other paneled and paned. Through the windows I can see nothing but dull black.

"What's back here?" I yell to Lo. He shrugs absently and sits down, cradling the basketball like a small child. Shooting hoops would cost him too much energy.

In my mind it unfolds. The gym is a honeycomb, a warren of doors and hallways, secret rooms and murder holes, and if I could cross the right threshold, I'd be free forever. It's inviting enough for me to close my fingers around the latch and tug again, but nothing happens.

I await the miracle a moment longer before turning back.

Svara's watching me with flat grey eyes, a python on a low branch. "Your status has been improving."

"Yeah?"

"Slowly." He rolls it around on his tongue. "No violent outbursts, at least."

"I'm a whole new me."

"Indeed." Svara weighs the words. "We'll see if you can keep it up, yes?"

"Sure," I say, ignoring the skepticism. "Hit me."

He glances down at his notepad for a moment. Somewhere in his pocket I can hear the light *whir* of the digital recorder, downloading my dreams into digestible chunks.

They'll never stop.

Phoebe's words come back to me, and then he presses ahead. "When we last met, you finished our session by warning me about someone called the Man, yes?"

His name, he said, was Marmalade. "I did."

"You expressed the fear that if you speak of him, he'll come?"

"Not a fear, no." My mouth was suddenly very dry. "An inevitability."

"Mmm." He taps the side of his mouth with his pen, his words stones down a well. "Let's test that theory."

"I told you—"

"So you did. Come now. Your release hinges upon it, so no more coyness. Do tell."

There's something about friendship that's hard to quantify. In the end, I think you open the door to your heart a bit and let someone come inside and tinker with the moving parts. And it's okay, you figure, because by then you've got your wrench out and are mucking about in their gears too. Where you stop and the other starts gets a little complicated.

I'm not sure that's a good thing.

Growing up, it was amazing. Ever since the day of the tea party—

What tea party? Please.

Anyway, it like was being friends with Arthur Gordon Pym, Nancy Drew and Batman, all at the same time. Yeah, it was kind of a downer that everyone else said they couldn't see him, but what did that matter? Reality's subjective. More than anything, I think that was part of what made it special.

Grade school flew by. When you're there, it seems to last forever, but now it's all clouded over and calcified. Weird how you have these moments, indelible, awkward glimpses into your formation as a person, but for the most part things just blend and blur in a washed-out palette. What I remember the most about the Man in the early days are moments.

How he made me feel.

Case in point: second grade. We were all having lunch out on the field. It was a grey, overcast kind of day, like so many of them are. The benches had been pulled over to the play area, some kind of recess-slash-picnic mixed into the same calculus, which would have been Ms. Abrams' doing. She was an aristocratic hippie with long brown hair and high cheekbones, always trying to "shake things up", break us out of our stuffy academic shells. Granted, we were seven, but her heart was in the right place. Last I heard, she's singing torch songs in a Reno nightclub now. Her partner doubles on piano.

Good for her.

We had lugged out these big coolers, giant industrial ice chests the length of a man that had to have the dust beaten off of them from whatever mothballed storeroom they'd been sent to die in. Everyone got to grab a sandwich from one, a snack from the second, and a carton of milk from the last, and we'd all rushed over to do this like the rapture was coming and dairy products would be your only ticket into heaven.

Somehow I'd made it to the last cooler and found the last little brown carton floating there, the miracle of chocolate bobbing free amongst the whole milk. I nabbed it and found a spot on the bench, watching the quick eaters already sprinting off to play catch and tetherball and red rover, smug and satisfied.

I had gotten three bites into my PB&J before the shove came from behind. I went sprawling.

The carton toppled off the table, hit the pavement, and bled its brown sugary magic onto the asphalt. Tears were already rising when I looked back at Billy McCrutcheon, who everyone called Cruddy. His reading aloud resembled putting together a stack of blocks during a mortar bombardment.

His eyes were a sick green. He laughed a braying snort.

Putting his hands on his hips like a lazy sitcom sheriff, Cruddy announced it to the world at large, "What's the matter, Prose? Didn't your mommy ever tell you not to cry over spilled milk?"

Another kid laughed, and then another, and like an infection of idiocy, it caught on.

My cheeks were burning red. I willed myself not to cry over Cruddy, who couldn't even read Dick and Jane, but by then everyone was howling. From over my shoulder I heard Mindy Cavanaugh's sly whisper. "*Look* at the *baby*. Bawl, bawl *baby*."

Somewhere inside me the dam burst. Hot tears poured down my cheeks. Ms. Abrams was already coming over, and I could see the smug satisfaction on Billy's face as he turned to go play red rover with the big kids.

The *hissssssss* came first, then the snap.

From out of nowhere, the yellow meteor ended its orbit, exploding with his nose in a leathery clap. The tetherball hit him so hard the air went out of the crowd.

Billy flopped on his ass, stunned as the blood began to pour from his nose and just-split lip. Then it was his turn to cry. It looked like he'd been punched in the face by a truck, and as the other children began to stare at him in horror these great whooping sobs erupted, braying cries that just wouldn't stop. The chuckles began as other teachers began to crowd around him with paper towels and a generally poor knowledge of first aid.

"Cry, *baby,* cry," someone whispered, and a nervous titter cycled around the playground. Just like that the bullying legend of Cruddy McCrutcheon fell down and died.

When I looked over my shoulder, the Man was sitting on one of the benches, knees up like he was on the courthouse steps. His long coat pooled around him, hair blowing around his cheeks in the breeze. He tipped his hat to me before pointing to the sandwich cooler.

He raised a finger to his lips. *Shhhhh.*

Cruddy had broken his nose in three places. His parents raised holy hell with the school, wanted me suspended at the very least, but there had been a score of witnesses on that field that could swear I never even raised a hand to him. No one could figure out why the tetherball line had snapped, or how the ball had gained such freakish velocity, but that was water under the bridge for Billy McCrutcheon. He never spoke to me again.

No great loss.

They found Mindy Cavanaugh fifteen minutes later when it was time to pack up. In all the commotion she'd gone missing, and no one could ever explain why she'd decided to stuff herself into the ice-filled cooler.

Or how she'd managed to latch it from the outside.

She survived. You've got that look about you. Sure, there was a trip to the ER, moderate hypothermia or something. To be fair, all that ice had probably slowed down her internal functions, saved her from suffocating.

I didn't say you had to believe me.

It would probably be better for both of us if I were making all of this up.

You want more?

All right.

Six months later, another grade higher. Most of the shock and awe from the year before had worn off. I was a good student, partially because my dad praised me and my mom was a relentless taskmaster, but also because I *liked* it. I liked learning, didn't matter about what, liked the approving nods and smiles from my elders when I passed a test or turned in a project or finished a book, and if my work had a certain morbid twinge to it, everyone was sure that I'd grow out of it. Gold stars and letter grades were the fulcrum of my existence.

What a laugh.

I liked history the best because I would love to imagine myself amongst a different humanity, surrounded by odd smells, weird clothes, and mysteries on all sides. English was second best, almost personal. Despite my father's diatribes about sentence structure and character development, I would devour everything I opened, cover to cover.

My bookshelf was a constantly overflowing paper mill, my trips to the library incessant. I guess I didn't realize that the *teacher's pet* brand was starting to stick.

My black-soled footsteps echoed against the linoleum of the dank hallway as I returned from the guidance counselor's. My art project, *War Elephant*, had raised more than few eyebrows amongst the faculty. The stammering guidance counselor had said that they only wanted to know more about it, but surprisingly the visit only consisted of questions about my parents and whether or not anybody was touching anybody else.

Oblivious and a little confused, I answered his questions. In turn, he was forced to agree that indeed the Carthaginians had fought the Romans to the point of their own obliteration, and that this was, in fact, worth sharing via the lost art of diorama, though possibly with less use of the color red.

The Man had slunk off shortly thereafter with a nod and was off wandering the grounds, doing something called *reconnoitering*, which is a word I still haven't bothered to look up.

I don't know where he went.

I *never* knew where he went. Or why he'd come back. I wish that I had, that I understood more, but every answer always led to two more questions.

Even with everything that happened, that never changed.

"Darling," he said to me once. "You're my best friend in the whole wide world, but you ain't my keeper."

Damn, I'm changing the subject.

So I was alone when I stopped for a drink of water outside Mrs. Campbell's third-grade class. It was the good fountain, just past the janitor's closet and sparsely used by the gum-chewing rabble. The janitor could be seen tinkering with it for at least thirty minutes a day, either his way of looking busy or the result of an unrequited crush on Mrs. Campbell, but the man had for some reason amplified the pressure to just a little short of fire hose.

Even with the hallway echoes, I couldn't have heard her coming.

My fingers pressed against the side of the fountain, and the cool bitter water was rocketing into my mouth when I felt the hand seize the back of my neck, palming my head like a basketball and thrusting it down. Her other hand shot out and crushed my own, jamming it fast against the button.

I heard a laugh, high and cruel as my sinuses filled with water, bleeding out my nose, and I tried to thrash loose. She was bigger and stronger and in the middle of a growth spurt, and there wasn't anything I could do short of flail and hope she got bored.

"Like your drink, baby?" she hissed. I barely heard her over the rushing water, but I knew the voice. I had no idea what had put me on her radar, but Grace was two years older and suddenly I couldn't breathe, couldn't do anything besides cry. She giggled. "Drink up, teacher's pet. Drink up."

"Let me go!" I blubbered. It came out *lemegorsh*.

She laughed again. My t-shirt had gotten drenched, my hair sopping, and even as black spots began to dazzle across my vision, she showed no signs of letting up. I screamed so loud in my head it felt like my eardrums would burst.

Someone had to stop this. My guidance counselor, Mrs. Campbell, the janitor who smelled like funny cigarettes, anyone.

But no one did.

Funny thing about drowning. It seems like it lasts forever.

Until the darkness closed in. My knees went weak and I slipped out of Grace's wet grasp, my head slamming against the metal rim with an audible *bong*.

The hallway lurched wildly for a moment. Grace stood over me, a nine-year-old titan, her look of triumph too malevolent to be a child's.

Time stopped for a moment. When it came back, I'd thrown up, salty tears streaming down my cheeks. My first real breath hitched and burned, the ache in my head given voice to an embarrassed, heartsick moan I'm not proud of.

The switch flipped. The look of triumph melted into *oh shit I'm going to get caught*, and with a kick she turned to bolt down the hallway, her steps already picking up speed.

Her legs seemed to lift out from under her. There's no other way to put it. Like something slipped an arm beneath her and scooped.

The front of her skull slammed into the shining surface of the fountain hard enough to dent it before she somehow propelled herself towards the janitor's door, which was rushed open to meet her with startling force. With a meaty *thud* like a major leaguer swinging for the fences, she caromed off the edge and smacked into the far stucco wall. Her slide to the ground was soft and boneless. She wasn't moving, and blood began to pool from beneath her gory scalp. I later found out the door had hit the wall so hard that it took a crowbar to dig it back out.

It could have been the water that made her slip.

Anything's possible.

The tears were drying when Mrs. Campbell finally exited her classroom, a large red-haired vision in green sweater and sensible slacks, shoulders like a linebacker and fire in her heart. I loved her so much in that moment.

Her third-graders peeked from behind her, taking in the scene with wide-eyed interest. Grace hadn't moved from the pile she lay in.

Blood was seeping into my eyes. I looked like a flood victim.

As Mrs. Campbell went to Grace, shouting something about what the meaning of this was, the Man stepped from the shadowed recess of the closet. His eyes were fierce, his clenched teeth shark-like as he touched a finger to the wide brim of his hat.

"Darlin'."

I looked from Mrs. Campbell and Grace to the third-graders clustered in the doorway.

Their eyes were wide, and more than a little afraid.

You're right. I am avoiding it.

I won't say his name. Speaking of him is bad enough. It might bring him here, but actually calling him—

Anyhow, Grace had fractured her cheekbone and left orbital, suffering a concussion that kept her out of school for the next couple of weeks. The widespread rumor started that I was a black-magic-slinging witch, which to be fair beat out *teacher's-pet*, and when she transferred out of the school district, *Spooky Prose Harden* had been born.

Wow. I'm not constantly interrupting you with bon mots, am I?

My father wasn't thrilled. Grounding, loss of privileges, all the parenting bells and whistles were applied, even though all I was guilty of was getting my ass kicked. It might have been better if I had hurt her. A normal kid gets into playground scuffles, all skinned knees and bloody noses. Instead, I'd put three bullies in the hospital without raising a finger, and no one over twenty was buying it as coincidence.

My mother started giving me strange, wistful looks that I was far too young to decipher. Dad couldn't be bothered with the real world right then, deep into rewrites on his fourth novel, *Stranger Than*, after the third had hit the market and died. My mother had all the time in the world to take my tangled web and try to unwind it.

That's not what I'm saying. You can go work on your jump shot with Lo if that's all you're going to add.

There was a rainy day in Mr. Weatherby's class later that year. I don't remember if that was his real name or just something I cobbled together from Archie comics, but Ms. Quezada was out sick with some kind of minor surgery. This portly, bespectacled fellow was the substitute, and he was all nerves.

At the drop of a pencil he'd start.

A burst of giggles and he'd whirl about, cheeks red and chalk raised.

He'd raise his voice at a seat creaking.

I'm just saying it was a good thing he was only with us for the two weeks. Four might have killed him.

Given the classroom, maybe he was a little sensitive too. Seeing a black mass untangle itself from the back corner of the ceiling and cast smoky tendrils towards your pupils is the kind of thing that might unnerve someone.

Even so, he should have guessed it was relatively harmless. The school had sat there for seventeen years without anyone being dragged off by the shadow fisher, so it wasn't worth overreacting, even if he could see it.

No, I don't think a lot of people did. The Man just laughed and called it Ol' Smoky, and the thing was perfectly content to be hands-off. Some of the things it whispered, though...

Sorry. I'm getting off topic.

It was cloudy outside, with crazy gusts of wind that shook the trees and sent dead leaves whipping through the air. We were getting back our English papers, and Weatherby kept sneaking glances to the far corner of the room as he walked between the rows, dropping our stapled assignments on our desks with vague words of encouragement or reproach. My paper had a red A stenciled in the upper right-hand corner, and he said something about my good work when I heard Marmalade clear his throat behind me, the rumble of a tiger.

"Figure you know better."

Frozen, it was as if a gear had just ground down in Weatherby. After a moment, he pressed forward, like a man determined to walk across the bottom of a pool. Drawing a red pen out of his shirt pocket, he glanced past me and marked a little plus sign next to the grade on my paper. His scurry to the front of the room could have won a forty-yard dash.

Spooky little Prose. I didn't make many friends.

Not that I cared. I don't want to give you that idea.

By then the Man was all I needed.

Svara had been scribbling like a spider trying to avoid the drain, but now he looked up with something soft at the corners of his eyes.

Pity. Oh, no, there it is.

"So, this man," he starts. "Your imaginary friend is some sort of bogeyman?"

I shake my head, concerned that he's missed the point, maybe missed all of it. I remember Marmalade pushing back his hat, letting some of his greasy brown hair float around his jaw. *'Maginary's a hell of a judgement to pass on a man.*

"Don't call him imaginary. Delusion, hallucination, schizophrenic embodiment of the id. Whatever psychobabble you need to work around it, fine. But never imaginary."

Svara smiles indulgently. My palm itches to slap his face. "You've told this to the police?"

"Whatever I told the police doesn't matter. I was out of my mind at the time, with the paperwork to prove it." I weigh my words. "Also I was a minor, being interviewed without a guardian present, and not having been read their Miranda rights. I'm sure anything I said is inadmissible, which is why Detective Holcomb keeps calling."

"Ah, Holcomb." Svara straightens his fedora. "The persistent gentleman."

Of course he's placed a call to your psychiatrist. Stay on point. "If you're ever looking for a case study on OCD, he's the one you should be talking to."

"Really?" The pen is poised, his eyes bright and expectant.

"Whatever evidence fits his theory he clings to like a remora. Whatever doesn't gets ignored or disappears. They probably teach classes at the Academy."

"Ah." There's something in his voice I don't like. "But you understand why he might have reached his conclusions?"

"No. It's lazy. He's supposed to be conducting an investigation, but instead he's firing an arrow and then painting the bullseye around it. My life's worth more than guesswork."

"Are you saying you're not responsible?"

My fingers tingle with unexpected frost. The creak of the rope reaches my ears, a discordant melody. "I think we're done here."

"Don't take it so personally," he smiles, as if him accusing me of murder is just poor sportsmanship. His teeth are a faint yellow against his mummy's grin. "It's just a question. Cheerfully withdrawn."

"Cheerfully." A dull throb starts behind my temples.

"When did you first realize that the Man was around?"

"When did I meet him?" I remembered Sarah in the tall grass, the woods at dusk as the Man stepped out. I wouldn't give him that.

"As you say."

My father had been locked in his study for most of the day during the tea party. Writing, he used to say, was like bleeding for applause. It left you weak and drained and, though I didn't understand it at the time, somehow wanting to do it again. After a big day, he'd need a glass or two of inspiration to keep his faculties up and running.

After I met him, the first thing the Man had suggested was amending the cupboard rules.

Dad had a glass of melting ice in one hand as he came down the slope. The Man had scooted the pink plastic table back a number of paces until we were almost touching the branches of the firs. M— the Man said he liked it better that way. I complained about it being too dark in the shade, and he laughed and said it for the first time.

"Darlin', we're all down here in the dark together."

While I didn't know a whole lot about friendship, I knew it was nice to let others have their way once in a while. It was there, then, that my father found us, a confused smile on his face and a dripping tumbler in his hand.

With a wave he had my attention. I loved my father so much.

"Evening, sweetheart," he said, the creases of a frown beginning on his forehead.

I smiled up at him, ecstatic to see him set free from his paper mill and patted an empty space next to me. My father shook his head.

Noticing his fixation on the table, I waved a hand theatrically. "Do you want to play tea party?"

"Not now, honey bunch." He leaned back, and I realized he was trying to see inside my plastic cup. I tilted the empty container to help. A mixture of relief and distress warred for a moment. "Did you have any?"

I shook my head. A cloud of emotions warred, and then he asked. "Why's the bottle out here?"

"M— said tea is for Yankees, Tories, and *sickofens*. We had to find something different."

"Sycophants," the Man murmured from his seat on the plastic chair. He didn't seem distressed that my father was ignoring him.

At the time, it did seem a little rude of Daddy.

"M—?" my father asked. "Wait, did you say sycophants?

"Affirmative." I smiled, happy that we were all on the same page.

He looked over at the Man's teacup. It was half-full. The Man had been taking his time. "Seriously, did you drink any?"

"I smelled it," I offered. "Your inspiration reeks of cat piss."

He turned a little red, his hands clenching, just before he threw back his head and laughed. With his free hand he rubbed his fingers through my hair before plucking the bottle and teacup off the table like a juggler. He drained the little blue glass in a swallow and wiped his mouth with the back of his hand. "Prose, this is just for mommies and daddies, okay? I don't want to see you playing with this stuff anymore."

"There goes the bourbon," the Man grumbled.

"Yes, Daddy." I patted the Man's hand in consolation. "It's okay. There are plenty more games than tea party."

The Man smiled. "Ain't you one to raise a man's spirits?"

My father's grin wavered. "Who are you talking to, princess? Sarah?"

"Sarah's sleeping, Daddy. This is— the Man." I presented him with a wide sweep of my arm like I'd seen on game shows. Something else seemed necessary. "He's very funny and has his own hat and knows lots of interesting stuff. We're going to be best friends."

"Well, isn't that something." My father glanced over at the Man's chair for just a second. The Man twiddled his fingers back in a middling wave. "Glad to have you aboard, M—."

"Oh, we've met," the Man said. I don't think my father quite heard him.

"Come on, Prose. Let's get you in for supper."

"Aw. We were just getting quainter."

My father smiled again. It lit up the night for me. "It's almost full dark. Come on. We can have hot dogs and yellow mustard and apple sauce. You don't want to get bit up by skeeters, do you?"

I would have drunk yellow mustard by the bottleful. "Can the Man come too?"

"It's a free country," he said, and so I followed my father up the hill with a skip in my step. I almost didn't hear the Man behind me.

"Worse things in the dark than skeeters, Thomas. Worse things by far."

"Heartwarming, don't you think?"

Svara presses his pocket, and I hear that digital *click* again. "It's not strange to you that you're the only person who sees these—"

"Irregulars."

"Yes. Did the name come from them, or did you derive it yourself?"

"Myself."

"Progress." His eyes gleam like a vulture looking up from its carrion. "Childhood capers are an introduction, perhaps, but we're going to have to bring this home sooner or later. Your parents, specifically."

"Yep." No great surprise there. He didn't come to the banquet so he could stick by the salad bar.

"In the meantime, I invite you to look around us. We've talked about your friend for hours now. Do you see him? Has he, as you feared, arrived?"

I'm not sure if he's having me on. With an errant flip of his hand, he urges me again, and I dutifully crane my head around the gym. There's Lo, playing on his smartphone, the basketball he's holding blocking it from whoever might walk in through those heavy double doors. The dark pair of doorways in the corner, empty with deep space. The hoop, an orange metal rim netless for over a week now since one of the teen boys had figured he could climb it and jump off the top. The pale wooden door on the far side with the EXIT sign shining over it in pale, tired red. The stage, black curtains enveloping the pocket dimension of the stage, a window to another world currently overstuffed with old files, lost possessions, and kitchen supplies. The—

One of the curtains twitches, a brief, unobtrusive spasm. I glance back to Svara, who shrugs as if waiting for a response. The curtain gives another frightened jerk, bunching and unfolding in a moment that seems to last forever. Four pale fingers close around the edge and tug, just a little. They are long and feminine, yellow and aged.

I force myself to complete the circuit, dragging my eyes along a cart of folding chairs, a shipment of donations stacked neatly in cardboard boxes, the other netless basket, the double doors again. "No. I don't see him."

Svara smiles, lips peeling back from his teeth. "That's good. Very good." He scribbles on his pad for a moment. "Do you want to play some basketball? I think you've earned it."

"I'm good." It's a battle not to look back at the curtain, hearing the low hiss of cloth as it brushes deliberately against the ground. Maybe I am crazy.

How many monsters can one building hold?

Distracting myself, I look at the pair of dark doors in the far corner. It occurs to me that as big as the basketball court is, the gym is much too large to only contain it. "Lo?"

"Yes'm?" Not looking up.

"Where do the big doors lead? I've been here for months, and we've never set foot beyond them."

Lo meets my eyes, for once looking interested. "Good question. You'd never need to. A lot of this building's been mothballed."

"Mothballed?"

He shrugs and turns the basketball over in his hands. "Not like, officially. More just out of use."

"Why?" A low melody had begun to drift from the stage, discordant highs and lows that were raising gooseflesh. I force myself to not react. Any information is good information.

"Everbrook was originally built to house way more kids. Like, a lot. And it did, I guess, until the occupancy laws changed. In the seventies, early eighties, the population used to hover between two or three hundred."

I do the math. "There aren't enough Lodges for that."

Lo nods. "Even doubling up the rooms, there's not. They had to get creative."

Creative isn't a word I want to associate with bureaucracy. "Are we talking Hoovervilles here?"

"I don't know that word," he sniffs. "It helped that kids had less rights then."

"Bully for you."

"Hey," he says, sounding genuinely wounded. "Do you really think we don't care about you? Want to help you?" When I don't answer, he shakes his head. "This afternoon Everbrook's housing eighty-two victims, all of who've suffered abuse. That number goes up on weekends and right before the holidays. Abused minors with explosive anger, severe emotional disturbances, extreme neglect, but we're expected to keep the peace with a six-to-one ratio and the budget of a small lemonade stand. They want us to create individual behavioral treatment plans but only give us enough manpower to treat you like cattle. If it weren't for charitable donations you'd be brushing your teeth with Borax."

"Yeah?" The song rises in pitch. I try not to betray my rising panic as something scrapes against the boards.

"Yeah. No one's here to get rich, kid. Everyone's doing the best they can with what they've got."

"Sorry." Lo's outburst is such a digression from the norm that I'm at a loss for words. Still waters run shallow?

"Anyway, I wasn't there in those days. Not a lot of old-timers left. Three to a room wasn't exceptional. Mattresses in hallways. When they were really pressed, this gym could sleep sixty like a fallout shelter." He bounces the ball once. Svara watches us with a faint curl at his upper lip. "They used to stretch cables across it, hang up sheets like clotheslines for a little bit of privacy."

A cold wind blows down my spine, and even the stage falls away for a moment with the memory. Figures pressed against the white linen, moving in secret, reaching through the fabric. The smells of pine and smoke. The cabin—

—he was going to give you back to them—

"Is everything all right, Prose?" Svara asks. His pen is pressed between his fingers. Numbly I realize that he's left-handed.

"Fine," I say. My voice comes from a distant place, worlds apart, and I try to focus on Lo. "How do you know all this?"

"Chapman showed me once. He likes to talk about it." Lo continues his vacant tour. "Behind the doors are another set of bathrooms. So are the group showers—

"Group showers?" My stomach rolls as images of late-night prison movies flit wildly through my conscious. Behind me, the singer takes slow brushing steps, the melody rising in volume.

"Like I said, it was a different time. Then came that Geraldo thing, and the nation was in an uproar. Anyone who'd try that now would be locked up." He smiles as if he's reading my mind. "There's classrooms, a locker room, a lounge. An old playroom for the toddlers with a door to the field. Stairs to the basement, to the attic. Storerooms beyond count."

"Can I see?" *Anything to be out of this room.*

"Don't have the keys. Besides, it's a maze back there. Creepy, too. A lot of the lights are burnt out and no one's gotten around to replacing them."

Svara clears his throat. "Is there anything else you'd like to talk about today, Prose?"

I can hear the dragging of cloth against the hardwood.

A long dress? A sheet?

A shroud?

"No, thank you. I'd really like to go now."

The subservience in my voice seems to throw him for a second, and he gives me a contemplative eye I don't like before he unfolds from his web amongst the bleachers. "Very well. Let's go back."

For the briefest second I feel something buzzing behind me, a high electrical circuit that I'm sure is about to rest its palm against the nape of my neck, and then I can't take it anymore. I jerk from where I'm standing, striding quickly to the foyer. Lo leaps from the bleachers in a burst of motion I wouldn't have thought possible, and I'm out the door before the lights die.

I don't look back.

Svara chuckles, as if at a joke only he could hear.

The dayroom is quieter than usual when I come in, an almost tangible pall lingering in the atmosphere. Chapman squats at the desk in the back, flipping through a logbook and jotting down notes onto a legal pad. He looks tired, which admittedly is better than the seething rage I've grown accustomed to. Harkness and a muscular girl with fantastic dark hair are playing video games, a siren wielding an unlikely battle-axe prancing about on the screen. Nellie and another girl are conspiring on the couch in a series of muted whispers, some teen romodrama playing on the big screen in the background.

Sandy sits across from them, scribbling some notes on a clipboard. *Incident report?* Jon raises a hand in greeting from his seat behind a pale-skinned girl in a grey sweat suit, who's sweeping her thick black hair out of her face as she attempts to reconstitute a jigsaw puzzle. I identify her as the screamer from the day before without much judgement.

Everybody gets one.

Graham nods at Lo, who slinks off to the couch, surprisingly intent on watching Miranda Cosgrove wade through the turmoil of high school. "You're my one-on-one?" I ask him.

"Exact-a-mundo," he tries. I give him a look that makes him wince. "Do you need anything?"

I look behind me to discover that Svara has melted away into the shadows. I don't even think he made it to the door. "Can I make a phone call?" I ask, and Graham looks at Chapman as if trying to get a read on him.

"Let me grab the phone," he says, stepping into the hallway. I follow him in.

"I want it to be private, please." Unless you ask, it's just assumed that you want to broadcast your business to the general public. Graham nods and pulls up a chair next to the desk. I feign pleasure at sitting so close to Chapman, the smell of his sweat and something darker tangible in the dim corridor. He radiates some kind of garbled concern as Graham asks me who I want to call.

They don't let you dial your own phone calls. Seriously. "Mark. My uncle."

"You got it." Graham punches in the numbers from the book and hands me the phone. "How was Svara?"

"Good," I offer noncommittally. The phone rings three times, four. Panic begins to rise in my chest, a high, wordless fluttering. Was Marmalade already getting closer? Worse, could he have found Mark?

Paranoid, Prose. That magical thinking doesn't even fit the narrative.

Maybe Svara was shrinking me because I was starting to wonder. Was Marmalade really just some fragment of my psyche? Someone to blame when I misbehaved or hurt someone, the devil on my shoulder?

The devil with a box of matches, maybe.

You know what he did.

Did I?

On the sixth ring, the phone picks up. The voice sounds tired, cagey. "Hello?"

"Mark? It's Prose."

"Prose." The word hangs as if he's trying to remember who I am. "Good. Good to hear from you, Prose. How is everything?"

"It's okay. I'm trying to be good."

Chapman raises an eyebrow at that as he jots something else down. I can almost hear Mark nodding over the phone. "That's—good."

"What are they saying in court?"

"So far it's okay. I've got full-time work right now, and they're taking that into account, plus your behavior seems to be more under control."

"I'm being good," I repeat, as if that would make it true.

"Listen, has the detective called you?"

"Not in weeks."

"Okay." He pauses, as if unsure how to proceed. "Prose, we might have a problem."

There it was again. "What kind of problem?"

"There's some kind of surveillance video from the cabin. At least he says so. Some kind of CCV anti-theft feed. They don't have to show us any of the evidence unless you're formally charged, so who knows, but still. He's claiming there's something tying you to it. Not DNA, 'cause you were clearly there. But something. Maybe he's just making noise, trying to scare us into some kind of deal."

"There's no deal to make."

"Prose, I'm not even your guardian right now. If you're charged, I might not be able to help you."

"Charge me with what?"

He pauses, weighing his words. I don't like it. "I don't know, but we can't afford a real lawyer."

"What about Thomas's money?"

"It's in a trust, and they're not going to just turn it over to his— look, you're going to have a shitty, over-worked public defender on a highly publicized trial miming defense in front of a jury. Worse, you're going to be tried as an adult."

My eyes begin to sting. *Because you're guilty?*

"That's not fair." It was childish and stupid, but it slipped right out of my mouth.

"Life's usually not. If they're willing to talk, we might be smart to listen."

"I didn't do it. I didn't do any of it."

He stops again, and it makes me hate him a little. "Okay."

"Okay?" Tears begin to tumble out of my eyes. "Okay?"

"You're not listening. Whether you did it or not—"

Whether you did it or not. It rings in my head like a bell.

"—doesn't matter. It's what they can show—"

"I have to go now." My eyes are wet, my voice croaking.

"What?"

"I have to go now, Mark."

He sighs. "Think about—"

I hang up the phone and place it on the desk. Chapman pretends not to notice. Graham hands me a tissue. "Not good, huh?"

"I don't want to talk about it."

"Do you want to hang out in your room?"

"No. I don't." *Because being alone right now instead of just inside would be too much.* "I'd like to just be in the dayroom, please."

"You got it."

My right hand aches smartly, a phantom throbbing without apology. In the dayroom, the air is full of different noises. Movie scores and electronic fights, open whispers and muted threats. Nellies filches me a dirty look from some recess of her soul as I walk past, and her lean accomplice on the couch tries to mirror it. My eyes don't break from the far spot on the wall. For once I acknowledge that the Lodge is actually pretty big, that I could probably do shuttle runs across the dayroom, and then the muscular girl puts down her controller in mock-rage and nods to Jon. "I'm going to take a shower."

"Shower!" Jon bellows to the back of the room.

"Shower," Sandy acknowledges. She slips from her seat on the couch and grabs a plastic chair from the back hallway across from the restroom, her monitoring position now secured, even though all she could see would be feet. Someone has to make sure no one's falling, hitting their head, or sneaking into each other's stalls.

The muscular girl gives me a pat on the shoulder as she walks by. "Hang in there, Spooks," she says.

It's strangely affecting.

Harkness spots me behind her and offers me the last controller. She's done something a little different with her black hair, fashioning it into a combination of spikes and waves that make her look like a lost anime character in a sleeveless black tee. "*Lamentations in Oakenshire*?" she asks.

"What?"

She gives me a bemused grin and presses the controller in my hand. "I'd ask your shadow, but he's already been proven my inferior in every way."

"Don't make me drop your level, sweetheart," Graham grumbles, but he's smiling too wide.

The controls of the game are insane and overcomplicated, so I fall into my age-old strategy of wandering the split screen and, when I encounter something, mashing buttons wildly. She gives me a look that probes the alcoves for clues. "Are you doing okay? Phone bad?"

I look over my shoulder for Phoebe, but she's either in our room or has somehow snuck out. *Lo was right. It really is hard to keep tabs on everyone without physically herding them.* "Accused of murder. Getting used to it. "

"Fuck," Harkness murmurs. Graham starts to correct her but falls silent. We play the game for a while, flashes of light and whirring blades and electronic music pumping. I've beheaded a goblin with a bat the size of a small telephone pole when she asks the question. "Is it true?"

"Is what?"

"Don't get that look. I don't really know you. I like you, but I don't really know you. You know?" Her left eye is scrunched up in concentration, and she's biting her lower lip as she enters a combination of buttons like a telegraph operator. The elf leaps onto the back of a dragon, the battleaxe swinging in a wide, haphazard arc, and the giant lizard is suddenly headless. Green blood sprays from the stump in a jetting arc. In a twist of video ingenuity, it spatters the inside of the screen. "The Red Orphan stuff. I mean, I don't even know what really happened, if you could do those things, but since you live next door, questions abound."

"Yeah. I've been told not to talk about it."

"Keep bottling it up until you explode? Sound parenting."

I smile in spite of myself. "Legal counsel. It's all a pretty grey area, but they're deciding where I get to live next. My uncle, foster care, emancipation." *Prison* gets a sound omission, which I'll worry about later. "Everything else is just a very red cherry on top."

"You mean the cops have cleared you, then? Cool. That's good."

Not just yet. "Something like that."

"Damn, but were you just born unlucky." Harkness gives me a brief little side hug, her fingers never leaving her controller. The casual warmth of the gesture stuns me, and I realize how long I've gone without anything like it. Fresh tears begin to blur my eyes.

Graham asks me if I need anything, and I wave him away. Poor, sweet Graham. I wonder how much longer he can last in a place like this, a combine that wears everything away to sarcasm and sullen edges. "Have you heard from Vanessa?"

Harkness blows a lock of hair from her eyes and scoffs. "Please. No, that airhead was supposed to call me if she got away, but I haven't heard from her. Seems to be going around, actually."

"Do you think they're all going to the same place?"

"Not a chance. People have lives outside these walls, at least until the cops roust them and bring them back. The only thing we all have in common is a couple of screws loose."

I giggle out of character, and Harkness gives me another little hug, and Graham mutters "Boundaries—"

"Oh, relax. You know you love it." Harkness lets me go. "You should laugh more, Prose. World's dark enough without it."

Darlin', we're all down here in the dark together.

A cold shiver courses down my spine. If she sees the ghost travel across my face, she doesn't ask. "Have you heard from Alisha, then?"

"Nope. Riders on the storm." Harkness glances back at Graham, then with a mischievous wink adds. "Between you and me, though, she said she was seeing someone. Planning to split with them at first, but then only her and Vanessa left. Draw your own conclusions."

The thought of Vanessa's solicitation occurs to me, and I almost put voice to it before something makes me choke it back. *It's not the time, not with Graham behind us.*

"You girls are having an uncommon amount of fun. Knock it off or I'll drop you both down to basic," Jon bellows from the table. The dark-haired girl doesn't look up.

Harkness shares a smile with me. It's the first real one I've had in forever.

For the next hour, I start to believe everything can be all right.

And then the lights go out.

How the hell did he find me so fast?

The light is sucked out of the room, an instant of stunned silence punctuated by nervous giggles as the screens die in white pulsars. My hand drops to my pocket before I remember that of course we aren't allowed to have phones, which means everyone's first and easiest flashlight is out of reach.

Chapman's bellowing for everyone to keep calm, knowing that half a dozen headcases aren't about to show the best coping skills. It has the same effect as shouting *Fire! Nobody move!*

I peek out the sliding glass door into the stygian world outside. Only the skeletal trail of the 'Sip is visible, the faint lights on their poles dead stars. The other buildings are only shadows, afterimages in the blink of an eye. I wonder about the emergency lights, why they haven't triggered on. Maybe maintenance wasn't in the budget this year.

Graham's triggered the light on his phone, and Jon is close behind. They're trying to regain order, and I can't help but notice that Jon has moved to block the front door. *Wily veteran*, I think, and then Nellie has plastered herself against Graham. In the dancing light her eyes are wide and wet, near panic as she clings to him. "Please," she whispers. "Please, the light."

A hand slips through mine, and my mind skitters.

It's a madhouse. Maaaadhouuuuuuse!

The silhouette of her flapper's cut marks her as she pulls me close to the far wall. Raised voices echo, and twin lights scurry sporadically as Phoebe lays a hand on my cheek.

"This is your chance, kiddo. Twenty-eight skidoo," she whispers.

"I don't know how," I whisper back, trying not to get swept up in panic. *Whether you did it or not*, he said. "I don't know the way out."

"Prose?" Harkness asks. She's somehow drifted over near Jon. Chapman's on the phone at the back desk, Sandy returned to the dayroom, and Phoebe shoots her a look that would have killed a cape rhino.

"You might not get another. Run for the wall by the field. There's a tree with low branches. If you hurry—"

"I *know* you."

The gravelly voice makes me whirl around. The newcomer's rasp is a funereal thing, birthed from a throat sick of screaming. "They know you, too. But I *know* them."

The black hair hangs in front of her like a mourner's shroud, making the new girl a faceless ghost in the dim light. "If you don't stop telling secrets, they'll make you pay, Harden. They'll fix you. Theta waves, you see."

I hear Nellie whimpering somewhere in the shadows, Graham grunting as he tries to pry her off. Phoebe pushes me towards the sliding glass door, her message clear.

Go.

She faces our newcomer with a snarl. "I don't know who you think you are, but you don't—"

"I know you *too.*" In a lightning burst of phone light, her smile is horrible. "Better than most, I think. *Qui videt vere videt.* There are sides. Not black and white but all the colors of the rainbow, and they *love*—"

I tug on the door, but it won't budge. Trying the catch, I give it another quiet yank. It might as well be made of stone before I see the heavy two-by-four responsible for blocking it in place. It's such a rudimentary stopgap that it catches me a little off guard. *Who are they worried about breaking in?*

Before I can wonder how subtle me running around with a board is going to look, there's a scream between the dayroom and the hallway. The shorter girl Nellie hangs out with, Victory, has her hands over her face, head firmly planted against the door. Sandy's trying to talk to her, but everyone's talking at once, and the newcomer behind me is still shrieking when I hear it, faintly at first but drawing louder.

—da da duh dee da—

A muffled melody, as if rising from a great depth. My knees pop as I crouch, hands tugging at the board. Swelled with age and Oregon damp, it sticks.

—da da duh dee da—

This one is loud enough to make me turn, if only to gauge the distance. I see nothing at first, and then a shadow begins to blossom on the ceiling, a curl of smoke that swells into shape. The volume intensifies with screams. Whether or not it's panic, hysteria—

Can they see it too?

"Everybody cool it!" Jon shouts, a patriarchal bellow that actually seems to help. "It's just the power!"

—the board pops free in my hands with a wooden *thunk* that I'm sure can be heard all the way to the gym. For a moment I imagine trying to club the black shape with it that even now has sprouted legs to mock gravity, strutting slowly along the ceiling, but I kneel and rest the plank at my feet. Discretion's always the better part of valor, my father used to say.

And when you need to get gone, *get gone*.

A hand loops around my arm, and I'm surprised to find my clenched fist ready to swing.

Harkness is inches away from me, and over her shoulder I catch a glimpse of those yellow eyes as the thing finds me, marks me. "Don't," she says simply. "The tunnels will be too dark."

There's a flicker, and then everything returns to blinding light, a rush of power that leaves everyone frozen in a brief still life. Nellie has her fingers clutched around Graham's wrist. Victory sobs in the corner. Eloise stands with a towel wrapped around her in the back of the hall. Too late, Chapman has loaded a pair of fresh batteries into a yellow plastic flashlight and waves it to resume command.

Jon is watching the two of us and the sliding glass door with paternal security.

Phoebe's fled, and the newcomer with no face is glaring balefully at the ceiling. The black shape on the ceiling extends a tenebrous length and strokes her hair, once.

There is a rush of breath, and for a moment I wonder if everyone can see it before it's simply gone with a muted pop.

—*da da duh dee da*—.

"Crazy," Jon bellows with a knowing look. "The power must have kicked the board out. Who'd a thunk?"

CHAPTER EIGHT
THE STORM BLOWS IN

The Eggshell Galaxy coalesces from a cloud of figures, constellations colliding from the dull swirls of dreams. I've slept in longer than I'd planned.

The day outside is patchwork, hints of azure poking through dark swaths of grey like hope through a veil of cobwebs. A couple of kids stroll by on the back path with an adult hovering behind them. One has a plastic pail, the other a tiny jar, and after a moment or two of poking around the trees I realize they're looking for caterpillars. The woman glances around, a watchful hen, and gives me a sharp nod that makes her tight ponytail shake.

I return it without enthusiasm.

Phoebe's sprawled out on the opposite bed, my copy of *Hangsaman* folded between her palms. She nods in my direction. "When you fall asleep, do you ever think you'll not wake up?"

"Sorry?" I process the question, still a little groggy. After last night's confusion, everything had taken on a brittle tone, and I had taken my meds as much to be done with the night as anything else. Sneaking a peek at the door first, I slide off the heavy bed and check beneath the leg. One-hundred-twenty-two pills, all shapes, all sizes. "I guess. Kind of abstractly."

"I do. I think about it all the time." Phoebe flips a page absently. "I think about it as my mind drifts and my eyes close, that this time will be the end of me. Consciousness gone, winked out of the solar system, and then the black comes. It's quiet there. Starless, and I rest forever. When the light flickers and I'm called back into existence, it's a terrible rebirth. It's not always welcome to open my eyes again."

I pull on a black DHD t-shirt and dark jeans. For a moment, my fingers pause, lingering over the lip of the drawer. I have an inexcusable sense that I'm forgetting something. It's come more and more often lately. It's beginning to worry me.

"No school today," Phoebe says, as if she hadn't been talking about the big sleep a moment before. It's so banal I laugh.

"Yeah, it's the weekend. No Stabby Academy."

"I hear there might be a field trip going out tonight." She says it with such mute disinterest that she's got to be yearning for it. "Graham's taking it out. For those on their levels and such, anyhow."

"Like you said, it's the weekend. Someone'll call out, and then Chapman'll kill it."

Phoebe shrugs, rolls over, and stretches, arcing her back like a great cat. "Maybe he will and maybe he won't. Just trying to put out some happy thoughts."

I haven't stepped past Control in over two months. The thought of being even temporarily outside Everbrook was more exciting than I could have thought.

Maybe. Just maybe.

"Doc showing up today?"

Had he mentioned it? "I think so. Sometime after lunch."

"Got some color in his cheeks now." She flips another page, biting her lip as she does so. Maybe it's the light, or maybe the aftereffects of antipsychotics floating around in my system, but her skin is pale, her lips blood red, a steampunk Snow White. "You ever think it's weird?"

"What's that?"

She pauses, a little unsure. "Wait. Why are you looking at me like that?"

I shrug. "You're almost glowing. I think the cowpoke is good for you."

"That's filthy." She smiles anyway, deep and secret. "I mean your click. How often he's around."

"Probably has quotas. Figure since I stonewalled him for a week or so he's probably behind."

"Yeah." She sits up, splaying the paperback open. "Was Osgood ever around this much?"

It's my turn to mull it over. "I'm not sure. Even with cheeking meds, my memory gets a little fuzzy."

"What do you cats talk about?" The luxuriant amber in her eyes doesn't quite meet mine.

"Everything. Mostly my childhood, I guess."

Phoebe raises an eyebrow. "That's it?"

"Yeah. And stuff. Phoebe, why do you care?"

"It's one of the reasons I tried to bust you out last night."

I laughed. "You pointed at the sliding glass door, Houdini."

"All right, so I'm out of practice. So what?" She laughs, and we're back to normal, a couple of goofs waking up on a weekend. "It's not their life, is all. Don't tell them everything."

"I wouldn't." *Couldn't.* There were some things that Svara, for all his threats, would never have. "Why so concerned?"

"Imagine the book deal if you disappear."

There's a rap on the door, and Monique's behind it. Phoebe goes back to *Hangsaman*, and I go ahead and shower early. My dirties go into the oversized canvas cart, an industrial relic that looks like a prison movie prop, and I brush my teeth and hair with equal precision. Breakfast is already cooling by the time I'm done, everyone crowded around the one big table, and as I bite into my scramble her words stay with me, a grain of sand slowly transmogrifying into a pearl.

I walk around the field in patient, perambulating loops. All around me I can feel autumn's fade, a brutal winter fast approaching. The clouds above me are gray and bruised, and eddies of cold wind gust about me with an abandon I'm beginning to feel. Dead leaves scurry across the concrete like rats, and even the grass has taken on a strained, yellowish hue. One corner of the walls peeks through, black and foreboding behind skinny, unsupportive birch and pine. Along the other side the gymnasium squats, a behemoth that slumbers dark and dreamless.

I wonder which of them would be worth trying.

We loop around the backstop and the bleachers again, and I half-expect Svara to call for a break. He's not getting any younger, and his beige suit and dark cap aren't the ideal outfit for a walkabout, but he doesn't even breathe funny.

Of course not, I think.

The ghoul feeds.

This is our second lap without me saying anything of substance or syllable, but he's content to let me work through it. Monique paces behind us respectfully, long-limbed and broad-shouldered. I hadn't seen her since the day I stormed back to the Lodge, that afternoon she shepherded the little ones inside where she looked at me with a mixture of mistrust and pity. A consummate professional, the event doesn't seem to have affected her attitude towards me in the slightest.

There's an explosion of sound as I pass beneath the branches of an elm, and my breath catches. A trio of crows escape the upper boughs of the massive tree, and whirl and circle before heading east. I watch them go, cawing in their alien language, and remember reading something about an experiment where they could recognize faces. Stranger still, explain them to each other. Since experiment is somehow synonymous with torment, in it a series of men in Dick Cheney masks would chase them with sticks. When the same men returned *sans* masks, the birds swarmed them anyway in a barrage of shadowed wings. It was worth noting, their tormentors said, that the crows didn't only attack their personal antagonists, but everyone involved in the experiment.

The ability to see through masks. What I wouldn't give.

Svara clears his throat, and for a moment I envision the birds vying for his eyes. The gory image is horribly real for a moment, and I stumble over a crack in the walk as I try to clear it from my mind. My cheeks flush red. "Is there anything in particular you want?"

"There are extensive notes in your file from a prior clinician. Berriman, I believe. You were discharged rather suddenly.""

"My old therapy? No psychobabble about disassociation today?"

Svara smiles thinly. "Perhaps later."

"It's your dime," I say, and wonder how many times Phoebe's said that to me since I've been here. It feels foreign on my tongue, and for a moment I wonder where she is, if the cowpoke and she are hiding out behind one of the Lodges or in the industrial laundry room. I wonder what it would be like to have something like that, someone close to you, to touch you, someone you could spill your heart to or bleed for on cue.

My chest hitches, and before he can ask why, I begin.

You walk through a doorway. The room is nice, modern, generously lit. The carpet is clean, free of stains, the walls hung with minor art and memories. A dog sits in the corner, its tongue darting between its lips with excitement and pleasure.

How, then, do you explain that something's not quite right? Off, in that certain sense of the word. Perhaps there's something grainy in the quality of the light, casting shadows that aren't quite where they should be? Perhaps a certain yellowing to the walls that calls to mind gnawed old bones? Perhaps the walls themselves seem, at least in part, insubstantial, as if there's a cheese-like softness, almost a thinness where a rigid object should instead exist? Maybe the dog's expression is manufactured, something else reflecting in its doleful eyes? The baseboards themselves, on closer exploration, might be just a little too far up, not quite meeting the ground. There's a certain fraction that might just allow something to slip through.

It was all of these things and none of them. Well, except for the dog. Algernon was long gone by then.

But how do you explain the sense of wrongness that a place can manifest? A house, a shipyard, a patch of woods? How do you make sense of something when logic can't be involved?

My stepmother's house was such a place.

Let me set it up for you better. You don't look convinced.

After— you know. After.

Like I said, we'd floated around for a while, trying our hand at motels and apartments, odd jobs in thin stretches. That my father met her was pure coincidence, if you believe in that sort of thing. At least he was happy again, the first time in a long while.

I'd like to think that.

There were always creepy feelings in that house, but after I saw the tongue in the closet, things began to move. Small objects, mostly. Keys and pens and pocket change would be on the counter one minute and gone the next, only to be found hours later in ice cube trays, high shelves, under cushions. My father thought it was me, though I don't think he ever openly said so. It was more of a look he'd give me when he thought I wasn't watching, a touch of sadness mingled with a twinge of disgust.

I didn't blame him. Any search engine you could fire up would give you hundreds of articles about children acting out, especially after serious trauma or grief. He was still waiting for me to get over it, to move on.

I don't think it really occurred to him that he could help with that.

Instead I'd spend long hours up in my room, reading, writing little stories, playing with my toys, waiting for my father to come in and make everything better with a little hug and ask his pumpkin if she wanted to play.

His work got darker, which is understandable too.

So much fucking *understanding*.

I'm so tired of that word.

I just don't want to paint him as some monster, some ogre who kept our heroine locked in her tower and supped on her tears. He was a good man, too. It was his idea for me to start journaling then, encouraging me to write down my thoughts, my feelings, gain perspective on my world. It would help polish my voice, he said.

Listen to me now.

Sure, a cynical person would say that. Scribbling them down also ensured that he wouldn't have to hear about them. But it wasn't like that. He had big plans for me in that sense, growing up Bronte. He told me that I could be a better writer than he ever could, and he'd marvel over the little stories I'd write for him, fantastic little episodes full of witches and unicorns.

Some had a certain Man. He never much cared for those.

Anyways, darker work, right? The so-called second phase of his career. *The Big Empty* was finished right after we moved into the farmhouse, and he was working through the preliminaries on *Breathing Deep*. It was going to be an ambitious, heavyweight project, the kind of thing that could make careers, and he had thrown himself into it like he'd tied an anchor around his throat. He was upstairs, then, when Rachel brought the VW Beetle home and asked me to help her put the groceries away.

She was dressed like she had just come back from work. Rachel was in marketing, part of a small firm operating out of revitalized Hawthorne, a vicious little start-up with a lot of new ideas. The farmhouse had been inherited, a gift from her grandfather who had practically raised her since her father had been killed in a freak industrial accident the night Nixon fled back to Yorba Linda. She'd never been particularly heavy with the details.

Not that I pressed. She was good to me and loved my father to death. A lot of strays should be so lucky.

Rachel had smiled and slipped a hand into her bag. When she retrieved it, she brandished a beat-up old hardcover of Poe's *Tales of Mystery and Imagination* she'd found on a rack outside a used bookstore by the place she got her nails done at. She knew my preference for half-decayed print, and the yellowed, funny-smelling collection in its little red cover made my heart skip a beat. I hadn't read it yet but knew it by reputation, and I hugged her with the fatal gratitude of a drowning woman.

She was always doing little things like that, considerate and thoughtful.

She didn't deserve what happened to her.

Rachel was going upstairs to see how my father was doing, which meant either his literary synopsis or general mental health, and I tugged two bags out of the boot and walked them back into the kitchen.

It's old world for trunk. Boot. Like cars are little people.

I just think it's cute, okay? Jeez. Let it go.

I propped the pantry open with an old brick we'd found in the yard when we'd dug out a bed for the pepper garden. The door hung a little strangely, but the repairs had yet to materialize. Hanging from a string was one of those bulbs that you'd turn on with a yank. As I filed things away in the narrow space, my mind was wandering with that particular trance routine gives you. Shelving cans and cereals, beans and veggies, cleaning stuff and coffees, my hands were doing their own juggling, and I was indulging in a little daydream when the light flickered.

My hand found the cord and tugged.

Off. On. Off. On.

Binary code. Everything seemed to work fine.

On my way out, a can of green beans fell off the bottom shelf behind me.

It didn't have my utmost attention. If it had, I might have noticed that damp, wet odor that seeped in, like old stones.

Rachel and my father were upstairs, voices a little raised, tempers a little blotchy. The smoldering shroud of terror fell over me, like it did every time their voices went higher. In my heart, I hoped he could see what our situation was, but he'd gotten leaner over the last couple of years, and a couple of rough corners stuck out where he'd just been tender and soft before. I think he had a hard time seeing the day to day.

Maybe that's where I get it from.

I went back out to the garage for another few bags and came back into the kitchen.

The slatted door was now shut.

The old brick lay alone before the pantry. Not the biggest thing in the world. Like I said, doors close. Doors open.

I peeked back into the garage, hoping somehow that Rachel had returned and was retrieving the last of the bags from the Beetle's boot. No such luck.

When I returned, the pantry door was open again, the brick squatting helpfully against it. A rush of gooseflesh crept up my forearms in a sudden chill that had nothing to do with autumn.

Open. Shut. Binary code.

I took a moment and just breathed, soft and silent in the threshold. Standing still, I could hear muffled voices. They may even have been Rachel and Dad's.

After a while, the bags in my arms started to feel heavy and the conflict cancelled itself out. If anyone else wandered by and saw me, they'd think I was having some kind of fit, and it was that more than anything else that forced me to move. The bumps on my arms settled and I hauled my load into the pantry, figuring it was best to be done with it and go rifle through the new Poe.

Setting the bags down, I began to sort out the cans, my mind already wandering to casks of Amontillado and still-beating hearts.

The scrape behind me took a moment to register.

By then it was already too late.

The brick spun merrily off towards the garage. The door closed with a dull finality like a coffin nail.

I dropped the can of diced tomatoes and heard it roll away as a thin rattling began behind me, not on the shelves but somewhere beyond them, like a train passing by on some distant and forgotten track. Ice water surged from the base of my spine and flooded my veins. The temperature had dropped so quickly that I could just see my breath before the bulb burnt out.

Behind me, I heard cans shifting, things falling off the shelves. In the dark I fumbled for the pantry door, tiny slices of light from the kitchen filtering through. A bag of rice exploded upon impact, casting bone-white kernels across the linoleum. Cans plunked over the side.

Still the door wouldn't move, wouldn't budge. My arms felt boneless, and the temperature continued to drop, the chill now seeping through my extremities. My teeth chattered and I cried out a plea for help, a curse at the door.

Something snapped off the wall behind me, and I turned to look.

The thing's eyes met mine, grey with fever in the crepuscular light, close enough to kiss. The reek of old pennies and spoiled meat bellowed forth as the misshapen thing lurched across the fallen boards towards me.

Where a wall of shelves had stood now stretched a funhouse corridor, twisting back at an unnatural apogee. Webs and dust coated the gritty walls like a second skin. Bleeding in from a source I couldn't see, a horrid purple light filled it.

Something in my mind bent with a sickening lurch. As I gazed down the unreal passage, I could just make out doors, black and gnarled things like old scabs. From somewhere beyond that came a faint melody. Something was singing in the darkness.

Then the pallid thing had a white claw wrapped around my bicep. It was somehow gentle.

Come and see, come and see.

A hopeless cry wrenched from my throat as I skittered off some mental cliff. The thing tugged again, impossibly strong, and I felt my feet slide without purchase across the rice-strewn linoleum. My fingers seized the door latch like a life preserver, and the thing tittered as it heaved.

Impossibly pale, somehow slick, my mind registered the thing as something like if a man and a spider could breed, though the specifics were mercifully lost. The wormlike tongue flopped out of its mouth again, smelling like old popsicles, and dragged along my forearm like an icy lover.

Wherever it touched, it burned.

I had the barest moment to grab the knob again, and then with another tug it was lost. The melody grew in crescendo as the delighted thing began to withdraw with its prize. My head hit the freezing linoleum, and it wrapped its other claw through my hair and began to drag.

No.

The door opened.

It was that simple, or so they said.

Rachel found me in the tall grass of the backyard, facedown at the edge of the woods, crying and bleeding and calling a name. She held me for what seemed like a very long time.

Then the county came crawling in.

Don't look so hurt. You knew you weren't my first rodeo.

My arm was a mass of wounds, sickly deep yellow-green bruises from my bicep to what looked like light burns scalding down to my wrist. The hand at the end was a mess of red and black, and I couldn't move it without agony lancing all the way to my shoulder.

My father came downstairs. I want to say eventually, but that probably isn't fair.

Rachel took me back to the living room and tried to comfort me as best she could, but apparently I was pretty wild until my father handed me a glass of iced tea. I drained it in two long gulps, the ice sending pitchforks to my brain.

I had time to think it tasted peculiar, kind of like licorice.

Waking up in a doctor's office was a violation, shirtless and wearing an odd smock that barely covered my breasts, what little there were at the time. Two police officers were questioning me, no guardian in sight, and Dr. Meltzer was hovering nervously behind them. Every now and again he'd interject a detail, some piece of medical trivia, and the cops would nod placidly and write something down on a pad. It's strange, the clarity with which I remember coming to: the uncomfortable look on the doctor's pallid, wrinkled face as he paced, the bored expression of the second cop with the pen, the almost fevered you-want-to-like-me intensity of the first as he grilled me with questions and promises he couldn't keep.

Surveying the room, it looked a lot like a doped-up half-naked teen with PTSD being interrogated by three men without an adult, and I clammed up in the middle of saying something like *"it drew its tongue along me"* so fast I heard my teeth click.

Looking back, I bet it looked coached. At the time I didn't care.

"I'm sorry. What was I saying?" My head ached with a dull fury, and my arm felt like it was smoldering from the shoulder down.

"You were telling us about a scary man in your pantry." The first cop glanced up at his partner. They exchanged a look that convinced me that the latter had been mostly either doodling or working on his screenplay. "It's okay, Prose. No one's going to hurt you. You can tell us what happened. What *really* happened."

The room grew colder and shrunk away. "I'd like my shirt back now."

"In a minute. Someone's on their way to take pictures."

"Now, or get my dad in here. I'm sure he's very curious as to my— examination."

There was another look, and they parted for me to retrieve my shirt. I grabbed it from the table and stood with my back to them before I realized that I wasn't going to be able to put it on without help, and so just wrung it in my hands like a towel before turning back around. Hot tears burned in my cheeks, and I wanted to scream, because I was old enough to know what this looked like.

"Do you—" The first cop tried again, his face a mask of sincerity. If he was offering to help me dress, he thought better of it. "I hear your dad's a writer. Makes sense. It's quite a story."

"I'll say," the second cop murmured. He didn't look up, scribbling something down on the pad. Notes for Act III.

"Maybe your pantry is pretty spooky. I don't know. I used to like scary stories myself when I was your age."

"Gravy," I muttered, looking at the door.

"But they're not real, Prose. They don't explain your arm." There was a burning earnestness behind the first cop's almond-colored eyes. "What was it that really happened? Did your daddy hurt you?"

"With all due respect, Mr. Harden has been coming here for years." Dr. Meltzer tried to interject. "I've seen Prose since she was—"

"People do crazy things," the second cop said. He scribbled something else down like an exclamation point.

"No." My arm throbbed, my thoughts greasy slow. I wanted my father and I wanted Rachel and I wanted to burn that farmhouse down, in no particular order. "I fell."

"Fell?"

There was a knock on the door. The police ignored it.

"Fell. Down the stairs. From the second story." It was like pushing through cobwebs. "I saw a spider. Big. Brown and black thing. I put my hand on the bannister and it scuttled onto the rail. Jerked my hand back. I must have lost my balance. Rode my arm all the way down."

The second cop shot the first a look. It seemed to say, *Well, all girls are scared of spiders. Her story checks out!*

"You fell down the stairs." The first cop was trying to keep a straight face, but I had a feeling he'd heard this song before. "What time was it?"

"Afternoon. Rachel had just gotten home."

"From the second story?"

"From work."

He sighed. "Was anyone else in the house?"

"Rachel. My father."

"Do your stairs have hands?"

What? "No."

"How do you explain the bruises, then? Prose?"

I didn't know what he was talking about, and for the first time, I looked at my arm. Really looked. It hung limply like a side of beef, and I turned it this way and that with ginger speculation. A raw red weal traced almost from my wrist to the crook of my elbow. Above it, a constellation of yellow-green ovals spread from my bicep to the curve of my shoulder like sadistic pointillism. Even to me, they were unmistakable.

Fingermarks.

Taking a deep breath, I surveyed my options. *Ugh.* There weren't many.

"Sometimes I get depressed—" I started.

They hung on my every word.

Svara must be made of kite parts and gasoline. He blows right by me on the path before he realizes I've stopped and double backs with surprising speed. While my legs ache and beg for reason, he's not even winded.

I wave us over to the bleachers, and he smiles as he sits, sliding across the corrugate metal and perching both long legs beneath him. In his glasses I can see dark clouds rolling in. "I started to see Dr. Berriman a couple of days after that. Social services got involved, but after a few home visits I think they started to believe me. To them if you owned a black t-shirt you were goth. Two and you were an emo disaster waiting to happen. It all fit nicely together."

"But I still had to go back to that farmhouse."

Svara taps the base of his pen against his lip. He starts to say something, then changes gears. "At this point, the Man wasn't there?"

"Is that all you want to hear about?" I ask. Somehow this seems important. "You won't stop bringing him up."

He shakes his head, and for a moment the wind threatens to snatch his hat. "No, but he's the commonality. The *deus ex machina*, as you will."

"You don't believe me." It's not as petulant as it sounds.

Svara smiles. "Does it matter?"

I pause, purse my lips. For a moment it occurs to me to tell him about Sinatra, about the yellow eyes I've seen at night, and then I bite it back. What help could he offer? Would he really let me out if he still thought I was seeing things?

Besides, a girl's got to have some secrets. "That's not an answer."

"So," Svara ignores me, glancing at his notes for the merest fraction. "This thing. In the pantry. Did *it* have a name as well?"

"I didn't exactly check its badge."

"And you really believe that you didn't hurt yourself? That your story was fabricated whole-cloth?"

"Yep." There was a tone to this that I didn't quite like.

"Mm. When you started this period of counseling, because you were '*attacked by the pantry ghost*', the Marmalade Man was not present."

"I never said it was a ghost. But no, not yet."

"But he came. Eventually."

"Like a bad penny. He always turns up."

He mulls this over. While he's calculating the rate of tea in China or the advance for his book, I glance over at Monique, wondering if she's listening, if any of this is of interest to her.

She sits at a respectful distance, her grey hoodie wrapped around her as the winds get worse. Ostensibly daydreaming towards the field, her head is turned at just the slightest angle to keep me locked in her peripheral vision. If she's amused or disturbed or outright alarmed, she gives no sign.

The doctor was a bespectacled, thick woman who meant business the minute I walked into her fourth-floor office.

The blinds were closed, and a dim little lamp from the desk cast the room in muted sepia tones that made me think of old photographs and crime movies about the thirties. She didn't rise from her desk as my father and I walked in and took our seats in front of her.

The supplicant comes, I thought. The Man had never liked desks, much less offices.

Tapping the rim of her glasses, she looked down at her notes. From the corner bookcase came the faintest hum. I was pretty sure we were being recorded.

"Prose Harden? I'm Dr. Berriman. Your case has been referred to me by the Department of Child Services for the state of Oregon."

I nodded. I knew all of this was coming, that my lie would mean jumping through hoops for a while, but there was something off about that room. Nothing tangible, just a weird feel at my temples that never went away. Somehow the air smelled gamy. Already I was doubting my choice.

My father squeezed my hand. It was meant to be supportive, but I could see the worry lines tracing their way around his eyes. For a moment I wondered what he thought, if he knew that the self-injury reports were a lie. He could always read me so well, but then again people believe what it's convenient for them to believe. The simple road is the easiest to walk upon, and there was no safer path right then than to get Prose some help and maybe some blue pills, then not have to worry about anything else.

My father wasn't a bad person, but sometimes I think he was just weak. And tired. Mom—

What happened to Mom took a lot out of him. I think part of him died too.

I really don't want to start crying.

I miss them both so much.

Already drifting, I started eyeballing her desk. On it was a single ornament, a Hummel figurine of a Dutch woman in the process of harvesting grain.

"*In the Dutch language!!!*" is still one of my favorite Lovecraftian stingers.

"As you know, today I'll be asking a series of questions strictly as part of the evaluative process. Your answers will help determine how the state wants to proceed."

We'd jumped right to scare tactics. The thought of waking up in a group home tomorrow steeled my reserve.

Yes, it really is that bad here.

Why don't we talk about *that* sometime?

"Understood," I managed.

The doctor showed her teeth. "Your father has the right to be present during this process to assist you with any interrogatives you may not either fully understand or be able to provide full answers to. Answer the questions truthfully and to the best of your ability. It goes without saying that a failure to do so will cast a black mark upon this process."

If she weren't worried about the whole truth, she would be soon. "What if you don't like what I have to say?"

"What you have to say will go a long way towards developing your overall treatment plan. This is only an evaluation. Are you ready to begin?"

The waxy light seemed to grow heavier. The Hummel figurine's features lengthened, became cronelike. The smell of old warrens and undisturbed air thickened around me, and for a moment I struggled to breathe. "Thrill me."

"What is your name?" She hadn't taken out so much as a tape deck. A sense of unreality washed over me. The position of the chairs and furniture like a set, the pair of us only actors in a stage play. *Plucky Madwoman Presents.*

"Prose Harden."

"How old are you, Prose?"

"Fourteen."

"Are you currently taking any medication, narcotics, or illegal substances?"

"Gummy vitamins."

"Any medications, narcotics, illegal substances within the last six months?"

"Not besides the gummies, no."

"Your father tells me you've been experiencing hallucinations?"

My jaw dropped as I whirled to face him. Thom Harden could have been carved from stone. "What have you told them?"

"You've got to answer the questions, Prose." His voice was impassive, reciting train times or stock prices. I could have cheerfully throttled him.

I turned back, flashing my winning smile. "That wasn't a question."

"Have you?" Berriman asked. Her hands were folded in front of her like she had a pistol right under the desk.

"No, I have not been experiencing hallucinations."

"Defined as seeing or hearing people or things that aren't there?"

"No."

"No?"

"No. They're there."

She paused, considering. "How long have you been experiencing these phenomena?"

I couldn't believe that my father had said anything. We barely talked about the irregulars, and for years never without one of us exploding. If he was just going to start throwing cards on the table, I was going all-in. "Since I can remember."

"Do they interact with you?"

Careful here, pumpkin. I heard the Man's voice so clearly I glanced behind me. Had the shadows grown longer? "Sometimes. They try to get my attention."

"Get your attention how?" Dr. Berriman was studying me as one would a mounted insect. In my mind, I could hear the faint ticking of a clock.

"Wave to me. Whisper. Come closer."

"Mm."

I sighed. "It's not that exciting. Sometimes they say things." *Horreeble theengs*, my inner Vincent Price quipped, and I tried to stifle a giggle. Before the doctor could speak, I cut her off. "Not like *join us* or *play with matches*. Just passing the time. Asking questions, every once in a while. Mostly I ignore them."

"Mostly."

I rotated my arm into view. The bruises were still a sick yellow-green against my pale skin. "Sometimes they get my attention."

Dr. Berriman slashed at her paper with a black fountain pen I was immediately envious of. "When did you first realize that no one else can see them?"

"I don't agree with that assumption." I shrugged, and my father cleared his throat. "Maybe you could, if you were willing to look."

"Prose." My father caught my eye, and for the first time I saw the genuine concern on his face. What kind of trouble were we in?

"Five. Since I was five."

"Your *hallucinations*." She put weight on the last word, and again I heard that slight tick. "Are they consistent, or do they vary?"

"To reiterate, I don't think they're hallucinations, but it depends. Some recur. Some I never see again."

"Is there a history of mental illness in your family?"

I opened my mouth to speak, but my father weighed in with a cough. "Her mother's uncle. He was diagnosed as schizophrenic. I believe he spent quite a few years down in Salem."

"Schizophrenia?" The pen slashed again.

"What?" This was news to me.

"Something like that. Prose never had a chance to meet him. And her uncle, but I don't know—"

"Indeed." There was a light in the doctor's eyes that hadn't been there before, and the feeling of being pinioned intensified. An uneasy feeling skittered inside my stomach and across my toes. *Soon. Soon all of this will be over, and you can go home to Dad and Rachel and—*

Oh yes. Your friend in the pantry. And somewhere beyond that is an opera, and they're waiting..

In the dark.

Darlin', we're all down here in the dark together.

I must have zoned out for the last question, because my father gave me a quick nudge that a blind man couldn't have missed. "I'm sorry, could you repeat that?"

A line had appeared on her forehead, a horizontal token of impatience. "Have you ever exhibited any of the following behaviors: bedwetting?"

"When I was, like, three."

"Setting fires?"

"Nope."

"A feeling of being watched, or some scrutiny from outside forces?"

"Who hasn't?"

"Disassociated lights or sounds?"

"No."

"Unusual or sourceless odors? Burning hair, for example?"

"Gross. And no."

"Cruelty or violence towards animals?"

"Ugh."

"We had a puppy once," my father added. "It disappeared."

The hell it did.

Dr. Berriman raised an eyebrow. "Thoughts of self-harm? Suicide?"

"Nothing serious."

"Nothing. Serious." The pen slashed again. "Self-injurious behaviors, including but not limited to cutting, auto-asphyxiation, burning, bruising, pinching, scratching, friction burns, bloodletting, extreme exposure to heat or cold?"

The figure in the Dutch hat leered at me as the light flickered overhead. I began to wonder if anyone else could see it, that sneering rictus. "It's why I'm here, right?"

"Show her your arms." It was almost a whisper from my father, but it carried an electric charge.

"She didn't ask—"

"Show her."

I rolled up my sleeve so Dr. Berriman could get a good look. I gotten back most of its use, but long, spidery handprints still formed a Rorschach up and down my arm. I didn't show her the other one.

He'd been back, you see.

Two nights before, I had awoken to the creak of the closet door, too late. His icy hands pressed down on my arm, the wormlike tongue lolling from its mouth. A sagging face the pallid color of old cheese hung over me with a look that was almost love, and in the distance, a melody held a promise.

—*come and see*—

I've read up on this sort of thing. That is, I've combed through the weak metaphysics sections of used bookstores, the Time-Life-Presents-The-Occult section of the library. There are a lot of sources for interpreting your dreams, finding love through candle magic, praying to the moon. There aren't a lot about ridding yourself of a rotting monster or closing a portal to a hellish netherworld in your pantry.

Believe me. I looked.

I wanted answers and found trivia. Fiction wasn't much better, though I got some great accounts of what might have been the cause. Extra dimensions rubbing up against ours, weak spots in reality. A lot of those stories are written in the past tense, giving the tellers the benefit of hindsight that only survival can give you. The worst ones— well, people vanish all the time.

And who's to say where they go?

It's not important if you believe me or not. Just remember your end of the deal.

I bleed, they read, right?

Anyway, my father muttered. "Dr. Meltzer thought her wounds were self-inflicted. A cry for attention, he said."

Because you've been going to him for a dozen years, Dad. I can tell you that it was certainly not *his first conclusion.* "Yep. Hallucinating, super-cutty me. Look-look-look."

Dr. Berriman laid her pen down on the table. It made a dry clacking noise that was somehow magnified in the small room. She leaned over the desk to get a better look at my right arm.

What slammed against the window made everyone jump. It was the sound of a bass drum struck by a sledgehammer, and the doctor raised a hand as if to shield herself from the inevitably broken glass.

The window held, but with the blinds closed, no one knew what had happened. Nevertheless, I'm sure everyone's mind filled in the gap.

Deep down, I knew who it was.

I sigh as the first patters of rain strike my face. Svara cranes his head towards the sky and shrugs his skeletal shoulders, dismissing the darkening clouds. "It will blow over," he says, and smiles. It is not an unkind smile, but there's something behind it I don't like.

Monique checks her phone and the weather with equal boredom. We've been out here for at least an hour and listening to me prattle on about cops and clinics isn't winning her over anytime soon. I guess she must overhear stories like mine a lot, and wonder how numb to it she's become. For the first time, I think of how she looks at us afterward. I remember Nellie throwing a coffee cup at her, it ricocheting off the bathroom door in a lazy arc to drench her.

Her smile remained bright and unaffected, even sopping wet. Her voice never raised in pitch. It must take a hell of person to go through all the drama and still treat everyone the same.

Maybe that makes her the crazy one.

I turn my head towards Intensive Girls, a blob on the shores of the mighty 'Sip. Everbrook's administration building lies further down like a port of call, and I remember the starfish girl with silver eyes. Had anyone else mentioned her? Even glanced her way?

With a numbness, I realize Mark hasn't visited in weeks.

A sudden gust of wind sends my hair billowing in loose tangles around my face, shadows against alabaster. Morning has slunk into afternoon, and everything I touch is burning around me. Cheerful reveries like these are what Svara pulls me out of.

"Why did you attack Osgood?" he asks.

It's so off-topic that it startles me back. "The book he was reading. It was one of my father's."

"Was he a fan, do you think?" The cold light in his eyes says all I need to know of his opinion.

"One of these days you'll get tired of asking questions you know the answers to. It's wasn't just any book. Not *Big Empty* or *Breathing Deep. House of Razors* is a betrayal."

"Quite a successful one, I think. Isn't that where *Red Orphan* comes from? The antagonist?"

"Have you read it?"

"I haven't the stomach." The sour smile says different. Osgood had been trying to gain some insight, and I bet he thought he'd go straight to the parental font. But that book—

"Things hadn't been great between us in a while." I measure my words. "I think that Osgood thought it was a shortcut. The keys to the kingdom, what makes little Prose tick. Instead he found a black mirror to hold up between us. Every secret I told him, every conversation we had, became reflected in that light. So I snapped."

Svara watches me from behind his glasses. I hurry on. "I don't feel good about it, but I don't feel bad either. He should have just asked."

He smiles again. "Your friend. The Marmalade Man."

"Don't say that name."

"Indeed." He raises an eyebrow. "You say he leaves you, sometimes for months on end. Where is it, do you think, that your boogeyman goes?"

I know what you're implying.

That he discorporates, or simply ceases to be. That want will bring him—or *need*. Not the case. There have been times when I wanted him desperately.

The pantry, obviously. Yesenia Flores' fifteenth birthday party, for example, where I broke Aedan Harcourt's nose after he tried to stick his hand down my pants after a few wine coolers.

The night we all snuck out to the abandoned club and barely got out alive.

He'd be the first to tell you. He's not a puppy. He doesn't come when called.

As for the trail he leaves—

When I was eight my parents began to worry. Snippets of conversation would disappear when I walked into a room, sudden hushes and wordy glances exchanged over dinner.

One day I walked back from the bus stop, the wind rippling the tall grass at the edge of the lawn. The air smelled of springtime and wildflowers, and Marmalade lay propped up against the old oak in the corner of the lot. He raised a hand in a half-salute.

I waved, climbing the steps to the door, one-two-three, and it wasn't until my hand closed around the latch that I heard him call out.

"Wouldn't do that, pumpkin. Two cats in a henhouse right now."

He hadn't even looked my way, just continued to stare out into the forest and its lengthening shadows like he was on the crow's nest of some vast ship searching for land. I paused and heard Mom distinctly through the thin wooden door.

"—Eight years old, James. Three fights already, and those are just the ones we know of. No friends—"

"She's doing great in school. You've seen the grades."

"What I've seen is the way the other kids look at her—"

My father sighed, audible even from my hiding place on the stoop. "This isn't about Mark—"

"Don't bring my brother into this. That was a long time ago, and this has nothing to do with him." She paused, as if gathering balance before plunging downhill. "She needs real friends. Friends who aren't— I don't even know."

"Those are fantasies, love. Ghost stories and fairytales. She likes to read. Better, she likes to read well—"

"I know, and I know how proud you are of that, but she needs real friends. Not Poe or Wells or Bradbury. Friends who'll be there for her, who she can tell secrets to, who she can laugh and love and play with. She needs something of this world to hold on to."

Why doesn't she understand? I have everything she asks for.

I have M—. I have the Man.

"She has us. She'll always have us."

There was the sound of paper rustling. My hand already raised to knock, I was going to go in and tell her so, tell my beautiful mommy not to worry about me, because everything was all right.

I did have somebody, well and truly.

His low voice came from behind me.

"You've got a good heart, pumpkin. Better than mine by far. But trust me. Don't step into this right now."

He put his hand on my shoulder, his lean figure eclipsing the afternoon sun. "Ain't a place for us right now. Come on, darlin'. We can play revenuers and rustlers 'til they settle down."

It all fell into line. "This is because of what you did, isn't it?"

"The joke?"

I nodded. "The noodle joke."

He sighed and ran one hand through his short stubbly beard. "Yes, and no. There's a thing in me, Prose, like a streak. I let it out more often than is best."

I folded my arms. "If you tell Mom you're sorry, maybe then she won't worry so much."

"You know I can't, darlin'. They see what they want, 'specially as they get older. She'd hear nothing but a fine breeze blowing, and that would be that."

"Why me? Why can I see you, then?"

The Man looked back towards the woods. "You'd be surprised what you learn, if only you stop to listen."

I've thought a lot about that. Mostly because of what happened after, but I thought I saw something in his face, a second of discord that's still stuck with me, even when so much else has fallen away.

You see, in that moment, I knew that he was lying.

Months passed. The arguments were there, my folks waiting behind corners and awkward moments to ambush each other with little bon mots and entreaties, but I managed to dodge more than I walked into. Finally I was making my way home from the bus stop only to find my mom sitting in a lotus position on the stoop.

She looked tired, a little drawn at the edges. Next to her was a box with a bath towel drooped over it that seemed to vibrate with life. It says a lot about me, but my first thought was that she had found me a tell-tale heart.

"Prose!" she called. Her smile warmed me from head to toe. I hadn't seen it in days. "How was school?"

"Good." Something more needed to be said. "We had a sub. The Man called him a black-hearted carpetbagger, but we managed."

The smile waned, just for a moment, and then it was back. "Is he here right now?"

"The carpetbagger? Or the Man?" I shook my head. "He had a rendezvous with Mr. Ortiz after school. He told me not to wait."

"That's nice." A line had appeared on her forehead. I could see the question blooming in her mind, but her lips smothered it back with that smile. "Your father and I were talking, and we thought it might be nice for you to have another friend as well. What do you think?"

"I don't know. The Man's pretty great," I said automatically.

To her credit, she didn't flinch.

"Maybe a friend that everyone can see? Someone you can share?"

The box hopped again. A stirring of disquiet began in my stomach. *Here it is,* she'd say, holding out the glistening muscle as it pulsed between her fingers. *Just like you wanted.*

But nothing is without its price.

"Maybe." I had come to a stop about four steps away from the stoop and eyed the box as it shifted again. Could I really hear its hideous beating?

My mother grinned, lifting the towel off of the metal crate with a flourish. For a moment, my mind stuck with the image, the red organ pulsating raw and wet inside the iron, and then I really saw what it was. A small brown terrier puppy, only a little bigger than both my palms put together, was fussing with his paw and batting at the inside of the crate.

The puppy saw me and made a small yipping sound. I was like the Grinch when his heart exploded.

My feet flew up the stoop without me as my mother slid open the latch on the crate and lifted him out. The tiny brown terrier had little stubby legs and the beginnings of a naval moustache. Held out to me, I froze, not knowing how to hold something that small and delicate. His tiny tongue raced across my face in hot sloppy kisses, and I took him from under his forelegs and hugged him fiercely.

He made a couple more excited yips, rolled over to his back, and stuck his tongue out in submissive doggie abandon. I rubbed his belly and looked up at my mother with warm gratitude in my eyes. My father had bemoaned pets as a pathological nuisance, needing constant attention and carpet cleanups, dwindling our resources with veterinary visits and constant kibble. A month before, he had put his foot down about owning a hamster.

My mother had stepped out onto a marital limb for me, and I loved her for it. She ruffled my hair, the puppy gave me kisses, and sunlight trickled down from the heavens.

She was never as beautiful as she was then.

As my mother started to explain to me how we'd take care of him, that this was a *big responsibility*, a breeze shifted behind me. I looked over my shoulder with a cool feeling tracing the nape of my neck.

Marmalade leaned in the shade of the big oak, watching us coolly, what might have been a faint smile creasing his stubble. I wanted to bring him the terrier, wave it around and have us all play together, but something stopped me. I knew that to go and flaunt the puppy to my best friend would hurt my mother.

Instead I wrapped my arms around her neck and gave her a big squeeze. She hugged me back, but when I looked up at her, her eyes were on the old oak, and the wind coming in.

The fourth-floor office had a level of quiet usually reserved for mausoleums. Dr. Berriman sat behind her desk on a thick leather chair, her black top and stern expression giving her the appearance of a provincial judge trying a horse thief.

My father was waiting outside in the reception area, lost amongst the stacks. Motes of dust flickered in the wan overhead light, flotsam from a celestial catastrophe.

The Department of Human Services had deemed our initial visit worthy of further investigation. That my father wasn't allowed inside spoke volumes, and he had been left grumbling with a cup of cheap coffee and a battered journal full of notes and chapter outlines for *Breathing Deep*. He'd given me a firm hug that I felt all the way to the base of my spine and whispered in my ear. "Be strong. We're going to get through this."

I admired his conviction. Poe knows I lacked it. Trying to get through an hour-long therapy session while staying true to your lie is a lot harder than you'd think. So many fabricated facets have to be kept in line that it really is just easier to tell the truth.

Bet that fills you with confidence. Right?

Anyway, my body ached and stung. I was sporting a fresh set of bruises down both arms and an ugly red scrape from where I'd hit my head off of a towel rod, courtesy of the thing from the pantry. To camouflage it, I was sporting a black paisley bandanna and a tight long sleeve top that made me look like I was either a gothic fortune-teller or looking to front a metal act.

Dr. Berriman wasn't buying it but hadn't called my bluff. *Don't volunteer information,* my father had said on the ride over. I thought he'd been reading too many crime novels, but I didn't say anything. Better to have a plan than to go in blind, even if the plan was stupid.

Things at my stepmother's house had gotten worse over the subsequent weeks. Whatever boundaries existed were wearing thinner and thinner, like a bald tire finally scraping down to the inevitable blowout. That peculiar melody seeped from the walls from dusk until dawn. Half a dozen times I'd awaken to the loathsome presence leering over my bed. There was a malevolent languidness about his touch that made me bite my tongue in revulsion. The dead grey eyes were contemptuous, and once or twice it tasted me.

I have the scars to prove it.

Worse? It was showing me it wasn't in any hurry, that it knew there was nothing I could do to stop it. Neither overt nor violent with its touch, it was simply letting me know that it remained.

I was being groomed.

What once was limited to the pantry or my closet was now a terror that permeated the entire second floor. In the dark, it became a nightmare to open any of the portals on the long hallway: the closet, bathroom, bedrooms, the study. I wouldn't dare go near the attic, that dreadful square hatch at the center of the hall.

Once I'd tried to get fresh dish towels for Rachel and found the linen closet replaced by a black and starless void, empty as the pit and just as deep. Below me, red lights seemed flicker and cant, dancing at the bottom of some abyss. When she checked up on me, I tried to scream a warning that came out a whimper.

When Rachel got the towels without being sucked into eternal night, the look of worried pity she gave me almost broke my heart.

Of course I'd started thinking about the Man again. It's all a little hazy. Part of me still loved him, part of me was scared, and part of me could never forgive him.

But I needed him. Needed him badly.

Sometimes I'd wake up with his mantra on my lips unbidden. Something he'd sing in his low, gravelly baritone when I was distracted by a book.

There was a man no god had made
His name, he said, was —.

No. I'm not going to say it.

Anyway, I'd hear it in my dreams, which were all tea parties and wyrms, black bags and burials. Before I drifted off to sleep, I'd wrap the dark comfort around myself like a blanket.

He wasn't lying. Not about that part, anyway.

The doctor sat behind her heavy desk like a bulwark, and from the bookshelves to my left came the familiar mechanical hum. I smiled with a mirth I didn't feel and asked her how she was.

"Very well," she managed. "How are you feeling, Prose?"

"Great," I tried. "Certainly not dangerous."

She sighed and folded her hands. Unconsciously I mimicked the gesture. The light above us, already low, seemed to dim. "Prose, roll up your sleeves."

My pulse thickened. "What if I say no?"

She gave me a sad smile that promised everything. Pulling up my sleeves, I rolled my eyes.

She was a professional. Only her breathing gave her away.

"Rotate your wrists, please."

I did as she asked, marveling impassively at the web of bruises that crept up my wrists and elbows, yellows and greens and deep purples like a masochist's motley. Only when she sat back did I realize how lucky I was to be even getting this second visit instead of rotting away in a foster home somewhere.

At some point, you stopped taking the parent's word for it.

Dr. Berriman clicked her pen once, pursed her lips, and asked me if my story remained the same.

"Absolutely."

"You maintain that these— injuries, have not been caused by a relative?"

"My father would have to come out of his office more, so yeah."

"Is your position still that they are self-inflicted? Inflicted by your hallucinations?" She checked a note scribbled on her legal pad. "Your irregulars?"

"They're not hallucinations."

"You don't consider them a projection of yourself?"

"No."

She sighed and straightened up behind her desk. Her eyes were empathetic, her tone soft. "Prose, you're not okay right now. A glance at your arms should tell you that, and I don't even know what else you've given yourself."

She'd guessed right. A crisscross of cold burns had been scraped along my stomach like cuneiform the night before, but I held my tongue.

"You come across as a 'hard' character, but deep down I know you're scared." I could hear the apostrophes dropping into place. "With your family's history of mental illness, it's understandable."

Did she say great-uncle last time? "I don't know what you mean."

She gave me a pitying look. I could have slapped her. "This is what I want us to do for today. First, I want you to promise not to hurt yourself until we meet again."

I was already tallying the drive to the county seat, more sessions, more afternoons for my father to stew in waiting room and count the pages he wasn't finishing. They were already forming a pendulum over us, the house the pit. "When will that be?"

"Does it matter?"

I thought about it. "Fine. No hurting myself. Got it."

"Second, I want you to come clean about these irregulars. Your hallucinations."

"It's your dime." I was lapsing into noir again, and tried to steer clear of Prose Harden, Private Dick. "I mean, go ahead."

"You said that they were physical manifestations. That is, they're fully visual and auditory."

"Olfactory, too."

"And now you're saying they can touch you as well. Prose, that's four out of the five senses, and I imagine that's just because you haven't tried to lick one yet."

"That's a common misconception, derived from Aristotle and the elements." When she raised an eyebrow, I continued. "Current science has demonstrated at least seventeen commonly used senses. Timing, for one, and magnetoception, and blindsight, and my personal favorite, proprioception—"

"You're stalling."

"It's the sense of where your body is in relation to the physical world around you." Yeah, I was a know-it-all then too. So what? "I just thought you'd like to know."

"Do you think it's odd that no one else can perceive them? Using any of these senses?"

"Honestly, I don't know that they can't. Everyone just wants me to keep taking their word for it."

The pen scratched something onto the legal pad. It looked a little like *paranoia*. "And you say that there are many different *irregulars*? All shapes, all sizes?"

"Mostly people-shaped. And I wouldn't say many."

The pen scratched something again. "Do you feel privileged that you can register them? That it gives you some kind of greater significance, as an emissary between us and them?"

"Hell no." It came out flat and immediate. "If there was an option, I'd rather not."

"Have you tried?"

I rubbed my burnt stomach, centering myself on the pain. "How would that work, exactly?"

The doctor ignored this. "Do you feel that they give you special information? Make you privy to things you wouldn't already know?"

Marmalade had taught me a couple of games, an appreciation for gothic literature, and how to pick the lock on the liquor cabinet. None of these seemed to be what she was looking for. "Not especially, no."

"Do you believe you have a supernatural ability? Or that you have other talents that no one else seems to possess?"

"No. The only weird part is that no one else claims to see them."

She scribbled something down on her pad. "Do you think sometimes you know what's going to happen? That you can predict the future?"

It's easy as keeping your eyes open, he'd said. "Not really. Beyond an educated guess, I mean."

Dr. Berriman paused and glanced at the window behind her, like she'd heard something settle. "Would you describe yourself as sociable?"

"Sure." It was a lie, and we both knew it.

"You would say you have a lot of friends?"

I sighed. "Fine. No, not really. Is this a therapy session or an inquisition?"

"Your educational record has recorded a number of violent incidents at school."

"Years ago." I thought back to Dominque Chau and her ride down the steps in September. "Mostly. And it wasn't me dispatching the violence."

"A minor tripped down a flight of stairs and collided with a concrete barrier after a pushing altercation between classes. Another who spread a particularly vicious rumor about your mother opened their locker door to have a five-pound sledgehammer fall out to strike them in the face, receiving fifteen stitches. A third fell twenty feet from the top of the bleachers after trying to pants you during gym last year. The child fractured their ulna and lost two teeth."

I had forgotten about the last two. Though I hadn't seen the Man in years, that didn't mean he hadn't seen me. "Don't look at me. Ask the witnesses. They found plenty."

"Children, not prone to tattle."

"*Now* I have friends to back me up?" Starting over in a new school had been rough, especially when you're dropped into middle school like a bucket of chum. Being a writer's kid, even one with the marginal success of my father, had raised enough eyebrows to give me a minor notoriety that one would normally have had to work on for years. Plenty of people were curious or envious, and it took a while for them to realize that I was just spooky little Prose.

"Are you familiar with the term *psychosis,* Prose?"

"Really?"

"Do you see how it might apply?"

I swallowed, my stomach tight and squeezing. "I'm not crazy."

Great. The first thing the insane have to offer, next to Pepsi requests. She didn't say anything. I tried again. "I mean, I get where you're coming from, but—"

"We're going to apply some medical tests. Physiological." Her voice was firm and dry. "There are ways that we can help you, Prose. I want you to understand that."

My cheeks were fully burning. "I'm not crazy."

"No one said you were. But you need help. Prose, we're going to try and give it to you. In the meantime, I have an exercise."

"What kind of exercise?"

Dr. Berriman pushed back from her desk. Pulled neatly from the legal pad were three pieces of paper. "Draw one of them, if you would. An irregular."

"I can't draw. I mean, I'll write you a poem or a saucy limerick, but I don't—"

"Just try. Chicken-scratch will do."

I'm going to make the chickens look really *good.* "I really don't—"

"Take the paper, Prose." A memory trickled through me, of an autumn day at the kitchen table, years earlier, my mother surprising me with a box of crayons and construction paper, the air full of freshly unsealed wax.

Everyone should have a picture of their family, right?

My stomach clenched. That day had been so beautiful and new when it started. I never imagined the horror show it would be by the end. "Do I have to?"

"Yes. You do." Dr. Berriman sat back and folded her hands. The lump in my throat was threatening to choke. I took the paper with pencil in hand and stared at it for what seemed like eternity but was probably something like thirty seconds. When you spend a lot of your time ignoring things that scurry through the shadows, trying to create a mug shot of one is harder than it looks. Eventually the pencil started to move.

It was a rough approximation, to be sure, but there was no mistaking it. The lazy hat, the faded shirt, the trace of beard, but mostly the smile. Even between the red and blue lines, the smile was unmistakable, a broad, weary love underlined with hint of devil-may-care. *I have a secret.*

We're all down here in the dark together.

I don't know how long I sat there for, studying my handiwork. The paper left my grasp and Dr. Berriman examined it under the wan overhead light. Maybe it was my imagination, but the shadows lengthened.

"Is this him?" she asked. Her eyes never left the paper.

"Who?"

"The man who marks you. Leaves the bruises."

"What?" The question took me by surprise. The Man had done a lot of things, but hurting me had never been one of them. Sometimes I think it would have been less cruel if he had. "No. Not that one."

She nodded once and handed me another sheet of paper. "More than one?"

Pencil already flashing across the paper, I shrugged. "Right now, I mostly see the other. With the tongue."

"So who's the other?" the doctor asked. I was trying to find a way to convey the thing's proportions, cheese-like flesh, and failing. She tried again. "Why did you draw this one?"

"He's where it started. I haven't seen him in a couple of years. He gets a little lost if we move around, he said."

"Did you name him?"

I let out a laugh, high and nervous. "Me? No."

She pursed her lips. "Does he have a name?"

"Yes."

When I wasn't forthcoming with it, she moved on. "Was he the first?"

I had almost drawn out the blind grey eyes, deep set in hollow cheeks, the droop of its long jaw. "No, but he told me he's the only one I'd ever need."

She said his name.

Yeah, I was surprised, but I assumed my father had told her.

"I wouldn't say that if I were you." I shrugged. "It'll help him find me."

"But he's not here right now?"

"I don't see him." The tongue stretched from his distended jaw, a third appendage to go with his clutching fingers. I flipped the paper back across the desk and felt a little bolt of pleasure as Dr. Berriman recoiled ever so slightly.

"And this?" she asked, taking in the portrait through gold-rimmed reading glasses. Dust motes flickered in the yellow overhead light, and I wondered how my father was holding up in the lobby.

"No name. I've just been calling him the Tongue."

"This is the one that hurts you?"

Nodding again, I slouched back in my chair. "Yes."

Dr. Berriman sighed and placed the paper between us, as if forming a stepping stone. For a moment I thought of old Dennis Wheatley paperbacks, nocturnal rites and stodgy Englishmen. "Prose, this is a goblin from a fairy tale."

My sleeves were rolled up, my arms inked in blacks and greens, and I mustered it up. "Look, the problem with therapy is that for you to think I'm making progress I have to concede that you're right. That they're not real. And I'm sorry, but I don't agree. Every experience I've had points to the contrary."

"You don't think the fact that no one else can see them calls into question their existence?"

"Frankly, it's immaterial. It doesn't change my experience in the slightest."

She nodded once. "Let's try something, shall we?"

The knot in my stomach turned to ice. "I don't think it's a good idea."

Dr. Berriman looked left and then right, a child preparing to cross the street. "Do you see any of them now?"

Sighing, I mirrored her look. The weak yellow light from overhead did little to diminish the shadows. "No."

"His name. Is it like Beetlejuice?" she asked. There was a long, wicked smile painted across her face. "Do I have to say it three times?"

"This is silly." I felt a weight begin to press in on me, a heaviness pushing the strength from my bones. Aching, my lungs hurt as my heart began to stagger faster. "What are you trying to prove?"

She said his name once, and let out a high, nervous titter.

"Look, I told you that no one's—"

Twice. My heart hammered in my chest.

"Could you *please*—"

Three, and now finished, she looked around the room with an air of satisfaction. "Now that he's on his way, I've got an experiment for him."

"I wouldn't." What a strange reunion it would have been.

I needed to get the hell out.

"Do you see this coffee mug?" she asked. I nodded. *Multnomah DHS*, white letters on black. "When he arrives, I'd like him to move it."

"That's not how it works," I started, but she cut me off.

"Of course not," Dr. Berriman nodded. "Empirical evidence never is, to one in your condition. We've got to free you from these delusions, Prose, from these hallucinations. You've got to concede that they aren't real."

She looked around the room again. "Can he hear me? Can any of the others hear me?"

I shook my head. "Probably? He always said it was a bad idea to invoke invitations."

"Can we agree that they— that your *irregulars—*" she said with distaste. "should be able to interact with the physical world? That they should be able to act independently, regardless of your admonitions. Please, move the cup."

"He's not here."

"Then another. Another *irregular*. They're not going to move it because they can't, Prose." She used my name like a cudgel, driving home the point with a firm *thwack*. "They don't have the power. None of these things you see do. You've got to free yourself, or else have one of them move the cup."

A cold tingle crept up my arms, danced along my collarbones to the tips of my pinkies. "Don't give them permission to act."

Dr. Berriman stopped and fixed me with a hyena's rictus. The tall grass was separating, and she was preparing to pounce. "That's what we want, Prose. For *them* to act, or *them* to fail, and in doing so we'll buy your freedom."

"Move the cup."

The shadows seemed to stir and lengthen in the dim overhead light. I tried one last time. "Look, he told me once that some of them would scratch your eyes into strawberry jam, if only to teach you a lesson."

"Prove to everyone that they're real or admit that they're not. It *is* all in your head." Maybe she noticed the light, or just had something in her eye. There was just the tiniest flicker of doubt when she turned to me. "If this cup moves, we'll be done here forever. Otherwise, you've got to start letting us help you."

I nodded and pushed back into my chair, back until I was touching the door. The black cup sat primly on the edge of the mahogany desk, a dark vessel on its maiden voyage towards the edge of the world. Dr. Berriman and I locked eyes in silence, and we waited.

"Idle as a painted ship," I murmured, and then the knocking began.

At first I thought it was my heartbeat, thudding towards some final terminal. Dr. Berriman's face had hardened into a war mask, etched and grooved with effort, and then I realized that the sound was coming from beyond the drawn curtain of the fourth-floor window. It was a dull, empty sound, coffin nails in concrete, edging upwards with grim determination. The raps beat along the upper panes, the painted wall, trailed along the wainscoting.

To her credit, she didn't flinch, even when they started across the ceiling.

In the yellow light, I could see the sick awe as the doctor licked her lips. "Are you doing this, Prose?"

Above us something snapped.

The room was plunged into darkness.

An object plummeted downward from the high ceiling, and I threw myself from the chair as the light fixture slammed into the desk. It exploded in a blossom of shrapnel.

Through the veiled light I saw Dr. Berriman throw herself out of the way, chair flailing backwards onto the floor, blood streaming from a dozen tiny cuts along her forehead, her cheeks, her jaw. I propped myself up on one arm before I saw it move. I heard something I will take to my grave.

There was an audible hiss as the thing descended, like a projector reel spinning unchecked. I could make out a vast, squirming bulk, chitinous appendages clacking together with rhythmic malice as the thing lowered itself onto her desk. What I saw was only shadows and suggestions, and for that I'm thankful. Dr. Berriman skittered backwards as the weighted horror swung what must have been its head towards her, but she might have been gaping at me. I'll never know.

With one grey tipped limb, it stroked the black porcelain of the cup. Something clicked and rumbled, deep in the hollows of its throat, and then her screams started.

It caressed the mug one more time before flipping it airborne, end over end in a fatal arc to collide with the far wall. Hot jasmine tea spattered against me as it shattered into a thousand jigsaw pieces. Whatever the thing was, it chittered once more and slithered upwards. I couldn't tell you where it went.

I suppose. For all I know she saw nothing but me having a freak-out, heard me making hellish, bestial sounds.

No one spoke for a long time.

When she did, it was only two words.

"Get out."

"I never saw her again," I finish, looking out at the old grey wall. "I don't know how she wrote it up, but DHS gave us a pass and we never went back. People might still be alive if she hadn't, but we'll never know."

The raindrops, momentary at first, shift into something more substantial. I cover my eyes against the impending storm.

Svara tucks his pad away. He looks older than he did this morning, and for the first time I wonder if something's wrong with him. Something terminal. "And you never had to deal with this— threat of diagnosis?"

"No." His eyes are the same color of slate as the sky, burning in deep sockets. I wonder what he thinks he knows, how all of this will look written down. I wonder if he'll send me a copy. "Not until now."

The pen taps against his chin. "Do you still believe what you told that doctor?"

"Some of it," I say. "Some, I know better."

"Your meaning?" he asks. Monique glances over at us, shielding her hair from the rain. It's begun to fall now, rich fat droplets that spatter against my face. The sound they make against the bleachers is a series of *pong*s, beating out a tribal arrhythmia. The air smells of copper and freshly cut grass. I take my time before I answer.

"How much longer is this going to take?"

"What do you mean?"

He knows exactly what I mean.

"This." I spread my arms wide, the drops starting to soak through. "I've been speaking for hours. How much more do you need before you start making calls? Before I get released."

"These things take time, even were I to have all I need." He stands, unfolding like a suitcase full of bones. "Which I do not. I want to know more about the Man, your mother. What happened in the motel, and then the cabin. There are doors still to be opened. How long that takes is up to you."

I nod, imagining myself a limp balloon, bled out across the bleachers. "I guess I just want to know that we're making progress. That we're on our way."

"Of course." He folds his long-fingered hands together. "We were saying. What is it you meant just then?"

I sigh and look back at Monique. She's got her hood up and has taken shelter beneath a neighboring tree, clearly wondering when this is going to be over. "Once I used to think I was the only one that could see them. It made me feel special. Later I thought I was the only one who chose to see. It made me feel strong. Now—" The words gather wool in my throat. I toss them out anyway. "I think I'm the only one who *doesn't have a choice*. And it terrifies me."

I roll up the shirtsleeve of my black hoodie. The bruises are in clear contrast to the paleness of my skin, a Rorschach test tribute to irrationality. "I need to get out of here, Doc. Sooner rather than later."

Svara does not flinch. "Soon," he says. I don't believe him.

Chapman's in a dead sprint as I walk back up the mighty Mississip, the rain really pouring down around us. He barrels past with a sour glance and barks something to Monique about being late and getting me back to the Lodge. If he's at that speed, there's trouble in another Lodge.

The drops pour around us in a spattering haze like a meteor shower in the orange sodium lights of the walkway. The empty Lodge squats like a haunted house on the edge of the walkway, its black windows the vacant sockets of a skull. The glow of the lit path doesn't extend that far, and the rest of Everbrook is alive like Santa's Workshop by comparison. In the fading light of dusk, something seems to shift behind an empty window, too deep in shadow to be sure, and something in my heart shudders.

Too old for portents, Prose. Whatever walks there, walks alone.

The dayroom is a bustle of activity when I walk in, and Graham catches my eye as Monique walks to the back desk. Harkness is filling a donated backpack with snacks from the pantry, little bite-sized packets of gummy bears and bags of chips. Victory looks as sour as ever, but she's got a pack of her own that she's zipping up. Eloise follows Graham like she's been surgically attached, and for a minute I wonder if this is the least inconspicuous escape attempt of all time. "How was therapy, Prose?"

I manage a weak smile. "It was okay. What's going on?"

There's a flash of disappointment that leaves his cheeks with a smile. "Field trip. Did you forget?"

"Isn't there some sort of crisis?" I ask. Monique's back behind me, a presence I sense more than see.

Graham shakes his head. "Nothing too crazy." His question is to me, but he looks at Monique as he says it. "We're going to the movies. Did you want to go?"

"Yes." There's no forethought, wondering where Phoebe or the other girls are right now or what we're seeing, just naked need. "Yes, please."

"She's got a one on one, right? I've been shadowing her all day." Monique asks. "Is Chapman okay with this?

"It was his idea," Graham says, the lie so transparent I can't believe it's coming out of his mouth. *Why?* "He said it was okay as long as you got back on time."

The look Monique gives him is part amusement, part suicide. "Well, if *Chapman* said it's okay. Just to make it clear: this is *your* Lodge, and *you're* making this call, right?"

"Chapman's call," Graham says again. "We've got to hurry if we want to make the trailers, though. They're the best part."

She sighs, and Harkness gives me an excited grin and an extended pair of crossed fingers from across the table. "Fine. Give me a second to get ready, okay?"

"Sure thing." Graham gives a smile that warms my toes, and the question bubbles out of me.

"Why?" I ask him, hating the mistrust in my voice.

"You behave and you try really hard, even though everyone treats you like a convict. You're not the danger people make you out to be, Prose. You deserve to have some fun too."

He checks his watch. "Hurry up and get ready. We've got sixty seconds before we've got to be out the door."

I rush to my room and find a dry T-shirt, peeling the wet one off with a careful flex of my shoulders. Phoebe's not in the room, but I'm too excited to wonder what that might mean as I hurry to the bathroom and run a brush through my hair. We're out the door and into the rising night in moments.

Stepping out of the van, part of me wonders how this is possible. Control had seemed a lot less optimistic about me leaving, but somehow Graham had smooth-talked our way past them and out the door. In the ongoing frenzy, I realize that I have no idea what movie we're walking into, and it doesn't really matter. A night outside these walls is something I haven't tasted in months. Even after we pull up, I'm not sure how to enjoy it.

My sneakers are soaking through, and Harkness and Eloise and I race most of the way to the theater in the dimming light with cheap umbrellas, splashing and kicking through puddles, laughing and giggling and finally remembering that there's a real world out there, somewhere. Graham is all smiles, and even Monique is having trouble hiding hers. It's the kind of joy that's infectious, and even if it's only an illusion, it's material enough for now.

In line we stand like normal people, without point systems, probation, or psychotherapy, and no one looks at us like we're weirdos or outright lunatics. The downpour seems to have washed the slate clean, and every breath is fresh and pure and full of glory.

Inside the theater it smells of popcorn and strangers and a hundred different perfumes. We find a row of seats as the lights begin to dim, and I think for the first time how impossible this all is, how much Graham put on the line to have us all here. I glance down at him in the reflected green light of the first trailer; he's sitting next to Victory on one end of the row, fishing a bag of chips out of a backpack. She leans over and whispers, and he smiles before noises erupt on the screen, flashing lights and loud men, and I settle back in my seat as Harkness passes me an honest-to-goodness can of soda.

Wonders never cease.

A teenaged usher drifts down the center of the aisle, plastic flashlight in hand. For a moment I expect him to call us out, to call us Maenads and madwomen, but he just smiles and saunters along. Harkness blows him a kiss and Eloise erupts into a fresh burst of laughter.

We're real. Inside those walls, sometimes it's hard to remember, but now it shines so hard it hurts a little. *We're really here.*

The bubbles of the soda tickle my nose as I retrieve a package of Red Vines from Harkness' black backpack. She leans over, breath warm in my ear. "Bet you never thought you'd wind up here, kiddo."

"Not a chance." I whisper back. "I haven't been to the movies in years."

"No shit?" She seems surprised. "What was the last one?"

"*Pacific Rim.*" I think back to the giant monsters, killer robots, cities going smash. My father had been aghast. "Our air conditioner broke, and it was on a second-run bill with *The Devil's Backbone.*"

Monique shushes the pair of us. The pause exists for maybe five seconds. "No, seriously? Nothing from this universe?"

I shrug. "My father wasn't a big cinephile. He said movies are for people with no imagination."

"Huh." She muses this over with a big swig of Cherry Coke. I'm starting to understand why adults hate teens in movie theaters. "No offense, but your father sounds like a bit of a prick."

I start to correct her tense, and then on the screen a man with a hefty jawline shouts in surprise as the camera lurches wildly to one side. Some kind of tentacle has seized the professor, and with a yank it pulls him behind the doors. Harkness shrieks, and Eloise leans over her. "Don't mind her. She had her inner monologue removed when she was eight."

Eight years old. Eight years old and—

My mother had sat me down in the living room without preamble that spring, the hard line of her mouth not setting off the warning bells it should have. My little legs swung freely off the brown couch as she tugged the coffee table a little closer with a grunt. There was time to reflect on the sepia light seeping in through the curtains, the dust motes swirling in their constellations. The loving smell of chocolate chip cookies baking wafted in from the kitchen, and Algernon barked excitedly as my mom handed me a small box of Crayolas, sixteen shades of wax.

"Do you want me to write you another story, Mommy?" I basked in the attention. Uncle Mark was in the other room, fresh-faced and back from college across the river, sipping coffee and talking with my dad about boring, trivial grown-up things, but my mom was taking time out from her brother's visit to do a special project with me.

Nervous, I ran my fingers through my hair and patted Algernon's rough fur as he rubbed against my leg in a puppy hug. Beneath the sugar baking there was a trace of ozone, like clouds were coming in.

"Not today, my little raven," she smiled. I had just discovered Poe the month before and had spent most of the interceding days reciting *Annabelle Lee* and *The Haunted Castle* to her at every opportunity. I still could, I think. "I wanted you to draw me something."

I nodded and fished the black crayon out first. She shook her head. "No crows or castles, Prose."

"C'mon!" I pouted, but only a little.

"How's your friend doing?" she asked, a little out of the blue even for her. I was a little taken aback. In all the years we had spent in that house, she had mentioned him less than a dozen times. These were strange, uncharted waters.

"Marmalade's fine," I tried. "He's out in the woods behind the house."

She nodded as if this was as expected and ran her fingers through my hair. "I wanted to know if you could draw him for me."

"I have," I grinned, not entirely having given up on the black crayon. "I hang them up on the fridge with magnets."

"Really?" She smiled quizzically, then came back. "Maybe a special one, then. Just for me."

"If you want."

She kissed my forehead. "I want that very much."

My mommy slipped back into the kitchen, and Mark said something to make her laugh. I furrowed my brow and concentrated. Algernon hopped up next to me, his tongue darting to my elbow in little puppy kisses as I patted him absentmindedly. Finally I just poured the whole box onto the table and got to work.

I had to start over twice, not happy with the lines I'd made or the way they crooked out of form, but by the end I nailed it. Wide dark hat, faded black work shirt hanging loose over worn pants. His stubble like a second skin, and his eyes, pale as hailstones on a cloudy day.

I might make it sound like I was Picasso's prodigy, but it wasn't the greatest. As a bit of a bonus I added myself, waist high and playing, with Algernon darting between us. It was a bit of fiction. Algernon didn't care for the Marmalade Man, and most appearances would send him scurrying to the other room to grovel between my mom and dad. It didn't bother me. When the Man was on one of his sojourns, we could play together anytime.

Once satisfied, I called my mother in. It took her a moment, and I rubbed Algernon behind the ears contentedly as I watched the low grey clouds roll in from the west outside the picture window. She appeared from the kitchen, a glass of wine in one hand, and Mark called something in passing that made her smile. I traded places with my mom and went into the kitchen to check him out.

They were sitting on opposite sides of the table, my dad and Mark, with two bottles of Widmer between them. He was different then, so fresh-faced and barely out of high school. My dad saw me coming and scooped me up in his lap, smelling of sandalwood and salt. "Hey, darling. Did you say hi to Uncle Mark?"

He twiddled his fingers at me, a ghostly precursor of the man he'd become. "Hello, writer's block."

"Now, now," my dad said, and ruffled my hair. My mom had yet to come back from the living room, but I didn't notice. "Mark's started university across the river. He's just down for a visit today."

I nodded. Mark gave me a little mocking grin that would vanish completely in six months. "Are you going to be a big girl and go to Chapelwaite like your uncle when you get older?"

"I think I can do better," I said, and both of them exploded in howls of laughter. They continued right until my mother appeared in the doorway, and something they saw hushed them both up in a second.

"Prose, can you take Algie outside?" she asked. Her face was a little paler than it had been a moment ago, her smile drawn. I nodded and went to the living room to retrieve my dog, hearing her pull up a chair and sit as she did so. The ruffle of paper was clear as she set it on the table between them, and then I was out the door and traipsing my way through the long grass of the backyard, Algernon bounding excitedly by my side.

I don't know what it was that compelled me to detour towards the kitchen. Clouds were starting to come in and throttle the afternoon sun, and the smell of grass and lightning were ripe in my nostrils as we meandered towards the big window by the sink. Below it were the thin and wavering stalks of sunflowers, and I bent over to pick one when I heard just enough. All the playfulness was gone, and what was left now bloody ribbons.

"—that's not possible—"

"—course it is—"

"—Uncle Hutch—"

"—the doctor said—"

"—he's still locked away—"

"—making a big deal out of—"

"—the same. I still have—"

The dull scrape of a chair pushed back against the tile.

"—it's not—"

"—is—"

"—figments of a child's—"

"—you know better—"

"—the same, Mark. Exactly the same—"

My father's face appeared in the window like a pop-up specter. Any trace of humor had been swallowed by worry, hard lines framing his mouth.

I would come to know that look all too well in the years to come.

I plucked a flower from the ground and offered it to him with my best, totally-not-guilty smile. His eyes were tired, but he smiled back.

Without a word, he shut the window.

I was preparing for bed that night, the Man draped over the little chair like a Southern gargoyle when I came in from the hall. A volume of Blackwood was laid open on the desk. My teeth sparkly and tasting of fluoride, I rubbed Algernon behind the ears as I walked by his bed nestled just inside my door. He let out a rumble of contentment, glanced in the Man's direction, and let out a growl of irritation.

Marmalade groaned, glancing up from the book. "That ain't hardly fair and you know it."

"He's just saying hi," I said, which was as bald-faced a lie as I dared.

"Course he is." The Man went back to his book.

I figured now was as good a time as any to try.

"Where do you go? I mean—when you're not around?"

He looked up at me slowly. "What do you mean?"

I chewed my lip for a moment. "I mean, if you're *imaginederry* like my dad says, why aren't you around all the time?"

"Imaginederry," he mused. "That's a hell of a judgement to pass on a man."

I shrugged. "You said to never be scared of words."

"Nor should you be. I taught you right." Marmalade folded the book and faced me, his fingers interlacing. His eyes were as pale as agate, a cold, mineral appraisal. "Do you also remember I told you never to ask me that?"

"I remember," I said. "Never mind. Just wondered."

I turned to my bookshelf and pretended to study the volumes. I had been on a *Choose Your Own Adventure* kick for the last month after my mom had overturned a bundle in a used bookstore. My father's thesis had been that they weren't worth the paper they'd been printed on, but since I'd made him a pick-your-ending version of *House of Usher* his tune had changed.

His eyes were on my back. The Man didn't have many rules, but I had just broken one, and if he left I was going to be well and truly alone. A catch caught in my throat, and the warm, bubbly tears started to rise from my chest.

The Man let me soak in it for almost a good minute, and then he spoke through a throat full of gravel. "Sometimes I wander. Other times I go dark."

It took me a moment to realize that he'd spoken. "Dark?"

He nodded. "The blackness between."

I nodded again, clueless. "I don't get it."

"Sometimes it's just me. Others, well—" He shook his head. "It's nothing to concern a girl with. You've got enough going on right here."

He glanced over at the closet. I could have sworn I heard something rustle inside. "You shouldn't have to go dark."

Marmalade grinned. It was one of the saddest things I'd ever seen in my life.

"Darlin, we're all down here in the dark together."

My cheeks hot, I chose *The Forbidden Castle* and pulled it off the shelf, determined not to show how much he was worrying me. "Do you want to go on an adventure?"

He unfolded his hands and nodded to Algernon, who still sat speculative by the door. "That all depends on your boy, there. Maybe he can be your co-pilot tonight." Marmalade cocked his head to one side, the wide hat sliding just a fraction. "When I'm not here, do you ever hear something in that closet? Maybe see something you shouldn't?"

I had been seeing strange things all my life. It was one of the few times I thought he was asking something ridiculous. "Like what?"

Not taking his eyes off of the wide slats of the closet door, he hissed.

I thought I heard something shift. "Why is Mommy scared of you?"

There was a flash of something in his eyes that I couldn't quite register. Confusion? Guilt? "Can't say I know, pumpkin."

I didn't think that was true but didn't say so. "Did you do something?"

"No. Never to her."

He unfolded from his chair. "Seeing things through older eyes, you'll realize that not everyone is so excited to unwrap the presents they got. Your Momma's one of them."

This didn't make any sense to me. "But she loves Christmas."

"You're going to have to excuse me for a moment." He stretched out his rangy arms and then ripped open the closet doors in one quick yank. Stepping into the toy box, he pulled the door shut behind him. I knelt down next to Algernon, rubbing behind his furry ears as he arched his neck contentedly, and leaned into my bedroom door, my ear pressing light against the latch. There was a noise, ever so slight, on the other end, and I mimicked the Man by tugging it open, suddenly terrified to see the wyrm.

My mother almost fully tumbled inside from the hallway before she caught herself, irritation and embarrassment fighting across her features. Straightening with simple grace, she asked me if I'd brushed my teeth yet. I nodded and she kissed my forehead. "You're a good girl, Prose," she said, and her eyes slipped sideways to the chair by the desk, the volume of Blackwood still stretched out before it. In the wan light of the hallway she looked tired, like the world had been placing weights on her back that were just getting heavier, and she tousled my hair with almost absent-minded abandon.

As I crawled beneath my covers, I saw it. Just behind her back was a bottle of baby powder. I didn't ask why she'd been listening or what it was for. Instead, I caught her hand and squeezed it twice.

"I love you, Mommy."

She smiled, that radiant light that could set the world aflame for me. "I love you too, Prose."

I didn't mention her arm, the spidery track of bruises crawling up it. Instead I watched her take the bottle of baby powder and sprinkle it gently along the hardwood floor, all the way back down the hallway.

The gooseflesh creeps up my arms, and Harkness squeezes my hand in a *Isn't-this-great!* gesture. Someone has been swallowed by a closet up on the big screen, the price of wandering around a dusty old mansion, after all, and I can't tear my eyes away as the door slams with a bang that threatens to shake the whole theatre. Harkness screams again, a high-pitched burst, and Graham shushes her with a smile and a laugh.

Eloise is scarfing down a package of Funyuns and staring at the screen with something like amazement. Victory has latched herself onto Graham, rapturous at the male attention, and keeps punching him in the arm every time something horrible happens onscreen, which is definitely rising in frequency. He pretends not to feel it, but I have a feeling that he's going to be sore tomorrow.

Leaning over the seat, Monique asks me if I'm okay. It must show on my face, and I nod, not wanting to explain how this reminds me of the city of dead light or the wyrm or the pallid thing from the pantry, really my whole life up to this point, and she smiles and goes back to watching the movie as the assistant throws open the black chamber, eyes red and weeping tears of blood.

It would be so easy. I take a sip of my soda, narcotically sweet against my lips, and try to push the thoughts away. *It would be so easy to slip over a couple of seats and just take off down the aisle.* Images cascade in a highlight reel: vaulting the row, Graham crying out as I fled, the empty theater I hide in, losing myself in a laughing crowd, dialing Mark's number from a borrowed phone, his old grey Volvo pulling up, flashing his lights like an old gothic—

He would turn you in the second he got here.

I push the thought away. The red of the EXIT sign is a lighthouse from the corner. No more Everbrook, Svara, Chapman, Sinatra. No more Nellie or levels or points. No more strangers sifting through my childhood for gold.

Looking over at Graham again, then at Monique, I know they would lose their jobs. Ninety-nine percent positive. *Bringing a mental case on suicide watch to a movie theater? To a horror movie about houses and tentacles and trauma, of all things. Good intentions or no, they might as well turn in a resignation letter.*

Harkness glances over and pushes a lock of ebony hair away from her face. "Wake up, Prose. You're missing the best part."

I nod and give her a smile as she turns back to the screen. Before I can I see a face, two rows from the back. Stubble creases his leathery jaw. The hat is unmistakable.

"Prose!" Harkness stage-whispers it loud enough to be heard in the lobby. I spare her a glance for an instant, and when I look back, I can't find him again.

Your mind's playing tricks on you, Prose.

Or you're running out of time.

Darlin'.

I slump back in the cushioned seat, my arms splayed against the plastic armrest. The protagonists stumble down a dark staircase, horrible noises screeching overhead as something approaches from the wings. I take a breath and lose myself in the film.

Darlin, we're all down here in the dark together.

When the final girl turns back to the cavern beneath the house, it is filled with the presumed dead, row after row of them. A last stinger and the screen goes black. The credits roll. Muted lights blink on from either side of the room and cue our departure, and Harkness squeezes my arm again and asks me if that wasn't the greatest movie on earth.

I'm almost certain it was.

We push out of glass doors and onto the sidewalk, ready to get in the van and cross the blocks back towards Everbrook and captivity, when Graham makes a big show of yawning and checking his wristwatch. The rain's let up a bit, only a faint drizzle past the warm cascade of light from the theater. Victory gives a squeal of delight and claps her hands, leaving me thoroughly confused.

"We've got a little bit of time left." Graham stretches his arms in an exaggerated pose, and I think for the first time, *drama queen.* "Is anyone up for some froyo?"

For a moment, I think he's saying Frodo, that we're going to be treated to some Tolkienesque fantasy, and then Eloise is hugging him with frightening tenacity. "Graham, you're the coolest!"

"Boundaries," he smiles, and then we're walking down the cracked sidewalk. Monique mutters something about boundaries again, and a lone streetlamp blinks off as we pass by

—ghostlight—

the cool night air pushing against us with the smell of dying leaves and precipitation. A harvest moon flickers yellow above us, ducking behind black clouds like the survivor at the end of a slasher movie. Harkness finds my hand and gives it a squeeze. There's a lightness in my heart that I can't quite process, a feeling that the world's been filled with helium, that it all might drift away. "What are you thinking?" she asks.

"That this is the happiest I've been in a long time."

The cocksure grin she gives me is its own reward, bright and full of mischief. It takes less than a minute to reach the ice cream shop on the corner, and Monique ushers us inside with a sideways glance at Graham. "Double scoop's the max," she says. "And everyone needs go to sleep right when we get back, capisce?"

We all capisce. They have flavors here I've never heard of, and I try to remember the last time I went out for ice cream with anyone. I split my choices between cookies and cream and rocky road before squeezing into a molded plastic chair. I can't describe how fabulous, how mind-numbingly delicious the first bite is, only that it's quickly beaten out by the second. Eloise is plowing through hers like it's an Olympic sport, and she smiles at me between spoonfuls. Graham says something to Harkness and she laughs. Sprawled around the table like vanquishing heroes, the moment is frozen in time.

Walking back to the van is like gliding. If my feet touch the ground, I can't feel them. The breeze rubs against me like soft down, the faintest trace of pumpkin spice and autumn, and the night that surrounds us is full of promise. We skip and we sing and we are, for once, ourselves.

Strange, then, to stroll back through the heavy double doors, enter under the harsh glare of halogen. The institutional tile reflects it as we pass through the lobby and get buzzed through the magnetically sealed door. Cheryl's left for the night, and a glance at the wide clock on the wall tells me that we're back way later than we should be.

A short, barrel-shaped man behind the counter gives us a tired smile and asks how our trip was. His heavy-lidded eyes drift disapprovingly over Graham as we cheer, and he reminds us to keep the noise down, that everyone else in the facility already went to bed. Harkness twists an invisible key in front of her lips and begins to mumble her assent through them, but Monique shushes her. We say our names, one after the other, and he checks them off of a clipboard. That feeling of normalcy starts to bleed away as we feel the walls come down, one portcullis after another.

Upon saying my name, the little man's eyes grow wider. Graham gets another look, this one more of a glare. The meaning is hard to miss.

A tired nurse in a white smock enters stage left, pushing his heavy blue cart before him. A row of wet paper cups and index cards are on the tray, and he gives us all a weary smile as his eyes slide over Graham like an old ghost. He calls our names, one after the other, in the timeless ritual of medical communion.

Beyond him, something moves the shadows of the little glass room. My memory drifts towards Mark, the last time we met. How long has it been? In reverie, I almost miss the flash of auburn against the glass, the little white hand like a starfish pressing against it.

I open my mouth to say something, that someone's missed one of the little kids up for a visit, and then I see her clearly. Her face pressing against the thin glass is pale and drawn, cheeks expanded like she's holding her breath. The glint of her eyes are like old silver dollars. Her smile shows too many teeth.

Don't make it worse. You can't have a breakdown in the middle of Control, or they'll never let you out again. I turn away and begin whispering *The Haunted Palace* to myself again, willing it away.

—*travelers now, within that valley*—
—*through the red-litten windows see*—
—*vast forms*—

Eloise is giving me a look. Stiffening, I smile back and I take my paper cup, sliding the mismatched pills between my cheek and teeth like a major league pitcher. The water is tepid, and I realize the whole display has been sitting out for a while. The nurse checks my mouth disinterestedly and reads through the rest of our names like he's taking inventory. Every one of us gets medication at night, I notice. I wonder how many of us are cheeking it.

As if Harkness can read my thoughts, her tongue flickers out, pink and wriggly. A white dot is floating in the middle of it, and she gives me a wink before she shuts her mouth and straightens up, the picture of innocence.

The cart wheels away, its strange proprietor trailing behind it, and we're dismissed. I make a study of the wall opposite the glass room. Though I don't look, I can hear her

—hullo poppet—

whispering like sugarcane, spun candy trailing after me as we follow Graham out another set of double doors, an airlock back into our world. Orange lamps dance like will-o-wisps in the mist, lighting our way back. The Lodge is as black and silent as an unopened tomb, and two strangers sit in the gloom of the hallway, guarding the center desk like ghouls their carrion. Graham pantomimes brushing our teeth and going to bed. There's an electric current as we do, forced, hushed mutters as we slip into the bathroom and Monique and Graham get ready to leave.

Something unusual happens as we spit out the cheap industrial toothpaste. Our eyes keep meeting through the mirror, everyone's giggles barely pressed back behind their lips, and then Victory hugs me. Then Harkness. Then Eloise, and then we're all hugging and telling each other good-night. It's like some crucible for sisterhood, some bond passed between us, and we replace our toothbrushes in time to see Graham silhouetted in the mist before the front door swings shut. We stalk down the hall like wraiths and dart behind our doors, the evening's ecstasy not quite done.

I have time to marvel, to contemplate what it felt like to be normal tonight, four teenagers doing teenage things, laughing and goofing around and just being alive. I think to myself six simple words.

This was magical.
This was freedom.
And then I find Phoebe.

CHAPTER NINE

EMPTY NEST

omeone's screaming. I want to tell that person to stop, it's not helping, and then I realize that it's me.

There are footsteps pounding down the hallway, muffled swearing, and then my wooden door is thrown open with enough force to put a wedge-shaped dent in the drywall. In the midst of changing into my pajamas, I pull my shirt down in a tangle of fabric that pins one arm to my chest in a haphazard sling before I turn around. That strange, terrible siren is still echoing in my ears as a lanky woman that could prizefight in her off-hours steps into the room, hands raised, shoulders square. Her hair is pulled away from her chiseled face in a high bun. For a moment, I think she's about to hit me.

"Honey?" she says in the low, measured tones I recognize as Everbrook's crisis communication. "Honey, what's wrong?"

She doesn't know my name, I think, and picture the other stranger rifling through the files at the desk, trying to get a handle on me. I still can't speak, and instead I gesture to what's wedged in the corner between the foot of her bed and the dresser, at the wall between them, at the floor.

At what's left of Phoebe.

My back hits stucco. She's sprawled against the wall, arms and legs at unintended angles. The left side of her face is gone, a raw ruin covered in sticky black-and-red that sluices down her neck and chest to meet her flapper skirt, which has fallen somewhere around her thighs. Her bangs adhere to the remnants of her forehead in a mix of dried blood and something darker, her remaining amber eye a dull signal flare that haunts sightless towards the closet. A single scarlet handprint grows on the door like a malevolent flower.

My stomach dances, threatens to erupt as the sobs hit me, doubling me over as the room starts to tilt on its axis. Part of my mind detaches helpfully, floating next to me on a neat little tether like a grey balloon.

You don't get to fall apart, the balloon tells me.

There'll be time for that later.

"Honey?" the lanky woman asks again. The other stranger finally appears at her side, a smaller woman, dark glasses framing a round, tanned face, and the lanky woman steps into my room, into the Eggshell Universe. Her hands are held out in front of her, palms up. She's not a good enough actor to hide that I'm freaking her out. "What's the matter?"

If I open my mouth, I'm throwing up. Maybe that wouldn't be a bad thing. Where my friend used to be lies an empty sack that used give me sass, tell me secrets, meet some cowboy wannabe after-hours. None of this passes my lips.

Instead, I nod my head to the corner and wait for the screams to start.

For what feels like minutes, I'm waiting, eyes red and wet, cheeks on fire. When the horror doesn't spread in some pandemic domino, I look. Out of the corner of my eye I see one spattered hand bent painfully back, her middle finger broken, outstretched. I can hear her telling someone to sit on it and spin, and instead of fresh tears I find steel.

The shorter woman wears a mask of concern as she asks me again what's wrong. At least she uses my name. All I can do is nod to the corner once more, and watch as they both turn their heads, not letting me leave their line of sight.

They're worried that this is a ruse. That you'll spring to your feet, dagger in hand, and open them up like dead letters, the balloon tells me.

The boxer turns and speaks to me like a child. "Prose, what's wrong? Did you see a spider?"

No, you dumb bitch, my only friend here looks like she went ten rounds with Jason Voorhees. What the hell's wrong with you? My eyes meet hers, incredulous, and see only confusion and caution reflected back. The smaller woman's the same. A cordless phone dangles from her left hand.

I force my head to turn, sobs subduing to whimpers. *Phoebe wouldn't want you to lose it,* the balloon advises. I can almost see it, bobbing merrily next to me, the irrational voice of reason. *She wouldn't want you to drop the ball, kiddo.*

Dispassionately via the floater, details are processed. She's in a heap in the corner. Lolling. Certainly not getting up. The room smells of ozone and some decadent pollen. The blackish-red puddle around her extends almost to the center of the floor, soaking into the worn grey carpet. I can see the boxer woman dipping the toe of her sneaker in its border and know the footprints she'll leave will drive me insane if I think about them.

"In the corner," I choke out, and both of them look again.

I hear the heavy front door close out in the dayroom. Knowing that they've summoned reinforcements, two courses stretch out before me, equally wide, equally fathomless, My mind races between options as time runs out. At the last second, the twins' expressions tell me all I need to know.

—*they don't see her. they don't see her but you do*—

—*what does that mean, Prose, what does that mean*—

—*they don't see her but you do*—

—*oh no oh no ohno*—

"A spider." The word twists out of me like a bad joke, and the relief on their faces makes me want to scream.

Plenty of time for that, the balloon advises. *Plenty of time for that later.*

"I saw. A spider."

"Hell of a reaction for that, honey." I could throttle her. "It's late."

So's my best friend. What a coincidence!

Bad balloon. You're not helping.

"I'm terrified. Of spiders. Locked in an old shed with them once. Check my file."

A flash of uncertainty creases the boxer's brow. The smaller woman looks like she wants to go back to the desk and pull the papers. "I don't see any spider."

"It crawled. Under the wardrobe." That particular piece of furniture is two hundred and fifty pounds of awkward metal bolted into the wall. Any refutation seems unlikely. "It was. Huge. And black."

And red.

"And its legs. All hairy." I spin around the room and try to look panicked while equally trying not to step in the still-spreading puddle. "I can't sleep in here."

A sigh escapes them almost in unison, as if this was my motivation all along. I could hear the shuffle of heavy feet out on the carpet, the backups beginning to relax. The smaller woman raises an eyebrow. "You want a room change? In the middle of the night?"

The boxer glowers. "Make good choices, Prose."

"Please." I try not to look at Phoebe again. That sweet smell has grown heavier. "I'd just be thinking. About it. I wouldn't be able to sleep."

"The day staff handle all of that," the boxer says, bureaucracy reasserting itself. "You can ask them in the morning."

"Please," I try again, real horror creeping back into my voice. All I want is to get out of this room, away from Phoebe's body, poor Phoebe

—who will go unmourned and forgotten because NO ONE ELSE CAN SEE HER WHAT DOES THIS MEAN PROSE WHAT DOES THIS MEAN—

and try to make some sense out of this. Out of any of this. The tears come back naturally. "Please. Please please! I don't want to be up all night."

Something about the words *up all night* seems to register with them. The pair exchange a look that's one part protocol, two parts spending their shift with a girl having a meltdown in the Eggshell Universe. Finally the smaller woman speaks.

"Get your pillow and blankets. Shake them out. Everything else needs to stay here until morning, and day staff can move you back or make the room change permanent. Okay?"

Nodding gratefully, I grab my bedclothes. As we step out of the door, I sneak an Orpheian look back at Phoebe, still staring sightless at the closet, at the single handprint left there in scarlet. A muffled sob escapes me. I need to know what it all means.

And I need to run.

A harsh knock on my door suctions me up from the whirlwind of my dreams, a downspout that had buried me so deep that I thought my heart would collapse. You wouldn't think that you could drift off after finding your only friend dead and invisible in an institution, but my mind had finally given out around four in the morning.

Thoughts had countered themselves and birthed conspiracies, forming and reforming until left with only two conclusions. The first being that I need to go, sooner rather than later. If Svara can help, that would be the smartest. If he can't, there has to be a way besides plummeting off a twenty-foot wall into a rough asphalt parking lot.

The second is haunted by the confused look on the boxer's face when I nodded to the corner. I don't care how incompetent or downright dangerous the staff could be at times; there was no way they were going to feign ignorance and just toss Phoebe's body in a laundry cart to wheel away when no one was looking. If they were some kind of sick serial killers who I'd interrupted, and that did cross my mind, the whole staff would have to be in on it, and no way would they leave me to sleep it off to report them tomorrow. The girls running away to never be heard from again surfaced, and it left me with some tough questions. It ached like a physical wound, but I was also my father's daughter, and that clinical scalpel came out of my reason to peel away the fantasy. My thoughts drifted back to the movies, at that potentially imagined figure in the back row. Has Marmalade found me at last? Was this his first salvo before he claimed me again, or was this the work of something—

—*da da duh dee da*—

—else entirely?

My dreams had been nightmare alterations. In the last, Rachel and I had been sitting in a purple room. When she crossed her legs, I noticed the black skirt that fell past her knees. Something was wrong with her face, like it had been roughly removed and then reattached as an afterthought. A strange, piping melody metered out from the antique piano. She didn't comment, instead offering me a stemmed glass full of purple light. At the corner of my eye, something writhed in flabby coils. *You missed the first round*, she said. *The city's missed you. We love you so much.*

Jarred awake, I stare up at the ceiling for a moment, lost by the change in constellations. The knock comes again, this time heavier, and the door opens with a misaligned creak. Chapman barges through the opening, his bald head like a battering ram. Lo lurks behind him like an ineffective ghost.

"I heard about the stunt you pulled last night." His overly white teeth grimace. "We don't take advantage of the night staff in this house. Get your stuff. We'll decide what your consequence is going to be later."

"What advantage?" I sit up, nightmares trailing away.

"There's nothing in your file about spiders," he says, glancing back at Lo. I almost laugh.

"Are you serious? Does it have what I ate for breakfast last week too?" I ask. "I'm scared of spiders. I don't want to go back to that room."

His eyes burn as he starts to say something, but he catches himself. "There aren't any spiders in that room."

I shake my head. It feels puffy, as if everything between my ears has swollen. "You can't know that. They're little. Itsy-bitsy, even. People write poems about it."

"Trust me. There are no spiders."

"I don't trust you, and I don't want to be in that room." I sigh, hating what I'm about to invoke. "When my click gets here, he'll tell you that it's not therapeutic and make you change it anyway. What's the harm in letting me? It's not like I have a poster of Rita Hayworth set up in here."

"Svara does come to see you a lot," Chapman mutters, as if it's the latest clue in a string of suspicions. "More than anyone I can recall, at least."

"I'm good company."

The strength is going out of his shoulders, the annoyance dying down. Finally he turns to Lo. "Watch her get her stuff and move it in here. If she gives you any trouble, she can stay in her old room, spiders or—whatever."

He turns and saunters off down the hall, pausing to give Harkness a yell to turn her headphones down. Lo stands to one side, expectant, and I remind him that young and nubile me is not going anywhere while dressed for bed. He closes the door in an embarrassed kerfuffle, and I throw on my jeans from last night, hands shaking as I work the belt. I don't *want* to go in there. I don't want to see what's been done to her again, the best thing that happened to me in the last year left in the corner like spoiled meat, and I can't watch as Lo traipses through the gore, oblivious and unseeing. But there is no choice as I step out into the hallway, the sun a bloody egg rising from the east through the dayroom window.

The old room is three doors down, the hallway unnaturally quiet. Everyone's sleeping in to the best of their ability. Jon sits at the far end of the hall, a sentry in a molded chair by the new girl's doorway, a paperback folded between his massive hands. He greets me with a smile that I shakily return.

Lo notices and tries the same. "You must be really scared of spiders."

Nodding, I duck into the bathroom, not ready. Lo stops at the doorway like a vampire without an invitation. What I see doesn't surprise me. My eyes are red and puffy and slightly crazed. My hair looks like a Halloween shock wig.

None of it matters right now.

"Come on," he says "Let's change your room."

I push past him towards my old door, throwing it open the moment my fingers touch the knob. I brace myself for the vision, for her ruined body to meet my eyes again.

There's nothing there.

Something below my waist goes weak and wobbly, and I find myself suddenly on the floor, chest heaving, heart racing post-marathon as the world caroms wildly before plunging forward. A mixture of feelings punch through me in no particular order: sorrow, outrage, relief.

The last curdles in my stomach, sour and shameful.

"Quick! Where is it?" Lo barges in with a rolled-up newspaper, eyes darting side-to-side like an antique clock. I'm beginning to think that I'm not the one with the spider problem.

"Nothing. I tripped." I pull myself up on the bed frame. The room smells freshly vacuumed and faintly of Lysol. There's not a mark on the wall, or on the carpet. The telltale handprint has faded away.

Phoebe's gone, like she never was.

—you're CRAZY Prose, just like everyone's always said, CRAZY—

Confused, I press my fingers between the blinds. In the rising sun I see a shadow, but it's gone before I can focus. My hands turn to the dresser cabinet, pressing palms against where her gory fingers had been, and in a rush I pull open the horizontal door.

Her side is empty. No clothes, no books, not so much as a stray hair to mark where she's been.

I turn to Lo, who's backed out of my room like a plague doctor. The question dies on my lips, and instead I ask him for a bag to put my stuff in. He seems all too happy to leave me to it. When I hear his footsteps streak down the hall to the supply closet, I prop my bed up and retrieve my secret pharmacy—one-hundred-and-thirty-eight strong now—and slip them into the pocket of my jeans. Some of them won't survive the trip, I'm sure, but it's better that than to be caught with enough antipsychotics to drop an elephant. When he comes back, my books are on my bed with my paltry selection of clothes. He tosses a green canvas sack next to them and pulls up a molded plastic chair, already powering down.

Snatching up the bag, I stow my items as carefully as I can before turning my back on Lo to shield my more delicate unmentionables. When my hands slip into my underwear drawer, pulling out cheap cotton and stuffing it into the bag, I make one last sweep of it and feel a rough, light object in the back, tucked neatly into the guiding track of the drawer. My heart thumps, and I glance over my shoulder at Lo, who's already staring down the hallway like I'd ceased to exist.

Graham would have noticed. Monique too. Even Steve.

It takes a moment to pry loose, a yellow slip of paper that's been folded into neat triangular creases. It could have come from any of the thousand cheap legal pads that dot the surface of the main desk. Unfolding it without tearing is difficult, but I manage, the paper dry and crackly beneath my fingers. Ten digits. Seven words.

It smells of dust and tombs.

Meet me at midnight, it says.

You know where.

In the dayroom, I watch the other girls bustle about their morning, already feeling worn out. Nothing's made sense in the last twelve hours, and it's all I can do not to curl into a ball and cry beneath one of the old institutional couches. Eloise and Harkness are wielding controllers in the corner, battling with giant robots and manga swords, while Victory and Nellie watch some teen drama about a quirky girl who moves to turn her life around. The new girl with the Ringu haircut I haven't seen all morning, though Jon lurks in front of her door like he's been chained to it. Lo shadows me from his post at the kitchen counter, where he's slurping cheap cereal out of a plastic bowl and mostly studying the movie. I feel a jagged ache where Phoebe used to be, and a tear runs down my cheek like it's making a break for it.

The note I hadn't been able to make any sense of. I'd turned the paper over and over in my hands like a puzzle box, letting the dry grain work against my fingers. Six words on one side, nothing on the other. No names, no addresses, definitely not a phone number, and still my heart fluttered against the weak bones of its cage with ill-advised hope. Was Phoebe alive? Had this all been some ploy, some remarkable design staged for my benefit?

Meet me tonight. You know where.

The thought of Phoebe's face, the raw, aching hole where her left eye had been, brings me back to center so hard I feel something pull inside me.

Be real, Prose. You know dead.
Out of everyone at Everbrook, you know dead.

What was it, then? A lovelorn note from a secret admirer? A conspiratorial memo from a partner in crime? A blackmailer's calling card?

Stashed back in my new room, I'd secreted it in the same spot. What the significance could be I wasn't sure, but having found it three feet from my dead, somehow invisible friend, I thought it had to have some meaning, as stupid as I knew that was.

Had it been written for Phoebe, some elusive note from her cowboy, or had it been there for months? Years? Despite my Poe, the meaning eluded me, which did nothing to stop the errant thoughts.

Chapman watches me for most of the morning, always keeping me in his periphery from his spot by the big desk. He's smart enough to know that's something's going on but short-sighted enough to think it has to do with Everbrook. Neither Graham nor Monique have shown their faces, which isn't a good sign.

I doze or dream for a moment. When I return, it's to him saying my name, close enough that I can smell the faint sourness of his breath. He passes me the cordless phone.

I hesitate. The black plastic box is wasplike, and I imagine the stinger slipping free, but by then it's been shoved into my palm. Chapman walks away, shaking his head.

Holding it up to my ear, I groggily imagine half a dozen horror movies. My words come out in a half-whisper. "This is Prose."

From the tone of his voice, my uncle hasn't been getting a lot of sleep lately. "Prose. It's me."

We exchange strained pleasantries before he comes out with it, coyly as a boy sneaking a kiss. "Have you heard from Holcomb?"

"Not lately." The detective hasn't called back since he called me a killer and promised to put me away. "What's going on?"

"Nothing, yet. Everything's in a holding pattern."

He yawns, and the toll this is taking begins to sink in. Being jerked around by the court, the police, the system, all to win custody of someone that at least part of you holds responsible for your sister's death. I wondered how badly the fight was going. Moreover, I wondered if he even wanted to win. "How are you holding up?"

He laughs like crackling leaves. "Aren't I supposed to ask you that?"

"You sound terrible."

"Yeah, well. We're still, according to Holcomb, in the evidence-gathering phase. The lawyer we consulted says they're probably interviewing old classmates, friends, going through your dad's papers. Diaries. Old school records. When they feel like they've built enough of a case against you, they'll spring it, and all the statistics look pretty bad."

I hadn't been near a computer in months, so there's been no way to research any of this. "What do you mean?"

"If they charge you with the big 'M'—look. Two of three murder cases lead to an arrest in this country. Of those, eighty percent of those arrested take deals for a reduced sentence rather than try to fight it in court." He paused. Was he gauging my reaction? "For those who fight it, and if we don't want a beleaguered, sad sack public defender it will probably cost every cent your father left you to do so, ninety-five percent are found guilty."

My heart sinks somewhere below the pit of my stomach. "But I didn't—"

"That's not even taking into consideration the sensational aspect of your case. All that Red Orphan shit is going to make it hard for you to get a fair pull." Mark just sounds broken now, voice heavy over the phone. "Blame CSI it you want, or NCIS, or JAG, or any of the other dozen forensic fiction shows where the detectives have magic computers. Most juries think that if they put you on trial, it's because you're guilty, whatever the constitution says."

A hot tear rolls down my cheek, unbidden. I turn and face the wall, the cordless phone a vibrating insect in my hand. "But I didn't do anything."

"It just comes down to math, Prose," he says, not unkindly. "Like you said, the police have fired an arrow and are painting the bullseye around it. If they had real evidence, we wouldn't be having this talk, but when the cops finish up trying to tie all the coincidences together, they'll look at the whole mess and guess if they can win. For your sake, I hope you didn't write any manifestos in your old journals. If everything isn't sunshine and roses, we're going to have a problem."

"Do you think I did it?" I blurt it out. In the moment, I just have to know. "Do you think I killed them?"

"Start thinking about it," he says, ignoring the question.

"What kind of a choice is that?"

"One that I hope you don't have to make. But you'd be young enough. You could still start a family, put a life together. It's not—"

He might being offering the philosopher's stone, the recipe for Coca-Cola, but I press the button and his voice ends with a dry click. I sit staring at the wall for a moment, beige cinderblocks, scuffed at the bases, and drop the phone on the desk. Without a word I move to the dayroom, not able to face Chapman right now, not able to weather a caustic remark without putting my nails through his eyes. I find a respectable corner and pull up a chair.

Lo is a cereal-destroying phantom to my right, chewing with the contention of a solipsistic cow. Words buzz unbidden between my ears like tiny wasps.

Good behavior.

Twenty-five to life.

"Is any of this real?" I ask. My head is down, staring at the divots in the boards.

The rain is pouring, hard enough that the field is a sloggy pond and the bleachers lightning traps. We've taken this session inside, and pendulous lights hang heavy overhead like the teleporters of alien spacecraft. If only they'd take me away from here, from dirty cops and apathetic counsel, away from a life whose mortar is flaking away an inch at a time. Holding my breath, I look up towards the lonely double doors at the far end, towards the black stage like a rip in the fabric of the world.

The doctor says what he has to say. The question might as well be rhetorical.

"No," I say. "What we're doing. Our deal. Is it real?"

Svara clicks his pen from his perch on the battered bleachers. He's tanner somehow, more vital. "I am a man of my word, child. It will happen the way I describe it." He looks over his shoulder at Steve, who bricks a five-foot jumper and chases the rebound almost to the wall.

"I'm more than ready to go."

"A head start, yes?" He smiles. "You don't think this is helping? To go through your past, tie the strands of time together?"

"It's already all I think about. Trauma and joy, blending into some kind of pain milkshake."

"Have your meds been helping?"

He knows.

The thought's irrational as I force my eyes not to flicker away, telling myself the alternate truth. *I take them every day. I'm a good girl.* "About the same. Mostly I just feel sleepy."

I nonchalantly turn my head, watching Steve make a lay-up and almost blow out his Achilles. Too much eye contact and he'd know I was testing him.

This place is turning me into a sociopath.

"Of course," he says. His steely eyes don't blink. "It's to be expected until we balance them out."

He checks his notes one more time and clicks his pen. "We were talking about your mother the last time we spoke, were we not?"

The closet door had creaked open sometime in the waning hours of the morning. Staring into the darkness, the shadows thick above my toy box, I marveled at the silence of it, the queer deliberation it must have taken to not topple the stack of books and coin-filled cans I'd laid at its base as a makeshift alarm. Weak moonlight wrestled its way through the thin drapes, the only way I had to guess at the hour. My nightlight was black.

I'd find out later that the bulb had been unscrewed.

My bedroom door was a thin crack leading into the barrow of the house. I looked to the desk, but Marmalade wasn't there. A chill shot up my arms. There was a dry, gamy smell wending from the opening, and it was this more than anything that caused me to slide out of bed.

I glanced into the hall, my anxiety climbing. The green fluffy bed we'd gotten Algernon was empty, his little sentry station outside my door an abandoned post. Not wanting to wake anybody, I whispered his name, then tried it a little louder, hoping to hear the scrabble of his clawed feet against the boards.

There was nothing.

Carefully, my pajamaed feet crept down the unlit corridor. The moonlight hadn't seeped past my door, and the darkness was thick and meaty. With one hand on the bannister, eyes squinting, I made my way to the top of the stairs.

That reptilian smell was stronger here. My toes curled against the carpet, not wanting to descend, and I glanced to my parents' bedroom, to their fortified door. I swallowed the lump in my throat.

Somewhere in the house I heard a door creak, the high, screeching moan of wood. My pulse quickened.

What was it that compelled me forward? The soft scratch of my pajamas against the carpet grated as I gripped the handrail, taking the steps slowly. I descended like the condemned.

The first floor of the house was glowering and dark. An unease began to creep through me as my mind yelled *Go back! Go back! This isn't for you!*, but its cries went unanswered. My soles touched the cool dry wood and plodded forwarded heavily. The front door was locked and bolted, the windows as well, but my steps took me past the living room, and there I stopped. The kitchen floor was icy through the cotton of my footy pajamas, and a foul, spoiled smell filled the room like the refrigerator had given up the ghost weeks ago.

That screech of wood came again, but that isn't why I stopped.

The backdoor was hanging open, a thin strip of moonlight against the cavernous shadows of the laundry room. It was always sealed, my father being fastidious about home security when he wasn't poring through the character motivations of *Breathing Deep* or watching the Mariners game with my mom, arm curled around her on the well-worn couch. He'd told me time and time again to stay out of the laundry room—neither chemicals nor lint the best companion for a child. Both doors hung open, the brand-new deadbolt turned impotently inward.

This is what it feels like to be pulled.

The thought came out from nowhere, and the door groaned open another inch. Almost against my will, I followed it to the outside world.

The dewy grass soaked through the feet of my pajamas as I took my first couple of steps, unsure of where to go. The creaking came again, louder, and in the night I wasn't sure from what direction it had come. In the weak moonlight I could just make out footprints splayed in the grass, and they led me winding around the side.

Silver clouds floated against a raven sky as the wind sent a gust of leaves against me, cackling as they blew by. I passed by the kitchen window and tiptoed gently through the tall grass to the front yard, its wet smell starting to replace the sickly musk from inside the house. The moon was a token of bone on the horizon as I turned the corner. That groaning creak came again, and I saw the old oak in the front yard.

It hadn't been the door at all.

It had been the rope.

He doesn't say anything for a long while. Behind us the leather ball echoes in an impotent series of bounces and misses on the hardwood floor. I awkwardly glance around the cavern, to the black stage, to the double doors that Lo had said lead into the older parts of the building. Part of me wonders if I were to just get up and sprint, could either of them could catch me?

The idea's brushed aside pretty easily. Visions of me wandering lost hallways and bouncing off of locked doors play through the most likely scenarios. A minotaur doesn't seem out of the question.

Too soon for that, and I think of my father in the good times before the rest.

When I was nine years old, he came in from his shift at the warehouse and found me sobbing at our secondhand table, feelings hurt and one Little Pony poorer. He'd picked me up in his arms and held me close before he said anything. I still remember that.

What's aching you, Prose?

I bet Suzy Van Houten my Misty that she couldn't go jump off the top of the monkey bars. But she went and did it.

Hmmm. Well, you were right to pay up. Did you learn your lesson?

That Suzy's mean?

No, Prosaic. If you're going to gamble, only bet on a sure thing, he'd said. *Do you think Suzy knew she could make the jump?*

Yeah.

That's just it, then. She wasn't gambling at all.

And neither should you.

"This must be very difficult for you." His voice is dry, a little parched as if some well inside him has cracked and drained all the moisture away. He clicks his pen in a moment's tic. "So you found her."

"I did."

"Do you want to stop? Take a break?"

"I want to get out of Everbrook. Whatever gets me there the quickest, doc."

He ponders this for a moment, as if unsure just where to go. I look back to the stage, wondering if the curtain just twitched. I could do without the company right now.

"What happened after that?"

I pick a point on the wall, unwilling to meet his eyes. I don't tell him about Algernon, or my suspicions, and the tears flow unbidden. "My father broke for a while. He really did love her, though sometimes he wasn't the best at showing it. For it to happen as it did—it left a lot of questions for him. For a creative, that can be poison. He couldn't write, the checks stopped coming. Eventually Chapelwaite cut him loose, and we lost the house a little after that. He made up for it with the drinking. He started to pick up shift work to make ends meet, and we started bouncing around Oregon for a while."

"I got really good at taking care of myself. I can grill cheese with the best of them." I force the smile out, then pull it back when I realize how ghastly it must look. "Eventually he flattened out, started pounding the keys again. Writer's write, you know? It's not like they have a choice. One day he got stable enough to meet Rachel, and that started a whole new chapter in his life."

"Did you resent him for it? Her?"

"No. The wicked stepmother bit goes all the way back to the Romans. People try to crowbar it into their own narratives, but that wasn't her. For all the good it did her."

"You were very young."

I shrug.

"Do you remember police involvement? Officers about the premises? Strange guests at odd hours?"

"The first day was a circus. Anyone could have been there. After that, it was all pretty cut and dried. I just stayed up in my room, a pencil in my hand and a blank notebook in front of me, ignoring the noises, the hum of visitors, exclamations of grief. All of the air had been sucked out of the world, and I thought I could suffocate while I wrote a letter to her. She was close, so close, and it I hurried I could cross that bridge too, bury my face against her leg and tell her how sorry I was. I wrote until my hand ached and my pencil was a shriveled nub. It didn't work. I don't think anyone thought to look for me until the sun was a bloody eye on the horizon."

"Do you think he blamed you?"

Shrugging, I glance back at the curtain.

He's silent for a moment. "What happened to the letter?"

I smile, sick to my stomach.

"How did your—friend take it?" The word startles me. He hasn't been that in so long.

"The house I had to myself for long stretches. My father was making arrangements, inquests, whatever. I'm sure the police were involved, but he wouldn't be home for hours on end. Not the healthiest thing, but there it was."

"Gone a lot, you say?"

"Shut up."

I was in the bedroom on the second floor, looking at her jewelry. There was a triangular box she kept things in on top of her dresser, and I'd dragged a chair all the way up from the kitchen to have a look. It wasn't the safest thing I ever did. My father's lucky he didn't have two corpses.

This was before he sent everything away a few days later, mind you. Not a word, not a do-you-want-a-remembrance. Just gone. I'm fortunate to have gotten there when I did.

Anyway, I was examining a necklace, a long pendant dangling on a silver chain, when it got caught on something. I leaned forward to free it and overbalanced. The chair tipped out from under me, and I knocked my head off of the corner of the dresser as I fell.

It didn't hurt, not at first, though the light seemed to have changed by the time I could open my eyes. My hand came away from my forehead warm and sticky, and there was a tacky red patch on the carpet. When I finally looked up, I found myself on level with the space between the dresser and the carpet. It wasn't much more than a couple of inches, but I saw a bundle of papers back there, tied up with a piece of black ribbon. Curious girl that I was, I took them out.

No. Not him.

I've never mentioned this to anyone.

Forgive me if that sounds stupid, but it's the truth.

I undid the knot on the ribbon. The bundle fell open like a dead thing, and I gaped at the first page. Then the second, then the third.

They were drawings I'd made, poems I'd written, little stories I'd concocted and brought to her, ever since I was five. They still smelled of her perfume, and I could picture her sitting there, cross-legged on the floor, poring over them like I was, looking for answers.

All of them featured M—. The Man. Black hat, long hair, beard, dark clothes. And the smile. Every one I'd done, from stick figure to pseudo-real, had that secret, winking smile. Some were of us fighting dragons, playing with Algie, wandering on Atlantean soil, but others struck home with a sickening clarity.

Our first tea party, Sarah lying in the tall grass like a pink afterthought.

The Man punching the tetherball into Cruddy's face.

Grace bleeding in a pool of water.

Dominique Chau at the bottom of the stairs.

There must have been hundreds of them.

For what seemed like hours, I must have sat there, wondering what it all meant. Why she'd kept these, and what they told her. The significance seemed strangely weighted, but every time I thought I was close it stretched away into the black. What would Marmalade say? That we're all down here in the dark together? I wondered if this is what he meant.

By the time I was done the tacky stain was a pale ochre. Putting the papers back, I tied them with the ribbon, got a damp washcloth, and scrubbed at the bloody spot until my hands were sore. They say nothing gets blood out, but elbow grease and remorse seemed to at least fade it a little.

I could still smell her perfume, her presence, when I took the steel wastebasket outside.

All it took was an old Writer's Digest and a couple of matches. I burned them one by one, watching them curl into dying leaves from the backyard. Embers danced against the autumn dusk as immaterial as ghosts.

The smell was the burning of dreams.

The last one I threw in was of Marmalade and I holding hands. We were walking down a forested road, away from a massive green fortress that I didn't recognize. Both of us were smiling. Our faces were dirty.

It went into the flames with all the rest.

I heard a car in the front drive and didn't care. Let him see what I'd done, that his only daughter was playing with fire in the backyard, that she's liable to burn the whole house down. I heard his heavy footsteps come in through the front door and cross through the living room, but instead of coming back to the kitchen, they went straight on up the stairs. I saw his bedroom light blink on through the window, and then shut off again. He'd gone straight to bed. No looking for me. Not a word.

Not even a goddamn thought.

I never felt so much like running in my entire life.

It was then that I realized I wasn't alone.

Did you— never mind. Just jumpy.

He emerged from the shadows of the grove, a worn black sack dragging in the leaves behind him. His face was dirty, and whatever he set down in the misshapen bag seemed to writhe. A confluence of emotions warred across his face. He took a step towards me.

"Don't," I told him. The flames were dying, blackened with the past. 'Where have you been?"

"Looking for something," he said, giving the bag a kick. 'Found it too late."

Teams were streaming down my face. Mixed with the ashes, I must have looked a wild thing, more on his level now than ever before. "Where *were* you?"

"Thought I had a job to do." He pushed the hat back and wiped the grime from his brow. "I was a fool. I'm sorry about your momma, Prose."

"Everyone's sorry," I told him. "Sorry's just a sad little word."

"Most of them are."

"Sorry doesn't get us back to normal. Not even close." I studied him, the tattered work shirt, the stubble on his cheeks. His pale eyes were haunted, but to my surprise they were more than that. They were resigned. "You always said we were friends. Best friends."

"So I did, and so we are. Forever and ever."

"There is no forever." I spat. "Forever was up in that tree. Do you know what I found?"

Marmalade looked at the trash can and took another step forward. I halted him with one hand.

"Stop. It hurts and hurts and won't stop hurting. I feel like someone carved out a part of me and left a hungry, aching hole in its place, and the worst is that I still feel like it's not too late. That I can do something, say something, that'll make it right, that'll fix everything, and she'll come walking down the steps behind me and ruffle my hair. We'll eat graham crackers and watch the Simpsons and maybe there'll be a bedtime story at the end of this. But there won't be. Not ever again. Do you know what I found?'"

He shook his head, either in denial or agreement, I still don't know which. I pressed him, raw and wounded. "You said she couldn't see you."

"She couldn't. Swear on all the southern stars."

I shook my head. "I don't believe you. I think she could, maybe just a little, and you scared her. Scared her so bad it made her crazy. And then you hurt her."

"Prose—" he started.

"I remember that day with the spaghetti. Your little *joke*." I couldn't stop crying. It felt like my whole soul was being washed away. "How many more *jokes* did you play, Marmalade? How funny did it get?"

He sighed, shoulders slumping. Defeated, he seemed to grow smaller before my eyes. "That's not what happened."

"I don't care." My voice was choked. I wanted to throw something at him, hit him, knock him to the ground. "We're all here in the dark together, right? I never want to see you again."

"'Prose-'" he tried, but I was already on my feet, kicking the trashcan over to roll down the grass. Slamming the door, I was in the musty closet of the laundry room when great shuddering sobs wracked my body, burst through my lungs as I slid down the wall onto the cold linoleum. I cried and cried until there were no tears left, until the sun came up outside and the world was new and he was gone.

I'd like to say I never saw him again. But of course that wouldn't be true.

That's my end of the deal, Doctor.

Time to follow up with yours.

I sit in my new room in silence, the rush of blood burning in my ears. The Beige Universe is like looking up through muddy water at unfamiliar constellations, and I concentrate on the window instead. What I'm looking for I'm not entirely sure, but I keep thinking back to the theater, the dark figure in the back of the room. Was it just an empty seat to everyone else, the sole black tooth, or was it him?

Has he found me again?

The thought sends a shiver down my spine. The fact that it's not entirely unpleasant worries me more.

I wonder if he could be the answer to all this, the flaming sword that slices knot and cart and earth apart.

They'll find you, part of me argues. The other shrugs it off.

Kids go missing all the time. Check some milk cartons and get on with your lives.

It wasn't that simple, but nothing ever is. Could the Red Orphan disappear? Slip through the cracks to Seattle, or Portland? Hook a Canuck and wash up in Vancouver? I was starting to think I'd have to find out.

For all his bluster, I was starting to doubt Svara. The walk back to the Lodge has been quiet, the abandoned building looming quietly on the right. Squatting on the dying lawn, it looked like a sick toad amidst the elms. Dead leaves scurried about, and I thought about the holidays. The year I'd gone trick-or-treating as Annabelle Lee with my father, resplendent in a tissue paper seaweed and a blue gown because I was convinced that she'd drowned, which raised many more confused looks than candy. Mommy letting me help with Thanksgiving, the kitchen full of rich and wonderful smells, turkey and cranberries and her secret gravy recipe I'd gotten to stir. Christmas by the tree when Algie got his leg caught in a low-hanging string of lights that nearly pulled the whole pine down on top of him. Tears started streaming down my face, not for myself but for the past, for what was lost. What we'd all lost.

Svara had said nothing, merely dropping me off at the door and taking his leave. Chapman had given me a once over, thrown a glance at Steve, and I'd mumbled something about my room and darted down the hallway. Once the door was shut, I'd laid my fist into the cabinet until my knuckles were raw and my heart was empty. Mercifully hollow, I'd sat on my bed until the knock came.

A faint bell of alarm surfaces, and I wait. The seconds drift by like flood victims, and I have time to wonder why my guest doesn't just push through and throw open the door. The staff have never played coy with me before.

Calling out, I creep over and angle my eye to the pane, a survivor of enough scary movies to never look directly through it. Who I see is enough of a surprise to pop the door open and usher them inside.

The newcomer glances about my room, disinterested. I haven't bothered to decorate, and so the only burst of color in the room is the smear of drying blood I'd left on the cabinet door. When last I'd seen her, she'd been yelling about theta waves and dark love. Her hair is pulled back, away from her face. It only serves to express the fullness of her cheeks and the dark circles under her eyes, giving her a spectral appearance.

I begin to question why I've let her inside.

Before I get a chance to speak, her eyes are upon me, deep pits the color of raw earth. "We haven't much time."

"I'd imagine." I glance back at the door, waiting to see Chapman looking through the panel, forehead red and fuming. "Where's your ghost?"

"Lo? Snuck off for a bathroom break. He thought I was asleep. But I never sleep, you see. Only wait." She had traded the dress for a pair of institutional sweats and a knockoff t-shirt, the unofficial uniform of Everbrook. It muted her somehow, no longer a high priestess but a fanatical devotee. "Thought I warned you, didn't I?"

"Warned me?" I didn't follow. "Warned me about what?"

"Not to talk out of class." She moves closer, and I realize that this was a bad idea. "They are never far. And always listening—" Her face draws near, and I can smell the staleness of her breath. Seizing my forearm, she wrenches my wrist around. Damn, but she's strong. She surveys my bruises with a clinical nod.

The metal cabinet is cold behind me. I can't back up any farther, but somewhere below my alarm is a budding fascination just now opening its petals. "Can you see them too?"

She shakes her head solemnly. "What I see? So much more. What I feel, what they do. The mind is a lump of clay, and they *squeeze*—"

"What do they want from you?" My pulse quickens. If she's not insane, we're on the brink of revelation.

She leans in, lips inches from my neck. Hungrily, she sniffs.

"Our fear. Drink it all up, but it's never enough. When they grow bored, they'll come for flesh."

"Enough." But she doesn't move, and my head snakes forward, the crown of my forehead missing her nose but bashing her cheek. She recoils in surprise, and I place both hands on her shoulders and shove. Her knee hits the corner of the bed and she spins, laughing, landing in a spry crouch reminiscent of a mantis.

"Prooooooose." She grins, her smile transforming her face into a death's head. "They love you. I love you. But no more stories, or they'll get angrrrrry."

There's a pounding at the door. I take a step forward. "Why are you telling me this? How does any of this help?"

"Darlin'. Why ever would I want to help you?" She giggles like something that crawled out of a sewer and pivots as the door opens. Lo and Chapman are both there, and I realize that I haven't seen Graham all day.

I'd never seen so many of them in one place.

Not that they dotted the hillside like a sea of bodies, but still. Not a swarm or a platoon, but they were scattered amongst the gravestones, faded and jutting up from the earth like discarded blocks from some cosmic playset. The sun was out for once, and I remembered how the grass on the slope seemed to sing with it, whispering low melodies with each gust of wind.

I was wearing a modest black dress, my hair pulled back from my forehead in a tight braid that was beginning to give me a headache, but I wasn't about to complain. My father stood next to me, more out of absentmindedness than any real sense of guardianship. His cheeks were stubbled, his eyes heavy. Those close enough to him could smell the sour tang of cheap whiskey and the desperation that surrounded him like a cloud. We'd barely spoken all day, and now that we stood in the old yard, a mound of raw soil to one side of the hole, there didn't seem like there was anything to say.

Mark's hair was longer then, blowing around his face in thin strands that escaped his ponytail. He had kept his distance ever since his old Subaru had pulled up to the parking lot, settling for a cursory handshake and a so-sorry that I had already become immune to.

I didn't cry. My tears had burned away with the fire.

A lot of people milled about the pit, most of them dressed all in black. A couple of family friends spoke in brief succession, eyes red, voices choked. We looked like refugees from a Cure concert. They spoke of my mother's heart, her vitality, her generosity, how she could light up a room by entering it or raise the spirits of her friends with a word. What they didn't say was that she left early, walked away.

What they didn't say was anything that would help my father.

It hurt to see him, the laughing, subtle man transformed now into just an aching question, and so I looked around. They were staggered about the old cemetery, but they were there. A balding man with patchy tufts of white hair in a beige suit. A little boy in short pants and a beret, a smear across his lips. A portly man that seemed to swell against the fabric of his sport coat. A naked thing so shriveled that it appeared almost sexless. A woman in a long gown that seemed to hover above the grass. Some were in rare sunlight, some in the shade of the willows and firs that dotted the landscape. All seemed to watch the spectacle with silent curiosity.

I ignored them and looked at the box.

I had read a lot of Poe much too young, but I wasn't stupid. Mom wasn't going to breathe in a startled, gasping rush of air and sit up, fate averted. This wasn't House of Usher. We weren't going to bury her alive.

They say he was terrified of that, you know. A lot of people were at the time, so maybe it was just the zeitgeist taking hold. Read up on nineteenth century medicine and you'd see why. When doctors had the same social status as field hands, it's not hard to picture their expertise being less than inscrutable.

I saw him just once, beneath the shadows of an elm, wide hat covering most of his face in the wind. He didn't say anything. He just watched as the box was lowered into the ground.

Mark looked over to me, overcome. He had been crying most of the morning, I think, and his cheeks were puffy. When he followed my gaze to the trees, he showed no reaction.

On the ride home, my father said nothing. Something inside him was broken.

I was waiting to see if it could be fixed. I was always waiting.

I'm not trying to paint him as some Bluebeard that kept me chained up in his closet while he toiled away. Far from it. What happened with my mother was devastating. To both of us. And he tried to deal with it the best he could.

We still did things together, read stories on the couch and watched lazy primetime TV, poking fun of the flawless detective work and their magic crime-solving computers. We went to a Ducks game out in Eugene the month after, the fall wind whipping at full strength, and laughed and cheered and drank soda as the offense ran up the score. He did dad-style cooking projects, things like lasagna, casseroles, tried to perfect a recipe for pork sausage chili. We were happy again, but something was irretrievable in his eyes, a jewel with just a little crack that can never be put right. Something told me part of him wanted to be with her.

Yeah. I do feel guilty. Sometimes I felt like I was keeping him here, in a place he didn't want to be anymore. Sometimes I missed my mother terribly. Sometimes the certainty crept in that it was all my fault.

Maybe if I'd been normal, if I made more friends, it might not have happened.

The Man? I don't understand the question.

Did I slip back there? I don't think so.

Maybe he missed it. Here's hoping.

For your sake.

I know what I said. And I blamed him. Maybe I was right, maybe wrong, but I did. The next few years were lonely, even though my father kept insisting I make friends. I moved around so much it was almost impossible.

The Man would show up from time to time, always in the background once we'd settled for a while. Once I spotted him behind the corner of Sudsy's Laundromat when I was crossing the parking lot. Another time he was lurking up the road when I closed my curtains for bed, silhouetted in an orange streetlight. At the schools I'd bounce around to, there were appearance in the fields, at the ends of a long hallways.

It takes him a while to catch up, you see.

Which is why you should worry.

Not that I could ever say that in front of my father. The times I did got out of control. His face would go red and the cords on his neck stood out, and he'd shout guilt at my damned imagination or throw something or both. If I upset the ship, he'd let me see how close he was to drowning. Just a little.

Part of him blamed me.

I mean, I don't know. I was just a kid when it happened. And with that on top of Algie, I don't blame him for selling the house. Too many bad memories. Too many ghosts in the corners.

The bruises? What about them?

We've all got bruises, Doc.

No, he never raised a hand to me. Not—

I see how you could think that. Human Services thought the same thing before they decided I was some attention-starved cutter. I thought I told you that the marks didn't match.

Believe me, they measured.

I roll the sleeve up over my right forearm, exposing my delicate wrist. It's not hard to see the bruises beneath the halogens. They stand out in stark relief, Rorschach inkblots on parchment.

Svara pushes his glasses a little higher up on his nose, craning over, and makes a *tssking* sound with his tongue.

"Why would they still be here after two months? Who'd be making them if it was always my father?"

His eyes meet mine. There's a depth there, a sadness I haven't seen before that makes me recoil. "I think we both know who's making them."

Something clenches inside me. It's as if my lungs have caught fire. "There's something else here, Doc. Irregulars at Everbrook."

"Like there was something in your childhood home? And something else in the one after that? And again after that?" He shakes his head on his long neck as if connected to some vast weight. "I was hoping we'd be farther along, Ms. Harden. This setback—"

My cheeks burn. Something is consuming the grief, the pain, the sadness, a phoenix pyre threatening to erupt. "I can't help who I am. Or what I see."

"If you can't try—" He glances back at Monique. She's perched on the last row of bleachers, checking her phone and glancing absently towards the big black curtain like she's waiting for the show to start. I wonder if she knows that she's doing it. "Ms. Harden, this will never end."

"That's just it," I say, pushing to my feet. "They've always been there, as soon as I was old enough. Why are we pretending that'll change? What can you possibly say that's going to keep away a bloody nightmare? Or that pale girl from the visiting room? What exactly are you going to do, Doc? How are you going to make it different?"

"Increase your medication, to start with. It's clear to me that it's not working, at least as well as it should. Perhaps a change in your environment. " He clicks his pen as he hedges his bets, so many neutral words, all the time.

"A change in my environment? I'm going to jail at the end of this," I spit. "How's that for a fucking change? I'm not stupid. Whatever pull, whatever power you said you have, it's all bullshit. You just found the perfect, desperate fool to believe it."

Svara smiles at me thinly. "What motive would I possibly have to deceive you?"

"We're just going in circles." I clear my throat. Something watches us from the stage. I think we peaked its interest ever since we started coming here to talk. "What's your theory, then? What's wrong with me?"

Svara's lips thin to a horizontal line. For a moment he calculates, and I realize that no matter how vital he seems, he looks like he's lost weight since this began. His loose grey suit makes him seem even more wraithlike. "Something you said caught my attention. A footnote from earlier, but I think it worth investigating."

My heart pounds in my chest as he continues. "You mentioned your great-uncle in a dash of conversation, no more, but it made me wonder. Hutchence, perhaps? Did you know him?"

"No. I never met him." Where was he going with this? I tried to control my breathing, which wanted to speed up and break free. "Someone might have mentioned him once or twice. We were a pod family. Not a lot of relatives around."

"Truly." The vast room seems to have gotten colder. I imagine my breath, white fingers of mist that wrap around his throat.

I don't want to hear this.

"If you repeat what I am about to tell you, I will chalk it down to your delusion and deny everything. Medical records are, after all, quite confidential, but you'd be surprised the great number of people who have expressed interest in your case.

Enough to bend a couple of lazy rules and leave some files laying around."

I say nothing. Part of me wants to call Monique and walk, but another pushes me down, keeps my knees bent. Whispers from below a railing drift back to me, eight years old and still in footy pajamas. *Uncle Hutch—*

"There are several things you might find enlightening. Information you have never known, I suspect. It wasn't the easiest thing to track down. Your great-uncle spent a great deal of his life in the care of the Spokane State Regional Center. Hutchence Charles Summers was a diagnosed schizophrenic, not unusual for a state-run facility."

"Stop." Nothing coming out of his mouth was something I wanted to know.

"He claimed he knew characters who could open doors. Show him things. Horrible things, by his account."

"I really don't need to hear this."

"And they'd hurt him, always hurt him, when he wouldn't cooperate. Sound familiar?"

I'm mute for the moment. "You're using the past tense."

"Indeed. He fell victim to his illness twenty years ago— am I upsetting you?"

A bark of laughter escapes my throat at the lunacy of his question. "No, no. Who doesn't want to hear that it runs in the family?"

"I didn't think I would get this reaction," he says. His eyes flicker over me, hungry.

"Fell victim?"

He shakes his head. "I think that's enough. Ask your—" and he stops, realizing what carrion is about to fall from his lips. "Your uncle, yes? Perhaps he would care to shine some light on the matter."

"Mark? He's never mentioned an asylum."

Svara nods and glances back towards Monique. The words escape the side of his mouth.

"Well, he would know, wouldn't he?"

In the first house, I still felt free.

Spring was blossoming, the air afresh with pollen and new life. The sun had gone behind a patch of wispy cumulus, and the ground smelled of wet earth and fresh rain. The Man and I were on a special, this-is-not-setting-a-precedent errand to our local little library to pick up research material for my dad, who was writing a short story titled *Ariadne, Get Your Gun*, and I'd stopped off for a Slurpee at the little Plaid Pantry on our way back. My backpack was full of Greek mythology and the Golden Bough, my little legs trudging gamely through puddles and wet grass.

I studied him as he walked, just a fraction ahead of me. His coat billowed around him in flapping gusts, and his boots didn't make a sound against the damp blacktop. Beneath the wide hat, his eyes were searching for something down the road.

A jackrabbit erupted from the grass and launched itself across the road with abandon. Neither of us spoke, but something in the set of his jaw unnerved me. When he was this quiet, it was like having a lurking shadow.

I planted my feet and folded my arms across my chest. "You're being weird."

He looked at me with a mixture of puzzlement and annoyance. "Certainly not."

"Sure you are." I stuck my lower lip out in a pout that was mostly pretend. "If you wanted your own Slurpee, you could have asked. I have another dollar-forty."

"Southern stars," he spat, and glanced back up the road. The rabbit was gone as if it had never been. "You can keep your chemical cola, darlin'."

"Then what's your deal?" I asked. "You haven't said two words since."

"May we walk?" He angled his head skyward towards the encroaching clouds. "Nature's not done with us today."

Firs and cedars whispered along the road. Grey streaks of cloud had started to solidify into zeppelins, threatening to block out the sun. I said nothing as the Man scanned the scrub of woods, content with the weight of books on my back and the cool chill of flavored ice in my belly, walking into the wind. A branch snapped somewhere in the forest with a crack like broken bone. Marmalade bared his teeth and hissed.

Curious, I tried to trace the sound. Was that a flicker of motion, the swing of an arm ducking behind a tree? "Keep walking," the Man growled, and I followed in the shadow of his coat.

There was something moving back there, almost a hundred yards away, too sly to be seen and too cautious to reveal itself. Angling between the trees, I caught a glimmer of knee here, a trace of elbow there. The Man's face had grown hard, teeth set in a thin line.

"What is it?" I asked.

He shook his head and kept us moving.

"I can see that," I said, and he turned on me. I gave him my seventy-watt smile, wide-eyed and Walt Disney, and after a moment he shook his head, a chuckle filled with gravel. Another branch broke. A low rumble of thunder echoed off of the hills, and the air filled with the smell of burnt ozone.

"What's eating you?"

He seemed to chew on the question for a while. Finally he spat it out, worn thin and palpable. "The books."

"Yeah?" When he didn't elaborate, I pressed. "I thought you loved stories."

"Everyone loves a story." His eyes darted back to the tree line. "Campfire tales on ice a couple thousand years, right?"

"I guess."

"Babylonians. Egyptians. Assyrians. Tcho-tchos. Each one with their own little stories about how the moon was hung, trying to explain how the world works. None of them stretching close. What does that tell you?"

It was an easy one. "People like stories."

"People like heroes, but they never do run out of monsters."

"Sure." I thought back to Odysseus, to Perseus, to the Argo and its crew. "But there are a lot less of them then when they start."

"Mm." Something shifted beneath the cedars, but he was too caught up to notice. "All you need to be a hero is humble origins and a disregard for human life. No one remembers the victims, the shepherds or crofters or millers who get turned to stone or lose sheep, sons, daughters. And where do monsters come from?"

I thought about it for a while. Dark clouds were beginning to circle overhead. "I don't know. They're just there."

Shrugging, I looked back to the forest. Something moved behind a scarred fir.

"Just window dressing for the truth. Magic thinking about bright lights in the sky. The truth is, darling, we're all down here in the dark together. And the dark is where we stay."

He took a step towards the tree line and waved me on. His coat billowed as the first raindrops began to fall. "Get on home. I need to see someone."

Without another word he disappeared into the woods. I looked after him for what seemed like minutes, but he was gone.

I felt that part of me was too.

Everyone's inside when I walk in through the door, the light drizzle outside enough to cage them. Chapman gives me a funny look from behind the kitchen counter, his fingers folding a sandwich into a wedge of compressed space. Like every other day, it's a free-for-all, and Nellie's watching a Disney channel movie-of-the-week while Harkness and Eloise blast each other into pixelated ribbons in the corner. Of the new girl there's no sign, but a couple of newcomers glance up at me with mild disinterest from the worn couch. They don't introduce themselves, which is par for the course at Everbrook.

Just passing through, people. Just passing through.

Harkness notices me and gives me a tense little wave, which Nellie notices with a scowl. She mouths something childish at me, but by then I'm crossing over. The dayroom smells of tater tots and yellow mustard as I pull up a plastic chair and watch two cartoonish figures on the screen race about and fling hellfire rockets at each other. With a raised eyebrow I wonder how much practice it takes to master the gyrations onscreen. The pair of them run through the levels like they'd created them.

Harkness flips her dark hair back and mutters a string of expletives as her character explodes. Over my shoulder, Monique and Chapman are speaking in hushed tones. I notice that Jon has slid quietly from his position by the back hallway to the couch by the girls.

The fact that I've grown used to so many people sneaking around disturbs me.

Svara passes by the window, humming a tune I can't quite catch. His thin hair is already damp and clinging to his scalp as he heads out to one of the other Lodges. I wonder who he's seeing next—if he's made deals with them as well. If any of what he said is true, it doesn't matter now. The walls are closing in, a fraction at a time, and I know that if I don't do something soon it will be too late.

It's Eloise's turn to contort in a wreath of flames. She grumbles something about camping and immediately launches back in. Unnerved, I try to whisper. The questioning look Harkness gives me makes me inclined to think I'm less than successful.

"Can I talk to you?" I ask.

"Shoot," she says. I roll my eyes towards Eloise, but Harkness shrugs. "What? Anything you have to say to me, you can say in front of Wheezy."

"When the lights went out. Do you remember? You told me something."

Harkness nods and glances over my shoulder to the kitchen. Monique and Chapman are still buried in conversation. "We look hella suspicious right now. Just watch the game."

"Thank you," Eloise grumbles. One of the cartoon figures dances merrily over the recent corpse of the other in a series of squats and jerks as we turn and watch the screen.

When Harkness speaks, it's out of the corner of her mouth. "What about it?"

"You stopped me from going out the slider. You said the tunnel would be too dark."

"That would have been the queen of bad ideas. I stopped you from screwing up." The other character explodes into a rain of pixelated body parts. Harkness wriggles in her seat.

I pause, waiting for a clarification that doesn't come. "What tunnel? What did you mean?"

"Old Everbrook legend. I heard it first when I was in Juniors from one of the older hellions of our time, Monty or something. Supposedly the big kids—" and she throws in a pair of air quotes, hands still wrapped around the controller. "—knew about a tunnel, or way out of the big gymnasium that lets out just beyond the fence. It's some kind of fire-code thing that they don't advertise."

The disbelief must show on my face. "There's a secret passage out of here?"

"Come on, Spooky. That's the goth in you talking." She says it not unkindly, giving me a little pat on the arm. "You're not going to go tilting a wall sconce and have a panel slide open. It's just there and they don't talk about it."

"So why would it be dark?"

"The same reason most of this place is. The gym's a Godzilla. Costs a fortune to run the heater, so they flip the circuits at bedtime to save power. Graham told me about it when we were shooting the shit one time."

"What happened to him? Graham, I mean?"

"Got in some kind of trouble for our field trip." She shrugs, a graceful roll of shoulder. "I think he's trying to stick it to the man."

"Stick it to somebody," Eloise murmurs. Harkness gives her a playful punch on the arm.

"Do you want to go look for it sometime?"

"You mean go exploring with you, or actually try to run?" Harkness pushes her hair back again, her little white teeth digging into her lower lip. "If I run, I walk right out that front door and wait for the cops to find me. There's no treasure hunt to do it. If you want to explore, though—" A mischievous light reflected back from jade eyes. "I think you've found your girl."

I nod, grateful, and some dark impulse comes jutting out of my mouth. "Can I ask you something and not have it get all weird?"

Eloisa groans. Harkness grins as another animated character is garroted by a string of pixels. "What's on your mind?"

"Do you remember my roommate?" She looks confused, and I try again, the tears filling my eyes. "Old school flapper cut, heroin thin? Caustically sarcastic? Stayed in the room a lot?"

Harkness reads me, and something cracks. Her arm slides around my shoulders as an animated figure is cut to ribbons. "Shhh. Hey. It's okay, Prose. It's okay."

My voice breaks. "Do you remember her?"

Harkness shakes her head slowly. "Can't say that I do, kiddo."

"Nope," Eloise offers, and then I'm really crying, hot stupid tears flowing down my cheeks in waves. It's too much. It's all too much.

No. No. Oh, no.

Crazy crazy crazy. You made it all up. If we only hurt the ones we love, you must have really dug her to cave the side of her fucking skull in. Maybe you should stay locked up.

How can something that never was hurt so much?

Not content to simply probe the edges of the wound, I mumble something about a cowboy. Nellie laughs, a sharp bark, and then Jon's there, taking me to the back hallway, getting me tissues. He makes soothing noises, but I can't really listen, because he reminds me of my father, the good version, and my feet take me away and flop down upon my bed, and for a moment I want to end it all before the light flakes away from the room and shows the dull grey matter of a rotting world behind it. Just like my father, my fictions are everything.

I sleep for what feels like forever.

If Ol' Yellow Eyes shows up, I'm too tired to care.

The second door swung open only to catch on the matted brown carpet, leaving me to squinch through the opening sideways. Mr. Grayson motioned me in with an annoyed frown from behind his desk. His sweater vest looked too hot for his office, and beads of sweat formed on his brow. Two filing cabinets framed him on either side like bodyguards. Hung diplomatically behind him against the yellow stucco was a framed diploma. I heard a muffled curse behind me and tried to ignore it.

"Prose, have a seat."

Beside me, my father's knees rose almost to his chest as he sank into in the undersized chair. He gave me a flap of the fingers that might be considered a wave.

What the hell am I doing here? goes unvoiced.

I glanced behind me in time to spot a tall shadow slipping back into the hallway.

Does he think I'm blind? "Dad."

"Thank you both for coming," Mr. Grayson said. His thick neck bulged against his sweater as if fighting a peculiar border war. I bit back whatever snarky comment I rising.

This meeting wasn't voluntary.

"Well, thank you for having us." My father drummed his fingers against his thigh. "Who got hurt?"

The bruises on my arms ached for a moment, and I remembered the purple light pulsating from the linen closet the night before.

—come and see, come and see—

Mr. Grayson looked surprised. "I beg your pardon?"

"To borrow a phrase, this isn't our first rodeo." My father nodded to the gray-green folder in front of Mr. Grayson, who crossed his forearms in front of it guiltily.

"No one is injured, Mr. Harden."

"So why am I—"

"At least not physically."

My father raised an eyebrow at this, a talent I was sure he'd cultivated through days at a mirror. It was brought out mostly for special demonstrations. Mr. Gray's three-act drama seemed to merit it. "Do go on."

"Your daughter's English class has been reading *Lord of the Flies*. As a creative project, they were asked to write a story about what would happen if they were shipwrecked on an island with their classmates. Five thousand words."

"I'm familiar with the novel. So?"

Mr. Grayson slid a stapled sheath of paper across the desk. "Most of her classmates wrote utopian fantasies. About teamwork, parental supervision, and new child-centric rules."

My father snorted and rifled through the pages. "You called it *Islander?*"

I shrugged. "There can be only one."

Mr. Grayson pressed on. "In your daughter's vision, the island is populated by a dark force that strikes a deal with her. To pick off her classmates one by one, leaving her the only inhabitant and the resources hers alone."

"Huh," my father mumbled, still flipping through the pages.

"It gets fairly graphic," the counselor said. "See the highlighted sections on page three, and six, and—"

"I can read," my father said. His eyes don't leave the page.

"She lures them into a series of traps with horrible consequences. In one, a boy is lured into a bog and drowned. In another, several children pursue her onto a high cliff before it gives way and drops them into the sea. In another—"

"Do you have the original assignment?" His eyes had changed without looking up. Something hard, something amused, and *was that pride?*

"I'm sorry?" Mr. Grayson pursed his lips. "I explained the assignment. You don't think this is—"

"Do you have the assignment? The paper that specified the details? I imagine you still use paper here, right?"

There was the briefest glance to a notepad in the corner of the table. "The assignment was made orally."

My father slid the paper back to him. "So I have your word, then, that some kind of rule was broken? Mrs. Sawa set out clear constraints regarding content?"

"I hardly think that this paper is appropriate—"

"You asked her to write a fiction by setting a couple of loose parameters regarding the setting and situation. That's exactly what she did. I don't understand your complaint."

"Is everything all right at home?" Mr. Grayson asked, folding his fingers into a virtuous pyramid.

My father stared back at him. "If you read that file, you have everything you need. Prose is a bright girl with an incredibly rich imagination. You gave her carte blanche to be creative and then, if you'll pardon me, cried about the result. You might as well ask her to make you an omelet and then bitch that she cracked the eggs."

Mr. Grayson stared back at him for what seemed like an hour. My heart raced at the profanity, at his attitude, but more that he actually seemed to have my back.

At last the older man spoke. "I hardly think that's fair, Mr. Harden."

"Why are we here?" my father asked. He had set the paper down at the very edge of the table.

"Your child's work this year, especially in English, has shown a rather morbid preoccupation. Black-edged fantasies. Tales of horror. Vengeance from beyond the grave."

"She does wear her influences on her sleeve, I'll grant you."

"She dresses in black. She quotes Poe to her teachers. Her art project two weeks ago was a diorama of something called *Pickman's Model*."

"And if this was a religious academy instead of a state-run school, I can see how that may be problematic."

"You've moved around a lot in the last couple of years, haven't you?" Mr. Grayson allowed himself just a fraction of a grin. "I did, after all, read the file."

"I don't—"

"She's been to a lot of state-run schools. Six, in fact, over the last two years. That kind of transience does damage. Trouble making friends, trouble fitting in. A permanent sense of impermanence. I look to your daughter's work and see a cry for help, Mr. Harden."

I seized up at becoming the focus of attention. I thought of the empty rooms of the farmhouse, so many doors, all leading to pale purple world beyond the pantry. *The city of dead light*. With the inevitability of the drowning, I was just waiting to be pulled inside.

"It doesn't matter," I said. "You've made up your mind. So has Mrs. Sawa. I'll take the D and keep going."

"There's no D." My father flapped the pages at the counselor, who looked more than a little perturbed. "Show me five papers better than this in her class. Hell, show me one. Just because you don't like the content doesn't mean it's not fantastic work."

"No one's—"

"If you don't like the results, I would recommend you make your writing assignments clearer. You know, *in writing*." My father's voice could have scuffed leather. "There's nothing wrong with my girl. If anything, I'd be concerned about a person who reads so deeply into seventh-grade fiction. Now, if you'll excuse us, you've done enough *damage* for one day. My girl and I are leaving."

He turned to me, and in that moment I wanted to hug him, tell him everything. Before I could, he put his hand on my shoulder. "She's going to be out for the rest of the day," my father said. "We're going for ice cream."

Hard to believe, then, that in a week everything would fall apart. I like to think that that was who my father was, really, before they took me and the world broke him.

It's an earth full of peaks and valleys, though, and you've got to be able to climb.

In the end, only darkness sees us through.

The day I read *House of Razors*, I was sitting on the concrete walkway outside the motel room in a borrowed chair, the corrugated steel railing supporting my feet and a pair of oversized sunglasses on my face. They made me look like a particularly surprised wasp, at home in the daubed mud and grit nest of the run-down two-story set back from the boulevard. Amidst the gnarled twist of blackberry bushes and scrub trees, the parking lot was so broken down beneath me it was turning back to gravel.

From my perch on the walkway, I could see the mobile home park on the other side of the road. It had rained earlier that morning, and old cars passed in and out of the puddles, spitting rocks and harming suspensions every couple of minutes. By the foot traffic, either two people on the first floor were selling drugs, or their Avon business was going through the roof.

The pocketknife was a cold lump of reassurance against my hip. There had been a decline in quality neighbors for the last couple of years, and our days in country houses felt like scenes taken from another life, a fiction culled from all the books I had left behind. The crunch of sand against concrete beneath my flip flops and the flaking paint felt realer than any of it had. My earth was a slung mudball hurtling through the cosmos, and I was just along for the ride.

I wasn't in school that morning, either because we'd just moved again and my father had forgotten about filling out the paperwork, or that he was just too busy to notice. Rachel had been gone for years, the detectives long since filed out of our lives. Her disappearance had raised some eyebrows at the time, but my father's alibi had been rock solid, and the fact that they had never *habeased* that *corpus* hadn't helped.

Neither had the early move to ignore the budding teenage lunatic in favor of the eccentric but essentially well-referenced widower. Later detectives would scoff at their incompetence, but hindsight's twenty-twenty and presumption a bitch. The Man was spot on.

Everything gets squeezed into a tight little narrative.

Take my father, who had either taken our beaten little four-door sedan down to Portland and the massive county library or was alternatively down at Pip's Corner getting lit. In those days it was fifty-fifty. Reality seemed to be thinning around the edges, and loose strands were starting to get in everyone's eyes.

I'd found the copy in an old valise he'd started to carry his notes in.

The lurid cover seemed to say it all.

The sun had slipped down past the clouds when gravel squelched in the wet parking lot and the sound of heavy shoes started to pace up the back stairwell. The smell of wet earth and wild berries fought each other for my attention. Two tweekers had already stopped by to hassle the skinny pseudo-goth with the art of single entendre, and if they'd come back for more I was ready to duck back and bolt the flimsy door.

When my father lurched into view, I wasn't sure whether to hide the book or throw it at him.

His eyes were red as if he'd been crying, a week's worth of black stubble drying on his cheeks. Over the last few years, his normally academic, almost prissy dress had been replaced with a caricature of the working class, and a once-white t-shirt and battered jeans hung off of him like a loose skin.

We both froze, as if seeing the other for the first time.

His gaze drifted down to the book hanging in my hand. I'm sure he recognized the spatter of red across the cover, even if he couldn't read the title.

"Whatcha' been doing, kid?"

"Reading." I gave him a brittle smile. "Your latest bestseller. Congratulations."

"Where'd you get that?" He took a tentative step forward, as if testing his balance.

"Amazon. Barnes and Noble. The fucking library. What does it matter?" My teeth bared as if suddenly too large for my jaw. "It's everywhere, Dad."

"Prose—" he started, but I held up a hand and flipped it to a dog-eared page.

"'*The darkness,' she said, 'has been here all along.' The noose grew tighter around her mother's throat, her windpipe drawing into a narrow singularity. She kicked at the girl feebly and almost lost her balance on the chair.*

The girl looked up, a shallow smile splitting her lips. 'Soon we'll all be down in the dark together.' The dark man nodded his assent, and the little girl kicked the chair away. As her mother's life beat a fading staccato against the air, the smile turned into a grin." I rifled through the pages. "Hold on, let me find another."

"I can—"

"'Her stepmother's screams were an awful lullaby as the last shovelfuls of dirt rained down. Already the storm was sullying the earth. By morning there would be no guide, no hint to as what she had done. It would be like the other woman never was, she thought, leaning the shovel against the side of the house. Kicking the mud off of her boots, she slid in through the back door, careful not to make a sound. The black spirit was her shadow now, and he was ever looming closer."

He stood there, arms folded. A blaze of crimson was creeping into his cheeks, but I didn't care. I flipped through the book at random.

"'The golden retriever yelped, a high and brutal sound. The orphan didn't notice. Rather, she took the second nail out of the box and positioned it just so, right beneath its warm brown eye. Madly, it licked her hand once as if in entreaty. Then the hammer drove it in.' Really? I killed the dog, too?"

"It's fiction, Prose."

"I *am* only halfway through, What does the Red Orphan do next? Torch a school? Poison a pancake breakfast?"

"It's make-believe. Fantasy." He spoke to me like I was a child, and I wanted to tear out every single page and feed them to him.

"It's your fantasy, Maybe you should be the one talking to the shrinks." My cheeks felt warm, on the verge of catching fire. I would not cry. "What's wrong with you?"

"It's not real. It's a novel." His chest swelled, his neck straightened. I knew what he was going to say before he said it, and I hated him for it. "It's very popular."

"And I'm your fucking inspiration."

"It's putting food on your table. A roof over your head. What do you want from me?" He took another step forward.

"Not to be seen as your demonic hellspawn, for one." I set the book down against the wet concrete calmly, willing myself not to explode. "At least this explains why there aren't a hundred vanity copies scattered around the room."

"You've never made this easy," he grunted. "The schools. Moving. Do you know how hard it's been for me?"

My jaw dropped. "Do go on."

He gathered himself in one rushing intake of breath. I raised my palm. "Maybe you shouldn't. Maybe we shouldn't say anything else."

"Prose—"

I pushed back from the borrowed chair and stormed back into our motel room, slamming the door so hard I was rewarded with a spray of peeling paint flakes. If there was wisdom in our family, he would have given me time to cool off.

Let it never be said that we were wise.

He burst into the room in another spray of powdered paint, his face red and his breaths heavy. "I have tried to be a good father to you, Prose."

"Try harder."

"But the fights, the psychiatrists. That thing you used to call your best friend." He swallowed, caught his breath. "Two people I've loved more than anything are gone, and all I know is that it had something to do with you."

The words swung in the air like a wrecking ball, a hammer finally given life. I felt something inside me give with the discordant melody of shattered glass. The room seemed to swell and contract like a bleeding pupil. I put my hand on the cheap table and felt the rough grain of unsanded wood. "Don't you pin this on me. Don't you dare!"

"Or what? You'll call your Man?" There was the faintest smile on his face, tight and cruel. "You've been sick for a while, Prose. I'm sorry, but I don't know how to get you well."

"Yeah. You've tried nothing and you're all out of ideas. How about being a parent for once?"

He ignored that. "I've told you. In writing, everything is grist for the mill. You take reality, give it a little twist, and it becomes another shape, another world. I can't ignore everything in our lives. I can't pretend none of it happened. But I can rework it into something. Something marvelous."

It came to me that he was standing in front of the only door. My heart beat faster.

"You used to be my little reader. You used to be so aware. I had such big plans for you, but something inside you was wrong." His hands were at his sides, two vicious slabs of meat he hadn't bothered to wield. "Instead of Tolstoy it was Poe. Lovecraft for Fitzgerald. Machen for Joyce. It's no wonder you started seeing things."

Don't defend yourself. Don't defend yourself, but still my voice found its way out. "Things? Do you remember my arms?"

"Your arms, and your mouth. That temper. We didn't have it easy, but there you always were, fighting for attention. Good or bad, in any way possible. Making up that Man—"

I whispered his name and hated myself for it. "His name was Marmalade."

"Your mother hated you for it," he said. His mouth kept moving, but something had ripped inside me, a well of blood and black bursting open, flooding all my senses. The tears came spitefully, around my defenses, and the world reeked of copper and salt.

My father looked at me, a hint of expectation on his red face. His fists were clenched, legs apart, the light outside filtering in around the shadow he'd become.

"Maybe once we could have had our happy ending," I said. "Instead it's just another horror show."

I pushed past him towards the door, my eyes burning, barely able to see. Half of me expected him to shove me backwards, knock me over the bed and onto the dirty carpeting, but he let me go.

Putting his hands on me would have required too much effort.

My feet bounded down the worn concrete steps, down into the parking lot and away from the motel.

I didn't return for three days.

It I hadn't come back, maybe he'd still be alive.

The knock raps three times, cliched but true. My lights are out, but I haven't drifted anywhere near sleep. As quiet as a cat I slip out of my cabinet, muscles cramped but confident. The pane of glass in my door shows nothing, and neither of the last two bed checks commented upon the lumps of clothes stashed beneath my covers.

She'd made this sound so simple, but now that it's upon us, my heart is pounding in my chest. As I crawl over to the window and put all my weight into it, the lower left corner comes away from the sill with a shriek of grating plastic, an inch, then another, finally bending outward and leaving a hole that seems way too small for any sane person to fit through. Harkness had said that the Lodge was falling apart, but until now I hadn't realized how badly. Sticking my feet through the opening, I wriggle down. Scraping my thigh, the small of my back, and for a moment I'm not going to make it through.

My shoulders are stuck tight between the thick sheet of plastic and the stucco wall. I picture myself jammed there until morning, half-in and half-out, and the air comes out of me in one colossal heave. There's a feeling of interminable tightness as I push again, and then my head pops out like an infant birthed.

I am free upon the world.

Well, not really. The dark walls loom in shadowed murk, and I have time to think that this is a tremendously bad idea. I didn't really think she could pull it off, but Harkness is nothing if not resourceful. She's lurking behind a bush, a tiny grey blur in a forest of them, and gives me a terse little wave. The screwdriver she used is already back in its hiding place.

"You okay? The third one was really stuck in there. I could barely get it loose." Her voice is a high whisper on a windy night. Elms buckle and shake around us.

"M'okay." I can't escape the feeling that I'm whispering too loudly. Before I can ask, she raises her left hand. Its contents let out a faint jingle.

"We've got forty-five minutes before shift change."

"What if he notices?"

"I'm sure he has noticed. He's just not going to tell anybody until he absolutely has to."

I nod and take Lo's key ring from her. It's surprisingly heavy and marked with a 46. At Everbrook, staff keys are picked up at the beginning of every shift and turned in at the end, without fail. Eloise claimed to have seen a new recruit, some twenty-something with a prominent chin and movie-star hair, almost lose it because they couldn't find their set of keys when it was time to go home. They ranted and riffed and searched high and low, but with no success. As it turned out, they'd left them in the cafeteria bathroom, but so sorry.

She said he'd never worked there again.

They had been surprisingly easy to pinch. All I'd had to do was walk past Nellie and mumble something, and the giant was on her feet and in my face before anyone had a chance to react. Trying to break up the resultant shoving match, it had been easy for Harkness to pluck the ring from the clip Lo kept on his belt. Chapman had hemmed and hawed at me before I went to bed early, but Harkness had slipped quietly back to her video game with no one the wiser. Lo wasn't likely to admit that he'd lost them. How we could get them back to him was another story, but it would have to wait.

The wind is an audible howl as we creep beneath the stars. Elms and firs shake with applause as we inch our way along the fence, the other buildings as indistinct as ghosts. The orange sodium lights float like will-o-wisps in the distance, and I'm faintly reassured. Anyone walking down the Mississip has zero chance of seeing past their glow to where we skulk along against the wall.

Something makes me turn and look. The abandoned lodge squats across the walkway like a tomb. A prickle of gooseflesh races up my arm, and Harkness hisses at me to get moving.

The delicious feel of danger begins to wash over me as we pass the last of the buildings and trace the fence across the field. The smell of burning leaves and turning trees is pungent, and damp grass sticks to my shoes as we squelch along the wet earth towards the gym. I want to bolt across the open space, to peel off from the perimeter and hurtle headlong towards the abyss, but it's not that late. There are still too many eyes.

I can see the flicker of lights in the Toddlers Lodge as the staff bustle through their nightly chores. At any moment, someone might decide to take the trash out or go restock supplies and step out onto the 'Sip, and how well hidden we are is certainly up for debate. It curdles some of the excitement and leaves me wondering how I thought we'd get away with this.

It's far too late for second thoughts.

As we stay folded to the fence, hitting the far corner and turning east beneath the canopy of pines, time wavers still. It's dark behind them, a secret hollow hidden from the world, and Harkness turns to me with a questioning look.

—we're all down here in the dark together—

Beyond us, the gymnasium rests like a sleeping giant, and I nod and take the lead. I can barely see my hand in front of my face, and in a dozen steps I almost turn my ankle on the granddaddy of all pinecones. Harkness stifles a giggle with the back of her hand.

What else is out here?

Past the knot in my stomach, a real question begins to raise its head. How many other irregulars could Everbrook host? And if Phoebe was never really here, how could you hurt her?

How does something that's not real to begin with die?

In the looming darkness of the gymnasium, the night has taken on a more sinister tone. The row of empty windows along the high wall glare back like soulless eyes, as if it's merely playing possum.

Harkness slips her hand into mine. Her eyes are wide and trembling. "I didn't think this old thing would give me the creeps."

"We're almost there," I say with a confidence I don't feel. We part from the wall in a suicide leap and head straight for the double doors. It's thirty yards that feel like forever before we're beneath the shadowed alcove and Harkness fumbles out the keys.

It takes a long time for her to find the right one.

The doors are well-maintained, opening with nary a squawk or screech, and we're inside.

The foyer to the gymnasium is black except for a pinch of starlight that pushes its way in through the reinforced glass. The meeting room on the south side is dark, the rest of the chamber a throat leading to the belly of the beast.

I've been in the meeting room before, the site of once-a-week church groups or arts-and-crafts showdowns. It's a rectangle with folding chairs, card tables, and a dry-erase board. Despite the locked doors at the end of it, the room doesn't interest me much, but it now looks far more inviting than the void where the court should be, an emptiness so thick you can cut it.

Harkness squeezes my hand. I hadn't realized we were touching until now. "Are we really doing this?" she asks.

I nod, then realize that she probably can't see it. "We'll be in just as much trouble turning back as we will pushing forward."

She nods, a shadow in a grove of them, and I pull a little LED light out of my pocket, the product of my Hangman championship two weeks ago with a youth group whose name I can't remember. It's a tiny round thing the size of my pinky. To call it a flashlight would be giving it far too much credit, but its feeble glow is nonetheless reassuring.

At least, until we step into the gym.

Passing through is like stepping onto the floor of some great ocean. The walls and ceiling are too far away to make out in the impenetrable darkness, and we're left with only the thick sound of our footsteps on the scuffed hardwood, echoing back to us as if across some illimitable gulf. I almost bowl into an iron rack, filled with deflated basketballs like rotten fruit. To my left I can just make out the short row of bleachers. To my right is emptiness.

I know somewhere inside it is the stage.

As if on cue I hear a faint melody, soft at first but picking up steam.

We move as if our eyes have been sewn shut. I can barely see the floor, and in the darkness it would be horrible to turn an ankle on some forgotten children's toy or old ball.

Somewhere out in the gulf are the double doors that lead deeper into the building, and on the other side the little tunnel that supposedly leads to freedom. It's a palpable tug to just run, slip across the river into Washington or the sands into Idaho, pick a new name and hide where even the Man couldn't find me, but it's a childish comfort. There are fingerprints and facial recognition software, DNA tests and drones.

The only places I could run to are places I could never stay, but the thought still warms my belly as I stick to the left and move slowly towards the double doors.

We're at half court when I hear it. A slow, steady draw of metal rings scraping across an iron bar. It's so alien that at first I can't place it, and then goosebumps sprout across my skin.

Someone is by the stage, drawing back the curtain.

Harkness stares into nothing. I squeeze her hand. Her eyes are as big as saucers. "Prose, there's somebody—"

"I know," I say, thinking of how much we must stand out with our little light, anglers on the floor of an ocean. *Here we are, making it easy since 1999.* My fingers press the little button, and then there's nothing, the two of us floating limply between the stars. I wait long moments for my eyes to adjust before concluding that they never will.

We stay there for what seems like hours, feet rooted to the boards as something moves in the darkness by the stage. Harkness' breaths are shallow, rapid things. Mine aren't much better, and I pull her towards where I think the doors should be. She resists for only an instant, but then follows like a wanton child on their way to school.

Time dwindles and becomes elastic. Her hand is warm, almost feverishly hot against mine. Countless times I jab the empty space ahead with my foot before setting it down. My free hand cuts the air before me again and again, like I'm trying to wave down help after a horrible accident.

It feels like an eternity of awkward motion.

Wave, step, repeat.

Wave, step, repeat.

All the while waiting for a cold hand to drape itself across my shoulders. It's hard not to simply bolt headlong into the darkness, racing into the sweet, certain oblivion that would come with plunging face first into the cinderblock walls. I think back to that other darkness, that other hall, that dead purple light seeping out beneath the cracks in the world.

What happened to Rachel in the mute spaces between?

My heart lunges as if a wild animal has found its way into my chest.

Harkness' grip is slowly grinding my bones together as the melody grows nearer. A mantra is being chanted right behind me in whispers that I can't quite make out.

Senses removed, it dawns on me.

Harkness heard it. *If not the song, then the curtain. What does that me—*

Fingers connect with splintery wood rather than stuccoed blocks. For half a second, I think it's an illusion, and then I fumble for the cold iron handle of the door.

"Keys. Hurry," I say, as if two inches of contracted wood is a bank vault against whatever's acting out in the void of the gymnasium.

I don't have to say it twice. She's next to me in an instant, grappling with the key ring, and I feel a warmth as the blood floods back into my hand. There's a metallic scratching that goes on for far too long, and then the old door swings open and we fall inside.

The heavy thud when it closes seems to shake the walls. There is no light in here, not even from the state mandated exit signs, and I reluctantly tug out the LED again. I click it on, and the weak nimbus it produces reminds me Bilbo and Sting. From the faint light, I can just make out a wide hallway, doors branching off of it on either side as far as I can see, and a swarm of shivers start at my spine and radiate upwards. The parallel between this and the dead space is uncanny.

Harkness starts off ahead of me. It's clear she's never come back here, either, and she tries the first door she sees. To the left of us is an old bulletin board, the cork kind you can stick pushpins in, and flapping in the dark are the yellowed ribbons of old fliers, their print faded to barely legible. They look like the fingers of some dark god, and I follow Harkness into the first room.

It's covered floor-to-ceiling in tile, and the rows of lockers bolted to one side remove any guessing as to the room's purpose. Two alcoves for group showers split off from the near wall, and another locked door sits at the far end of the room. In the center of the room are cardboard boxes, a massive stack four or five feet high. The showers are full of them too, and Harkness steps towards the stack with an eerie reverence. A patina of dust rests on every surface.

"What do you think's inside?" she whispers, her fingers playing along the cardboard. I shake my head, but she's already taken the keyring and slit through the tape.

"Someone'll know we were here," I say, but she shakes her head right back.

"If they ever come back here, all they'll find is this," she says, and draws back the flap.

Stacked neatly from top to bottom are boxes of Tide, the little baby-sized ones good for one or two loads. Harkness picks one up, shakes it, and sets it neatly back into its slot. "Exhibit A," she murmurs.

Before I can say anything, she's cutting through the tape on another. It's filled with miniature bottles of body wash, familiar because I've used one every night since I've been here. She slides over to a third, and I stop her. "It's just donations, Hark. They're using the space for overflow."

Her eyes are wide in the little nimbus of light. She's looking at the alcove where the group showers would have been. The flickering shadows are surely a product of the strange reflections and the dancing LED, but it's enough add a sense of urgency.

The next door is a spur to an adjoining locker room that mirrors the first. His and Hers, probably. Another leads into an abandoned office filled with old toys, another to a janitor's closet home to at least eight breeds of spider native only to Oregon. Harkness gives this one a grimace and locks it tightly shut behind us before wrenching open the next.

This door opens onto another office. File cabinets line both walls, a lone desk standing sentinel between them. Plastic flowers and a nameplate teeter on the edge, in danger of being jounced to their deaths by a stack of cardboard boxes reaching almost to the ceiling. Years and alphabetized groups are marked on their sides in black sharpie, and it wouldn't take Holmes to deduce where the file overflow room is. Harkness slips inside and ignores the deep cake of dust and cobwebs to begin rummaging through the drawers. I prop the door open with the nearest box and follow, my stomach starting to twist into knots. Something is wrong here and wants us to know it.

My fingers trace a pattern in the dirty surface of the desk as Harkness shoves aside papers and office supplies. Eyeing the boxes, my heart begins to sink. So much information at my fingertips, but where to begin? What to look for? I feel like I'm on the precipice of a revelation that I can't quite scale. Tracing along the years, I think of old movies I'd watch on the sofa downstairs, sneaking down in the middle of the night to watch masked killers stalk coeds and ghosts fling sharp objects at the unsuspecting. They'd always find a newspaper clipping or a file, some missing piece of the exposition that would give them the origin of the mystery. *Starfish Girl, died in 1973. Mauled by kittens and teased to death, it seems. Look, here's a picture!* Instead I'm staring at half a ton of poorly organized ditto paper and trying to bury the urge to bolt back to the Lodge before somebody comes looking for us.

Harkness finds what she's looking for as I slip an expensive looking pen into my pocket from a cup of them. What's a journey without a souvenir, right? She waves a half-full pint of Elijah Craig at me triumphantly, pulled from some unknown recess, and grins. "Someone's been getting naughty on break-time. I knew this couldn't all be detergent and baby wipes."

Uncapping it, she takes a deep swig, her cheeks reddening in the blue light, and wipes her mouth with the back of her hand. She stretches her arm to hand it to me and raises an eyebrow at my hesitation. I shake my head. *Breaking and entering, stealing, drinking hooch. If we start making out the guy with the machete will be here in no time.* "Come on, Prose. When are you going to get this chance again?" Her smile is electric. "Drink to sisterhood."

I roll my eyes but nod all the same. The bourbon is sweet and hot, burning a trail to curl sullenly at my core. I manage not to sputter wildly. Harkness sneaks another sip and then tucks it away, pushing the drawers shut behind her. There's a moment when her eyes meet mine, a question, and then we're back in the dim hallway, the door swinging shut behind us.

At the click of the latch, I hear something faint, almost imperceptible. Before I can tie it down Harkness is trying our key in the second to last door on the left. She wrestles with the knob and then we're inside. It's not what I expected.

We're in a broad room with a rubber floor. Our light gets magnified, reflected by the wall-length mirrors lining the walls. There are stacks of boxes, sure, but along the floor lie old toys and children's books, yellowed and stained.

There's a slight rise on the far side of the room, separated by a baby gate. Harkness walks towards it before I can grab her arm. Something's wrong with the mirrors. Something's wrong with our reflections, but she doesn't notice. Her eyes are focused on the far end of the room.

"Hello?" she whispers. I can't see what she sees, only the funhouse way her reflection seems to twitch and stretch beyond her. I step over a stack of plastic rings and try to pierce the darkness, but the far side of the room is impenetrable, the abyssal night between the stars. When Harkness whispers again, it seems very far away. "Hello?"

"Harkness." A chill whips its way across my shoulders, freezing fingers. "Leave it alone."

The words surprise me. I'm not sure what *it* is, or what I think she'll find, only that it feels like a very bad idea to keep going. Everbrook is a place of secrets, and like any some of them shouldn't be stirred up.

She glances over her shoulder and almost trips over a plush dinosaur, eyes gone dusty in the gloom. "There's someone back there."

I squint, trying to see over the baby gate. My legs feel rooted to the spot, but Harkness keeps winding through the central stacks, Theseus without the string. Out of the corner of my eye I catch it, some shadow moving against the greater black. Feet squelching against the foam rubber floor, I start after her. "Nobody should be back there, Harkness."

"Shhh." Three-quarters of the way there, she never turns. In the faint glow her breath is a misty halo.

Harkness places her hand on the railing at the other side of the room. Hurrying past cardboard stacks and over old toys, I can make out the rotting tops of cubbies, a pair of doors hanging precariously from a cupboard. But then the darkness begins to coalesce, not fleeing the light but facing it, almost drowning it. I imagine the melody a moment before I hear it.

—*da da duh de da*—

I can't tell what she sees, only that it must be very bad, very bad indeed, because she just starts screaming, any vestiges of her hard exterior torn apart. She flops back, lands on her ass, and begins to scoot across the foam rubber. A bubble-pop lawnmower snaps beneath one hand.

Beyond the baby gate it slips from the ceiling, landing on what passes for feet with liquid boneless grace, black as the space between howling stars. It tips me an obscene yellow wink before it comes.

My mind is awash with panic, but somehow I rush to Harkness. Her hand is bleeding against my shirt as I slip both hands under her arms and yank, feeling something shriek in my back that I'll worry about later. For a second we teeter on the brink of collapse, and then her Chuck Taylors find purchase on the rubber and we're bolting past the mirrors, the boxes, neither one of us looking back.

Tripping over a plastic table full of blocks, I sprawl hard, thankful for once of the foam rubber. Scrambling to my feet, I see it already halfway across the room, a floating nightmare reflected to infinity before Harkness throws open the door and yanks me out into the hallway.

We turn towards the gym before my hand finds her shoulder. Something is pressed against the glass, too smudged to make out. My mind traipses back to the purple city, that space between the spaces, and have just enough time to think *We're trapped* before instinct kicks in and I'm pulling Harkness in the opposite direction, towards the big stairs at the far end. Her eyes are wide and white.

The hallway seems to have grown darker as we stumble against the heavy doors at the opposite end. Nothing budges.

Under the burned-out sign of the emergency exit, some genius has wrapped a padlocked chain through the handles.

There's a door next to it, locked as well. I pull Harkness towards the stairs. Our footsteps thunder against the bare wood as we reach the landing and keep going, rushing up the steps before slamming against the solid door at the top.

I whisper for Harkness to hurry, and it seems to break her out of a trance. She fumbles through the ring. Beyond the glow of the LED, shadows entwine and thicken below us.

Something dark moves at the foot of the staircase.

There's a scrape of metal on metal, and Harkness yanks me through the yawning doorway. We slip past stucco into an empty room and immediately try to seal the door behind us. Heavy and thick, it feels like it should belong on a battleship, but eventually it thuds into the jamb.

Soft footsteps slither outside, so faintly that I'm not sure if it's my imagination. I hold the LED up like I'm offering it to the night, and my breath catches.

The room stretches back and away across the length of the gym, a massive attic split evenly down the middle by a series of shelves placed back to back. The object nearest us is a standing metal cabinet adjoining a large desk, the kind you'd find in a public school that had started to run out of special bequeathments.

What's on the shelves can wait, because I'm already shoving my back against the metal cabinet, pushing with every ounce of muscle I have. It shifts with a metallic groan against the bare floor, and I can imagine the grooves I'm tearing into the linoleum, but that doesn't matter now.

Harkness sees me and puts her weight behind mine, and in under half a minute the cabinet is braced against the door. I hear the door jostling as someone tests its strength, but I'm already behind the desk and forcing it onto the barricade. Harkness slides in next to me like a forgotten twin, and we give it a heave that sends it grating towards the cabinet. A rusty leg snaps off, sending a corner crashing to the ground. Drawers yawn open madly, but a final push hammers the desk into the cabinet. I wipe my brow with one hand, my balance gone, and Harkness catches me before I can fall.

"I don't know how we're getting out of here," she says, "but at least this is Disneyland."

I look at the shelves for the first time in the faint glow of the LED. They must stretch all the way back to over the gym, but it's what's on them that gives me pause. There are hundreds, maybe thousands of children's toys adorning the cases, piled high like a store stockroom. On top of that there are hygiene products, art supplies, batteries, comic books, canvas bags, heaps and heaps of goods going all the way back past over the gym. I take a step towards them, jaw agape, not too jaded to marvel at the vast stores in front of me. Harkness is already rushing ahead, out of the light, and I think of some fairy story, some supernatural ruse to ensnare the unwary, but even the pounding at the door behind me doesn't deter the wonder of this treasure hidden atop a lonesome building in the middle of an institution. I start forward, only to have my foot catch on the rusty track of the fallen drawer.

Glancing down, I forget completely about the toys, the wonder, the possibilities.

A numb horror fills the pit of my stomach and radiates outward. Muted voices struggle outside the door, but they seem millions of miles away as I kneel and scoop up the first item that's spilled out onto the floor.

Dangling from their chain, I find Vanessa's dog tags.

CHAPTER TEN

TEACHING LEVEL

The setting sun had turned the horizon blood red on the afternoon that he finally found me.

We'd been in the farmhouse a while by then, sometime after I started getting glimpses of the city of dead light and after Berriman. I had taken too long at the library, staying away from home as long as possible, and having gotten immersed in Machen or Blackwood or one of the other weird minds that blazed along the turn of the nineteenth century, was straggling home along the country road at a much later hour than I should have.

My father had been in a mood, revising the third draft of *Breathing Deep* and punctuating breakthroughs with the crash of flying objects against the office wall, and so it had seemed best to get out and escape into a world even stranger than mine. Walking back along the low wooden fence at the side of the road, watching the leaves whip through the tall grass, I began to wonder if finishing the book would calm him down, at least for a while.

If I'd been paying attention, the silence would have worried me. Sometimes even the world around you holds its breath.

I'd cut through the field behind the elementary school and across the little bridged creek to a side street that was a testament to Machiavellian city planning. One of the first things I'd done since we'd moved was map out any number of alternate routes between the library and the farmhouse, sorting them out for speed and efficiency. Staying on the main road meant ascending a series of suburban blocks and plunging back down along a wide, sweeping curved before I'd even reach the farmhouse. This route was decidedly more direct by swinging me past a number of Christmas tree lots to a forest trail to the rural road. It was quiet, secluded, and parts of it were straight out of high fantasy, Lothlorien or Winterfell.

Away from all the people, it was easier to think, even easier to lose myself.

My fingers played connect-the-dots along the bruises on my arm as I made my way down the shoulder. They had morphed into a fascinating yellowish-green, and I kept gingerly poking at them. I wasn't sure what I would say to Rachel if she noticed. My father never would.

Novels were tough on him, and tougher on us, but his agent was convinced that the current one was lightning in a bottle, sure to put him over the hump, and his dedication to it bordered on obsession. I thought fleetingly back to Mom and the old house, how Dad used to smile like the world was clapping him on the back when we all sat down together. I wondered if those times would come again, superimposing Rachel into Mom's place in the picture.

I hated myself for it.

From one of the sporadic lampposts, a crow cawed. My head snapped up. A shimmer of dust blew across the asphalt and sent the pines and firs sighing, but there was something thick in the shadows below the boughs. The gravel crunched against the asphalt behind me.

A truck was sitting halfway off the road, a dark, rotting green. Dull streaks of rust dotted its side like dried blood, and it stank of diesel and exhaust. An icy tingle crept from my tailbone all the way to my fingers.

A squat round man leaned out of the driver's side, his jaw patchy with beard but otherwise bald. He had on huge round glasses that distorted his eyes, and there was something unnerving about the way he was looking at me, like he was measuring components for some chemical experiment.

His smile was a wide sliver of teeth, astonishingly white in the fading light. "Good evening, miss."

I stared at him dully, waiting for the feeling to come back to my toes. He looked up and down the street. The wind picked up. "I'm not from around here," he began.

The same crow cawed again.

"The main road's back that way," I heard myself say, and pointed with a hand that felt like it was full of balloons.

He nodded as if that was how it should be and reached across the dashboard. "Thing is, I'm trying to find my way to Oregon City, and I got all turned around going down that big hill and past that antique store with the crazy windows. This is supposed to be a shortcut through to the highway, but I've got no idea what hill I'm on now. Street, I mean."

"Juliani," I said, feeling like I was being drug through a play in which I'd forgotten all my lines. "This is Juliani."

He nodded again and unfurled a giant road map against the wheel, the kind you could get at a gas station for eight bucks. It struck me as odd, like some kind of cloak. We were in the boonies, but it wasn't *that* boonie. He should have been able to get bars.

The man rubbed a big hand across his bald pate. "Could you show me? I'm terrible with directions."

I'd really only heard the first part, *I'm terrible,* and my feet found their strength again. "Just head that way and go right. It'll take you back to Foster."

"Could you show me?" He flashed me an embarrassed, aw-shucks smile and raised the map again. The sun was lower, sending red streaks across the orange sky, and the shadows were beginning to lengthen. "I really don't want to get lost out here."

"You'll manage."

Your imagination's running away with you.

These serpentine roads cut through forests and hills, farms and buttes. Thick patches of forest removed the sky in places, and there was more than one abandoned road or house squatting in the thick of it. It was easy to get turned around on the back roads, and I'd gotten lost plenty when we'd first moved. If all he needed was a couple of directions, it didn't seem like much, no matter what my paranoid heart had to say about it.

Impossibly, I had taken a step towards him before I saw how he was holding the map. One hand bunched at the upper corner, draping the length of him all the way below the wheel. The other hand was nowhere to be found.

A knot was forming in my throat, and it was my turn to look both ways.

No cars.

No people.

"I really have to get home." But my feet didn't move, and I realized that getting back to the farmhouse meant turning my back on him.

"Why do you have to be like that?" the man said. His cheeks drooped in a comical pout. "Aren't you a nice girl?"

"No," I said, and started walking. "You'll be okay."

I heard his door open behind me, the screech of old hinges. The crow cawed again, and I heard a grunt as he rose out of the truck. I looked over my shoulder to see him huge against the road, bigger than I expected. One fist was still wrapped in colored paper that rippled in the wind.

"Don't be like that," he said, and took a step forward. "Maybe I can give you a ride."

"I said I have to get home." This was bad, stranger danger bad, and I flew through my options with a cold, analytical precision, my body a million miles away. There was already too little distance between us. If I fled, he might just get back in the truck and run me down. Leaving the road for the woods or the field of trees meant abandoning all hope of passerby, and while big, outrunning him wouldn't be a gimme.

If he caught me, there would be no one to see. No one to help. "Get out of here."

It was a crazy thing to say, but crazier still was the smile it brought him. The map still wrapped around his fist. "Why don't you let me give you a ride?"

"That's my house, right over there." Gesturing vaguely over my shoulder, I didn't stop to see if he looked, but coiled, an instant from bolting.

He made a weird clicking sound with his tongue, and then the map was knifed away by the breeze. Where it had been was a small insectoid box, like some undiscovered species of beetle. It took me a moment to realize that it was a gun. "Get back here. Or I'll put two in your little kneecaps."

I froze. What I knew about pistols was precious little outside of hard-boiled detectives and westerns, but I had no reason to doubt that he could do it.

No one would see. No one would know. And he'd do it again. *There's no reason to think this is his first rodeo, darlin'.*

The voice I hadn't heard in forever. Outrage churned inside me at the sick cruelty of a universe that could let you be reading *The Willows* in the library thirty minutes ago and dead in a ditch the next. My shattered corpse was all I could picture, a gory reflection, ants in my hair, blood in my eyes, and my father turning the thing over, losing another girl, losing his mind. I was sad and sick and furious.

"Fuck you!" I shouted for maybe the third time in my entire life. My hands balled into fists. "Who the fuck do you think you are?"

Grimacing at the sound, his eyes flicked sideways as he took a step towards me. Madly, fists clenched, I somehow took one towards him.

The look on my face made him pause, just for a second. Then the black shadow burst from the woods and flew into him, tossing him up and into the truck's door with a burst of motion I barely had time to register. The pistol went off, thunder echoing through the low hills before the stranger hit the pavement with a meaty thump that seemed to shake the road. The pistol went skittering into the grass.

The stranger pushed himself to his elbows before he was thrown into the air again, harder. This time I heard metal crunch, glass crash. There was a dodgeball-sized dent in the door as the stranger struggled to his knees. Glass shone from his cheeks in embedded flecks, blood streaming down his face in the sunset.

Marmalade tilted his hat and delivered a kick to the stranger that sent him hurtling into the wheel well. The sound it made was like a bell. The Man's grey eyes seemed to burn in his haggard face as he appraised me for a moment, then he snarled and kicked the stranger again. "Run home, little raven. Run home and forget about this."

I couldn't say anything. This wasn't any reunion I'd ever dreamt of, but then he swept up the larger man by the lapels of his overcoat. The stranger's face was now misshapen, reds and scarlets streaking wild colors through his beard. The frame of the oversized glasses had buried itself in his cheek.

The Man didn't seem to feel the stranger clawing at him, trying to scrabble free. His wide hat was a black halo as he pulled the stranger closer. The driver gibbered, wild words, threats and apologies as Marmalade embraced him tight. Something inside the larger man popped like a knot of cordwood burning, and then another. He screamed, high and girlish.

Marmalade looked back at me. "Go."

Something else exploded inside the stranger, folded, and a gout of something dark ran from his mouth and down his chin. My feet stumbled, tentative steps, a disjointed jog. He might have said something else, but then the stranger was a siren as he was pulled closer, closer, and I could look no more. There was a sound like branches breaking, one after the other, and then I bolted, an echo following me the whole mile home.

I told myself that it hadn't been laughter.

The light is streaking through dirty slats as I wake, casting late morning shadows along the Beige Universe. My head hurts and my throat feels scoured. When I look around, the room is bare except for a single change of clothes on the top shelf of the cabinet. I suppose it's a new consequence, and I groan. Something cold and metallic rises with my chest. Pulling it forward on its chain, I think of Vanessa, and it all comes struggling back to me.

Eventually they had gotten enough manpower together to shove the desk and cabinet away. There had been nowhere left to go in that little treasure trove of riches at the top of the gym, but for all I know it was a rescue. I'm sure Sinatra could have found another way in, the black jelly seeping up through the floor or slithering down through a crack in the shingles. Maybe I should be thankful they found us when they did.

What spilled out onto the floor kills any gratitude. Vanessa's dog tags. Rings. Pendants. A bracelet or two, silver or gold or steel, in different sizes and shapes. One I recognized from dangling around Alisha's wrist an eternity ago. There must have been two dozen in all, and I'd slipped the tags around my neck as the door burst open, Chapman throwing himself into the room, half a dozen bodies stumbling in behind him.

I crack open my door to find him perched in a molded plastic chair, directly across from the door. He looks hungry as he raises his eyes to mine. I say the only thing I can think of. "Sorry about last night."

"Not as sorry as you're going to be," he grumbles. He catches the eye of someone I can't see and gestures towards the kitchen. "Can you get her majesty the royal breakfast?"

"Where's my stuff?" I ask, fearing that I already know the answer.

He doesn't respond, but hands me a roughly stapled packet of paper and a number two pencil. "Schoolwork. Do it by shift change to get credit."

"Okay," I agree, not clear on what's going on but sure that it's not going to win any awards. "My stuff?"

"It's being looked through for contraband."

"Searched?"

"We aren't trained to search. We're trained to look for contraband."

I roll my eyes, but he continues. "You can earn it back as we go. You have no idea how serious what you pulled last night was. Stealing someone's keys. Rifling through the gym. Trying to run. None of it's going to help you."

The last doesn't quite compute, but I'm not going to say so. Was there really a way through the gym that passed outside the fence? Was that what the little door in the corner was for? "I'm sorry."

He nods as if this is how it should be. "You and your co-conspirator will be given one on one supervision until such time as the clinicians choose to take you off of it. You will remain on intensive teaching level for three days. Passing each shift depends on following all the rules, modeling pro-social behaviors, and completing behavioral packets. During this time you will have zero contact with any of the other residents of IG or each other. Failure to follow any of these rules means you will automatically fail and begin the whole cycle again. Do you understand?"

There is a light in his eyes I don't like. More than any rule I had broken, something I'd done had offended him. My thoughts drift to that drawer in the attic, the cheap keepsakes that came spilling out. He takes my silence as moody consent. "Good. Monique's heating up your breakfast."

His eyes shift sideways in a gesture I'm becoming all too familiar with as he leans forward. "You're skating on really thin ice right now, kid. There's already talk of kicking you out to juvie, and when you start trying to take our other clients down with you—" He shakes his head, a toad readying its tongue. "Everything you do here goes to the cops. It won't take much to get you behind bars while they're deciding what to do with you. Understand that. If you think it's bad here, if you hate it so much, you haven't the slightest idea of what goes on in juvenile detention. You need to show them you're a model, *model* citizen or you'll be fighting the bangers and crazies in your sleep."

I nod and try to close the door. His hand reaches out and seizes my wrist. I'm shocked into silence, more by the line he's crossing than his touch. "One more thing," he hisses, low and venomous. "People lose their jobs over things like the shit you pulled. People with families. People with kids of their own. If you can think about anybody but your precious little self for a minute, think about how much trouble you got Lo in. We're people too. And we don't forget."

He releases my hand and I hurry behind the door, slamming it harder than I'd meant to. *Is he responsible? Does he know?* But I'm not sure what the drawer means, why anyone's things had been there in the first place.

I creak the door open a crack. "Chapman?"

"What?"

"Why are there bags and bags of people's things up in the attic?"

He's quiet for a moment, as if mulling it over. "Get to work."

The door closes in front of me. I take a breath, then push it back open.

"Chapman?"

"No contact means me too."

"That's ridiculous."

The door's closing when he reaches for a clipboard. "One more thing."

"My manacles are in the mail?"

Chapman's eyes meet mine, the color of raw earth, and I don't like what I see there. "What does the name Phoebe mean to you?"

"What?" I put on my best innocent smile as my heart races. It does nothing but crease his brow.

"Phoebe. I didn't get a last name."

"Who?"

"Who told me? Doesn't matter. Who is she?" He shrugs.

My poker face must be atrocious because he shakes his head. "We're trying to help you get better, Prose. Keeping secrets doesn't help anyone."

"Agreed." The idea springs before I know it. "So why don't we trade? I'll tell you my secret if you tell me why those bags are in the attic."

"Really?" He grimaces, fingers doing a brief dance on the clipboard. "Fine. When people run, it tends to be with whatever they can carry. The rest of their stuff gets bagged and stored for when they come back."

"When they come back?"

"I admit it's been a bit of a dry spell lately, but they all get caught. Eventually. When they do, they get sent right back here if they don't wind up in juvie." He gestures down the hallway. "Believe it. I've known Harkness since she was twelve."

"Eleven!" calls a voice from the far end of the hall.

Chapman stares furiously for a moment at a spot in the ceiling. "Your turn."

I take a deep breath. Somewhere in my scramble for a convincing story I end up with the truth. "Phoebe was my roommate when I first got here."

"What?"

"She was my friend. She left a while ago." Which is partially true.

—don't think about the red ruin of her face, what happened to her—

The tears well up in my eyes unbidden, and his face relaxes, the scowl gone. For the first time, there's something different in his eyes, and the pity is somehow worse. "Kid, you're a potential danger to yourself and others. We would never give you a roommate."

I finish breakfast with a plastic fork and the door shut. The hash browns are soggy and the eggs scalding, but since I don't want to think I devour everything before starting in on my packets, behavioral first and the schoolwork second. Both are patronizing, remedial at a kindergarten level. I can only hope that they didn't pay good money for them.

As untethered as my head feels, though, answering the questions of a pedantic five-year-old helps to put things back into focus. Before long, the whole room smells of graphite and copy paper, and I'm answering essay questions with aplomb as I try to avoid the only thing that really matters right now. There's something broken inside of me, and I'm not sure if any of it will really help.

I read once that the first indicator of insanity is simply asking yourself if you're crazy; once the question comes up, it's already been answered. While I'm not sure if that's true, I've got enough unanswered questions right now to fill a coffin, and time isn't on my side.

Sighing, I tear the back page off of the behavioral packet, confident that it won't be missed, and begin to write as objectively as I can. Contemplations of a hundred times before, I try to connect the dots and know that it's probably fruitless.

I wish Phoebe were here.

If she was just a hallucination, what does what happened to her mean? If she were an irregular, she could be hurt, maimed, torn apart. Somehow that's existentially worse, and *can I use that?* Fingers drumming along, I scribble down scenarios and try to support them.

Scenario One: The Irregulars are ghosts.

-Supporting: No one else seems to see them.

-They dress all funky.

-A lot of them seem to hang out in the same place constantly.

-Contrary: Other people see ghosts. Some constantly.

-Distinct lack of horror movie behavior, chains rattling, direct haunting, et al.

-Defined personalities and actions, not just booing at me.

Scenario Two: The Irregulars are a product of your sick mind, Prose.

-Supporting: See funky dress, invisibility, lurking.

-Violent fantasy, product of early childhood trauma.

-A sick girl, lonely and looking for friends, who's best childhood friend is a sociopath in a black hat.

-A sick girl who reads too much, wants to be special, feel unique.

-Occam's Razor cuts deep.

-Contrary: What about your uncle?

-Hell, what about what happened to the man on the side of the road? Your father?

Scenario Three: It's a conspiracy, and people pretend not to see the Irregulars.

-Supporting: See funky dress: costumes?

-Not invisible.

-Motivation's a big question.

-So's coordination.

-Contrary: This is stupid.

Scenario Four: The Irregulars are something else.

-Supporting: See funky dress, invisibility, lurking.

-Have own agency and motivations. Some follow. Some go away and don't come back.

-Can be hurt? Killed?
-Some hurt.
-Some kill.

There's a low knock on the door, and I slip over to the door with as much silence as I can muster.

Graham's taken up residence in the plastic chair. The grin alone makes me want to hug him, and it hits me how much has happened since that wild night at the movies. "Morning, runaway."

"Shut up." I say, risking a glance down the hallway. Chapman's nowhere to be seen, but Sandy's position mirrors his at the far end. *Harkness.* "Where have you been?"

His eyes cloud for a moment at that. "Been working in other lodges. Rotating around."

I think back to our less than stellar reception at Control, at some of the things Monique had hinted at. "We didn't get you into trouble, did we?"

Graham waves a hand. "Just office politics. How have you been?"

"Exploring." I hand him the first two packets, minus the back page, and feel another smile when he initials the covers and shoves them under his chair without bothering to check.

"Besides that." He grabs a bottle of water from under the chair and hands it off to me. I could walk over to the fountain in the by the bathroom at any time, but it's a nice gesture. It's cool and I take a half of it in one long swallow. "There's talk, Prose. Of sending you out of here. Putting you away from the other girls. What were you guys thinking?"

It's hard to explain, even to myself. "We weren't trying to run. We just were looking to see if any of the stories about the gym are true. That there's a tunnel out."

He starts to say something, then stops. "Whoever gave you that idea?"

It's my turn to cover up. "Fire code. There's got to be some kind of emergency exit, or we'd all burn to death."

"So you were looking for a way to run away, without actually planning to run away?"

"Exactly." There's an earnestness in his eyes, a hint of laughter, and I come out with the rest of it. "We found something else, too."

"Yeah?" When I hesitate, he spreads his hands. "I've never even been back there. Never had the occasion to go exploring. You tell me."

"There's all sorts of supplies back there, old rooms that don't ever seem to be touched." The resident monstrosity, I think, seems like a good thing to omit. "Full of soap or detergent or whatever, and there's a massive hall upstairs full of games and books and action figures—"

"Toys in the attic?" he asks. His grin is infectious.

"Shut up. The point is that there are piles of bags with people's names on them."

"Really?" he asks.

"Chapman told me they belong to the kids who ran." I give him my best raised eyebrow.

"Everything gets bagged and tagged." He takes a minute and mulls it over. "I guess it has to get put somewhere."

"Right," I say, and reach to the chain around my neck. I take a breath and pull out the dog tags. "But there's a whole drawer of stuff that people wouldn't leave."

He stares at me blankly.

"These are Vanessa's," I say, and raise it out for further inspection. "She wouldn't have run without them."

Though maybe she would. Maybe you're jumping at a lot of shadows, Prose. Maybe you want the world to be a story so bad you're raising conspiracies where there are none.

Graham eyes the item, reaches out and turns it. "It looks familiar. But people forget all sorts of things when they run, Prose. Whether they're meeting someone, trying to get high, or on their way to Vegas, they're generally not super calm when they do it."

"Then why aren't these labeled?"

He pauses, then spreads his hands again. The smile's back. "Maybe they got dropped somewhere on campus. Maybe your drawer is a lost and found for valuables."

I sigh. What deep secret did I think a drawer full of baubles really held? "Maybe."

"Yeah," he says, then holds out a hand. "If those really are hers, maybe I should get them back. I can put them with the rest of her stuff."

"I'm going to hold on to them for a while," I say, unaware of it until the words come out. "I'll get them back to you when I'm ready."

The hand doesn't go anywhere.

I try again. "Please. We were friends. It makes me feel like part of her's with me right now."

Graham frowns but nods. "Let me know when you're ready."

I'm ready to close the door when I think of it. "Graham, can you go look?"

"Look at what?"

"Up in the attic. They were all in the bottom drawer of the desk unless someone moved them." *Chapman*, I think but do not say. "All little trinkets, personal things. There must have been twenty, at least. Can you go look?"

He sits back. "Prose—"

"You've all got keys. Pretty please. I wouldn't ask if—if it didn't feel like something weird is going on."

"Like what?" Graham seems both defensive and mildly confused. "What do you think it means?"

"No idea." It's true, at least that part of it. Synapses are stretching, trying to find each other and coalesce. I almost tell him about the note I found when I changed rooms, but what would be the point?

Meet me at midnight. You know where.

"People run, but never call. Never check in with their friends, even though they can. Never get caught and come back. And somehow they all forget something important, and it all ends up in a drawer—"

What are you saying? That there's some serial killer hiding trophies over the gym?

Please, but that's not that far off.

What if Sinatra's why people are disappearing?

What would it have done if it had caught us?

I shake my head. "It was dark and loud and crazy. Maybe I didn't see what I thought I did. Maybe the tags are it. But I need to know." My eyes are wet again, and I'm furious with myself. "I need to know if I'm going crazy—"

"Okay," he says, and starts forward like he's going to hug me before he thinks better of it. "If this means so much to you, I can go up there after shift and look. But I'm promising nothing, okay?"

"Thank you."

"Get some rest and make sense of it later, okay? I'll let you know."

It's a full day of isolation and packets before Svara's next visit. In the hallway, he looks like he's lost weight but gained more color. It stretches him, makes him loom taller against the low ceiling. Faintly I hear the sounds of the dayroom, video game explosions and the muffled chatter of a movie playing. There's been no more contact with the outside, no more word of Graham, no calls from my uncle or the cops or the Tooth Fairy. I'm not sure if they're deliberately screening my calls or if everyone's genuinely keeping their distance.

The Red Orphan strikes again.

Svara makes his way down the dim hallway with a bit of limp, a subtle dragging of his right leg that makes me wonder if he's hurt himself or if I'm just noticing it for the first time. Steve vacates the chair across from me and goes to stand next to a nearby bank of lockers as the tall man folds himself over the molded plastic. He appraises me with eyes the color of gunmetal.

"You've been busy, yes?"

"Not so much." Truth to tell, the walls are pressing in. Thirty minutes of outside time, confined to the small patio with its rusty basketball hoop, and I'm starting to appreciate *The Shining*. "Can we go somewhere?"

He looks up at Steve, who standing isn't that much taller than the old man. Steve shrugs his shoulders. "Flight risk. She's supposed to stay here."

"Then I'm not going to talk. It's too personal." My eyes flicker down the hallway, searching for the overruling vote. Sandy's down at the far end with Harkness. "I don't want everyone to know my business."

"The last time you left you tried to run. My answer's no."

"I wasn't trying to run." My eyes roll of their own accord. "No one tries to flee by locking themselves in an attic."

Svara nods, as if this makes all the sense in the world. "May we appeal?"

Sighing, as if against a great weight, Steve calls for Jon. He sticks his head in from the entrance to the dayroom. Even his presence is reassuring. "What's up?"

"The doc wants to know if they can go outside." Suddenly it's Svara's request, but I don't say anything. "I told him about the program she's on because she tried to run."

"Prose?" Jon asks.

"Yes, sir." I say it with great deference.

"You weren't trying to run before?"

"No, sir."

"Knock that off." He sizes me up, measuring something inside me. "Promise me you're not going to run?"

"I will take full responsibility for her," Svara offers, but Jon doesn't seem to hear him.

"Promise."

"I'm not going anywhere, Jon. I promise."

"That's good enough for me. Steve's still got to go with you." He gives the younger man a nod. "Gym's okay. Have her back by dinner."

"Sure, Dad," Steve grumbles, but I'm already back inside my room, fumbling my shoes on. I barely bother with the laces before I'm back out with Svara, walking towards the door. Focused straight ahead, I barely hear Harkness say *no fair*, barely glimpse the dayroom with a few new faces. Stepping through the door and onto the 'Sip, I assume Svara and Steve are trailing but don't care. The cool air brushes against my face, the afternoon cloudless and stark. I realize that I'm not even sure what day it is—if Halloween's entirely passed us by. The leaves on the trees by the field are vibrant reds and orange, autumn bleeding through.

Svara's at my elbow as if an apparition. "A lot of talk lately. About what's best for you."

"Yeah?" It feels so good to be walking anywhere, feet against the pavement, that he could tell me I was to be burnt at the stake tomorrow and I'd still take it in stride.

"Mm. They speak of sending you over to the juvenile detention. Of course, unless you're formally charged, that is not quite an option, but still, they discuss it. Meetings and meetings."

"Should I feel special?"

"Sarcasm is a poor defense."

We're almost to the gym before he speaks again. In the daylight it's just a building, not some slumbering malignity. "We've been talking about increasing your medication."

"I'm sure you know what's best." I push open the big double doors. The foyer is bright, fluorescents working overtime, almost the polar opposite of a couple nights ago. The doctor says something else involving milligrams and long names, but I tune it out. Increasing the meds would only affect me if I were taking them.

Finding a perch on the bleachers, I position myself to see both the doors and the stage. It feels as if it had been years and not just days ago. The haunting melody, the fluid shadow, the way the walls had seemed to fall away seem so dreamlike, and yet the cold metal around my neck proves that we were here, that some of it might have actually happened.

The leathery *sproing* of a basketball hitting scuffed hardwood breaks the spell as Steve dribbles away to work on his field goal percentage. Svara places himself a respectful distance away from me and folds his hands, his long legs resting several steps below him. "Something is wrong here, I think."

"What do you mean?" Trying to pierce the darkness behind the double doors, I catch only the last part.

"I speak of raising your medicine, of isolating you from the other girls for a time, and the most I get is your feigning of ignorance. You are planning something."

"Just trying to get through Intensive Teaching," I offer. Already the seed of something is forming in my mind, germinating just beyond my ability to grasp it.

"These *irregulars*. I cannot help but feel that they made an appearance on your big night, yes?"

I nod, not bothering to lie. "Sure. They do what they do."

"Yes?"

"There's something else here." The words spill out of my mouth. "It's like a man but like a liquid, some kind of big black cloud. Sometimes I think other people can see it, like the new girl, or Harkness. Other times I think it's only me. It likes to scare people. It likes to hurt."

Svara pauses, the pen hovering. "What is this new thing?"

"I don't know. They don't come with their own bios." I roll my sleeve up. The bruises are faded, a sickly yellow-green.

"No, I suppose they wouldn't." He raises an eyebrow, takes his time. "How long has this been going on?"

Forever? A few days?

"I don't know. A while now. Probably weeks."

"And you are—the only recipient? Of this attention?"

"There's an urban legend about this place, but no one besides the new girl said anything about—it, about it, and she could be just loony." His eyebrow wags skyward again. "It's hard enough being here without everyone thinking you're actively crazy. I don't think it would help to tell stories about the boogeyman."

The pen is back up, poised. "Does this new one have a name as well?"

I shrug. "I call it Sinatra."

A touch of curiosity wrinkles his brow. "Why?"

"It hums when it's around, kind of a big band song. *Da da duh de da, da da duh de da*, that kind of thing."

"When do you see it most?" Something about my rendition must have been hilarious because he's trying not to smile.

"Night. When I'm in my room, alone. It walks the hallway. Once or twice it's come in."

"Any others?"

"When the power blew out. That night in the gym."

"When you see it, what does it do?"

"Scratch at the door. Mock me. Like it's trying to scare me." My breath feels hot, rushed. "When it can't get that, it's settled for pain. What should be its hands, touch me—"

"Hence the bruises, yes?"

I look at him with eyes warm and wet. "There's no *hence* anything. It's like living in a fucking nightmare with no way to wake up. I'm tired of this. Of all of this. I just want it to stop."

He leans forward, his face hollow. "And it will stop. With the proper medication—"

"Fuck medication. You said you could get me out of here. But I'm still waiting. Waiting most nights for that thing to finally grow bored and kill me, or worse. You're not holding up your end of the deal, doc."

"Prose, listen to yourself. How many stops in your life have had malign spirits? Left mysterious injuries?"

"Berriman thought the same thing."

Looking over my shoulder, I see the ever-present pad in front of him, pen poised. There's already a rash of scribbles across it, spidery arcs that can't be translated upside-down. "I don't know how much more of this I can take."

"You say you think it's marked you? That this poses a danger to your life?"

"I think it's a danger to everyone. All the girls who have never returned, waking up with bruises they can't explain. People run away constantly, and with the kids already crazy, no one will believe them."

My fingernails dig into my palm. "It's picked the perfect feeding ground. Maybe it's why no one here ever seems to get better. Maybe it's making everyone here worse."

He's quiet for a long moment. In the background I hear the leather ball bouncing, the occasional vibration of the backboard as Steve launches bricks with quiet determination. Finally the pen finds its way to the pad. "You said *or worse*. What did you mean by that?"

It tried to shatter me completely.

Ever since the pantry I'd tried to be careful, but there were doors in that house. Most of the time they would open onto spare rooms, closets, stairwells. Sometimes they'd open onto— well, nothing.

They were gateways.

Late at night, I could sometimes see a fetid glow seeping out from beneath a doorframe, never more, never for more than thirty seconds or so. I'd lie in my bed and imagine I could hear them scurrying in the walls, behind the baseboards, scrabbling in the attic. I loved my father, and I loved Rachel, but I was terrified of that house. Something in there wanted me. Something there wanted me all to itself.

It wasn't confined to the night. Setting the table for lunch, I opened a cupboard onto a hollow void, some ancient crawlspace that bled magenta and madness into our world. I'd be reading in the big easy chair but hear them calling me, a low, gravelly whisper between the eaves. Sometimes I'd catch strains of a cacophonous melody that would drive me mad if I listened too long.

I know, I know. Looks like I listened too long, right?

I began losing weight, losing sleep. My father chalked it up to some growth spurt that wasn't happening, part of becoming a woman or someone insane fatherly paradigm of puberty. I'd begun my 'lady troubles' with a calm anticipation the year before, but he acted like spectral paranoia went hand-in-hand with pads.

Rachel sensed that it was more than that. The long-sleeves and hoodies had come out, and the kids at school had added whispering hushed tones to their general avoidance of me.

Not the regular irregulars had won me a lot of friends, mind you. There were still wanderers, lost souls straggling about the long roads and forest trails and empty hallways. I'd seen a man in a rumpled Halloween costume in the parking lot of the post-office, looking confused and angry. A cat-headed woman had strode across the play field of junior high in the middle of a soccer game, imperious legs pounding through the turf on her way to some unknown destination. A thing in rags haunted the alley between the thrift shop and Bella's Coffee and cried when the moon was full. This isn't a complete list, by the way.

Not by a long shot.

But I'd gotten better at avoiding them. Ignoring them. Pretending that I couldn't see them. Over the years I'd learn not to let them latch on, turn a deaf ear to their wails and their demands.

I didn't have the Man to protect me.

It was freezing that day, maybe the middle of February, where the wind came whipping out of the Gorge and every gust was like a flurry of pins. Berriman had already granted me the clean slate, if only because she never wanted to see me again.

Yeah. Kind of talking about you, too.

Read into that.

I'd just gotten out of the shower and thrown a towel about my shoulders. Tying another around my hair, the steam had cleared just enough to spot the condensation on the mirror. I didn't give it a second thought until my eyes adjusted. Circles and symbols and branchy shapes, as if someone had taken their finger and sharply scribbled across the glass.

Were they runes? If it was a message, I couldn't read it, but it startled me, enough so that I pulled the door open to the hallway without looking, without thinking. If I had, I would have noticed how cold the knob was, enough to numb my fingers as I yanked it free.

A sick purple light like bruised flesh leaked from the rotting corridor that stretched beyond it. Black doors hung from either side, and it tilted madly as it stretched to some darkened center. It was different this time, some other branch of this celestial labyrinth, and something inside me moaned with realization as the piping melody began again. Something was singing at the dark heart of this

—*city it's a city*—

empty place, and worse still, some part of me wanted to explore

—*come and see, child, come and see*—

to pull it all in and let it fill me, pour from my eyes and ears and ragged mouth.

I know it doesn't make sense. I don't think I can explain it, but it was there all the same.

The unseen black door raised from the floor like the lid to a dumpster and that pallid *thing* came scuttling out. Its skin was white and grubby and slick, as if it had crawled forever beneath the earth and never seen the sun. Its eyes caught the light from the bathroom, and chittering, it smiled, raising the corners of its flat, spade-like head.

It licked its lips.

Somehow I became aware of the icy latch. As the misshapen thing scurried towards me, I threw the door shut with enough force to shake the walls, or maybe that was the thing slamming into it. Off balance, I wavered, slipped in the water. My temple caught the hard corner of the towel bar with a meaty *thunk* that sent white lights dancing before my eyes.

Stumbling to one knee, I finally gave up the ghost and went down.

I don't know how long I was there. All I remember is Rachel opening the door and finding me, naked and shivering on the linoleum floor. Blood had clotted through my hair and splayed dry and sticky across the floor. We washed it off in silence, Rachel full of questions she didn't know how to ask, me full of answers that no one would believe.

We were quite the pair.

I loved her for it. She tried so hard to make it work. I wonder if my father knew how lucky he was to find her.

What the hell was I talking about? Right.

It wasn't the only time they'd managed to trick me. The creatures were sly, right out of the gate. Defying pattern, sometimes they'd wait for weeks between episodes, other times drawing close three times in an hour. The only pattern I was ever able to discern was that they wouldn't stray far from the doors, as if afraid to venture further into— the house? The world?

I don't know how to explain it.

Having found me again, the Man had taken to lurking. No doubt about that, though he tried to hide it. Ever since that day on the deserted road, I'd catch glimpses. A flicker of long coat turning a hallway corner. The brim of a hat sliding behind a wall.

Heavy footsteps on the floor above me, or the light aroma of vanilla and bourbon when I woke up.

In between everything else, I had no idea what to do. If I could force him to leave.

And if I'm honest with myself, the little girl I had been wanted him there. He was safe, if only for me. He would protect me.

By the time I started seeing him more often, I needed all the help I could get.

Svara taps his pen against the pad of paper, humming faintly. I hear the hollow ring of one of Steve's bricks caroming off of the bleachers, but I don't take my eyes off of him.

My face is hot. For some reason it matters what he says next.

"Did your father know?"

"No." It's not entirely true.

After the first round of bruises and the allegations, I tried. My explanation had been light on drama and sketchy on the details, a kind of half-assed *Amityville*, but how do you explain the frailty of chaos? That ninety-nine percent of the time opening the cupboard would get you Oreos and gummy bears, but that the one percent would open onto a violet hellscape where some skittering thing beats the shit out of you and tried to drag you away?

It was a madman's lottery, but still. The man wrote thrillers and horror books. If anyone could step outside the confines what they considered sane, you'd think it could be him.

Instead he just shook his head and muttered about how Rachel wasn't trying to replace Mom, and how I needed to stop hurting myself. He got me a copy of *The Merciful Scar* and that was the end of it.

"He didn't seem like he'd be very receptive."

"You're holding on to something." When I don't reply, Svara leans forward, pen tapping against his chin. "You never speak of your father."

"There's not a whole lot to say."

"From all you talk about him, I'd imagine he's your Marmalade." The pen slashes downwards, scribbling a faint note I can't make out. "I would imagine there would be plenty to say. It is what put you here, after all."

"You've been warned about that name," I sigh. "There's really not. He was pretty self-obsessed to begin with. Except for—" Something catches in my throat, and I push it out. "We grew farther apart after the farmhouse. It's hard to talk about lessening interactions."

"From what you say of your father, he seems to have had a hard time with your mother's death. Perhaps even before then. Certainly depression."

"If I've said nothing about him, what exactly are you basing—"

"Your father. Your uncle. Your great-uncle, of whom we have spoken so little but may be the most illustrative of all." He flicks up a finger for each, marking a place. "Perhaps even your mother. Do you sense a commonality between them?"

"Can I charge by the hour if I do?"

Svara shakes his head, and scribbles something on the notepad. I can feel myself wearing down, like a pebble in a vast ocean.

"You're a very unusual girl, Prose Harden." His eyes meet mine, the color of wet slate. "Let me speak of the usual."

"Whatever."

"These issues, these injuries, come from attention. Too much or too little. Am I making sense?"

I shrug. "Why start now?"

"Too much attention, and I would think that one or both of your parents is hurting you. Too much discipline, too many unrealistic expectations, coupled with a loss of control. I'm sure this is what your previous doctor anticipated."

I say nothing.

"Too little, and the child creates problems. Tries to force their parent to act the parent. One of the parent's utmost responsibilities is to keep their little one safe, yes? So bruises.

Scratches. Little things, caused by phantom boogeymen, all as they wait to be saved."

"Hey—"

He raises a hand. "That is not what I am saying applies here. Only illuminating, yes? For the purpose of comparison."

"If you say so." My eyes drift towards the stage, the black curtain hanging so out of place at the side of a basketball court. Memories of the gym at midnight slouch towards me, and I try to push them away.

"In such cases, injurious behaviors persist. It has become a comfort, after all, putting the child at the center of attention. A hero beset upon all sides by monsters."

"Stop that."

The doctor spreads his long hands. "If it sounds false, please elaborate on why."

For close to a minute I say nothing, listening to the scuff of the leather against the hardwood, Steve dribbling out NBA dreams at the far end of the chamber. I study the ripples of the curtain on the stage, the void between the two halves. Something's back there. A round shape, six feet off the ground. Something familiar.

"I'd like to go now." My voice sounds weak, even to me. "I'd like to leave here, please."

"Have I struck too close?" he asks. His hands fold like paper swans, but my feet are already under me, a tad shaky but climbing down the corrugated bleachers all the same. I don't slow when I hit the hardwood, my breath coming in shallow gasps, a wild butterfly beating against my chest.

Svara might be saying something else, *Stop her, you fool!* or *We're not finished!*, but I don't have time for it now. The only thing that matters is leaving the gym, breaking through those doors before those boots clack down against the boards. Poe forbid he calls to me.

Steve's yelling something as the basketball pounds against the backboard and voyages off towards the far wall. I raise my hand towards the foyer and manage something about going back. I think he gets the gist of it, but I don't care. All that matters is putting myself behind those walls, behind as many walls as I can muster.

Hoop dreams forgotten, he catches up to me, walking briskly if only not to look stupid. I take a deep breath as I push open the heavy doors. Sometime in the past hour a storm has blown in, and dark clouds squat heavy against the earth with the promise of rain. As I walk, step after purposeful step, back to the Lodge, there's a smell of copper in the air. Burnt ozone.

That, and just a hint of vanilla.

We had started a tradition the summer after second grade, the Man and me.

Before things started to fall apart for good, before the decaying spiral really started to plunge downhill, I'd pretend to go to sleep until after all the lights were out downstairs, my mini-flashlight presiding over my thrift-shop paperbacks of Dumas or Maupassant until the noises ceased and the big door at the end of the hallway creaked shut. I'd stick my head out from beneath the covers to spy Marmalade more often than not, perched on the chair by my little desk, waiting for something I wasn't always sure was me.

I'd tip him a wink and slide out of bed, feet silent against the wood in my footie pajamas. With precocious silence, I'd make my way across the corridor and down the stairs to the kitchen below. The first floor would spread out before me, dark and dappled in shadow, and I'd feel more than see my way past the family room and through the narrow door until my hand had gripped the smooth handle of our old refrigerator. Giving the room a once-over, muttering half-conceived hopes that this wouldn't be the time my father was sitting at the kitchen table, hands folded, his frown all the discipline I needed, I'd pull, bathing the room in radiant white, and snake my hand down to where he kept his beer. There was always a twelve pack of cans on the lower shelf, initially Pabst or Coors but recently venturing off into more colorful cans and labels.

If he'd noticed that occasionally one went missing, he'd never said anything.

I wonder what he thought was happening.

My fingers laced around the sweaty can, I'd madly shuffle my way back. I'd started to catch old black-and-white movies on cable, and some of the histrionics melded with my gothic phase into a cocktail of dramatic swooning and wild accusations. I was confident that my parents and even maybe my teachers would be at the top of the stairs, judgmental fingers pointed, eyes wide, possibly screeching.

When they weren't, an odd mixture of relief tinged with disappointment used to settle in my stomach as I hurried up and shut the bedroom door behind me.

He'd be watching me, tiny desk chair beneath him. I'd smile and pop the top of the can before handing it to him, and in my lowest whispery voice, I'd say "Tell me a story."

His eyes would catch the night light (my *reading* light, or so I insisted) in a strange way, almost as if they were turning inward, and as he took his first sip he'd usually begin.

I've thought a lot about one story in particular he told.

"This was in another land and another time, a place of mangroves and moccasins, appaloosas and alligators. Sweet earth on either side of a fertile river, and on one patch there was a big white house, willows and cypress towering around it. But that wasn't theirs.

"That was the product of man who'd pounded ingenuity and ruthlessness into a spade and set about to change the world. They grew a couple of other things, but mostly they grew cane."

"Canes?" An image of curved stalks with rubber tips came to me, being harvested and wheeled into old folks' homes.

"Sugar cane. Like they pile into all your damn breakfast cereal. May I continue?"

"You may." I folded my legs under my knees on the bed and leaned forward.

"The family was not that family. The family ran the bellows, handled the horses, ran odd jobs. There were other people there, of course, some free, some not, and between them all it was like a little kingdom, set a hundred yards off a mighty river, ruled on the whim of the man who couldn't wait to change the world."

"Funny thing, though, is sometimes the world goes and changes on you. Such is what happened to the Beauxreveres."

"What was our family called?"

"Hush." He took another long swallow from the can and elaborated. "The man who would change the world married and had himself some young ones, two sons, two daughters, but what started out sweet then spoiled. Within the confines of the kingdom, they were known for generosity and cruelty in equal parts. The family watched this with growing concern and spoke long after the candles had gone out. Pa had a trade, after all, and he could practice it anywhere, but they would be furious if he left. Even if he just thought about leaving."

"He wasn't sure how, exactly, only that the moment they started packing their wares the Beauxreveres would fall upon them, calling them traitors and worse. He'd seen enough bloody backs and swinging men on that patch of land to know what would come. The Beauxreveres were in good with the local governance, paid their taxes, greased whatever palms needing greasing. As a result, they were free to do as they pleased, being a full day's ride from the city and nigh impossible to find. The family found itself on an island, and it was all they could do to keep the tide at bay."

"As the world changed, though, the waters began to rise. The Beauxrevere children grew harder, their appetites stronger, but more and more ignored the world outside. When the split happened, I don't believe they paid it any mind."

"That is, until the day the boat came down the river."

I was leaning forward, so wrapped up in the story that I barely heard something in my closet shift. Marmalade whipped his head around and bared his teeth. "It was a strange thing, so unlike the steamships and barges that ferried their crops back to the city that at first all it did was give them pause. They sat on their high balcony and watched it wend their way, weathering the eddies and twists and cross-currents that made that river so ill-tempered. Sipping their juleps and sours, they made light of the whole thing, unaware of the hush that fallen around them."

"Pa felt it, the heavy weight now teetering to one side. Without a word, he left the bellows for the riverbank, and his boy went with him. Something momentous was coming."

"It took them a while to draw closer. The river was a treacherous thing, and no one foreign to those parts ever had an easy time of her. But work had died off in the fields. The kitchen staff had come out onto the porch."

"The entire kingdom was holding its breath."

"Flying high and proud off the mast of the ship was their flag. Pa saw it first and had gotten a head start back to the bellows before it even neared."

"Everyone put it together at the same moment. What followed was the most awful silence I ever heard. A pindrop would have been a gunshot as everyone turned the possibilities over in their heads."

"Then the man who would change the world barked something at his wife, another at his children, and they all disappeared inside the house. Pa told the boy that it was finally time and sent him into their little shack to gather whatever they could."

"The men had started to come in from the fields, mindless of their overseers. Most of them gathered around the house, silent as the trees."

"Who was in the boat?" I asked.

He shook his head. "Beauxrevere's lackeys fanned out across the property, treasures in hand, and set about to burying anything they could. Paintings. Jewelry. Coin. They hid them in the walls, in the fields, in stacks of hay. Dug them shallow graves in the woods or covered them with manure in the stables. The weight was on the scale, and it was finally wobbling to balance."

"The boy was returning to the smithy when the second son found him, carrying a lockbox full of wages and the locket from his mother. The bastard snatched him up from the ground by the back of his shirt as he ran. He was the kind that'd pull the wings off flies, and he swung the boy like he was about to skin him then and there. The second son might have said something clever, or something stupid, but he spun him around as if to march him back into that mansion."

"I snatched up the second son and shoved. The boat had docked by then, a man in clean blue hailing the house in clipped tones, and he went sprawling into the smithy, bouncing up to his feet in a hurry. I told the boy to run. Not to his father, not to the shed, but run. That he found himself a horse and did is why there's a story instead of a secret, I tell."

"Without a word, the Beauxrevere son drew the pistol hidden his coat, this hideous, stupid grin on his face. Yard full of workers, house full of kin, made no difference as he cocked the hammers back. He screamed that he always knew that I'd come for him. It didn't matter."

"It was too late the minute he pulled the gun."

The Man looked over at my closet, brow furrowing as he finished the can and slipped it back to me. I waited on the edge of my bed, electric with the story and feeling that twist you get when it won't finish when it ought to. A familiar voice drifted down the hall, soft and feminine. His head snapped towards my bedroom door before he looked back at me. "That ain't your mom. Don't pay it no heed."

There was a question there that I left unasked. "What happened then?"

"Everyone was peachy thereafter," he grumbled.

"Come on." I tried again. "I'm old enough."

He sighed, as if all the wind had gone out of him. I couldn't see his face in the shadow of the hat.

"Pa was down by the waterside, trying to hail the blue men. I believe he thought he could buy passage, or make a full report about the horrors that had been going on there, but the one with little ropes on his shoulders was only shouting towards the house. Half a dozen scuffles had broken out, dust clouds whirling around overseers who could tell which way the wind was blowing and slaves who'd had enough to last them a lifetime."

"The second son had time to get a single shot off. Three things happened."

He licked his lips, face hidden by the faint glow of the nightlight. "The horse the boy was on spooked and bolted for the fields. What tangible weight hung suspended over the field then fell with the smell of powder, and the whole yard erupted into one massive riot. Decades of suffering boiled over, and people went at it with fists, with teeth, with tools, the timing of which would seem in a moment like a cruel joke. The actual bullet itself punched right through the canvas tent of the smithy and flew an infernal, random course that couldn't be duplicated in a thousand years. It was dumb chance that it hit the corporal."

"The man with the little ropes started shouting something, his old flintlock coming into his hand. Those boys in blue scrambled about like ants after the hill had been kicked, but he paid it no mind. He sighted down the barrel, picked the man closest to him, and fired."

"They weren't there to save anyone."

"They never had been."

"A single red rose appeared on Pa's forehead. He dropped down on the riverbank like a puppet with its strings cut.

"By then the boys in blue had formed a line, rifles levered to attention, and the shooting began. One row'd fire as the other'd reload, like an engine set to deviltry. The air erupted into thunder and smoke, the reek of gunpowder burning nostrils."

"The closest to them were cut down almost at once. Those in the middle had time to rush them, to try to fight, but they were malnourished beggars against a polished infantry. They didn't have a chance."

"I finished with the second son in time to see them marching up through the yard. The Beauxrevere's were firing back from the windows, not giving a damn who they hit. On the lawn, anything resembling resistance had dripped into the earth, and the soldiers were wading through slaughter. Those on the edges tried to escape into the fields, into the swamp. Some might very well have made it."

"The boy brought the horse back around for his father. A bullet went wide and took off most of his ear."

"He barely twitched. The boy looked at me strangely then, one of those instants that seem to last a lifetime. There was something like terror, and something like blame, but there was also a choice. A very adult look had come over the horrified child, and these two faces warred over each other before he turned and disappeared into the trees."

"It took me forever to find him again," the Man said, and fell silent, inspecting his folded hands. His wide-brimmed hat obscured his face in a black halo.

I waited and heard that voice again, calling from somewhere downstairs, separate but distinct.

"What happened then?" I whispered. "At the farm?"

He shook his head. "Farm."

"Most everyone died. The blue boys took anything of value they could find and shot everything that moved. I heard stories later of things they'd found in Beauxrevere's house, down in the basement, up in the attic. Things that aren't right to tell a child, even one as precocious as my raven."

He paused, as if savoring a scent long forgotten. "They didn't get all of them, though. The swamp went deeper, and out among the flotillas there were plenty of places to hide. One got away for sure, maybe the father, but that's a tale for another time."

"What happened to him?"

The Man was silent for a time. "Do you understand?"

"Understand what?"

"Authority's just bully who changes masks. Someone else won't save you. When the time comes, you need to make your stand or ride like hell. Sometimes there's no difference between the two."

He straightened like a shadow unfolding. "Time for bed, little raven."

The voice from downstairs had fallen silent again. Straining, I could just make out a faint shuffling against the boards of the foyer. "What's making that noise?"

"Don't you fret." He disappeared out into the hall, as quietly as he could, the door shutting behind him.

I lay back against the pillows in the faint nimbus of the nightlight, hands folded, imagining the land of Spanish moss and tall houses, the stink of mud and the sweet flavor of the river. The scenes unfolded before me again and again, and only when I was drifting off on the edges of sleep did I realize that Marmalade had narrated the entire tale, but never said why he was there.

Not once.

I wait the afternoon and most of the evening in the Beige Universe, trading my "outside time" for more in, not wanting to subject myself to the whipping wind from the gorge. My reflexes are askew, leaping at small starts. Every shadow on the wall predicts his coming,

I try to tell myself I didn't see it.

The assignments they send are remedial at best. Upon my arrival back there were two fresh packets, twenty-five pages apiece. The work takes maybe thirty minutes, and then I'm alone with an Agatha Christie paperback and the increasing flutter of my panicked heart. Sandy draws first watch and sits in the plastic chair across the hall, thumbing through her phone and glancing increasingly down the hall for something of interest. She glances at the packets I turn in and places them under the chair with a nod, and that's the whole of the interaction. Nobody talks to me. In the silence my thoughts begin to bounce off of each other like atoms in a collider.

Between chapters, I study my window and roll the piece of paper from the cabinet between my fingers.

Meet me at midnight.

Whose number is it? Can I really expect that whoever left it would drop everything to come to the rescue of a perfect stranger? Even if I were willing, what kind of person would do that?

And what would they expect in return?

A cursory check shows that they've fixed the heavy plexiglass panel of the window. It doesn't give an inch under my weight, and some nonchalant patting is as far as I'm willing to press the issue. The staff might be disinterested, but they're not amateurs.

I try to think about how many young women have passed through here, slept in this bed, worried between these walls, watched Chapman scowl from the corridor. There must be some trick to surviving. If I can get my mind around it, maybe I can too.

The knock at the door startles me, makes me realize that I've been staring out of the window at the encroaching dusk for minutes. My eyes feel dry and uncomfortable. "Yes?"

Jon's at the door, trying not to take up the whole frame. The plastic phone seems tiny in his hand. "Your uncle's on the phone."

It seems like years since the last time we'd talked. "Thanks, Jon."

"Keep your head up," he says, and hands me the phone, dropping back to the plastic chair in the hallway. I lean in my doorframe and try not to let everything bubble to the surface.

"Hello?"

"It's Mark." Something's weird about his voice, like he'd just run a marathon or was on the verge of collapse. "They tell me things aren't going so well for you over there."

"They're fine. Just a misunderstanding."

"You get into those a lot, don't you?"

There's a pause. I can feel him trying to center himself, willing not to swing, and I let it go. "It happens."

He sighs. "Look, I asked you to cooperate with them, right? That it would make it easier?"

Something cold sinks into me, like a tumbler clicking into place, and suddenly it's so clear. "It doesn't matter, Mark. They're never going to send me home with you."

"What? You can't just give—"

A wash of ice is coursing from my spine to the tips of my fingers. Even my tears feel cold. "They're not going to send a disturbed teenager home with a sporadically employed ex-mental patient and just hope for the best. That's not how things work around here."

"You don't know that, Prose. You can't just give up." Another pause. "Mental patient?"

"My doctor's been doing some digging." My words come from a loudspeaker, miles and miles away. A piece of me, a core chunk of my heart, is turning to ice. I watch it with bloody eyes.

"Enough happily-ever-after. Did you want to tell me why *you* got put away for a while, Mark?"

"You don't—"

"Or Uncle Hutch? I've never met him, Mark, but *the stories*. It's really therapeutic to hear about dark secrets swinging from your family tree. Any comments?"

"That's not—"

"Fair? Bit of a foreign concept right now." Cold streaks are dotting my cheeks right now, at best incidental. "Do you want to talk about your sister? What you used to whisper about when you thought I was out playing with Algie or lost in a book? There's a whole world out there, a whole universe behind this curtain you raised, and I've never had a chance to see to behind it. You're the last family I have in the world, and you won't tell me the truth."

"Damn it, do you know why she did it, Mark? Do you?"

There's silence for a minute, a long minute, and then I kill it, tossing the phone to Jon and shutting the door. The world burns hot beyond my window, my heart thudding away in my chest, and I wait until the room's no longer streaming red and violet.

—now you've done it. Your one chance, and now you've done it. He'll never save you now. He'll never even think about you, not one thought—

But it can't be heard over the crashing of the planets, the asteroids of the Beige Universe dancing the Armageddon hop as I flop back on my bed and try to still the beating of my heart. If he found me now, my black protector, my dark guide, all I would ask is that he stop dragging it out. Send me off with the rest of my tattered family, for better or bloody worse.

I just want it to end.

And then there's a knocking on the door again, telltale rapping, and I want to scream for them to go away but something's catching in my throat. Instead I just watch through the little glass panel as a new face appears.

"You okay?" Graham materializes from outside the glass. I shake my head, and he opens the door a fraction. "You've got another visitor."

"Tell him to go away." Svara can keep his stories, keep everything scratched down in that little notebook. The realization is clear and immediate. I'm through talking, through sifting fragments of my past through a dirty sieve.

Something inside me has changed, warped, and the part of me with faith in tales and stories seems to have bent beyond repair.

Graham sighs. "He's not the kind of visitor I get to tell that too."

I pause, confused. "Who?"

My feet have already taken me to the door when he puts a hand on my shoulder. The contact is strange, warm. "You're already upset. Don't say anything right now that you're going to regret. Better yet, don't say anything at all."

And then he's behind me, and I'm walking past the blue room with its magnetic lock and the big desk towards the dayroom, when I turn the corner and stop. I've only met him twice, both times in a dingy cinderblock room that reeked of stale smoke. A table had squatted between us as the camera rolled, and I hadn't said much then either.

The detective spots me, a graceful hulk that might have been carved from broken rock. My feet want to backpedal, but I'm aware of Chapman and Sandy behind me. A few of the other girls glance my way and turn back to their movies or talk. *There are so few of us now*, I think, but then he's crossing the room.

"Prose Harden?" It isn't really a question, but he throws in that little rise at the end almost as an afterthought. He's wearing a mask that's slipping badly.

"I'd like to go back to my room now," I say over my shoulder, but no one seems to hear.

"Prose?"

"Drop the act, detective," I say. "You know who I am."

"I was just in the neighborhood. Thought I'd stop by." He looks past me to catch Chapman's eye. "Is there somewhere we can talk?"

"No need." My voice seems stripped, raw. "I'm not saying anything to you without my lawyer. Sorry you made the trip."

The detective gives me his best *aw, don't be like that* smile and steps forward. It's hard to imagine that working. "I've got a couple of questions. Since you're the only survivor, Red Orphan, I figured you might know."

His smile says differently. His smile says that there's a team of men in white coats who are likewise privy. I take a step backward, but there's nowhere to go.

From somewhere down the hall Harkness shouts, "Fight the power!" I love her for it.

"Come on. Do you really want to do this here?"

"No," I say. The room is filling with electricity, a crackling tension that's beginning to course from witness to witness. "I think it's shitty that you show up at a place where I'm literally being held against my will and acting like we're going to plan a bake sale. The last time we spoke you accused me of killing my parents. Where do we go from there?"

"Rachel—"

"Then arrest me." It comes out in a growl.

"All in good time. Who started the fire, Prose?" He asks like he's commenting on the weather. "Where did you bury Rachel?"

I turn to Chapman. "I'm going back to my room."

I shoulder past him, see him raise his hands for a moment before limply putting them back at his sides. I hear Nellie on the other end of the room, muttering *killer killer killer*. Behind me, Holcomb smiles. I can hear it in his voice. "Time's running out, Ms. Harden. Then no one'll care what you have to say."

The corridor is a blur as I stumble to my room, dropping onto my bed and putting my head between my knees, willing the universe to stop spinning.

It's lies. He's just trying to rattle you.

Maybe there is a lab report somewhere about the fire, some arson investigator who's been bought and paid for, but they can't know about Rachel.

No one can.

When she sent me down to the cellar, it had been raining for three days straight. Most of my bruises were healing, striping my arms with camouflage patterns of yellow and grey and green that were stubbornly refusing to fade, and the scab in my scalp was still sticky-rough enough that I had to brush my hair a different way to hide it. The power had checked out earlier that morning, a fallen hemlock dragging down the cables just up the road. We were down to one working flashlight and a stream of candles.

Dad was still clacking away upstairs, apparently having switched the word processor out for the old Remington he still kept in a black suitcase beneath his desk. Deep into the third act, he was only taking short breaks now, and I knew from experience it was best to just leave him be until he got the whole book out of his system. To do otherwise was to invite that scowl and furrowed brow.

I had been sitting by the window, watching the rain spill down upon the fields and flowers, the long wet stretch of green that traveled to the little fence, thumbing through a Stephen King novel and getting lost between the fields and Derry's Barrens. When she asked me to go find the battery stores, I thought fresh lines might have appeared on her brow over the last couple of weeks. There was something deferential about her tone, and when I asked she gave an embarrassed grin and said she'd never liked the cellar, ever since she was a little girl. Generations of her family's antiquities were stored down there in grotesque piles, and the deep shadows... well, she'd had quite a fright once.

At least that's how she put it.

I could sympathize.

Not doing anything crucial, I took the last flashlight and paced to the end of the hallway. I wondered what had disturbed her so much that she'd send an unstable preteen in her place.

I tried the handle, the memory of purple lights and dark corridors pressing in so hard that I had to catch my breath.

The old white door didn't open.

"It's locked," I called. There were sounds of rummaging in the kitchen, and then she appeared with a key. A loop of old lavender ribbon ran through the top of it.

Pressing it into my hand, Rachel retreated to the safety of the living room without a word.

It was strange, and stranger still that she felt the need to lock it. A vague feeling of unease stirred through me that I was starting to get used to.

But finally I had the chance to help, to do something for her. Conscripted into motherhood by my father's distance and whatever the hell was wrong with me, she had never complained, never a dark word in defense. If she wouldn't go into the cellar, more power to her.

The doorway yawned open like a black throat, a wet, earthy smell seeping up from the stairs like dust and old fruit. My flashlight looked pitiful, a firefly entering the void. That creepy sensation began again, and I hurried down the steps before I lost my nerve.

Rachel hadn't undersold the state of the cellar. The grey stone walls dripped with sweat, and across the uneven floor were haphazard heaps of boxes and detritus from across the ages, looming to the ceiling as if giving support to the house above. Some cantered contentedly against the walls, but most had been placed at random and teetered on the verge of collapse. Upon a few more swipes of the beam, I saw that some of them already had. The overarching affect was of a labyrinth set in a cavern, and it took another moment before I could will myself forward amongst the shadows.

The batteries were nowhere near the foot of the stairs. Knowing my father, why would they be? A pile of old toys and boxes leaned close, hobbyhorses grinning malevolently in the flicker of the beam, and I staggered around a pile of old furniture, gingerly stepped over a collapse of grotesquely swollen books.

In the damp cellar, questions about my father's mental state began to drift unbidden to the surface. Ever since Mom *left*, he had spent more and more time alone, punching away at the keys, trying to make something out of nothing. The distance between us had grown, the bridgework increasingly difficult. Bizarre edicts and odd choices had become the norm, but now that he had found Rachel, I found myself seriously wondering if he could keep her. I tried to think back to the last time I'd seen him that hadn't been at a meal. A thin ribbon of guilt had snaked its way in between us.

Some childish part of me wondered if I could still stay on with Rachel.

—in the purple between worlds—

Something moved at the back of the chamber, a dull scrape against concrete, and I froze. My trembling fingers somehow held on to the flashlight.

"Hello?" I called, wanting to kick myself.

There was no response, only the grating sound of leather on stone, closer this time. I took a step back and tripped over an edition of Baum's *Wizard of Oz* bloated to the size of a phone book, landing on my butt and something damp. Scurrying to my feet, I glanced around for anything I could use as a weapon.

As long as it had an allergy to mold, I thought I could take it.

My hand closed around an old hobbyhorse, its head a runny mess of cotton and snapped strings. Glimpsing the dark shape moving behind a pile of old boxes, the stairs to the cellar were impossibly far away. My grip tightened, muscles curling like a spring.

The thing slipped from behind the nearest stack of old papers. I swung, my heart jumping, eyes half-closed with the effort. I put everything I had into the blow.

It caught the wooden pole in one callused hand.

"No self-respecting monster on this earth would allow itself to beaten to death by a children's toy, little raven. By the southern stars.."

It was even worse than I thought.

Letting go of the pole, I took another step back. "Get out."

He reached into his coat and tossed me something heavy I caught out of habit. It was the firm plastic shell of a box of batteries.

Tilting his hat back, the Man studied me. "Little raven, you should know better than to wander around in places like this."

"I told you I didn't want to see you again."

He hadn't aged a day. The same scruff of beard, same weary eyes. I remembered him being bigger somehow, but it didn't take long to push that aside. My surprise was already giving way to anger, my mouth already a thin hard line.

"Since when have I ever done as I was told?" He glanced over his shoulder at something only he could see in the thick emptiness of the cellar. "You should know that's not how it works."

"What do you want?"

"For your father to not store comestibles in the nightmare basement."

My mind was fighting a brief and emotional war whose only survivor was a sense of weariness. "For a while there, they'd convinced me I'd made you up."

He sighed. "Imaginary's a hell of a judgement to put on a man."

I shook my head. "Marmalade, what do you want?"

"To take you out of here. Make things how they were, but that's a second. We have to go."

"I'm not going anywhere with you."

"By all means, go by yourself." He frowned. "Look at your arms, little raven. Your head. Tell me you're safe here."

I folded my arms across my chest. "I can take care of myself."

"You're tough. Tougher than I could have hoped. But that doesn't matter here." He nodded towards the ceiling. Water dripped onto his wide-brimmed hat. "Do you know what this place is?"

My frustration was mounting. I still spotted irregulars, caught glimpses of things I couldn't explain, but could wave those off as the occasional hallucination or mental disorder. Here he was, though, not a glimpse or figment but larger than life.

Having a conversation was like driving a spike deep into my temple. "An ancient burial ground? Ley lines? What?"

The Man looked towards the stairs. "It's a place where the world's thin, darlin'. Another place has started to rip through. You've taken steps along it. Heard the tunes. If they take you again, I might not find you."

A chill rushed up my spine independent of the cold. "Good."

I turned to walk up the stairs and a hand closed around my wrist. His touch was cold iron.

"Trying to respect your wishes, little raven, but there are times comin' when you're going to need a friend in your corner. This world will swallow you whole if you let it. Leave me, by all means. But you need to go."

"Thanks for the heads-up." I pulled out of his grip and started up the stairs.

"When has ignoring things ever made them better, Prose?"

"Who are you trying to save, Marmalade? Me, or yourself?"

I didn't look back until I got to the top.

By then he was already gone.

The batteries I left on the counter as I resumed my spot by the bay window. Picking up the book, I'd crossed through another few chapters before I saw him at the tree line, hat drawn low, slouching against the fence. The rain continued to pour, so heavily that I couldn't see his face. Couldn't tell if the rain was touching him or not.

Through the floorboards I heard something move.

The knock comes around seven.

At least I think it's seven. There aren't any clocks that I can see, but the sun has finished bleeding out over the horizon and the darkness now is absolute. I've been lying in bed, gazing out the window for men in hats, trying to decide whether he's really come back or if I just really need to take my pills, and the knock comes again.

Towards the end of the remedial work I've just started drawing pictures. Greeks pulling Trojan horses. Alexander's problem-solving skills. Hannibal and the Alps. Medea and her poisons. My mind seems stuck in a neo-classical mope, even though the drawings are rough and unskilled. Every stroke of the pencil seems the wailing of a chorus.

He wouldn't knock, though.

I'm surprised to see Monique behind the panel, and I lurch out of bed to greet her.

She doesn't look thrilled. "Hey, Prose."

"Hey." I wait for something else expectantly.

It needs to be pried out of her. "If you want to take a shower, now's your time. But it's got to be now."

I nod and grab my stuff from the cabinet drawer. Monique leads me down the hallway to the small stand of lockers that hold my soap, shampoo, toothbrush, all of that. The corridor is dimly lit, with only the red glow of exit signs on either side and the light seeping in from the dayroom. From the bursts of sound and the smell of popcorn, everyone's watching a movie, most likely a CGI apocalypse.

Chapman's sitting at the desk in his big chair, eyes so heavy-lidded that they might very well be closed. The light in the blue room is on, the door open, light reflecting off his bald head. The faint smell of disinfectant leaks out. He doesn't say anything as I walk past.

Graham's supervising the dayroom, leaning against the double doors, and I try to catch his eye. He sees me, starts to say something, and Monique says his name. Just once, an old cobblestone plunging into a well.

No love lost.

He just shakes his head.

No, there was nothing there. You're cracking up, kid.

I nod and look past him to the dayroom. I can't see what they're watching, but I can see them on the couches. Eloise I know. The rest are total strangers.

"Whatever happened to that new girl?" I ask. "The one with the long dark hair that looked like she walked out of *The Ring*?"

"She left yesterday." Monique doesn't seem inclined to say anything else, then glances back at Chapman. "She went to the hospital to get better. Were you two close?"

The idea is so ludicrous I have to stifle the laughter, but on its heels comes a numb revelation. *They watch us twenty-four-seven, all the time, but they don't really see. Some of them don't see anything.* "No. Just wondering. We talked a couple of times."

Monique nods as if that's all there is to it and pulls up a plastic chair outside of the bathroom. It's a long shoebox you enter via a door you can wheel a stretcher through, with three stalls, a long sink, and three shower stalls along the back wall so that people walking by can't glance in for a dose of eighties cheesecake. I grab a towel off the stack and go to the far corner, turning on the water in the far corner stall. It pulses tepidly against the gray tile with all the fury of a garden hose. It doesn't occur to me that the door to the nearest toilet is closed.

I strip, steel myself, and get in, pulling the plastic curtain shut behind me, determined to get this over with as quickly as possible. The shower is dim, the cold water sending chills racing up and down my spine . I try to think of summer, of warm days, hikes in the woods and trips to the lake. Faintly, I hear Chapman call Monique over to the desk as I lather the two-for-one shampoo into my hair, and then another sound, fainter still against the beating water.

And then the curtain rips away. My first instinct is to cover myself, which laughably leaves me exposed as something explodes between my eyes. The world goes wobbly for a moment, and then something hits me full force in the stomach, doubling me over and knocking the wind out of me. A knee finds my chin, and I'm suddenly on my ass against the wet tile, half in and half out of the stall.

A foot pistons into my side, and then another. Face down, I can't even get my bearings, much less what's happening as a hand wrestles its way into my hair and shoves my nose into the tile. Something wet and warm is covering my lips, my chin. I croak a ghastly noise, and maybe Monique hears it because I hear her footsteps down the hall, her calling my name, and then a startled cry, a heavy slam, a groan.

"—that, bitch?" I realize whoever's on top of me has been yelling throughout, but it's harder and harder to hear. My forehead bounces off of the flooring and white lights dance. "You like that?"

My hands are wet, weak things that can gain no traction. She mounts me and begins rabbit punching, aiming for kidneys, the back of my head, anything. There's a commotion in the hallway beyond that I hear as a distant rustling, a windstorm blowing past. Nellie keeps swinging, but I don't feel it anymore, don't feel anything except for the cold beneath me and the warmth on my face. Everything seems like it's happening someplace far away, to a stranger I barely know.

Idly, I wonder where the man in the black hat is.

Then the long darkness closes in.

CHAPTER ELEVEN
THE LOST LODGE

The first thing I realize is that all of this is wrong. The constellations are off, as if someone has moved the stars. Navigation is nigh impossible.

I'm not sure how long I've been lying here. Time became a little runny, with nothing to mark it but the grainy light from a dirty fixture overhead. Of pain, I feel none. My leaden limbs don't want to respond to my derelict synapses, which would worry me if I could still think. I might have been lying here for days.

Maybe I have.

There are dim recollections. Flashes.

Simple meals served at a card table in the hallway. The nurse wheeling in her heavy cart, administering ointments to my face and so many pills to my throat. A pair of yellow eyes floating in my doorway with laughter like broken glass, telling me that my moment is coming. My mind so full of cobwebs it's hard to string anything together.

A noise comes from the door, the first thing I can remember to break the monotony.

Part of me realizes that I don't have to go back. I can live like this, empty amongst the clouds, a thin tether connecting me to earth but flying free and clear above it all. My mouth moves, but it doesn't matter.

The door opens anyway.

A lanky man with hair in rough spikes is there. Some disassociated part of me remembers Steve. He winces and doesn't meet my eyes. "Lunch is here."

I nod and crawl out of bed. One look at his face makes me realize that I'm not fully dressed, and he shuts the door in a hurry. I put on the only thing I can find, a pair of baggy sweatpants, not so much moving as floating from state to state.

In the stale air of the hallway, it's obvious there's something awful at work here. It's still a Lodge, the same basic design, but gone are the decorations, the nametags, the lockers. The walls are a different color, and where the heavy desk sits is a folding table with a couple of chairs next to it. There's no sound but my own breathing. The dayroom beyond is devoid of items save for a pair of small couches, and the rest of the space is full of boxes, chairs, and collapsible furniture piled up against the walls. I feel like I've slept through Armageddon and woken up in some dystopian future.

Sandy winds her way out of the kitchen, navigating beyond piles of cardboard taller than she is. The tray in her hand contains a sandwich, some fruit, and a carton of milk that she sets down at the table. I fall into a chair.

"Thank you," I say. Something feels wrong with my lips, and it hurts to swallow as I begin eating. The pair of them watch me from a safe distance, not saying a word.

I have trouble forming a coherent sentence, giving me just enough space to wonder what meds they must have me on. The peanut butter sticks to the roof of my mouth. "Where are we?"

"Lodge," Steve says. "The empty one."

"We've told you that," Sandy says, a little more firmly. "They're separating you from the other children until they can decide what to do with you."

"Yeah. If Nellie wants to press charges."

Some warm little ember at my center starts to simmer, fog be damned. "What?"

"Don't play dumb." Sandy has the right tone but won't meet my eyes. "You soaped up the floor of the bathroom entrance and jumped her. Monique slipped and hit her head trying to break you two up. It's a good thing she was able to get away from you when she did."

My laugh is a crone on a midnight mountaintop. Images begin to blend into memory. "She's got sixty pounds and six inches on me. The only way I'd attack her would be with a two-by-four."

"Everyone's read your file, Prose." Steve's studying a spot on the far wall. "You've got a history of violence."

"Good thing I'm really bad at it, right? Is that why you won't look at me?" The food has stopped tasting of anything, and that furious coal is starting to burn through the cotton. My teeth feel weird, a little loose. I'm beginning to wonder about mirrors.

"Prose—"

"I didn't touch her. If I did, I wouldn't be the one who looks like this. I want—"

There's the sound of wheels over uneven tile, and we all turn to the door expectantly. Eventually the blue medical cart emerges, with a nurse I haven't seen before pushing behind it.

Pills on Wheels.

I get up before I see the doctor trailing behind her in a faded brown suit. He seems stronger than before, something pulsing beneath his skeletal appearance. Svara gives me a curt nod and motions me over.

The unnamed nurse sets two dixie cups on top of the blue cart. One is full of whites and blues and oranges, the other tap water. Neither is inviting.

"What are those?" I ask. Did I ever take the oranges or blue-tips? "Or those?"

"The court has agreed that we will increase your medication for the time being." The sympathy in Svara's eyes is sobering. "Please."

All eyes on me, I can't picture a way out of this. Instead, I take both cups and down their contents. The doctor checks my mouth after the nurse does, a lot more thoroughly. "Good," he says, and leads me to the small couch in the center of the room. Leads is not too strong a word; already my knees feel wobbly. I almost career through a stack of folding chairs before finding myself on the cushions. The sound of those wheels rolling away is already a distant memory.

"Can I call my uncle?" I'm surprised to hear myself saying it. There's a purpose behind those words, but I can't really remember. Something about a detective, but what? "He's supposed to be getting me out."

"In a little bit." Sandy says, retreating to the card table in the back hall. She and Steve are having a brief discussion that I can't make out.

"—spooky—"

"—way easier after the meds—"

"—place gives me the creeps—"

"—done with this—"

"—lock her up—"

"—lock her *up*—"

Svara folds himself onto the other couch, presses something in his pocket, and places his hands together like a penitent. "I'd like to speak more to you about your stepmother—if you don't mind. Whatever happened to her?"

"Don't want to." Already I feel the barrier loosing, my tongue priming to speak.

"Prose," he smiles. "We had a deal, remember?"

"Not fair. The drugs." But against my will, the secret surfaces, a bubble rising from a vast depth.

Svara shrugs. "Whoever said life was fair?"

no.

don't.

don't. it's a

The dust from the attic had started to scratch at the back of my throat, but that didn't matter. Neither did my dirty shirt sleeves, rolled up over my elbows, or the sweat soaking into a black bandana tied around my forehead. We were on spring break, and Rachel and I had spent most of the last two days up in the attic, less of a spring cleaning and more of a purge. It was also us time, girl time, if you can dig it, and there was a closeness and camaraderie between the splinters and cobwebs that I hadn't felt in years.

The space above the house was just one long room, with a couple of deep nooks and crannies thrown in for no reason that I could see. Despite the sunlight and open window, the assortment of boxes and stacks were a strange mirror of the room beneath the house. Piles of family knickknacks, old photo albums, cardboard boxes, stacked randomly to the ceiling, creating their own alcoves and blind spots. Stranger still were the piles of old paintings, heaped horizontally in random patterns. As above, so below.

Anyhow, most of it was getting tossed, and it was slow going. Did you throw out the tattered photo album when you couldn't name nine out of ten subjects? Was Rachel's grandmother an artistic genius whose work needed to be preserved for posterity? Are the old Chaplin dolls junk without checking eBay first? Once the broken furniture had been removed, our progress had dwindled to a crawl.

Rachel was perched on an old rocking chair, her laptop glowing open beside her as she carefully removed a porcelain doll's calico dress to check for a manufacturer's stamp or markings. I took the moment to wander over to the space we'd cleared by the window. Although I'd hate for my ancestors to turn art critic on me, we'd formed three piles of paintings: hangable, questionable, and rubbish. The master heap was pressed against the wall, and I was idly leafing through them when I came upon it.

The colors were off, faded and chipped by decades of weathering, but the backgrounds were the same. An old, faded metropolis from some witch-haunted perspective. Twisted corridors with black doors. An alley where hatches swallowed the ground. Ancient buildings teetering impossibly over empty streets. Even a few shades off, I recognized the design.

Hell, I recognized the subject.

In the last one, he was there. Not the central figure, not by a long shot, but in some warped concert theatre the pallid thing squatted, looming in a balcony over a wavering aisle, almost out of perspective. White, gleaming skin. Long flat head. Its tongue, improbably long, lolling from its mouth.

I shoved the painting back. Then shoved it again, as if I hadn't quite vanquished it. My mind was reeling, my breath driven from my lungs. One hand went out to steady myself on an old television the size of a pony.

"Prose?" Rachel looked up from her computer. Gulping, I stumbled towards her. "Are you all right?"

"'S okay. I think I just need some air." The attic temperature had dropped ten degrees. Squatting down, my hands fumbled with the latch in the trapdoor.

"You're worrying me," she said, her brow furrowed. If I had looked down just then, maybe I would have noticed. Maybe I would have saved us all, but instead my eyes were meeting hers when I pulled the door open.

"It's okay. I'll be fine." I said, then saw the glow on my hands.

The pallid thing seized my arms, digging deep before I had a chance to scream. Cold and wet, the smell of spoiled meat filled my nostrils as I kicked my legs out, trying to find purchase on either side of the opening. What passed for a face gibbered as the music rose.

It had been waiting, you see. For the time to be right.

With another yank, I cried out again, wrenched almost in half as it tugged me down. Gravity was on its side.

Already my arms were numb, but I finally managed to plant my knees against the lip of the trapdoor. My legs quivered with the strain, my mind with revulsion as the thing's tongue sagged out of its mouth and caressed my wrist like liquid nitrogen.

Rachel was behind me, then, her hands scooping beneath my arms, her weight thrown backward. She was calling my name, calling for my father, and I realized *It's cut us off from the whole house.* If my father raced down the hallway to the attic, what would he see? Would there even be a door there to let him up? Even be an attic?

It pulled again, my face dipping almost even with the portal. Below me I could see more doors, black and withered things. As I watched one threw itself open. Another creature scuttled out. A ruined town stretched behind it, tapering spires and abyssal gorges

—come and see, come and see—

and something that could have passed in dim light as a lodge, a castle. The agony was almost crossing into numbness.

"Rachel, let me go. Let me go!" Another claw took hold of me, and together they heaved. Something tore in my back, another strain gave way in my arm, and then I was toppling forward, saying his name.

The city of dead light.

"Marmalade."

"No more."

My eyes feel heavy, my limbs like lead. Moreso than the tightness in my chest, the tremors in my hands, I can't shake the feeling that there's something wrong in this abandoned Lodge, stacks set up like a warehouse fire sale. A strange texture bleeds through the air, like ammonia and fire, and I find myself peering into shadows, waiting for the inevitable black mass to unfold.

"You must," Svara says, scribbling something down on his pad I can't make out. "Get it all out, yes?"

My mouth starts to move. I have just enough time to wonder what they've given me.

I landed ass-first in a puff of ash. The melody was a piercing whine in the back of my skull, and the flat face peered closer. Its breath was a gagging cloud, and where the pallid thing had touched me burned. Dimly aware that another pair of hands was pulling at me, I tried to turn away as that wormlike tongue emerged, trailing across my cheek in awful tenderness.

Part of me hoped they would tear me apart right there, devour me on the spot, but the two grub-like things showed a casual cruelty that somehow unnerved me more.

The scream came from behind me, overriding the demon lullaby. Rachel, bless her heart, hadn't let go of me, for all the good it had done.

She'd landed in the burnt muck behind me and was clearly unprepared to discover that her stepdaughter had just needed a good dose of relocation therapy. The second pallid one was larger, bulkier at what could be called the shoulders, and he pawed her onto her feet.

Tears stung her cheeks, and I could see the welts the thing was leaving upon her arms. I forced myself to stand, a twinge of pain shooting through my knee that made me think that walking would be a problem for next few weeks. Of course, I'd have to live that long.

My eyes drifted upwards, and I forgot all about them, about Rachel for a moment.

I forgot about everything.

The diffusion of purple and shifting lights was coming from somewhere just above the horizon, a malleable luminesce that reminded of me of submarine movies or underwater documentaries. Everything smelled like ash, and clouds of black flakes rippled up with every step. What could be called buildings lilted and canted at all angles, covered in something like black mold, creating some imperceptible labyrinth. The sounds, the lilting of the pipes—

It was hypnotic, is what I'm trying to get at. More so than the gruesome twosome, the city had this mental weight to it, if that makes sense. Just being there was creating this psychic strain, some cognitive dissonance that grew and tore until it threatened to shatter the whole. You felt your mind pulled, rejected whole senses out of hand. It—

The smaller one made a harsh, squalling noise, and a rough claw shoved against my back. A couple more jostles and they were herding us along the deserted streets. I tried to keep an eye over my shoulder trying to remember where we came in, but we quickly turned down a dark alley, then a broken door, then out a hole in a moldy wall, then down a side street lined with black portals. The teetering buildings leaned against each other so closely they blocked out the sky. Seeing the real world disappear behind me was bad enough, but worse still was the knowledge that I would be lost—

—in the city, city of dead light—

and never find my way back.

Rachel asked me where we were a couple of times. I couldn't answer, and she didn't seem to mind. My heart was breaking, not for me but for her, who'd tried so hard to be the best stepmother she could be and now found herself lost within this broken metropolis. Tears streamed down her cheeks, her hands rubbing frantically at her eyes every time one of the pale things touched her. If she'd been frightened by the cellar, I couldn't imagine how she was coping with this.

"I'm sorry," I said, and she sniffled back. I realized with a start that this was somehow unsurprising, as if I'd been waiting my whole life for one of the irregulars to bring me here, drag me away with a sick lurch out of this half-life.

I'd never thought they would take someone with me.

The turns were never-ending, looping trails up fractured stairs or down splintery holes. The pervasive melody grew more insistent, pleasantly eager. I wondered between bouts of delirium if we really had any destination or were just wandering until one of them grew tired of the game. They jostled and prodded and poked us along the way, and I found it was easier to just give in, let the music sweep through you, before we forked left between a pile of detritus and a stone wall and emerged into an impossible courtyard.

Inside the stone oval, the black building was certainly remarkable, a series of spires and balustrades that emerged from a narrow base like a spiny fungus in a display of architectural impossibility. Windows were set at irregular intervals, a feverish light seeping out into the ruins like oil from a drum. Nothing leaned against it. No other structure dreamed of touching it, and my mind pulled dangerously as I followed it up and up against the purple sky. Rachel laughed behind me, tears in her eyes.

From somewhere near the earth a fracture opened, and then I saw that it was two parting doors, a diagonal slash along its face. Without prodding we moved towards them. There was a warmth to the light inside, and our hideous guides let us go unmolested towards the door.

Rachel was mumbling words, sobs racking her frame, but she did not waver in her approach. I realized my mouth was set in a horrible line, straining at the corners as we paced over the dark stones to the gate. Forms moved inside, terrible silhouettes just out of reach.

Is this all they want? Is this the way home?

I hesitated at the opening for an instant, the music murmuring in my ear. Rachel smiled sadly at me, and then she stepped inside.

I rushed after her with an eagerness bordering on dementia. The world seemed to spin, light burning at the edges, and then the gate closed behind us.

The chamber inside was circular, roughhewn walls of stone carved by no earthly mason, with a sphere of light distending from the high ceiling. At regular intervals were—images. There's no better word for them, no way to describe the impossible creatures they represented, as if Noah's Ark had gotten creamed by a semi and someone tried to glue all the animals back together again, set high up in the walls and angled down at us. A wide table was in the center of the room, just beneath the light, and at the table was seated a woman.

At least, it was shaped like a woman. Something heavy and chitinous covered the top half of her vulpine face, a dark shadow that wove into two colossal points and turned her eyes into deep hollows. She was as pallid as our captors, maggoty white, and when she rose we could see that she was covered in a strip of black plate that ran from the tops of her breasts to the floor. She took two jittering steps towards us and gestured for us to sit with a hand whose fingers were far too long.

The music had grown louder, more insistent, and I realize that it makes no sense that we obeyed. The chairs felt wooden, hewn from a prehistoric giant that had once towered over a mountainside, and slid back into the massive table effortlessly. Rachel took my hand beneath their gaze and gave it a squeeze. I squeezed back tightly as the glow above us grew brighter.

We realized that we weren't alone.

There were others sitting at the table, set as if at the points of the compass. A middle-aged Pakistani man with a mustache and sagging eyebrows. A beautiful woman with ebony skin who looked as if she'd fallen out of a fashion shoot. An elderly man whose face was skeletal in the dim light. An aging dowager in a sensible evening gown. A corpulent giant who looked as if he should be protecting a quarterback's blind side. A uniformed cop, hair tucked back in a ponytail, badge pinned to her lapel. We all looked at each other with the same sort of dazed resignation, as if this were a dream we were all waiting to play out. The melody became quicker, more convoluted, and the woman-thing clapped her hands together twice like an exotic starfish.

They came out of the walls and around the table, more things like our abductors. In the wan glow, they merely appeared, scuttling forward from nowhere and around the table. Everyone seemed to shrink back from what was happening across from them until they realized that the creatures were behind them as well. Capering, tongues sagging from distended jaws, the pallid ones moved with ritual purpose towards the table.

Steeling myself against their touch, I was surprised when each set an item onto the table before scurrying back.

Goblets.

Plates.

Bottles.

Courses of broiled meat, ribs, whole cuts, roasted potatoes, fried vegetables. As the largest one of them began to pour, the glass looking strangely natural in its claw-like hand, the group visibly relaxed.

Clearly this wasn't real, because what possible purpose would it serve?

The aroma was beyond delicious as the meal was set. Every now and again, I wake up and catch just a ghost of it. Even though I know what it contained, what the price was, my mouth still waters for a taste.

Something that looked like wine filled our goblets, and the woman-thing sat at the edge of the table, forming our group into a nine-pointed star. She raised her glass, and the melody strained behind her, chaotic now and lilting. The creatures that surrounded us became agitated, jostling each other with broken claws. Finally the largest one took up his neighbor in one misshapen hand, spread his jaws wide, and crushed the other's head like an overripe grape.

Gore splattered, and suddenly it was carnage around the table as the servitors began to tear each other to pieces. In the center of the slaughter, nothing had changed. It was oddly calming, like being in the eye of the hurricane.

The woman raised her glass again and drank as if nothing was amiss, and as if on cue the dinner guests began to drink. Rachel squeezed my hand once more and let me go, bringing the goblet to her lips with an almost sexual satisfaction.

"Prose," she whispered, and human speech was so foreign at this point that it took me a moment to decipher.

"It's like heaven."

With her fingers she plucked out a cut of meat and dangled it into her mouth. All around us, surrounded by raging violence, the other guests did the same, a look of such contented decadence on their countenance that I felt my hand closing around the goblet and raising it to my lips. I watched one of the things rip its brother's tongue out by the root and wear it like a shawl, and I only glanced placidly into the cup. The golden liquid was thick, almost like honey, and I was about to drink when I heard a sound like a thunderclap behind me.

It was just a brief break, a record skip in the music, but I turned all the same. The doorway had reappeared, and he was forcing his way in.

The dark hat obscured his eyes, his coat flowing around him in some unseen breeze. Something black was dripping from his ears, his mouth. When he raised his head, I saw it seeping from the corners of his eyes.

"Put that down, raven," he growled. His gravelly voice somehow drowned out the melody, and I paused. His hands were covered in black and red. A dozen or so wounds had ripped through his clothes, bleeding some dark liquid I couldn't name.

One of the surviving servitors stepped towards him, claw up in a salute or warning. Marmalade took his arm and wrenched. It came off at the shoulder with a hideous pop and a fresh spray of gore as the thing howled.

The woman-thing was on her feet, chittering some horrible warning, but he crossed the room in six steps and scooped me up before the others could react.

If the dinner guests noticed, they gave no sign. They were laughing to each other as if not surrounded by an abattoir and shoveling more from their plates. Grease coated their fingers, their mouths.

Rachel looked up at Marmalade and smiled at me. It was the last time I ever saw her. "Is this your friend?"

His hands tightened as he drew me out of the chair. With a soporific slowness I realized what he was doing, the goblet falling from my hands as he turned for the door. I reached out to Rachel, my fingers just tracing her shoulder as the Man pulled me away.

"Where are you going?" I screamed. In the hall, the sound seemed unnatural.

"Ain't no help for her." There was a mournful quality buried in the growl. "Wouldn't have been for you either, darlin.'"

The bloody giant stepped into our path and put out a warning hand. Marmalade pulled my chair out as if it weighed nothing and buried in the creature's skull. I barely had time to register the impact, the gout of blood, and then we were out in the courtyard, racing away across the uneven stones.

"You can't leave her here!" I pounded my fists against his back. He carried me like I weighed nothing, my thin cotton T-shirt already sopping up the hot wetness that was pouring out of him. So much, so fast.

"She's already gone." Behind me I could see the woman-thing streak out from the diagonal doors, her carapace shining in the purple light. She barked something, and the city came alive behind us.

Like ants from a kicked hill, the pallid ones poured from the ruins, from shattered windows and collapsed doorways, from beneath black hatcheries and dark alleys, streaming in pursuit.

Through the street beyond, Marmalade took us darting through alleys, jogging past narrow lanes, rushing through the corridors of abandoned houses, choosing passageways seemingly at random. The music blared, as if pleading with me to stay, and I let the melody lull me, relaxing in his bloody arms.

This was all a dream.

All that was and shall be, just a dream.

Maybe I would see my mother soon.

The things were drawing closer. It was their city, after all.

Beneath everything, I knew we were going the wrong way, that the door to the attic was somewhere else. But my warning wouldn't come.

The Man turned right, then left, and we were in front of what may once have been a schoolyard. He rushed to the top of the broken steps, sick light cascading across his face, and glanced over his shoulder. With a languidness I wouldn't have thought possible, I saw the flood of them behind us, a sea of pallid flesh and cruel claws, and smiled.

"It's too late," I said dreamily. "Wrong way."

He shook his head, dark fluids spattering from his eyes. "We may be in the dark, little raven," he said, and kicked the door open. "But I will never leave you behind."

There's a period of silence that seems to stretch, or maybe that's just the meds doing their thing. Svara clicks his pen and scribbles something down on a pad now full of jotted notes. I hear Steve whistle from the back hallway.

"I knew she was crazy, but *wow*."

I hear his indignant squeal as Sandy presumably elbows him, but my eyes are locked on the vampire, daring him to interject. When he says nothing, I start again.

"We came out in the basement from behind an old water-soaked pantry door off its hinges that was just leaning against the far wall. The Man spun around and kicked it, and the thing was so moldy it split in half. Just like that, the dream fell away.

I wrestled free of him. 'Where's Rachel?' I screamed. 'You have to go back for Rachel!'".

"He just shook his head and sank to his knees. Whatever fueled him, there wasn't much left. "There are rules, darlin'. Rules even I have to follow.'"

"The Marmalade Man sagged to the ground and didn't move. A puddle was already forming around him."

"By that time the house was filling with smoke."

"I wandered the basement, completely dazed. My father ran across the top of the basement stairs, cardboard boxes in hand,

and almost by accident I was drawn towards the light. He passed me again, empty-handed, and did a double take before plunging down and taking me up in his arms. He said something so saccharine sweet I can't quite remember it, something about how much he loved me and how glad he was that I was safe, and my father ferried me out onto the porch and down the steps to the front yard. He didn't ask about the blood, or the black stuff that was still coating my tee shirt, or about the dazed look in my eyes, but only yelled Rachel's name and plunged back into the house."

"The attic was an inferno, by then, flames pouring from the little window and licking the roof of the old Queen Anne. The turret was burning like a beacon fire, and the pillar of smoke it sent across the pale blue sky was so beautiful that I felt something in my chest snap. Sitting down hard, my cheeks aflame, I started to cry. My father came back out with another pair of boxes, and I realized that I was sitting in the middle of them, his papers stacked around me like some poor man's Stonehenge."

"'Have you seen Rachel?' he asked. He gave me a little shake. 'Prose, have you seen her?'"

"I just shook my head. There was a wildness in his eyes, the precursor of the years to come, and he ran back into the farmhouse. I watched him go, tears flowing out of me the whole time. I cried until there was nothing left."

"The Man had trapped her, you see. No house, no doors. No way out. For whatever reason he'd chosen me, and in doing so killed her."

My cheeks are hot, my breath heavy in my chest. I look to the windows behind the stacks of refuse and wonder where the sun has gone. Svara nods patiently. "The house?"

"My father survived a few more trips before the other floors caught as well. He'd managed to nab a box or so of my stuff, his stuff. It wasn't all manuscripts. He wasn't that bad yet."

"We sat in the yard as the sirens approached and watched it all burn. As the flames took to the other floors I thought I could see purple flashes inside the fire, strange glows like will o wisps, but I'm pretty sure that was just my imagination. By the time the fire department made it all the way out to the farm there was no saving any of it. The farmhouse burnt completely to the ground."

Svara clicks his pen. "And your friend?"

The word is so foreign to me here that I have to scramble to understand his meaning. "Friend?"

"Your accomplice. The Marmalade Man."

I shudder.

"I didn't see him escape. For all I know he burned to a crisp with the rest of it." The last part is a lie, but he doesn't have to know that. I feel so empty now, so scoured clean. All I want is to skulk down that dark hallway and go to sleep.

"Thank you," he says, and unfolds from the couch. "That will be all for today, I think."

"Meds aren't playing fair," I say, and sink lower into the hard cushions. My eyelids are heavy, my breathing shallow.

"I know," he smiles, and walks away.

In the dead of night, the clouds part for me. I don't know how long I've been in the abandoned Lodge or what time it might be now, but my face feels like it's knitting itself back together and the ache in my back and legs has faded to a dull moan. Fresh though, are the bruises on my arms, dark green Rorschachs that ache when I move. Blurs of visitors and questions, dreams that aren't dreams of black shadows and yellow eyes, mocking smiles and brutal truths, I don't know what's figment and what's fact for the last few days.

This amount of clarity is unfamiliar.

Someone must have forgotten to give me one of my pills.

I slide out of bed with the furtiveness of a cat burglar and risk creaking my door open. The hall is as dark as the void between the stars. Not even the emergency lights are running by the doors, which have been blocked off by heavy industrial laundry carts. I can just make out the huddled form of a man sleeping at the desk, head buried in his arms, and the faint glow of the other night staff reading by flashlight in the other room.

For a moment I think of running. Not with a destination in mind, but just going, rushing past the person in the other room and towards the gym, keys or no. The idea dies down as quickly as it started.

Where would I go?

Silent, I shut the door behind me and sink back onto the bed. From my window I can see an unrecognizable corner of Everbrook, trees pushing up to the wall, the bushes and briars having overtaken one of the old walking paths. The smothered orange glow of a lone surviving lamp wavers in the gloom, the last beacon preparing to be blown out. Folding my arms, I try to pierce the shadows beyond it, not quite admitting to myself that I'm looking for a dark hat, a faded coat.

I don't believe in Svara anymore, I decide. I'm not sure I ever did. Whatever angle he's playing, whatever bigger purpose is at work here, if he's trying to shill his findings to the cops or writing a tell-all or draining the life out of me isn't clear but getting me out of here and placing me with Mark is a lie. Why did I ever go along with it?

What had Phoebe said?

Just thinking of her makes my heart ache. True or imagined or somewhere in between, it doesn't matter. The pain is real, the loss is real.

She would want me to survive.

She would want me out of here.

As if on cue, a dark shape moves behind me, not bothering to be coy, humming its familiar tune. It flows into the room as I'm sure it has for many nights, and I slip out of bed and into the cabinet, forming a tight little ball and shutting the door behind me. Its yellow eyes are full of murder.

With a piercing groan, a less-than-material hand pools to scratch against the door, but it's already bored. Nails scrape down the metal surface, a terrible grinding that's supposed to set my teeth on edge. I shut my eyes in the darkness of the cramped space.

I shut my eyes and begin to plan.

Eventually my time is up.

My entrance back into Intensive Girls goes without fanfare or distress. With a couple of extra bruises and nights tucked in the closet, I served whatever sentence they thought was just. If they ever explained to me what that was exactly, the haze of extra medication and sleepless hours made sure it didn't stick. I'm as surprised as anybody to be led by Lo and Monique one afternoon out of the abandoned Lodge and into the gray sunlight of Everbrook, to walk the short path down the 'Sip. There's a chill in the air even during the hottest part of the day now, and dead trees greet me with leafless arms.

Chapman's sitting by the desk, arms folded, brow furrowed, bent over the logbook. For all I know, he could have been sitting there since I left. Sandy's getting something ready by the kitchen as I'm escorted through the dayroom and down the hall to the same old quarters. The padded door to the blue room is open as if I'll suddenly attack, the smell of stale moisture undercut with disinfectant radiating down the corridor.

"Really?" I ask to no one in particular. "You're afraid I'm going to jump you?"

My eyes catch the log board, scramble down the roll of names. The one I'm looking for isn't there.

"What happened to Harkness?"

Chapman doesn't say anything, but lets his eyes drift over to Lo, who clears his throat. "She ran. Right after your thing."

"Probably thought she was next," Chapman croaks. I let it go.

Monique follows me back to my old room as Lo splits off down the hall. I lean back against the cabinet, head against the window. Lo comes back with a green canvas sack and shuts the door.

Inside are my clothes, my books, my notepads. The contents of a life stripped away. Freed from the chrysalis of drugs and isolation, they're almost unrecognizable.

I dutifully begin putting them away.

With a peek back at the glass pane in the door, I check beneath the leg of the bed. The castoff meds are still there, one-hundred-fifty-seven white and blue and orange tabs that could put all the pain away once and for all. It takes an effort to replace them and start setting the Agatha Christies away, so much so that I almost forget the little note tucked between the lip of the drawer and the cabinet wall.

I'd almost forgotten about it. The same scrawled-out set of numbers. *Meet me at midnight. You know where.*

There's a knock on the door, and I cram the note down into my pocket before turning. Lo's propping the door open, the black shell of the cordless in his hand. "Phone's for you."

"Who is it?" I step out into the hallway after him, but he just passes the phone to me and goes back to the big desk that divides the hallway.

"Last chance to say you did it." His gravelly words send a cascade of ice down my spine. Holcomb must be able to sense my breathing. He acts like I've responded. "I've got it on good authority someone's been getting chatty over there. Talking a little too much, one might say."

"What are you talking about?"

My voice sounds stronger than I feel, but he laughs. "Really? You're going to play dumb with me now?"

I don't say anything, thoughts racing. He presses. "After you got your ass handed to you by that dairy farmer, they set you up by yourself for a while, right? Loneliness can make people open up, I hear. Maybe say some things they shouldn't?"

The blood pulses out of my head in an instant, leaving me numb and dizzy. *Who else visited me? Who else asked me questions?* The memories are locked behind glass. Only broad strokes are visible, no faces, no names.

The detective laughs again. "Don't ask how I know. Confidentiality, and all that. Point is, you fucked up with your little mouth. Now it's come time to pay."

"I didn't do anything." The words rush out like I've opened a vein. "I was drugged out of my mind the entire time. I barely remember being there. Whatever they say I said, they're lying."

"I wouldn't drag hearsay in front of a judge, Prose. Would I?"

This hits home. Hard. *Tapes? Svara?*

Another part of me screams that it's a trick, that the detective will say anything to try to get me to confess, anything to catch me off balance, and that part of me grabs the panicked half and begins shaking her wildly.

"Simple deal. Give me the confession now. You're a juvenile and likely batshit crazy to boot. Chances are you roll this into a reduced sentence, you get out while there's still time to enjoy what life you have left. Fight me on this and you won't see the light of day until you're wearing diapers again."

"I didn't kill anyone."

"Do you know what the conviction rate is when there's a recorded confession? You'll be going away for a long, long time. I'm trying to help you here."

"I can see that."

"Decide. This time tomorrow the option's off the table."

"You don't have anything." The idea is suddenly clear, as if it had risen from the depths of a frozen pond. "This is all just a game to you."

He laughs again. "Do you want to take that chance?"

The phone's dead in my hand, the dial tone startling me back to life. I realize that my hands are shaking. *He's bluffing. He has to be. Who would have helped?*

The answer, of course, is anyone. I glance up the hallway. Lo's thumbing through a logbook. Chapman for once is nowhere in sight.

With shivering fingers I pull the note from my pocket and punch in the numbers. It rings and rings as I nod my head, pretending I'm still talking to the detective.

There's a click as it goes over to voicemail. It's standard, you-have-reached-this-number, but that's not what makes me drop the phone.

I recognize the voice immediately.

Graham.

CHAPTER TWELVE
HERE AND NOW·

When I'd slunk back to the motel, it was without purpose. Days, I'd spent at the library or wandering through the woods. Nights, I'd slept in an old treehouse I was pretty sure no one alive remembered set a quarter-mile or more back in the woods off the 84. I'd stumbled upon it by accident while out walking, trying to clear my head of persistent ghosts. It was moldy and wet and smelled rotten when the wind hit it, but it was better than open spaces that summer.

It was better than home.

The questions kept sifting, never answered. Part of me wanted to go home and throw my arms around my father and tell him everything would be all right. Part of me wanted to stand on the shoulder of the road, stick my thumb out, and never see him again. I knew I still loved him, in spite of the book, in spite of the fear and guilt I now had every time I looked his way, but something between us was broken.

Neither one of us knew how to fix it.

My key still worked, and I paused with my hand on the latch. I didn't know if I was going to grab a change of clothes and bolt or stick it out and wait for him to come back. In this moment of indecision, I noticed something tucked between the door and the frame.

The note was simple, scrawled in an inelegant hand that I barely recognized as my father's. The contents were a disconnected apology of sorts that seemed out of place, written maybe days before. I'm not going to get into what it said, just the usual platitudes without the remorse to back them up. Unwowed and still a little monster in his heart, I pushed open the door to find him absent, his laptop open on the bureau, notes scattered across the desk.

Neither had any interest for me at the time, though I find myself thinking of them now in the haunted hours before morning with disturbing regularity. What secrets could they have kept? What was his fractured mind thinking? Instead I stripped, threw on fresh clothes, and dragged myself in to flop down on the rented bed.

My eyes must have closed, because in the next instant I was aware of a presence in the room. At first I thought my father had come home, but that couldn't have been true because he opened the door mere moments after. I started at the sound of the latch to find that the light had changed, the shadows lengthened. How long had I slept for?

He came into the room in a dirty shirt and jeans, the stubble of the last week a charcoal smear along his jaw. There was something disjointed in the way he moved that at first I attributed to alcohol, then just to exhaustion. "Little raven," my father said. "I wasn't sure you'd be here."

"Just passing through." I watched him slump next to the table, his hands shoving through his tousled hair. He swept his notes into a loose pile and pulled a cardboard six-pack onto the wood. "What time is it?"

"Afternoon." He drew out two bottles and twisted off the caps. "C'mere."

I did as I was told. There was just enough room to pull out the other chair without putting a hole in the wall. He slid a Widmer over to me. It smelled murky, bitter. "What's going on?"

"Drink," he said. There was a sourness that wafted off of him. I saw the dark circles under his eyes, the thin line of his mouth, and wondered when the last time he'd gotten more than an hour of sleep was. Something in my chest twisted guiltily. "Can't a father be there when his daughter drinks her first beer? 'S magical."

I nodded, not wanting to tell him that this wasn't my first beer, thank you very much. Some of the other motel kids, vagrants and vagabonds we all, had pulled a case of PBR off a truck a couple of months prior and invited me down to the creek with them to finish it off. In a rookie maneuver I'd thrown up in the bushes after the first three before my stomach settled down. Pushing some kid's hand off my ass, I'd wandered back to our room to go straight to bed before my father could smell it on me.

There was something else that night, some darker shape glimpsed in the shadows of the woods, but in my hurry I hadn't paid it any mind.

The thought stirred unease in me, and I raised the bottle to my lips and drank. The amber was complex and cold, dank vegetation and something bitter beneath. "Sheer sorcery."

He frowned. "I'm not a bad guy."

"No, you're not." I took another sip, this one easier. "I love you. But I need you to be here for me and you can't. You just can't, Dad. I'm not sure you were ever able to."

"That's not fair." Rigid and unmoving, he might have been carved from stone. "Someone had to provide. Someone had to make it all work."

"Cause that's what's important."

"I don't want to fight you."

There was a noise outside, something heavy running into the wrought-iron railing, and my father started, peeling back the curtain to look. He shook his head after a moment. "What do you know, though? About doctor bills and mortgages? The costs of psychiatric care? What do you know about having decide between an hour playing or putting food on the table? When your money comes from your imagination, you'd realize. There's only two things there's never enough of: time and money. You can't have too much of one without running completely out of the other."

"Pretty easy to see which end of the spectrum you opted for." I waved my hand around the dingy room, my beer half gone. It felt light, almost airy. "Welcome to the manor house."

"The mouth on you sometimes." He settled his forearms on the table. "I didn't raise you like that."

"Some would argue you didn't raise much of anything." My tongue was a razor now, casually flicking across his face, opening wounds that would never heal. I loved him, but there was a perverse satisfaction at play. I couldn't stop if I wanted to. "The most important things in my childhood were a ghost in a black hat and a stack of library books."

Strangely disconnected, I spat the last part out and stared at him. Something wasn't quite right. The room felt like it was slowly rotating around us, a wheel loose on its axis. My father frowned and opened another beer. "I always wanted a special child. Some little reflection of my hopes and dreams. And here you are. You're everything I thought you were and more."

"Yeah?" My voice seemed to be coming from further and further away.

"What happened to her?" he asked. "Rachel? What did you do with her?"

I couldn't stop blinking, my eyelids heavy and languid. "We went to the city."

"Please."

"Inside the house. She ate from the table and the doorways burned behind her."

Things were blurring together now as if I was crying, but my eyes were dry. I put a steadying arm on the table and almost teetered off into the wall. My father leaned closer. "I know what you did. I know you started that fire."

"No." It came out in a whisper.

"You took her away from me. Like you did your mother, Prose."

"No."

"I'm the only one left." He walked around the table and picked me up, my body a limp rag. The bottle fell out of my hand and skittered frothing on the floor. "I'm the only one left who can stop you."

"Daddy?" I asked, and the world went dark.

The next few hours stretch into infinity. Daylight refracts off of the windows, casting grainy shadows into the Beige Universe, but I can't sleep, can't do much more than lie there, eyes open, and look for a place between the stars. I don't bother to unpack much, but simply shake out the contents of the bags into my cabinet and crush the door shut, throwing the nylon sacks back into the hallway in a jumbled mess. With any luck no one will notice that one of them is missing, crumpled into a tight little ball in the bottom of the dresser.

Lunch is a revelation, grilled cheese and tater tots with a carton of funny-smelling milk. The knock on the door startles me when Monique delivers it, and she doesn't bother to make conversation. I ask her if I'm going back to the Academy later, but she just shakes her head and leaves me with a copy packet of remedial schoolwork which I could have aced even on the magic cocktail they'd been giving me.

I don't bother but slide the pencil between my bed and the wall.

When I set the plate outside my door, I scan the hallways. Chapman's still manning the big desk in the middle, the only person visible on the hall. I wait until he looks over before ducking my head back inside, trying to push the panic down. This has to work. It has to work.

Crossing over to the window, I'm not sure what I'm looking for, only that time has become a problem. I barely notice the starfish girl, staring silently into my room from beneath a tree out on the lawn. She's unusually pale, and I wonder what she's doing outside of Control. Her hand is raised and her lips moving, but it's too far away to make out what she's saying. I motion her forward, but she shakes her head. We watch each other for a little while and then I steal over to the cabinet, sneaking a peek to make sure I'm unwatched as I cram essentials into the bag: clothes, notepads, money from my uncle pressed between the pages of Christie's *And Then There Were None*. As quickly as I start I shove the bag into the bottom drawer.

When I look up, her hands are pressed against the glass, pale little starfish. Her lips move again. There's something horrible about her eyes, unblinking silver marbles, but I can read her just the same.

He's coming.

Eyes pressed shut, I turn away. She casts no shadow into the room.

When the door opens, there's no noise, only the diamond of light shifting from the pane. Chapman is standing there, not saying a word, just watching me. I meet his gaze. I have no idea how long he's been watching me, but finally he turns and shuts the door behind him. When I look for the starfish girl again, she's gone.

Hours pass, enough to make me nervous. I hear voices coming and going, a new shift beginning, the noise of play and mischief in the dayroom. Finally I stick my head out and try to study the corridor. No one's sitting next to my room, which seems like a mistake. Only Chapman rests at the big chair, guarding the desk like a state secret. After a while he waves someone over to watch and walks off of the hall. There's a terrible second of anticipation before I see who it is. The last tumbler falls into place.

Graham.

My breath catches as I wave him over. Eventually I get his attention and he flashes me a winning smile as he crosses the hall. "Hey," he says. "How are you feeling?"

For a moment I can't say anything, my breath caught in my throat, and the flash of concern across his face seems genuine. "Jeez, Prose. Are you okay?"

The words don't want to come out. Instead I unfold the slip of paper and hold it out to him, palm up. It takes a second before he looks down. When his eyes return, it's as if someone else is standing outside my door. "What's that?"

"You know exactly what it is." My voice surprises me. With my heart leapfrogging against my ribs, it's doing the opposite.

"I don't." He tries the grin again, easy and carefree. "What's it say?"

"Meet me at midnight if you want to run. Your pal Graham. I may be paraphrasing."

"Come on." Graham glances back down at the paper. "Can I see?"

I shake my head. "The only person who's going to see this is my lawyer. It's your number, Graham. You can't deny that."

"No, it isn't." Earnest eyes find mine. "I've always had your back here, Prose. Why would you make something like this up?"

I don't answer.

"You're having delusions, kid. It's okay. I'll get somebody."
He nods and moves back to the big desk.

My feet grow roots as I watch him go. Everything rides on
this.

He makes a show of checking the logbook, rummaging
through papers, picking up the phone, talking to somebody. I
can't tell if it's real or pretend. Minutes pass before he finally
shrugs and comes back to my room.

"Step back from the door," he says flatly. When I don't
move, he lets out a huff of impatience. "Anyone stepping onto the
hall can see you."

"Wouldn't want that." I make it sweet as I withdraw, my
hand now comfortable inside the frame. He looks me up and
down, a red flush in his cheeks. His hands are balled by his sides.
Any minute now I expect him to slam the door in my face.

When he doesn't, I know. I know it all. "Where did you find
that?"

"Worried there might be more?" I ask. "Worried not
everyone took theirs with them? Threw them away?"

He looks up the corridor. Whatever he sees there reassures
him. He whispers the next like a stage director. "Lift your shirt
up."

"Excuse me?"

Graham stares at me like something in a reptile house. "Lift
it up. Or this goes nowhere and I take my chances."

It's my turn to gape at him. In my wildest dreams, I didn't
expect this. He glances back down the hall and makes a twirling
gesture. "Come on. I need to know there's no wire."

For a moment I wonder if he's asking me about
undergarments, and then I put it together.

How much trouble does he think he's in?

Hell, how much trouble is *he in?*

But beggars and choosers are diametrically opposed, and so
my hand slips down to the hem of my shirt. I lift it unartfully to
my neckline and let it drop. He shakes his head.

"More."

Sighing, I raise it again, feeling the heat in my cheeks as he takes me in. "Turn," he says, and I make a twirling 360, willing the embarrassment away, willing myself into ice. When I come full circle, I let the thin cotton of the t-shirt fall. He nods. "Okay. You haven't said anything. What do you want?"

"I need out of here. Tonight."

"Tonight? What kind of trouble are you in?"

When I don't answer, Graham smiles, the ghost of the charmer he's let us all see. Once more he looks around, making sure we're alone, and then the words come fast. "I'll jimmy the door to the gym open before I leave tonight. Make sure that it won't lock. You'll go out through the little fire door in the back. Move the stuff out of the way, go down the steps, and go all the way through. There's a field. Cross it. In a hundred yards there's an old logging road. A van will be there, and I'll take you to the bus station. From there, you're on your own."

I nod, but he doesn't look away. "Okay."

"This isn't a charity," he growls. "You think you've got something on me, and maybe you do, but there's still a price. Understand that."

Swallowing, I nod again. Wordlessly he puts his hand out for the paper. I shake my head. "Tonight."

He sets off back down the hallway and plants himself by the big desk. I let the door fall shut. My mind is racing, and I need to sit down. Like a diver, I've put my foot out into the void, and now all that's left is the fall.

Tonight.

In swaths of white, the sunlight burst through the window, glowing like a nimbus and filling my skull with sharp bolts of pain. The air smelled of disinfectant and some vague plug-in freshener. My tongue felt draped in cotton wool.

Shaking my head, the first thought I had was that I was back home, but I quickly dispelled that. The floor was hardwood or something like it, and wherever I was, someone had tacked crisp white bedsheets to the ceiling. Their skirts draped almost to the floor, forming four walls around me. Beyond the space, two fabric passageways stretched, their walls rippling gently in the breeze. Somewhere a window was open, and the smell of the forest, decaying leaves, was sweeping in.

The world seemed to dip and buck as I got to my knees, and my stomach lurched in a ball of heat. I was quietly sick against the bare boards, fighting off the night that pressed in against the edges of my vision. My nails pressed against my palm to the point of pain, trying to drive me to clarity.

Wiping my mouth, I sat up. The room seemed to swim less, and I looked around for some clue as to where I was.

The motel was gone. In its place was a labyrinth of white linen.

The rippling ghosts of the walls were unnerving, casting lengthy shadows and pockets of pitch about the room. I couldn't see anything, and I was loathe to begin wandering through, my mind instantly picturing hands pressed against the cloth, faces upon the cotton, reaching, biting—

Instead, I pushed through the grainy soreness. Sitting at a table. The skunky aftertaste of beer. Dirty floor mats. A car, gliding soundless through the forest. My father.

My father.

I stumbled to my feet, the ache in my heart contesting the one in my head. I needed to get out of here, needed to flee, needed to find help. Whatever he'd done

—drugged you prose you've been drugged—

something wasn't right. He needed help—

Something shifted at the end of the hall. That room was dark, the sheets spectral fingers in the wind, but something moved between them, their footstep a quiet thing against the boards, then closer still.

"Raven." The voice was a wretched thing, croaking from some unknown depth. "This is going to hurt me a lot more than it hurts you."

There was another sound as it moved, wood dragging along wood. The room still rocked like a ship's cabin in a storm, but I put one foot in front of the other and started down the opposite passage, the billowing curtains brushing against my ankles. Whoever was behind me was in no such hurry.

"It's not your fault. Everybody's got a nature," the voice reassured. "Shame yours is poison."

Closer now. The hallway was hard going, a moving walkway that rippled with strange fingers and shifting lights. My balance was shot, the world rotating around me. Each footstep was a daring effort into the breach.

"We're going to cure you," the voice echoed, and that dragging sound of wood against wood grew louder. "I promise."

A sheet billowed out in front of me, and I screamed in frustration, hands tangling as I thrust it aside. Why the hell had they put them up?

But running into one was like drowning. Worse still was the feeling that not every space was empty, that there were things pressing in against these flimsy walls, waiting for me to pass. The footsteps intensified behind me.

"Don't fight it. In your heart, you know this is what you want."

My feet tangled, and I stumbled into the sheet at the end of the passage. As I pushed off to the right, it seemed to curl and loop around me. The drum of feet drew closer.

The white linen corridor continued, ceiling to floor, herding me onwards. Maybe it was whatever I'd been given, and maybe it wasn't, but I started to see them, faces and hands bulging beneath the sheets, howling and grasping as I dragged myself by.

"They say a thing like you is rare, raven. So's what I'm going to do. They've all come to see."

The corridor forked again, walls billowing in the wind. There could be an army behind them, but I pushed on, my heart hammering sickly in my chest.

I wouldn't say his name. I wouldn't.

Following the hallway, I glanced back at the turn, at the figure methodically following. Their face was irretrievable in the pressing shadows, as was whatever they dragged alongside them. Brushing against the linen, I was almost positive I felt something scratch against me, jostling me upright.

I went faster, the ache in my head becoming a roar, the turns coming quicker now, short jaunts left and right and—

The corridor opened up into a wide room, draped bedsheets forming four walls along the perimeter. At the center of the room was a low table. A brazier of lit coals smoldered behind it, the pungent smoke tasting of incense and some exotic spice. No adjoining passages split off. No doors were visible. The curtained room was the end of the line.

Running my hands along the cloth, I tried to ignore the sensation of grasping fingers and gaping mouths, trying to find some hidden exit, a knob, a latch, something. It felt like fumbling through a crowd, but I was still in some kind of house. No one would build a room without exits.

The fruitless search had taken me halfway around the room before the figure caught up. He stood in the mouth of the passageway, fabric whipping around him in a strengthening gale. With one hand, he tapped the sledge against the floor slowly.

"Lie down, raven." The voice was almost mournful. "Lie down. This can all be over."

"All I have to do is call him." I don't know where it came from, but my voice sounded stronger than I felt.

"Your demon?" The bat tapped again. "How do you know I'm not him?"

"He wouldn't do this. Not to me."

"Little raven, I have protection against such things. I read a lot, remember?"

My father stepped into the room. There was something horribly wrong with him, his face distorted, ruined and terrible in the flickering light. "They told me so many things, once I was willing to listen."

"Why?"

He shook his head, and I saw that he was almost on the verge of tears. "They said I could have her back."

For the first time, the sledgehammer came off the ground. "Lie down, raven. I'll make it quick."

As crazy as it sounds, his voice had a bizarre gravity to it in the smoke-filled room. I almost drew closer to the table.

They're all gone, Prose.

Everyone you cared about. Don't you want it?
Don't you want to join them?
"Daddy?" I asked.

"Shhhh." His feet traced a wide semicircle in the salt. Beyond the walls I could hear a vast rushing, like the beating of some cosmic wind. "I've seen it. This is what has to be."

All at once the sheets lifted, flowing inward from the pressure. Horrible dark figures blew in on some abyssal hurricane.

Skeletally gliding, called forth by some invisible tether, their awful faces were mercifully masked. Draped in black, they filled the edges of the room.

My knees buckled.

I pitched forward.

On my knees, then, the cool surface of the table pressing against my cheek. My eyelids fluttered in the soporific smoke. Dimly, I was aware that they had closed a ring around me, all waiting behind my father.

—irregulars all—

His feet came into focus. A vast rustling surrounded me, like a twister bursting through a field of cornstalks, and the sledge left my field of vision. Over the roar I heard him suck in breath, and three words came to me.

"I love you."

Something crashed, as if a hole had been torn open in the universe. The voices shrieked in a demented chorus as they withered aside. The sledge fell, clanging off the edge of the table, ripping off a chunk of its surface. I rolled over to face the ceiling, consciousness gladly fading.

Marmalade had my father off the ground, face red, rough hands clenching as he kicked. One foot collided with the brazier and toppled it, sending coals skidding along the hardwood.

One brushed a curtain with a finger of flame.

"Don't." The words bubbled to the surface as if from some great depth. "He's all I have."

Marmalade met my eyes as the darkness filled them.

When I woke, my world was shattered.

He was gone.

The hardest part is waiting until shift change.

I complain of a stomachache and hide beneath the covers, mapping the new universe and wandering between the stars while outlining the steps in my head. Three possible roadblocks exist, even if Graham is as good as his word. The way he had looked at me with his lizard eyes made me cringe at the empathetic mask he'd always worn.

How many girls had taken him up on this offer? Had Harkness?

And how many had paid the price?

The first obstacle is easily cleared. When the time comes, I manage to cheek my meds and add them to the collection, most now wrapped in a sandwich bag in the tight little bundle stashed in my bottom drawer, and I await the witching hour to spill forth. Forcing myself to flip through Shirley Jackson, I'm positive that anyone walking through on bed checks would see the electricity in my eyes, the way my fingers dart with ecstatic life.

All I need is to maintain the facade of normalcy until the time comes.

The dayroom finally quiets, doors shutting on the hall around me, and I still wait, minutes stretching by with the ropy elasticity natural to great events. I sneak glances out my window, sure that I'll see him there, his black hat slightly angled on his head, cold eyes peering in through the window. The trail of blood he'd left had claimed everyone I'd cared about. Worse still, I was sure now he'd done it all for me.

At this hour, I sincerely doubt I was worth it.

I know that I'd called him, said his name to Svara.

I just want to be a memory by the time he gets here.

A floating head passes by the panel of the door, noting me and moving on. I slip out of bed and angle myself against the wall, trying to peer down the hallway through the thin slit of glass. Just able to make out the edge of the central desk, I make out the first of the night staff, a hulking man with bifocals and his hair tucked up into a samurai bun. The slight woman who'd walked by my window was out of view but probably doing bed checks on the other end of the hall. Patiently I wait. Eventually she returns to the far end of the desk, pulls up a rolling chair, and makes small talk while they sip from massive mugs of coffee. No one else appears.

I get beneath the covers again and wait. Bed checks are every fifteen minutes. Trying to feign sleep, I hide here, counting and being counted. Three, four...

The door doesn't make a sound as I step out onto the hallway. Two pairs of eyes whirl about to mark me. "Bathroom, please." I say, surprised at how level my voice sounds.

The hulk nods before picking up a magazine. The slight woman puts her cup down and moves to one side of the bathroom door. Making my way down the hallway, I slow down as I pass the desk. Her mug sits just on the edge of it. The blue powder slips from my fingers in an imperceptible drift.

I step into the first stall and snake my hand into the corner of the toilet paper dispenser. The second dose is right where I'd left it before. Counting to a hundred, I flush, wash my hands and walk out. The slight woman has already lost interest, a paperback novel flapped out in her hand.

Pressing myself to the desk, I lean over and pretend to steal a peek at the big man's magazine. His head turns and my other hand snakes the dose into his glass. He growls. "Bedtime."

"Sure thing," I nod, and saunter back to my room. It hadn't been hard to grind down some of the blue tablets of benzo from beneath my bed, but my only worry had been the dosage. At the end of the day, I just guessed. Quadruple seemed about right.

In near blackness I get dressed and sit cross-legged on my bed.

—We're all down here in the dark together—

and wait. It doesn't take long.

When five minutes have gone by, I press my face against the panel of glass. The woman is slumped against the desk, her head resting on the crook of her elbow. The hulk had gotten a little farther and sprawls as a mountain by the water fountain. The cordless phone lays flung from his hand like an upended beetle.

The insane thought that they might be faking it occurs to me.

I jostle it aside and grab the nylon bag from the closet. As I turn, I see the starfish girl pressed against my window, a pale moon watching soundlessly. I take a deep breath and step out onto the hallway. Her eyes follow me with no expression, and I have time to wonder if she's a portent or just curious.

In the end, it doesn't matter. I flash her a wave and shut the door behind me.

My feet seem unnaturally loud as they scuff along the carpet. Blood is pounding in my ears. This must be what it feels like to freefall.

Past the blue room, I reach the desk and have the mad urge to take my file, to flip it open and read the lies about myself, the half-truths and disinformation pouring forth. What had they been told?

It occurs to me that I could also rifle through the sleeping pair's pockets, but time is rushing by already.

Just as well.

You know who you are.

The hulk snores in deep throaty rumbles. I wonder if it's loud enough to wake anyone as I step over him and past the water fountain. The dayroom is empty, just a shell with couches and a couple of screens. It's been so long since I'd been out here that the freedom gives me pause. I feel like some deep angler from an oceanic trench, rising to the surface until it explodes.

Shaking it off, I head for the glass door to the outside and the 'Sip.

A lone footfall raps against the tile.

I freeze. The room seems to spin around me as she steps around the corner, heavy hands already wrapped into fists. Her head is lowered and her cheeks a bruised red, breathing in heavy puffs.

I should have known, I think.

Chapman.

"Back to bed, Spooky." Nellie's hands flex like fleshy pistons. "Or you'll be pissing blood for a week."

I try to make my voice as hard as I can. It's not great. "You don't have to do this."

"Yew don't half to do dis," she mocks. "Bitch, I want to do this. I want to kick your spoiled little superior ass. You think you're so goddamned better than the rest of us, but guess what?"

She nods at the night staff. "You screwed up this time. They'll put you away for real, bitch."

"Just step aside." I swallow, hating the tremble in my voice. "You'll never have to see me again."

"But I want to," she said. "I want to watch what they do to you."

She takes a step forward and I flinch back. Her grin is a crawling white worm. "I caught you trying to run. After you hurt them. Then I stopped you. I'm a hero."

I backpedal, sure now that this is it, eyes racing for a way out. If I can make it to the 'Sip, I can outrun her, no question, but everything is undone if I can't get around her.

"What are you going to do, Spooks? Call your ghost man?" There's no time left as she puts her hands on my chest and pushes. The couch behind me hits me in the ass and I go tumbling over it backwards. The room rushes by and I land in an awkward roll, my knee jarring against the thin carpet.

I rise to a crouch shakily. "Last chance." I growl. "Let me go."

"Fuck you." She's already stepping over the couch. "I'm going to enjoy this."

I scamper backwards towards the far wall as she gives me a kick to the side like a soccer hooligan. The air rushes out of me in a gasp, then I find my feet and fumble along the counter for anything I can use. A stack of board games are left out and I toss the first one her way. She bats it aside with a snort, pieces exploding in a confetti of plastic and paper cards. DVD cases are next, but she doesn't even bother to dodge as she closes the distance between us. Something explodes in my right cheek and for a moment the world is full of bright shimmering light, but when it clears I'm face down on the tile.

She kicks me again, harder this time. Again, I take it, rolling onto my side. In a mad scrabble, I scamper for the side door.

I hear a laugh behind me as she comes. My knees slide across the tile as I try to tug open the slider, but it's still blocked by that old two-by-four. Fumbling for the board, I jar it loose as she steps onto the linoleum. "Ready for more?" she asks.

My fingers wrap around the wood. Pivoting, I swing the two-by-four with everything I have.

"I am now."

Still coming at me, her face is a pale ghost of surprise. It takes her in the side of the head.

The meaty *thunk* echoes across the confined space.

She grunts, steps, and drops to one knee. A ribbon of blood becomes a river down the side of her face. Nellie shakes her head to clear the cobwebs, and a freshet of fine red drops spatters the glass.

"Bitch," she says, and starts to rise.

I am aghast, like I'm watching from outside myself, but another part of me, a shadow Prose, is smiling. She doesn't care in the slightest.

Maybe I am the Red Orphan.

The next swing catches her behind the ear, a dull reverberation I can feel all the way to my shoulders. For a moment she stays up, then Nellie's eyes roll back to show their whites.

She pitches bonelessly forward onto the tile.

Heavy breaths pump from my chest, but I don't move. The board stays in my hand, and I try to ignore the hair and blood matted on the end of it.

Part of me is positive she's faking.

The other is positive I've killed her.

You don't have time for this.

In the end, the little rises of her torso might mean she's still breathing, or maybe I'm just trying to make myself feel better. Either way, I shove open the door and bolt into the night.

In doing so, I leave Intensive Girls forever.

CHAPTER THIRTEEN
THE END OF THE WORLD

The 'Sip is a chalk outline in the darkness. The wind is bitingly cold, rustling the trees so violently that it might be trying to raise the alarm. Pale orange ghosts light the path, and I run as hard as I can, the vinyl bag bouncing at my side. All I need is for someone taking out the trash to notice me, but the alternative would be skulking and sneaking through the shadows. There's no time for subtlety now. If someone finds the night staff and Nellie, it's all over.

The gym looms before me as I race past the field, a hungry Sphinx. Out here in the open, I take no time getting to the double doors, half sure that this has all been a setup, that any moment Holcomb will step out of the night with a round of mocking applause before slapping the cuffs on me.

Only when I pull the latch and the heavy doors swing open does that last vestige of doubt break.

Graham is as good as his word.

What is his price?

I push the thought away as I step into the darkened foyer, half sick. I think I already know.

The night seems to have followed me in, a cloying glove, and I can't see more than a few feet in front of my face. It doesn't matter. If anyone saw me running down here, I don't have long.

Shoving open the double doors to the basketball court, I set off into the void in what I hope is a straight line, corner to corner. The massive room is pitch black like the bottom of the ocean, and my footfalls echo distantly off of the far walls. An errant basketball right now could twist my ankle, kill this night, but I try not to think about it.

From a short distance, I hear the melody coming from the stage. I don't bother to look but concentrate, one foot in front of the other, trying not to break my pace. The air could be full of monstrous forms, a surrounding ballet of horror that whirl and sway around me, but the darkness is

—we're all down here in the dark together—

also a blessing. Had I just been psyching myself out? Or is Marmalade watching from the curtains, marking me?

Part of me, the shadow Prose, hopes that he's here, that any unpleasantness in this midnight ride could be mitigated by his presence, but I know what that will look like. Fire and blood, blood and fire.

I've been down this road too many times.

The darkness is amplifying my thoughts, turning them upon each other with eager abandon. My hands are out in front of me, and I keep expecting something to press up against them, something wet and cold and covered with—

Stop it, Prose. Just stop.

—but these are elastic moments, stretching out forever. Logically I know that the gym can't be more than a hundred yards lengthwise. It can't take me more than a minute to cross it, but it feels like I've been walking through the void for days.

Time holds its breath before my hands find the wall. On impulse, I go left, sliding my hands against it until I hit a corner and turn, knowing that I might be headed for the bleachers or directly back to where I started, but it doesn't matter. The melody is growing louder, like whatever's creating it is drawing nearer, but I can barely hear it over the thumping of my heart as I step carefully.

Then the handle's there.

Unlocked, it opens beneath my touch, a slick maw of stygian blackness against an ocean of pitch, and I shut the door behind me. There is no light in the confined space, and I almost wonder if I've been tricked, that this is some janitor's closet they'll find me locked in come morning, but hands on the walls, I step forward.

Blind, I walk a long way, waiting for something to step out and take me. Sinatra with his glowing eyes, Holcomb with a pair of handcuffs, Chapman, but there is nothing but cautious steps, my hands trailing along the cold brick.

I shiver as my fingers find another latch, certain that this one will be locked, certain I should have taken the night staff's keys after all, but when I press it opens before me. My feet find a set of steps leading down, and I clutch the railing as a lifeline before I find myself below the ground. The air smells of dust and disuse, and the darkness is absolute. I can feel emptiness on both sides of me, and I wonder where else the tunnel might lead, where it might let out to.

Conjuring a map in my head, I count my steps, trying to determine which way the wall should be. In the end I pick a direction and go, turning, turning, and turn again. My thoughts turn to grues and other nasties, open pits and shallow graves, anything waiting for me in the absolute void between the stars my paces take me through.

And then there are more stairs beneath my feet, tripping me up, pitching me forward and bloodying a knee. I crawl up them, not trusting myself to stand, and there's another door beneath my hands.

Mercifully, it's unlocked as well.

With a deep breath, I push.

The doors swing open.

The cold night air breathes against my face as I step out of Everbrook, an autumn wind soughing in the branches above.

The cold sickle of the moon smiles upon me as I step out onto the grass.

The van is right where Graham said it would be, just visible across the field and tucked behind the first stand of scrub trees before the forest really finds its footing. I pause, at first of unsure of the time, but in this moment equally unsure that I want to go with it.

You could stick to the woods and follow the main road out. Hitchhike once you hit the highway. You don't owe him anything.

You don't owe him anything.

The urge to run is overpowering, a chemical taste in the back of my throat, and I'm ready to run when the lights flash, a simple blink that tells me that he knows I'm here.

Cops will pick you up in the next thirty minutes without him. They'll find you and bring you back.

Certainty a cold stone against my heart, I start across the clearing to the stand of trees, the wall a receding facade behind me. I'm plunging again, a lump in my throat.

There's some vital facet I'm missing.

I'm turning the plan over and over in my head when he gets out of the van.

He's dressed all in black from head to toe, and for a fraction of a second my heart stops. Before I realize that the height's all wrong, he could be the Man, but then Graham walks around to the back of the van and opens up the hatch. Like Orpheus, I look over my shoulder. Everbrook is already just a shadow behind me, a grey and unimpressive specter.

"Come on," he hisses. It occurs to me again what very real trouble Graham is in, but shadow Prose silences that train of thought. *You're the one blackmailing him, genius.*

My sneakers crunch against the gravel of the shoulder as I step out from the trees. The smile he gives me is not reassuring. When I try to climb in, his hand snakes out to block my path. "The paper," he says.

Hands searching my pockets, for a moment I'm petrified that I forgot it, that he's going to drive off without me, but then my fingers close on the slip of paper.

I hand it over and he tucks it away. Without a word I clamber up into the back of the van.

It comes to me then.

The other girls, Prose.

The one who have never been heard from again.

No.

Not Graham.

Then who else?

The doors close behind me. There is no latch.

Almost to myself, I whisper a name.

We drive for thirty minutes, maybe more. He sticks to back streets and lost highways, not a lamp or signal to be seen as we pass through old forests and forgotten haunts. Hemlock and fir sway in the cold wind, and the last mile or so has been up a winding dirt path whose shoulder plummets into an empty abyss of black and starshine. Gravel pings against the undercarriage in a failing chorus as Graham ignores most of my questions, only telling me that we'll go to the bus station when we're through.

I don't know if even he believes it.

When the van pulls to a stop, I prepare to act. Running blind through the middle of the woods would probably be fatal, so I clench my fists and look around the van for something to brain him with. Besides a crumpled-up sleeping bag, it's been cleaned out thoroughly, without even a candy wrapper or bit of string curled up in a corner.

It's so he doesn't leave any evidence, part of me whispers. I hush it. There's no point in pondering why we're backwoods off a logging road, either. For all I know he just likes his trysts to be private. If he were stable, he wouldn't be picking up runaways in the middle of the night.

The driver's door opens. Graham steps out, looking around. Pinecones and old needles crunch beneath his feet as he comes around and pops open the hatch, sitting on the bumper. The moonlight glistens off a small flask that he offers my way.

"No thanks," I say, thinking that being roofied would be the perfect end to the evening.

"Suit yourself," Graham says, and looks back over his shoulder. The smell of fresh leaves and mountain air is unmistakable, almost bittersweet.

"When are we going to the station?" I ask, willing to keep the pretense alive.

"Soon." He says it softly. "I need you to do something for me first."

The only thing I plan to do is wait for an opening and crush his skull. The ghost of hitting Nelly travels up my arms, and revulsion and righteousness wrestle against each other. I'm through with these games and it shows in my voice. "Yeah? Like what?"

He smiles and scoots closer. *If he touches me, I'm going to scream. I don't think I can help that.*

"So direct." He smiles, and I wonder how I ever thought him kind. "Relax."

I straighten my fingers, forcing my fists to uncurl. "This is very charming."

"You can be nice," he whispers. "Nicer than this."

Before I can respond, a ribbon of light cuts a swath through the darkened forest, shadow leaves and branches fleeing in its wake. I have enough time to wonder if I'm saved before it disappears. Whatever lone wanderer was passing along the dirt road must have sought higher ground.

Graham peers out, eyes prying apart the night. My hands are raised to shove him and run when he turns to me and smiles.

Who was he expecting?

He wipes the corner of his mouth with the back of his hand. "Where were we?"

A hand like a side of beef comes out of the darkness and seizes the back of his jacket, yanking him backwards and spilling him out of the van. For a moment there is just the sky, dim and black and bottomless above the open door. I scurry forward on my hands and knees as I hear a grunt and Graham cries out, then again. Leaping down, my feet hit the deep leaves with an audible *crunch*, and for a moment I can't believe what I'm seeing.

A little overgrown, the clearing is otherwise just as I remember it. Jutting timbers and blackened boards are all that remain of the cabin my father took me to, ruined and spider-like at one end of the drive. The roof has caved in, and through the broken windows I think I can make out the tatters of a white sheet like a burial gown in the moonlight. Firs and cedars crowd the canopy overhead, but before I can process why he chose this of all places I take in the strange scene in front of me.

Graham is on the ground, curled up into a ball and taking the worst of a kicking. The heavy figure doing the damage looks like a buffalo crammed into a black hoodie, and in the dim light it takes me a moment to recognize him.

"You piece of shit!" he barks at the huddled figure and gives him another kick. "I knew it!"

The buffalo turns to me, broad chest rising and falling. "Stay in the van, Prose."

I shake my head and take a step to the side, speechless to see Chapman come to my rescue. "How did you know?"

He uncrumples a scrap of paper. I don't have to read it to know that Graham's been less diligent than he thinks in covering his tracks. "I didn't. But I had my suspicions."

He swings his boot again, hard. It connects with Graham's ribs like a mallet hitting meat. "It wasn't hard to follow you up here. Guy's not half as smart as he thinks he is."

In the moonlight, I wonder. It could be shadow play, but the fallen branches in the corner look artificial, the stage too carefully set. Graham groans in the dust and broken leaves, and I take another step towards the road.

"Come on," His beady eyes find mine, glimmers of onyx in the creases of his broad face. "We get you back to Everbrook and this guy to a police station. I'm sure you're not the first he's tried this with."

"I can't." My feet scuttle back of their own accord. I keep my eyes locked with his, hoping Graham left his keys in the van.

"It's okay." Chapman puts out a conciliatory hand. "You're safe now, kid. He can't hurt you."

Graham makes a noise. Dark stains mute his face in the pale light, but he doesn't move. Only smiles.

"You think this is funny?" Chapman leans forward, and then I hear it too. Facedown in the bloody leaves, the counselor is laughing.

The big man moves to kick him again, and just like that the shadow unfolds from the canopy, dripping from the trees like an oil spill. It's a blackness that swallows the night, and Chapman has just enough time to put his boot on the side of Graham's face before inky tendrils pour around him and yank him skywards.

There is a soft humming beneath the screams.

I recognize the melody.

Something hot and wet spatters my face before Graham gets shakily to his feet.

"Guess swing shift just got a lot more fun, Spooky." One of his eyes has already swollen shut, and a sheath of blood and dirt covers the right side of his face. A final piercing keen comes from the leaves above that descends into a damp rattle, and Graham glances upward with bemused indifference.

Shaking, I can't even ask before he looks for something past my shoulder with a strange curiousness. The crunching of leaves presages the stranger stepping into the road.

"You're getting sloppy, I fear," the skeletal form says with a *tsk*.

"Guy's had it in for me a while." Graham spits something red into the undergrowth. "No great loss."

"Still," Svara says. "One hopes to avoid making such a mess, especially where they dine."

I gape as he steps forward into the clearing in a beige linen suit, impossibly gaunt, a brown recluse amongst the trees. As the black shape seeps into form behind him, my heart sprouts blades of ice.

Its jaundiced eyes meet mine as everything falls into place, tumblers in a lock.

Phoebe, I'm sorry.

Stupid. I've been so stupid.

"Hello, Prose," he says. The flowing mass over his shoulder hums a couple of bars, but he doesn't seem to notice. "Congratulations. You're free."

I say nothing, my eyes casting about for a weapon, something to hammer this impossibility away. The doctor doesn't seem to mind. White and black, he and Sinatra form a nightmare yin-yang in the moonlight.

"Come now." He fetches a piteous smile. Icy needles slide into my heart. "Did you really think you were the only one?"

My feet stumble back, recoiling.

"You never did finish your story, you know. What happened to your father." His thin arms stretch impossibly wide. "Here, then. A fitting place to end it."

"Why?" The lonely word stumbles out from between my lips.

"Reasons? Still? The world's not a novel, silly girl. If you were to grow older, you'd learn it defies expectations." He smiles, a little sadly. Graham pushes past me to rummage through the van. Whatever glee he'd embodied with the two of us alone has escaped. "Your case came across my desk. Delusions, possible schizophrenia. Deaths. I know how much trouble *my* friend can be, and I wondered: is there really another?"

"Of course, I also thought: here is one that will not be missed."

I scan the clearing, searching for a trail, a path, anything. Any way to run. "It was all a lie."

Svara shakes his head. Behind him, the oil slick shimmers and weaves. "Not at all. I have many friends, who owe me a great many favors. Freeing my little murderer, though, was never going to be one of them."

My cheeks burned. I wondered what it was Graham was looking for. How much time I had left. Even if I sprinted from the clearing, I wasn't sure I could outdistance Sinatra.

Drops of scarlet still dribbled from the canopy, spattering my arms. "Then why? Why bother with any of this?"

"Simple. I wanted to know if it was true."

My heart lurched. "What'd you come up with?"

"Truly? I'm not so convinced." He pushes his glasses up on his nose as he raises an eyebrow. "Not that it matters now."

I swallow. The black shape slides forward in a wave. It reeks of bad pennies and smoke as the doctor raises his hand, the creature now inches away. Sinatra's yellow eyes affix me, full of horrible familiarity. It hums a funereal dirge.

—*da da duh de da*—

—*da da duh de da*—

"The irregulars—"

"Ah, yes. Your word. He's never met a one he didn't like." Svara looks past me, checking on Graham. I don't have time to wonder what's taking him. "Quite unusual. Like having a fish that eats the other fishes."

"What?"

"Those he catches out, of course. Everbrook was quite the aquarium when he first arrived."

"He feeds on fear." It's not a question. My eyes dart around, looking for anything I can use in the dim light between the trees. There's a promising-looking branch as thick as my wrist four or five yards away. The wind picks up, carrying the musty scent of dead leaves and rich cedar with it, and I take a single step towards it.

"In earnest, I don't believe he has to, but he's developed a taste. Like the cream in one's coffee, yes? It's not really what he wants, though."

"Everbrook's just a hunting ground."

"Quite." Svara studies me, his eyes in a squint, "And he's been so hungry lately."

"The other girls—"

"People run away all the time. The streets are littered with them."

"Not all, though." Graham calls out from somewhere inside the van, and a flash of annoyance creases Svara's brow. "Some? Sure. Don't want you to get the wrong opinion of me, Spooks. But the doc pays pretty well, and he's right. You'd be surprised how little you'll be missed."

"How long have you been doing this?" Subtly, I shift another foot towards the branch. The black shape bobs ahead of me, tendrils darting and taunting.

"Please." Svara nods towards the van. "For all your stories, for all your city of dead light, somehow you understand nothing about them. What you call *irregulars*—"

Graham steps around the rear bumper of the van, There's a needle in his hand, its contents cloudy in the moonlight, and I leap for the branch, sliding through the husks. My palms close around the branch and I heave it upwards.

It doesn't give. Longer than it looks, I only manage to shake some leaves off of it, the other end pinned beneath a fallen log.

Cold fingers trace lovingly against my back, and Svara laughs.

"Come now." The patience is dripping out of his voice.

I try again, the branch levering a little further, and suddenly there's a great *whoosh* that knocks all the air out of me. My feet leave the ground before I can even register the impact, a momentary feeling of weightlessness, and then I collide with the side of the van in a brutal crunch, a bright flower of pain exploding in my hip, my shoulder. My fingers go numb as white lights shimmer across my eyes.

I'm face down in the frigid undergrowth, dew soaking through my jeans.

"Easy on the van," Graham growls. Stunned, reeling, I nonetheless let out a hysterical giggle as I struggle to a knee. I'm about to be murdered by an oil slick on the surface of reality and he's bitching about his paint job.

Everything aches, the forest swinging off balance, and I see his boot coming but can't avoid it. New pain blossoms hot behind my eyes as the world flickers on and off for a moment. Something hot and salty is streaming across my lips, and I stay down for a moment, trying not to vomit. When I look up, I'm facing the cottage, its burnt ruins the skeletons of the past.

Dad, I'm coming to see you.

Coming to see you soon.

"No need for that." Svara's walking towards me by the sound of it, but I'm transfixed on the bare bones, the jutting timbers. Shadows rise and fall before my eyes.

Some rogue shape moves inside.

The tendrils press against my shoulders, a different kind of pain. Sinatra spins me around so that we're almost face to face, its yellow eyes like cracked amber peering into mine. The stench of smoke and copper pours from it. My arms begin to sear.

Sinatra begins to sing in a guttural croak, the tune timeless as Graham crunches through the leaves towards us.

Like an invocation, the name leaves my lips before I can stop it.

The wind catches it and sweeps it away under the moonlit night. Stars glare down at me from their dead affixations, watching my life unspool with dread indifference.

I'm shivering with the pressure. Nausea surges, and the world is just beginning to fall back into focus when Graham grips me by the bicep and yanks my arm forward. "Can't take me by yourself, can you?" I growl.

He pauses, hypo in hand. "I have every intention of it, yeah. Mostly while you're asleep."

Drawing back, I spit in his face. He wipes it away with one hand, amused, which is when my foot comes up and kicks him squarely between the legs. Graham makes a grunting sound, staggers but doesn't fall.

A smoky streak of oil turns my chin when I hear Svara gasp.

From between the trees, a man walks forward. A low dark hat hides his face, his old work clothes a frayed black. Stubble coats his weathered cheeks, and the icy smile he gives is a sickle of moonlight.

Svara crows, and the smoky mass is gone.

"Little raven." The man's pale eyes meet mine, a trace of amusement flickering behind them. "Who're your friends?"

"What's happening?" Graham yells, leaning against the van. He's looking from me to the doctor, red flushing his cheeks. If he remembers the hypo, he shows no signs of it.

Svara smiles in a skeletal rictus, glee barely contained. "I did not think it possible."

Marmalade gives him a glare that would set tallow flowing. "I'll get to you in a minute."

Doubt lies on the floor, eviscerated and twitching. There's a knot in my stomach that's yearning to be untied, fear and guilt and underneath it all, familiarity. "How did you find us?" I ask.

"Didn't. You came to me." The barest hint of uncertainty wavers between us as he looks from Graham to Svara. "Get the keys. We're leaving."

"Leave?" The doctor rises to his full height, and Sinatra flops from the trees like a black tar. "Things have just started to become interesting."

For the first time, I realize that beneath his cold plastic interior runs rivers of bubbling crazy, like an old doll infested with spiders. Undaunted, Marmalade bares his teeth and starts forward.

Sinatra draws up into the approximation of a melting man and steps into his path. Black clothes rippling, Marmalade reaches for him with one worn hand. The shape blurs backwards, once, again, drawing him forward.

Too late, I realize that none of this is coincidence.

He's baiting him.

There is a whir and a mechanical chirp. A dull grinding starts between my eyes, a dark ball of pain like a negative flare, and Marmalade halts. A loud humming is coming from inside the van, and the Man puts his hands up like a grizzled veteran doing the world's worst mime impression. Fists clenched, he batters at something only he can see before he glares at the capering old man.

"Decades of work. Research." Svara smiles. In the moonlight it's only a grinning skull. "I don't want to bore you with the details, or how many of you have died to make this a reality. Suffice it to say, a lifetime of obsession is finally bearing fruit."

"Who are you talking to?" Graham's leaning against the panel of the van, hands on his jeans, struggling to catch his breath. There's a growing unease shifting his features into something almost childlike. I have maybe thirty seconds at best before he gets back in the game and beats me bloody.

Svara casts a disapproving glance. "Hush. Grownups are talking."

Barely visible beneath the canopy of trees, I spot a metallic cylinder buried in the leaves, no bigger than a stake for throwing horseshoes. Once I see it, I see them all. There are five in total, vibrating at such a rate that they seem to shimmer and blur. The wind picks up in a roar, shaking the soughing branches, and in the gust of leaves I spot paint along the forest floor.

It's a trap, I think. *It's always been a trap.*

The old man creeps over to Marmalade. I notice he's still cautious enough to stay out of reach. "From her stories, you're quite the bogeyman. To be honest, I didn't think you were real, and even if you were, I wasn't sure if Sinatra could take you." He pats the flowing inkblot almost parentally. "He's a hungry thing, but like most predators not that interested in a fair fight. Nor am I, for that matter."

"This won't hold me." My old friend spits the words. His beard has grown longer in the years, his cheeks more sunken, but his cold eyes still blaze like the heart of a blizzard. "Parlor tricks."

"More than that, really. You're missing the best part." Svara reaches into his pocket and presses something. The air seems to pressurize around him, grow thick with shadows and something else with the smell of burnt wiring and dragon's blood. The darkness seems to intensify as Marmalade stiffens, his teeth grinding together in a thin white line. Silent, his eyes never leave the old man's, not even when they begin leaking black.

He begins to shake, the fluid running from his ears now, his mouth. Sinatra glides over, flowing like a dark stain across some invisible dome as the old man looks on. Its hunger is an almost palpable need as it spreads itself thinner and thinner, until at last it's coating the invisible field like a black veneer. Before he's entirely obscured, I see Marmalade fall to one knee, his visage now one long streak of gore.

—*da da duh de da*—

—*da da duh de da*—

A rough hand jerks me back against their warm body. "What the fuck is happening?" Graham hisses, wide-eyed. I have just enough time to register that he's gaping at the clearing, at Svara grinning maniacally at what must to him seem thin air, and he's scared out of his mind because he can feel it, something horribly, utterly naked in the world.

I take the opportunity to throw an elbow into his gut and twist.

His hand comes away with part of my shirt in a scratchy *rip*, and I scurry for the branch one last time.

His footsteps crunch after me, and for a startling second I remember all the people they think I might have killed, all the things I'm responsible for. *Whether you did it or not,* my uncle said, and something coils into steel inside me.

My hands grasp the rough bark, and I wait until the last second before I yank it free and swing.

It almost doesn't go, and I imagine his needle sinking in between my shoulders before the branch bends and the weight is suddenly, deliciously free, coming around with the momentum of something escaping orbit.

In a savage arc, I bring it around. Not an ounce of force is wasted.

I bury it in Graham's face.

His look of surprise is obliterated in a crunch of blood and bone. The wood shatters his nose, obliterates one cheek. The jagged stump of an old offshoot buries itself in his left eye. Stunned, he doesn't even scream as his hands come up to cover his ruined face, one eye gaping at me madly in surprise. I don't hesitate but bring the log around again, colliding with the other side of his head. In a crimson spray he sinks to his knees, inaudible below the hum of the machinery. I remember his leer, his promises, and I hit him again.

Behind me, Svara stands before the black dome, his creation, arms spread wide in the moonlight as if in anticipating a boon. If he noticed me caving in his henchman's head, he gives no sign but drinks in whatever dark glory manifests itself here tonight. Beneath Sinatra's shadow, Marmalade is invisible and silent.

For all I know, he's dead.

The van rattles slightly on its tires, and I fumble through Graham's pockets for the keys before ghosting over to the sliding passenger door. Beneath the mildewed sleeping bag lies a small metal cube, no bigger than a foot on each side. A green light winks balefully from the top, and it vibrates slightly with the whirring of mechanized innards. I've never seen anything like it before, and the heavy branch is raised—

Wait. This is a mistake.

What?

This is your chance to be free. He let them die, *you know.*

Did he? The more we talked about it, the more it felt like shedding skin.

Your only chance. The Man can stay buried here forever, and you can be free at last.

Something burns within me, a chrysalis conflagration. Part of me tears free.

Isn't that what you've always wanted?

A normal life, to be out of this horror show and into the light?

His words come back to me, and I realize.

I am free.

It's my choice.

It always has been.

We're all down here in the dark together.

I bring the branch down hard. Something pops and hisses inside the container, and I hammer it again. The top panel dents inward with a hiss of smoke, and the little green eye blinks out. The thickness in the air seems to dissipate, and I clamber into the front seat of the van to stick my head out the window.

The cylinders' gyrations have grown wobbly, and the ebony dome falls silent. Sinatra is still, humming infectiously. Svara wavers, a fraction of doubt creasing his skeletal features.

He doesn't seem to notice when I turn the key in the ignition.

The van rumbles to life.

My hand hesitates for just a moment, and then I pop the van into reverse and floor the gas. It jerks backward with a lurch, gaining downhill speed faster than one would have thought possible. The wheel turns slightly in my hands as I line the doctor up in the rearview mirror.

Svara sees me coming at the last second, enough to drop his hands and reach for something. The crazy notion that it's his pen flits through my mind as the bumper of the Dodge picks him up, a steel wall plowing through him at thirty miles an hour, and throws the doctor the twenty feet into a gnarled old elm with a crunch I'll hear for midnights to come.

There's a moan then, a gurgling breath that makes me think the doctor's trying to tell me something, but I pop the transmission and roll forward. The rear windows are coated with a red spatter before I throw the van into reverse again, just to be safe. After I strike the tree a second time, there are no more sounds.

Beyond me, there's a scream in three-part harmony. Sinatra flows from the broken dome, drawing itself upward and back down into something shaped like a melting man. Yellow eyes burning, it stalks towards me, a puppet with its strings cut.

It takes a step forward, murder blazing in its gaze. Then halts.

Its yellow eyes go wide as it realizes that something's not quite right. Then it looks down.

A large hand protrudes from its chest, and Sinatra stares at it with a blank curiosity before the other hooks its fingers into his mouth.

"Start spreading the news," Marmalade says, and rips the thing's head from its shoulders.

In a spray of shadows and ichor, his free hand yanks upwards, and the black mass explodes. Ebon chunks of something unwholesome and wet rain down amongst the undergrowth. They're both black shadows in the moonlight, and when the Man collapses I find myself out of the car and running to him.

His face is a bloody mess when I turn him over. Even though there are no obvious wounds, whatever the device did must have been catastrophic. I stare at my boogeyman, my benefactor, my friend, and something deep and dark tears inside me as I take his hand. "I'm sorry, Marmalade. I'm so sorry."

"Fuck that," he sputters, and opens his eyes. "You did what you had to. I've never been so proud."

A bolt of shock traverses my spine. "Are you okay?"

He smiles with bloody teeth. "Little raven. I'm the Marmalade Man."

The moon is sagging below the trees by the time he's done smashing the remaining cylinders. I clean the worst of the gore from the back of the van with Graham's jacket, each breath of the frosty air scouring the months away.

I realize that no one knows where I am, or what I've become.

Dead stars shine down indifferently upon me in the clearing, the forest soughing with the night wind. With another name, the possibilities are endless, the universe so very wide.

For the first time, I can finally be free.

Marmalade makes his way around the clearing with a pronounced limp and inspects our handiwork.

"We've made quite a mess," he grumbles, prodding what's left of Graham with the toe of his boot. "People will look,"

"Let them." A new fire was blossoming in my heart, fanned by possibility. The petals of the old Prose, the Red Orphan, the prisoner, all were even now curling into fingers of ash.

"Figure. World's a big place for a girl starting out on her own."

"Where will we go?" I ask, starting for the van. We'd leave it downtown with the keys in it, a quarter mile from Union Station. With luck, it might never be tied to us.

"Anywhere," he says. "Anywhere at all."

"Are we still down here? In the dark together?" I hop into the front seat and scoot it up until my feet reach the pedals.

The Man's already in the passenger seat. I slide my hand over his.

"By the southern stars, no." he says, and kisses me on the forehead. "The future's bright."

ABOUT THE AUTHOR

Roland Blackburn is a father, IPA enthusiast, and author of *The Flesh Molder's Love Song* and the upcoming *Seventeen Names for Skin*. He lives in Troutdale, Oregon with his wife, two children, and multiple dogs. While not strictly imaginary, his assumption of the human form is irregular at best.

ALSO FROM BLOODSHOT BOOKS

Missing for seven months , fifteen-year-old Ted Wallace wakes by the river with no memory of where he has been or what has transpired during his absence. He only wants his life to return to normal, but soon he realizes the chaos that his disappearance caused, and that his return has only made matters worse.

His sister, feeling like an outcast from the family, finds solace in old friends and becomes a victim of horrendous bullying at school.

His mother is torn apart by conflicting emotions: concern for Ted given his life-long heart condition and anger about his disappearance which she diverts towards the local oddball.

Worst of all, his father, no longer able to contain his drinking problem, becomes convinced that the boy who has been returned is not his son at all, but a doppelganger with an insidious purpose.

As other missing persons return, Ted discovers where he has been and what he must do, but the sinister influences around his family threaten to tear them all to pieces before he can do what is necessary to bring their lives back to normal.

Available in paperback or Kindle on Amazon.com

https://bit.ly/NormalPB

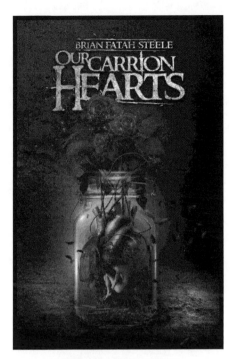

MONSTERS EXIST

Vampires, Witches, Faeries, Djinn, and Wendigo. These five tribes have held an uneasy truce for centuries, united for their mutual benefit as the Carrion Court. But now the collapse has begun.

Daniel Hale has been summoned back to his hometown to investigate the disappearance of another Wendigo. Rumors are circulating that his kind are going feral, hearing voices in their primal form. To make things more complicated, a young psychic woman seems somehow involved.

Meanwhile, Kelsey Radu and her family are acquiring an impressive body count. The teenage Witch has a plan, one audacious and brutal. It doesn't matter how many die out back in the shack, she will not be stopped until the ritual is finally complete.

Daniel and Kelsey are on a collision course that could determine the fate of the world. Wendigo versus Witch. Neither of them are heroes.

Available in paperback or Kindle on Amazon.com

https://bit.ly/OCHearts

HALLOWEEN, 1988

A gang of twelve-year-old boys are trick-or-treating in London. Off in the distance, they hear the discordant chimes of an ice-cream truck. It seems strange to hear on a cold autumnal night, but their thoughts of maximizing their candy haul soon dismissed its incongruous melody... until they saw the rusting hulk idling in the shadows at the end of the street, its driver a faceless shadow.

That was the night he took one of them.

OCTOBER, 2016

Years later, Halloween is fast approaching and Tom Craven is still haunted by the events of that dark night, especially the fact that their friend was never found. Increasingly plagued by horrific visions, Tom returns to the place where it all began, only to discover he's not the only one who can feel it. His friends have already arrived and are preparing for a battle which could get them all killed.

The Ice Cream Man is back... *and he's come for the ones that got away.*

Available in paperback or Kindle on Amazon.com

https://amzn.to/2YihXkt

ON THE HORIZON FROM
BLOODSHOT BOOKS
2020-21*

Soundtrack to the End of the World – Anthony J. Rapino

BioTerror – Tim Curran

Birthright – Christine Morgan

Cracker Jack – Asher Ellis

The Obese – Jarred Martin

Cluster – Renee Miller

Pound of Flesh – D. Alexander Ward

Crimson Springs – John Quick

Popsicle – Christa Wojciechowski

Schafer – Timothy G. Huguenin

Revival Road – Chris DiLeo

The Amazing Alligator Girl – Kristin Dearborn

Fairlight – Adrian Chamberlin

Ungeheuer – Scott A. Johnson

Teach Them How to Bleed – L.L. Soares

Blood Mother: A Novel of Terror – Pete Kahle

Not Your Average Monster – World Tour

The Abomination (The Riders Saga #2) – Pete Kahle

The Horsemen (The Riders Saga #3) – Pete Kahle

BLOODSHOT BOOKS

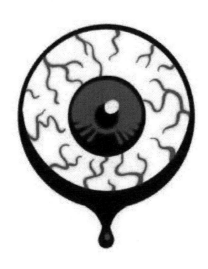

READ UNTIL YOU BLEED

Made in the USA
Middletown, DE
23 October 2020

21668860R10196